THE GALLANT MRS. STONEWALL

The Gallant Mrs. Stonewall

A NOVEL BASED ON THE LIVES OF

GENERAL AND MRS. STONEWALL JACKSON

by Harnett T. Kane

DOUBLEDAY & COMPANY, INC., Garden City, N.Y.

With the exception of actual historical personages identified as such, the characters are entirely the product of the author's imagination and have no relation to any person or event in real life.

Library of Congress Catalog Card Number 57–11426

CONTENTS

PART I

A Special Providence

. . . I cannot but look upon it as a special Providence that led me there to meet him.

—*Mary Anna Morrison Jackson*

CHAPTER 1

Anna Morrison had no reason to guess, as the stagecoach jolted around a curve on that shining May afternoon, that the tranquil town of Lexington in the blue-green Valley of Virginia would ever be more to her than the scene of a pleasant visit.

Several years were to pass before she would realize that the settlement, nestling among the soaring mountains, would eventually and indirectly bring her a husband, and thus fulfill one of her mother's purposes in planning the trip. Many times Anna would wonder with a musing smile over the odd situation that had made it possible for her to know the future "Stonewall" Jackson so well and to go about with him as she did. Had matters worked out only a bit differently, had there been even a few weeks' delay in her arrival, her life would not have been the same.

But on this early summer day in 1853, the bright-spirited Mary Anna Morrison thought mainly of the reception that awaited her and her younger sister, the twenty-year-old Eugenia, whose light, tousled head fell against hers as the stage rocked on, bringing them nearer to Lexington and to their older sister, Isabella. With her husband, Major Harvey Hill of the old Washington College at Lexington, Isabella was to receive "the pleasure of a sociable stay," in the words of Mrs. Morrison.

The driver on the seat high above them gave a blast of his horn to notify the distant town of their approach. Eugenia stirred briefly and then fell back into placid sleep. Anna gave the girl an affectionate look. A head taller than Anna, the serenely beautiful younger sister would probably be married first; Anna accepted that prospect with good cheer, as she accepted most things. When the two of them walked down the street together in their native North Carolina, the boys glanced casually at her, then stared at Eugenia.

Well-developed though her figure was, Eugenia had an almost childlike air, with her plump cheeks, small mouth, rounded blue

eyes, and easy amiability. "You do it, Anna . . ." "Any way you
think best . . ." For most of their lives Eugenia had been saying
that. Because their ages were so close—Anna was two and a half
years older—the sisters spent most of their time together, and a
special bond had grown between them.

As the high, bumpy coach swayed like a canoe on a rough river,
the woman on the opposite seat took out her mirror. For a moment, Anna caught a glimpse of her own dark brown hair, drawn
back to a knot beneath her bonnet, and the sharp line of her chin.
She sighed. She had her own looks, and she needed nobody to
tell her that. It was only that Eugenia was so much more handsome.

At home, their energetic and resourceful mother had worked
for hours over Anna's costumes for the trip. "This brown is right
for your eyes, a close match." "Child, a cream shade brings out
that clear complexion of yours." Anna shrugged inwardly in recollection; with Eugenia such matters never arose, because practically anything became the younger girl. Anna's thoughts went
to their two older sisters, Isabella and the quick-minded Harriet,
who sent her writings to the papers. Both Isabella and Harriet
were so clever that . . . Half-guiltily, Anna stopped; she had been
on the verge of an unsisterly thought. It was only that—well, there
always seemed to be a Morrison who was *something* more than
she was!

Ten children who had lived, including six daughters . . . And
the fact that Dr. Morrison was a Presbyterian minister did not—
some thought—make Mary Morrison's task of finding husbands for
her girls any easier. Years later Anna would smile wryly when a
friend called her mother a "remarkable woman," adding, "Not the
least of her feats was that she got all six of you married, and married well. Several of you brilliantly." But now, in the early 1850's,
Mary Morrison was, if not worried, at least slightly concerned.
Only her two oldest daughters had thus far gone to the altar.

The family had "certain advantages," which in Mrs. Morrison's
broad terms meant a great many things, all of which she used
for her purposes. "There's nothing better for anybody than travel,"
she had observed, and Anna nodded. Now the young woman remembered, with a flicker of hurt, her mother's first question after
Anna's return from her last year's trip to Washington City. "My
dear, didn't you meet some nice young men? Ones that were—
interested?"

"Mother, anyone who gets around the White House as I did sees a lot of nice young men. They weren't especially interested, though. Nor was I." Anna had chuckled, and Mrs. Morrison had shaken her head. "Now don't joke about such things; it isn't becoming." But a moment later her natural good humor had returned as her daughter described her four months in the capital. "Uncle William opened practically every door in town . . ."

William A. Graham, who had been governor of North Carolina and Secretary of the Navy under President Fillmore, had made Anna his house guest for her first close look at Washington's brightly fashionable world. Only recently Uncle William had run for Vice President, with General Winfield Scott as presidential candidate, in a bitter race which had left scars. But in spite of his defeat, Anna had realized that her uncle was still an influential man. How much attention he drew as he moved about in his old-time costume of knee breeches, long black stockings, and silver-buckled shoes! "I'm just an ancient Whig, the last of a dying breed," he had told her with a good-natured laugh. "No, it's a fine breed, and it's going to go right on living," she had assured him.

In Anna's eyes Washington was a place of spreading magnificence as she went to receptions, dinners, and concerts. Her brother William, for years her uncle's private secretary, was a bachelor with a polished manner and the unmarried male's easy entree to Washington drawing rooms, and William had also done his part.

"You know, I've always liked a party," Anna had explained to Mrs. Morrison, and her mother's eager nod reflected the same feeling. Mary Morrison's family had a less solemn outlook than her minister-husband's, and Anna suspected that her mother had once known a highly festive social life. Reliving the weeks in Washington, Anna had continued, "I heard more music than I've ever heard in my life, and I enjoyed it all—overtures, waltzes, polkas. Though I didn't dance, of course."

"Of course not." Her mother had nodded quickly, but her glance had been enigmatic . . . Today, on her ride toward the Virginia town, Anna closed her eyes and returned for a moment to the damask-hung rooms and the hallways banked with flowers. This time she was not an onlooker, but joined the dancers in a swift polka, a slim youth moving by her side, his gaze fixed on her large brown eyes. Then with a start she reminded herself again: a Presbyterian minister's daughter never dances.

By now Anna had seen enough of the world to understand that the Morrisons occupied a somewhat unusual place. Although Mrs. Morrison occasionally informed strangers, "We're country folk," her daughter sensed that she did not quite mean it. True, their Cottage Home estate stood fifteen miles from Charlotte, but both sides of the family had connections in many other places, and most of the Morrisons spent a good deal of time traveling back and forth from visits. And in the title of Cottage Home itself, only the word "home" could be considered strictly accurate; it was a big, spreading establishment.

Dr. Robert Hall Morrison was part minister, part Southern planter, and looked like both. His lean, handsome face, well bearded, had the thoughtful air that Anna associated with a man of the cloth, and on occasion he could thunder against abuses around him. At the same time, his management of the property had given him a certain calm command, most evident as he rode about his land with his hunting dogs. Father and those dogs . . . Anna mused fondly. Except on Sundays, when one of the Negroes locked them up, they were seldom far from him.

At what age had she first gathered that he held high rank among his people? She could not be certain. But from her early days she had watched the procession of her father's callers, and among the portraits hanging on the walls of their home, Anna could name a dozen or so Scots-Irish Morrison ancestors, usually a minister or two in each generation. In a day when comparatively few went to college, Dr. Morrison had attended the University of North Carolina and Princeton. He became a minister at twenty-two, published a pioneer religious paper, and then scored his master stroke by creating Davidson College, the state's first Presbyterian institution.

And what crowded, argumentative years had followed! As Davidson's president, Dr. Morrison had to cope with all kinds of problems—student troubles, money troubles, factional troubles. When he fell sick, he had resigned, yet even now he had a strong interest in the college. Ever moving, ever organizing, he maintained three pulpits in a circle outside his estate, and managed the Cottage Home property and the twenty or thirty slaves who had come from his wife's family, the well-to-do Grahams.

Most of the dark people still considered themselves "Graham

folks" and talked largely of Graham glories. Only a week ago
Anna's maid Hetty had reminded her solemnly, "Your pa, he married well. Us Grahams is quality." Anna smiled in rueful amusement as she recalled the scene.

A voice broke into her reverie. "Child, what's so funny to you?"
It was their escort, the elderly Mr. McDowell, who was on his
way to the North and had agreed to watch over the Morrison
girls until they arrived at Lexington. She flushed. The old gentleman leaned forward and added affectionately, "You'll never learn
to hide what you're thinking, Anna. One glance, and everybody
knows."

She shrugged. As a matter of fact, she was nearly always bright-
humored—so much so that one of her dour-faced women cousins
had recently informed her, "My girl, I'm afraid you smile more
than a minister's daughter should." Before Anna could respond,
the cousin had gone on, "That's your father's fault, with his peculiar ideas about learning for women. A girl shouldn't know too
much, *I* always say."

Though Mrs. Morrison had given her a warning glance, Anna
had responded on one of her quick impulses, "Just how much is
too much?"

The lady had turned huffy: "It just doesn't help you if a man
thinks you're a bluestocking."

That meant, of course, that it would not help her get herself
a man. Still, Anna had no intention of throwing herself at anything in pants that passed her. Twenty-two . . . At that age, many
people believed, a young woman should feel a certain concern.
Well, Anna was not concerned. In time, she expected to meet
somebody who meant something to her, but she had no intention
of being forced into a marriage.

Her mind went back to the busy days she had enjoyed at the
strict yet cheerful Moravian school at Salem, North Carolina.
There she had been drilled in the old-fashioned rules: prudence,
economy, the enjoyment of quiet pleasures, and—not least—order.
She could still repeat the memorized words: "It is entirely contrary to good manners to run in a great hurry into a room, or in
going out, to slam the door after you."

In contrast to the sobriety of the rules and regulations, Anna
had welcomed the happy Moravian ceremonies, the days when
parents and patrons visited the school and received great sweet
cakes and mugs of steaming coffee, while the students appeared

before them in white dresses with long sashes and lace caps tied
by ribbons under their chins.

At odd times Anna's thoughts would return, as they had today,
to this interlude in her life. Even if she sometimes found it hard
to live up to the strict regulations, she had profited by the routine
of industry with needle and broom, the myriad duties in class and
garden, the hours of silence followed by soaring song. Whether
or not she could trace it to the Moravian school, she had a particular love of music, of singing and the piano. Even now, when she,
like Eugenia, might be dozing through their ride, she hummed
quietly to herself.

A shout drew her back to the present. "Whoa, whoa there!"
The driver tightened his reins as they moved into the outskirts of
Lexington. Anna gazed out of the window at the rolling green
earth, at the deep ravine on one side and at the leafy richness
of a fruit tree against the sky. This was a neat, clean-swept, hilly
place, the streets going up one elevation, sloping down another.
At regular intervals brick houses rose behind white picket fences,
and ahead stood the first of several imposing-looking isolated
homes. The early Revolutionary town, where some of the first
fighting with the British had taken place, had a peaceful air, for
which Anna would always remember it.

Now that they had almost arrived, she wondered how her sister
Isabella, and Isabella's husband, Major Hill, would react when
they saw her. Usually their mother sent out the Morrison girls one
at a time, and since Anna had visited in Washington only recently,
Eugenia was to have made this trip alone. Then at the last minute the younger girl had run up to their room: "Father says you
can come, too!"

Anna had cried out in immediate delight. To see Isabella
again . . . It was a joyful prospect. The first of the sisters to leave
Cottage Home, she had a place of some authority in the family;
six years Anna's senior, the ever efficient Isabella had helped Mrs.
Morrison in supervising the younger children. She had intervened
on Anna's and Eugenia's behalf the time Dr. Morrison rose up in
chill disapproval because they laughed at a rawboned visitor from
Texas. Working resourcefully as a kind of assistant mother, Isabella smoothed their way then and on many another occasion.

During the past few days, however, Anna had puzzled over the
matter of this visit to Lexington. Was it Eugenia's dependence on
her that had led the family to make the change—or the feeling

that Anna needed a second chance? The latter reflection was not
flattering.

As for Isabella, the crisply businesslike sister had found a husband of high promise. Though short and of an unprepossessing
appearance, Harvey Hill had made a name for himself a few years
earlier in the Mexican War. Originally from South Carolina, he
had left the army after the war to teach mathematics at Washington College in Lexington, the old school that George Washington
had endowed. Anna recalled the family stir whenever the Hills
visited: "Now Harvey says . . ." "Major Hill always tells us . . ."

For a time Anna had considered her brother-in-law almost overpowering, as sharp-tongued as he was sharp-minded. At nineteen
or twenty she had quailed when he greeted her, "And how is the
little Anna, the very little Anna?" She had stood it for a while
until one day her temper had flamed: "You're not so big yourself,
my dear brother. In fact almost a bantam!"

Harvey had looked at her in mock surprise, winking at those
around him. Still he had said nothing more, and from then on
she and the Major had gotten along without difficulty.

The stage ground to a halt outside a drab hotel in front of
which was gathered a waiting crowd. Anna rose, shook the dust
off her skirts, woke the tired Eugenia, and peered from the window until she made out the lean form, the head of shaggy graying
hair, and the pair of spectacles which came first to her mind when
she thought of Harvey. In spite of the war and his West Point
career, her brother-in-law always seemed to her much more the
teacher than the soldier.

"Oh, Harvey, Harvey!" As old Mr. McDowell helped her down,
Anna tried to draw the other man's attention. When he caught
sight of her, Harvey's thin lips fell open in astonishment. Moving
toward her with his shambling walk, he seized her hand. "Anna,
we thought it would be . . ." At that moment the placid younger
sister thrust her head out of the stagecoach door and he grinned:
"Well, we expected a shower and got a cloudburst of Morrisons!
Two of you are better than one."

Still wondering if her arrival would complicate the Hills' plans,
Anna bade a hasty good-by to their escort. Then she helped
Harvey to find their mud-splattered bags. "Isabella is as impatient
as a horse nearing water," the Major told them as they rode off
to the house. "She has a full schedule for—for both of you." When

Anna laughed at his hesitation, he changed the subject. Pointing out of the carriage window, he began to describe the sights.

"Washington College, my school, and a fine-looking place, isn't it?" He indicated a series of simple white structures in a stately row, and Anna commented, "My brother William went there some time back, you know. But where's the other place he talked about —Virginia Military Institute?"

A few minutes later Harvey showed them the second school at the end of a slow rise—"that big Gothic building with the others around it." In years to come Anna would know every line of the Institute's heavy structure; today she gave the turrets and double tower only a casual inspection. "Looks a bit new, doesn't it?" Harvey said, in his nasal voice. "Well, it is, not quite fifteen years old. They used to have the state arsenal here, till they had the idea of replacing it with the school to serve the same purpose and more—a sort of West Point of the South."

He smiled. "The two schools used to have a lot of feuds, but that's over now. Haven't had a row in—well, a whole year! You're going to meet people from both schools, especially my friend Tom Jackson from the Institute. The one from Western Virginia, that I've written about now and then."

Vaguely Anna recalled that Harvey had mentioned a man with whom he had fought in Mexico. "We helped chase the enemy after Chapultepec and met in the City of Mexico." Harvey's tone was warmly affectionate. "Old Jack made a fine record in the war, even though most people around here don't know it and don't care, if they do." Harvey's irony was apparent, and Anna gave him a curious glance. What did he mean?

"Oh, Jack's . . . well, if not a diamond in the rough, something close to it. I've never known anybody like him—an odd one from the word go." He stopped, but Anna's look prodded him. "Sister, he's had a lot of trouble. I got interested in him in Mexico, after a friend told me a little about him. It seems that Tom Jackson arrived at West Point as badly prepared as anybody who ever attended. Poor and country-looking and scared, and without enough real education to qualify."

As the carriage rolled on, Harvey Hill shook his head. "Still, Old Jack went to work with the determination of a bulldog. Got a low ranking the first year; he was barely able to hang on. But he got a fair ranking the second year and a good one the third, so that they said if the course had been a few years longer, he might have rated first. As soon as I came to know the fellow, I could believe it!"

With that Harvey grinned. "Nobody has ever called Tom a beauty. Great big feet and hands, and doesn't ride smoothly though he's been on horses most of his life, and walks as awkwardly as anybody in shoes." Anna did not let the Major see her own amusement. Was anybody less graceful than Harvey himself?

Her brother-in-law continued, "Ah, Tom's not a very good teacher and I suppose he'll never amount to very much. But I'm right fond of him. A fine fellow, with all his—limitations."

Anna's interest heightened. "If he's as bad as that, how did he get here?"

"I'm responsible, I guess." Harvey's small eyes brightened. "After the war he plodded along in the army, one post after another. He had a bad time in Florida. Then about four years back there was a vacancy over at the Institute. The superintendent and the board wrangled, and when they finally agreed on somebody, the man himself said no. The fight was about to explode again when I happened to drop in at the superintendent's office on a casual call.

"He handed me an army catalogue and asked me to suggest somebody. My eye hit on Jackson's name—he mightn't be ideal but he'd try like fury." The Major smiled: "So they picked Tom as professor of natural philosophy—that means subjects like optics and mechanics—and he instructs in artillery tactics too."

Turning in his seat, their brother-in-law gave a high-pitched laugh: "Anyhow, don't you girls get your interest up. Old Jack's already practically on the marriage shelf." After a moment's reflection, he cautioned them, "Oh, oh, I wasn't supposed to tell that. Please just forget it. Miss Junkin doesn't want anything known yet."

Anna forced back her curiosity. Harvey's remarks about Jackson's "troubles" and his unnamed oddities—the whole picture he had presented—piqued her interest. And in spite of that, "Old Jack" was getting himself a wife. . . . At that moment she saw, on the corner just ahead of them, a pleasant white house with a deep, sloping roof and many windows. In front of the porch stood Isabella. As soon as the carriage stopped, Anna jumped out and caught her sister to her.

"Both of you! We'll have an even better time," Isabella cried out in delight; and then, close to tears, she talked on. "Is everybody well, and is Father still taking his medicines, and what do you hear from Uncle William?" Even in a time of emotion, the efficient Isabella asked about essentials. A moment or two later she stopped, reached for her husband's handkerchief, and proceeded with a brisk air to the duties at hand. "You two take the upstairs room, and after we have a chat you're to sleep two or three hours and tonight we're going to a faculty party . . ." A few directions later Isabella remembered a message for Harvey. "President Junkin hopes you can go over at six tonight for a little talk."

Anna caught these last words as she started up the stairs. She did not miss their meaning. President Junkin . . . Obviously, "Old Jack" had not done badly for himself. As she paused, a shout reached her, and down the stairs ran the Hill's son, Morrison, now approaching three. Anna had expected the boy to be diffident; instead, she received a welcome so loud as to make her blink.

"Don't go up now. Sit down and play—play with me!" The lean, high-strung boy shrilled at them, and to Anna's further surprise Isabella and Harvey gave in. A few minutes later, sitting on a chair beside the overeager Morrison, she told herself with an inward sigh that, however expert his mother and however sharp-sighted his father, Morrison had become a spoiled child.

Shaking herself free, Anna went upstairs with her two sisters. There she sat up in bed for a time while Isabella talked on: "There'll be boating and a picnic next week, and meanwhile . . ." Both Anna and Eugenia were dozing, and, giving them a fond look, Isabella slipped out.

Dusk had already fallen when a noise from below made Anna open her eyes. Eugenia was sleeping heavily, her flushed cheek against a pillow. Almost at once a dark maid carrying a bucket of hot water materialized from the hall to help Anna prepare herself for the evening. The newcomer to Lexington quickly established a rapport with the dark girl. "Miss Anna, you jus' a han'ful an' a half o' lady," the dark, thick-bodied maid told her in a whisper.

Anna took the remark as a compliment. Holding up her arms, she drew in her breath as the girl tightened the corset and lowered her gray silk dress with its trimmings of red braid. Though less low-cut than many she had seen in Washington, the gown displayed more of her arms than she usually showed. Taking up a box of light powder, she applied it sparingly. She shook her head, how-

ever, to the offer of a curling iron. Long ago she had decided that
question: "I have straight hair and there's nothing to be done
about it."

Directing the maid, she nodded as her helper parted it in the
center, drew it tightly back, braided it, and twisted a coronet into
place. When the maid lighted the lamp, Anna's almost black hair
had a soft shine, and so did her eyes.

The maid cocked her head in approval. "Them eye' bright like
two big button'," she beamed, "an' if yer jes' keep out'n the sun
yer never have trouble wid' that white-white skin o' yourn."

Moistening her lips, Anna studied the mirror critically. Her
nose, small and regular, had a faint hint of a bulb at the end; her
lips were fuller than some liked, but her rounded figure appeared
good enough. "Your mouth gives you almost a French look," a
friend had once confided. Many would consider such an impression out of place in a Scots-Irish preacher's home, and several of
her neighbors, Anna knew, would not approve of the final touch
which she added today—the small pearl earrings.

They were her pet indulgence. One or two austere callers at
Cottage Home had murmured that such ornaments had a suggestion of "worldliness." To this Mrs. Morrison had responded instantly, "If my children do no worse than that, I'll be satisfied."
And her quiet smile had removed any offense. . . . Tucking in a
stray hair, Anna went downstairs as the maid prepared to assist
Eugenia. In the early evening her steps echoed through the empty
hall. Harvey must have gone to President Junkin's, and Isabella
was probably supervising arrangements in the kitchen.

At the foot of the stairs Anna glanced into the parlor, to discover
there a tall man of about thirty in dark blue soldier's coat and
white military trousers, his face in profile at the window. There
was something almost rigid in his stance, in the way he held his
head—up and a trifle back. Short brown hair with a hint of a curl
ended in brief side whiskers, the clear skin was sunburned, he had
a high forehead, and a small mouth cut across the narrow face.
And the blue-gray eyes had a look—Anna searched for the word—
close to solemnity.

For a moment she felt an impulse to retreat; it was almost as if
she spied on the stranger. Then, suddenly aware that she was
watching him, he turned, flushing heavily, and Anna sensed an
almost agonizing shyness.

"Oh, I'm sorry," she apologized.

The man said nothing, but simply stood there, his large hands hanging at his sides. His constraint communicated itself to her. Then with an awkward movement he advanced across the room, and she had the feeling that he would have preferred to be anywhere else at this moment. In a low voice he stammered, "I—I thought the Major would be here, and Mrs. Hill too. They're— they're somewhere else, though . . ." He spoke quickly, tensely; by his manner Anna placed him as one who came from an isolated, almost frontier, section. Now the thin lips tightened and the newcomer merely stared.

With an effort Anna took charge. "Of course, but the Hills will be here soon, and why don't we sit down? I'm their sister from North Carolina, and you're . . ."

The light skin reddened again, and this time the words came more stiffly than ever. "Miss Morrison, I'm Thomas Jackson—Major Jackson."

Her first reaction was one of surprise. Why, this Major Jackson wasn't at all as bad looking as her brother-in-law had implied; he appeared almost handsome. In later years thousands would argue over descriptions of him, calling him everything from scarecrowlike to gaunt to commonplace. Anna's own opinion was to alter several times, but from the start Tom Jackson gave her the impression of a certain clear strength, and with it a suggestion of some underlying melancholy.

Going to work to lessen the strain, she delivered what was essentially a monologue.

"My sister and I will be here until August or September. . . . This part of Virginia's much different from Richmond and the Tidewater. But still it isn't as mountainous as your section, is it?" As she chattered on, Anna noticed her guest's position: he sat so firmly upright that his spine did not touch the back of his chair, his hands were folded on his lap, and his uncrossed legs rested squarely before him. All at once she was sorry for him. Couldn't he relax?

Receiving little or no response to her opening conversation, Anna turned to her trips, her taste for different locales; and for the first time the light eyes revealed a quickened interest. "Travel . . ." As he murmured the word his long face brightened. "Miss Morrison, it's one of the things I like to do most in life. Some day I'm going to see Europe, a great deal of Europe."

He spoke with unexpected decision, and her surprise must have been visible. Major Jackson's heavy eyebrows lifted. "You don't think I'll do it?"

Before Anna could protest, he exclaimed, "I've made up my mind to, and I will. Unless God wishes otherwise, of course, and then I'll accept what He orders." In a solemn voice he assured her, "We can do anything we want in life, Miss Morrison. I learned that some time back, and I've never had reason to doubt it."

As he went on, his eyes shone and his lips tightened, and Anna felt sure that this man was completely convinced of what he said. Recalling her brother-in-law's words about his determination, she commented softly, "Major, you've proved that several times."

For a moment he sat silent, and she thought she had offended him by letting him know he had been a subject of discussion. But Major Jackson showed no annoyance. "Yes, I think I've proved it." He nodded earnestly and seemed about to add more when the narrow lips compressed again. Clearly he did not talk with ease of himself, or for that matter of anything else.

Reaching for some other topic, Anna recalled that her uncle, William Graham, had gone to Europe a few years back, "and I wanted to be taken along no matter how young I was. But when I jumped up and said so, in front of the family, they all laughed. It sounded silly to them, and I was so embarrassed I cried and ran away to hide for an hour."

Although Anna chuckled at the recollection, her guest did not. Instantly sympathetic, he shook his head: "I can understand just how you felt. There's nothing worse than having people snicker at something you say honestly and—and . . ." His quick sentences trailed away, and in his eyes Anna read such comprehension of her earlier misery that she was touched.

After a pause Tom Jackson cleared his throat and mentioned her brother-in-law. "The Major's made things so much—so much better for me here. I won't ever forget it." His voice thickened with emotion. "I've had times when I was restless and—and unsettled and troubled in my mind, and the Major and several others in Lexington helped me. Directed me to God, too."

Again Anna's surprise was evident in her eyes. Most people did not speak so readily of their religious beliefs, but Major Jackson went steadily on: "The Hills told me you were Presbyterian, and I was glad to hear of it. Oh, I wasn't born to it; I chose it after I looked around and—investigated. It wasn't until after I came to Lexington a few years back that I joined the church."

The caller's eyes darkened, and his face took on a suggestion of harshness. "I moved around a lot when I was a boy, from one relative to another. It was an aimless life, then and afterward as well." The narrow face held a hint of pain, and Anna's sympathy grew. "I didn't have any real religion, and I didn't think a great deal about God." Suddenly and unexpectedly, Tom Jackson turned to Mexico. "My stay meant a great deal to me, Miss Morrison. I was there nearly two years in the war and later, and I met some good families, and called on the archbishop, and thought for a while of taking that faith."

Before Anna could absorb this, he continued, "I believe strongly in prayer and its effect; without complete faith in the Heavenly Father I couldn't have gotten along . . ." He hesitated. Anna was stirred by his complete, fervent faith, and his simplicity in describing it. She saw new marks of his tension: one hand was clenched around the arm of the chair, his shoulders were hunched, and despite the chill of early evening, Major Jackson was perspiring heavily.

Here, surely, was a complex individual. Her pity increased; he worked so hard and with such set purpose for things that others were born with or had acquired so easily. And there was no polite dissimulation about him, but a directness she liked. She thought of several drawing-room types who had visited her home. If they had some of the Major's simplicity, and he had some of their polish . . .

A step reached them, and both Anna and Tom Jackson gave a start. Eugenia stood poised in the doorway with an expectant smile. Her hair piled lightly at the top of her head, her well-scrubbed skin shining in the lamplight, the girl had a softening glow as she waited before them, and her older sister felt a quick admiration. She noted that Major Jackson too was impressed, his eyes widening as they fixed upon Eugenia. Stern though he appeared, it was obvious that he had an appreciation of women.

Anna introduced them, and almost at once there came a jarring note. Taking a stand between them, the Major uttered what must have been a speech planned long in advance. "Young ladies," he said, "I will be here a few more weeks, and I want you to consider me as an older relative, to take you around under my—my brotherly wing." Anna understood his kind intentions and was grateful for them. Nevertheless she writhed inwardly; the phrases had so stilted a sound. And Eugenia, with all of youth's lack of consideration, tittered.

With a rush of relief, Anna saw the Hills approaching, and the awkwardness passed as greetings were exchanged. When everyone was seated, Harvey and their guest talked of Mexico and their service there. Soon her brother-in-law snorted derisively, "Ah, all that sand and rock, and fleas too!"

Almost involuntarily Tom Jackson protested, "Major, it's a beautiful country, and you know it. Don't you remember those flaming red plants, and the way the mountains stretched to the horizon?" The warmth in his voice made it clear to Anna that the Latin country had an even greater importance in their guest's life than he had previously indicated. He used two or three Spanish phrases with a liquid accent: "This *hombre* found everything *simpático*, and the people the kindest on earth."

Major Hill shrugged, as if such remarks by Tom Jackson were an old story, and Eugenia inserted a question: "Were they as *simpático* as all that, Major—including some *señorita?*"

Harvey guffawed and gave their guest a long, meaningful look. Though he managed a grin, Tom's face turned a furious red. Obviously the question had touched a memory. Anna would never know, but often she was to ponder the question: Had Tom Jackson first met love in Mexico?

For the moment, however, she felt a quick anger. Her sister had behaved in so juvenile a fashion, and so hurtfully. The Major's manner became more uncertain than ever, and after a few minutes he retired nervously from the house. As he left, Anna told herself that he was obviously not at his best among those he did not know well.

In their room several hours later, the younger sister glanced over from a pad on which she was writing. "Oh, did you ask the Major about his engagement to that Miss Junkin?"

Anna's head went up. "Why, I didn't think about it. Not once."

"You didn't?" Eugenia's laugh let Anna understand that she did not quite believe her words.

CHAPTER 2

The next few weeks were crowded ones, with commencement festivities at Washington College and at the Institute—dress parades, receptions, field sports, ceremonies formal, informal, and those "in between," as Anna classified them. She liked Lexington for the special atmosphere with which she was familiar from other school communities, its lively social hours, good conversation, and quiet enjoyments.

It soon became evident that their energetic older sister planned to have her and Eugenia meet practically every man in Lexington between the ages of nineteen and thirty-nine. The day following their arrival, Isabella and Harvey Hill talked together for a long time in their room, and Anna suspected that they were canvassing the "availables." Once Major Hill's muted words ended in a derisive guffaw, followed by a shushing sound from his wife, and silence. Soon afterward Isabella emerged from their room, pointedly sent Eugenia on an errand, and drew Anna to a window seat.

"While you're here you'll have a good time," Isabella began in a confidential tone. "You always do, Anna; you can talk to anybody. But I want you to make *use* of your time. You know you could have been married a dozen times in the past few years, if you'd only taken a little trouble." Before Anna could respond, her sister gave her a sharper glance: "One or two of the men who'll be here this week would make a good husband for somebody."

Anna smiled. "You mean they haven't been spoken for already?"

"Don't be flippant." Isabella's assistant-mother look deepened. "If you'd only make the——"

"Well, suppose I don't want to make the effort?" Anna shrugged. "I'm satisfied with things as they are, and if you and Mother would only relax and see what happens——"

This time Isabella broke in. "Anna, you don't get a husband by relaxing. Not in these days."

"How are these days different from the others?"

At that unreasonable inquiry Isabella sighed. "Everybody's busier today, more pressed, and I suppose there must be more women and fewer men around. Anyway, these are the 1850's, and

men are warier than they used to be." Isabella became earnest:
"You'll try to show some interest, now, won't you?"

Anna felt her temper rise swiftly within her. Then she heard
her father's solemn words: "Anger, child . . . It's unbecoming
for anyone, especially for a woman. Curb it as you would a sin."
While sometimes she did not succeed, Anna generally managed
to keep her temper from flaring. Now she nodded slowly. The
only way to handle this situation, she decided, was to submit, or
at least appear to submit.

The next day the whole Hill household went to work to arrange
the details of Isabella's "little party." Activity extended to practically every room of the airy, comfortable house. Clearly excited,
the precocious Morrison asked several questions about "the soldiers that's coming." Anna was puzzled by the child's remarks,
but she soon had her answer; today Isabella was drawing on the
military. The first arrivals were three uniformed young men.

The oldest proved a vapid character whose conversation
seemed to consist entirely of a catalogue of his ancestors. The
second nodded silently through everything. And the last, a pim-
ply, nervous fellow, had evidently accepted the invitation because
he was a junior colleague of Major Hill. As she studied this fidgety
lad, Anna told herself with an inward smile that he might be
willing to get married in order to keep his job.

Although Anna carefully "made the effort," she soon sensed that
even Isabella had come to share her conviction of the futility of
this afternoon. As the first hour passed, Anna saw, over her teacup,
the three young men gravitating toward the soft-voiced Eugenia;
but while Eugenia nodded and asked polite questions, the girl
could not conceal the fact that she was far from fascinated by any
of them. With young Morrison occasionally underfoot, Anna concentrated on the other guests. When the party ended, two of the
young officers lingered beside Eugenia so long that Major Hill almost had to invite them to leave.

Amused, Anna sat afterward with Isabella. "It doesn't matter,"
she chuckled as her sister frowned dejectedly at the floor. "I never
expected you to produce a 'prospect' as easily as that." Isabella
responded with an upward lift of her head. "I haven't started to
work yet, and we'll see about that."

The following afternoon brought a more formal affair, a garden
party at a neighbor's. Anna was often to speculate over the chance
that drew together several of the people she met that day. Had

she known how closely their lives would be connected with hers, she might have paid even closer attention to the two clans, the Junkins and the Prestons, to whom she was introduced.

Preparing to leave for the party, Anna attached her earrings and thrust several flowers into her dark hair. At home she would have been more conservative. A month earlier she and Eugenia had appeared on a Sunday, each with a pair of roses in her hat, and at the sight of them Dr. Morrison had frowned. "You don't mean anything worldly, I'm sure, but, daughters, on the Lord's day . . ." Contritely, the girls had reached up to remove the offending objects, but Mary Morrison's hand had touched her husband's arm, and Anna had read a silent appeal in her penetrating eyes.

"Well"—the bearded man had hesitated—"well, one rose each." Today, intending to enjoy herself, Anna tucked in three of the choisest blooms from the Hills' garden, and Eugenia followed suit. With a feeling of triumph they set out beside their sister and brother-in-law.

A few minutes later, in the side garden of the large house at which the party was taking place, the girls temporarily lost sight of the Hills. As they walked about, their attention was drawn to a group clustered around a very small, auburn-haired woman of indeterminate age. "Why yes, Miss Junkin," a man exclaimed, and Anna stared at the tiny figure on the bench.

So this was Major Jackson's fiancée! Anna could not cloak her surprise; at closer range she judged the lady to be ten years or so older than she. Her eyes went over the somewhat irregular features, the thin arms held not altogether gracefully at the woman's side; Miss Junkin was rather less than handsome. As the Morrison sisters approached, the tiny creature continued to talk swiftly, nervously, her attention upon the man closest to her, and Anna watched the pink lips with something akin to fascination. Such a flood of words, chosen with such care and spoken so crisply! And then Miss Junkin mentioned the name of Tom Jackson.

"He isn't like some of us, but I can't agree with you, sir! Major Jackson will be heard of in the future, and by a great many people. You mark my words."

The speaker's intent eyes, under the fringe of wiry hair, almost cut into the face above hers. Such outspoken comments were unexpected; here was a highly unusual individual, one who spoke her mind like a man. A moment later the speaker's pointed fea-

tures softened, and Anna assured herself that this was someone
who really loved the Major.

Miss Junkin, she observed, was dressed a little differently from
the other women around them—primly, in a severe, untrimmed
waist and an all-but-shapeless skirt. A phrase rose in Anna's mind:
old maid. She tried to check her ungenerous thought. Nevertheless, Miss Junkin had it stamped upon her, and what did Major
Jackson see in the lady?

Harvey Hill stepped up and drew Anna and Eugenia forward.
"My dears, I want you to know the brightest mind in Lexington,
Maggie Junkin." The woman on the bench turned, and the intense
face underwent a transformation.

"Of course, this must be the gentle Miss Anna." Margaret Junkin
gave her a quick, bright look, nodded to Eugenia, and returned
to Anna for a probing scrutiny. The oval-shaped blue eyes held
both candid inquiry and a clear intelligence. Miss Junkin would
not be an easy one to fool about anything. As she murmured a
greeting, Anna repeated to herself the words that had fallen so
casually: "the gentle Miss Anna." She was not sure she liked that
description; it made her sound like—like one of those milk ices
on the buffet.

Others came up, and Major Hill took Anna to a small circle of
ten or so young people of assorted ages, all Junkins. "There are
twelve sons and daughters, and most of them are in or around
Lexington at the moment," her brother-in-law explained. "Sometimes I can't remember them all." The Junkins stood near the
dominant sister as if on guard, and Margaret peered over them
with a kind of fierce possessiveness, like a hen with a large brood.
And all of the Junkins, Anna noted, had a certain resemblance to
one another, a sharpness of face and a sharpness of attention as
well.

Leading Anna toward a newcomer, Harvey explained, "Maggie's really a learned one—she writes stories and articles and
poems. Began to study Greek and Hebrew under her father when
she was only six, they say. He saw she had a brain, and he trained
and trained it—too much, maybe." Major Hill's eyes were merry:
"A dictionary in shoes, or maybe a hothouse flower, and sometimes I think she'd wither if you took her into the open. Someday
somebody may try it."

Anna felt a sudden uncertainty. A woman who "appeared in
print"—she had brushed against one or two of the sort in Washing-

ton City, and counted bruises as a result. With a backward glance
at the little queen of the Junkins, she observed to Harvey, "All
of them have a way of talking that's different from ours."

"They should have." Harvey's tongue sharpened again. "They're
from Pennsylvania originally, though they've lived in Ohio and
other places." He shook his head half-severely, half-affectionately.
"Wait till you meet Dr. Junkin, my president at the college.
There's one for you—as strong-minded as anybody I've ever met,
and a good man. But not the easiest in the world to get along
with. You know, girl, you've got to take these Junkins on their
own terms."

"Indeed," Anna's temper flashed, and she fought the impulse to
add, "provided you have to take the Junkins at all."

A step sounded behind them, and Margaret Junkin herself approached, a broad smile on her face. "Miss Morrison, here are two
late arrivals. My younger sister Elinor, and our friend Major Jackson." Anna swung around to see Jackson in his blue uniform next
to a girl whose arm touched his. Her first glance made clear her
error: beyond any doubt it was the junior Miss Junkin to whom
the diffident Major was to be married. But what about the older
Miss Junkin and her feeling for the Major? The question would
rise more than once in Anna's mind.

Meanwhile she turned to Elinor Junkin: "My dear, you're
lovely." She spoke, as she often did, on quick impulse. The young
woman before her had a soft, full-lipped beauty that could not be
missed. The silent Tom Jackson gave Anna a grateful glance, and
when he faced Elinor again Anna read a tenderness that was un-
mistakable. This girl meant a great deal to him, and he could not
have concealed the fact had he tried. At first Anna had observed
only Elinor's blooming complexion, the dark reddish hair and the
chiseled nose—and the look of calm well-being in the deep eyes.
After a moment she realized something else: Maggie and her
sister were gowned almost identically. But in spite of the plain-
ness of her attire, Elinor Junkin's charm could not be dulled.

At that moment another man appeared, and Maggie Junkin
took charge of the conversation: "Thomas was talking yesterday
about the Mexican War and the storming party against Santa
Ana's force, weren't you, Tom?" Anna noticed that Maggie
Junkin's manner was as rapt now as it had been earlier when she
spoke of Jackson.

"Why, yes. It was just that we . . ." Jackson flushed as his eyes went around the circle of people, and Anna began to suffer with him, much as she had at their earlier meeting. In his face dismay became alarm, then panic. Elinor Junkin gave him an encouraging glance, and Maggie stood silent until the wait grew interminable.

"Well, Tom may have forgotten, but . . ." And Margaret Junkin quoted the unhappy officer in flowing sentences that he would hardly have used. While Anna still felt for poor Jackson, she marveled at the way Maggie, gesturing with birdlike hands, held the group's attention. Here was a true storyteller and romanticist; she had the crowd laughing one moment, intent the next. "Our side set the siege, gathering every force, and it must have been superb. Tom here . . ."

Anna sensed an undertone of amusement among some of the men. Jackson, the central figure, stood dumbly by while his admirer swept on. At the edge of the group Harvey confided to Anna, "It's funny, but Maggie's right. Though Tom looks almost sleepy as he goes around town, once a shot's fired, he's another man, eyes flashing, face alive, shouting. I think he actually enjoys war more than anybody I've ever seen. . . . In Mexico he fumed that the war would end before he had a chance. When he got it, he pushed ahead of everybody around him, advancing our colors, taking impossible points."

Anna blinked. It was hard to picture Tom Jackson in such a role. She was about to ask several questions, but stopped when her brother-in-law stared across the garden: "Look who's here—Major Preston and his wife."

Taking Anna forward, Harvey whispered, "I think you could call him *the* man of the town. Remember the big house we passed yesterday? That's the Prestons'. John used to be a lawyer until it bored him; then he did more than anybody else to get the Institute started, and now he teaches languages there, runs an estate, and——"

"And Major John T. L. Preston also keeps his hand in everything else in Lexington." Lightly Isabella completed her husband's sentence. "How Miss Sally got him here today I'll never know. He's a rule to himself, and he hates parties."

Despite the critical quality of some of their observations, the Hills' voices were friendly. Her curiosity stirred, Anna gazed toward the tall, heavy-set figure. The man was handsome; his manner had flourish. In his stylish dark costume, his head cocked to one side, he had an air of importance. At his elbow was a large woman, matronly and quiet-mannered, who deferred casually to her husband. Behind them Anna made out a sight that left her smiling—a covey of older and younger Prestons in an uneven file.

Proudly John Preston nodded as Isabella named each of his children in turn, and then he addressed Anna in a cultured voice: "So this is the Miss Morrison we've heard so much about." There was a certain kindness in his manner, yet also a touch of imperious patronage. He seemed almost to be saying that he had expected something more imposing, and Anna struggled to keep down her momentary resentment. Who did this one think *he* was?

At that point the woman beside him slipped her hand unobtrusively into his. "And everything we've heard about Miss Morrison is true, isn't it?" Quietly Sally Preston invited her husband's agreement, and to Anna's surprise the big man surrendered with a pleasant, ungrudging smile. Confused by the change, Anna gave an uncertain smile, and at a signal from Isabella, the group moved toward the others, the line of junior Prestons following like a royal train. When they stopped before Margaret Junkin, she was still going on about Mexico.

"Why, if it hadn't been for Major Jackson——"

"You mean, Maggie, we'd have lost the whole war?" Major Preston's softly modulated voice cut into the monologue, and he gave Miss Junkin the stare of a man who has only amusement for a brainy woman. A dozen faces turned; few people in Lexington, Anna surmised, would break so abruptly into Margaret's remarks. Not the least astonished was the speaker herself. Anna saw her sudden hurt; twin circles of red flamed in the thin cheeks. Clearly, Miss Maggie had a temper, and equally clearly, it was about to erupt. In the momentary silence the two clans, Junkin and Preston, faced each other.

"I certainly said nothing about our losing the war!" The pink mouth formed a narrowed circle, but before it could reopen, Mrs. Preston stepped deftly forward again. "Why, not the war, John," she corrected her husband. "But our friend certainly helped win important battles, didn't he, Maggie?"

Major Preston shrugged elaborately, as if to say that there was no way to defeat these women. Maggie nodded, her annoyance slipping away, and Tom Jackson merely looked from one to another as if he had missed the preliminary steps in the clash that had begun and ended around him. But now, advancing toward Jackson, the imposing Preston spoke blandly to him of military

matters, and let his eyes move over the group as if to challenge
any who might want to belittle his friend Tom.

More puzzled than ever, Anna read a warm, almost tender note
in Preston's manner. Behind her, Isabella whispered, "John Preston's been one of Tom's best friends, practically like an older
brother. And John's nearly the kindest man I know—once he has
his way. And he generally gets it." Anna glanced somewhat ruefully at her sister; if Major Preston did not get his way, she
gathered that his opponents had better head for the storm cellar.

Here was an odd situation, with both Preston and Miss Junkin
in support of the silent Jackson, yet far from united. To inspire
admiration in such firm-minded individualists, Thomas J. Jackson
must be quite a fellow. Anna's thoughts returned to Preston and
to Maggie Junkin. She had changed her mind several times today
about each of them, and she still did not know precisely how she
felt. What would it be like, she asked herself, if that pair ever
met head on?

Toward the close of the afternoon, Jackson, Maggie, and
Elinor Junkin left together. As the three started off in the half-
gloom, Anna saw Major Jackson's hand slip around Elinor's waist,
and he drew her against him. When they had disappeared down
the street, Anna turned away suddenly, and her sister Eugenia
frowned. "What is it?"

"Nothing at all." The sight had disturbed her for a reason or
reasons she could not have named. And all at once Anna was
very tired and glad to go.

Before the week ended, the two visitors learned that Tom Jackson was an intimate in the Hill home, one who dropped by every
day or so. He had long talks with Harvey; he rolled on the floor
with the excitable Morrison and strove (usually unsuccessfully) to
curb the overindulged child. And he made it clear from the start
that he wished to please the Morrison girls. On his first call after
the garden party he paused hesitantly before them. "Are you
young ladies at leisure this afternoon? Of course, if you aren't . . .
But if you are . . ."

At this nervous approach Eugenia giggled, and Anna intervened firmly, "We aren't busy, Major, and we'll be happy to go
with you, if that's what you mean."

It developed that Major Jackson had in mind a walk around
town. "I'm something of a walker," he observed, and they

promptly learned that his remark was an understatement. They strolled together up the hill to the Institute, inspected Washington College, and went past a row of houses. "That last one is a nice place for a couple expecting to have a good-sized family," he told them, and added self-consciously, "I believe in marriage for everybody."

Eugenia's eyes danced in merriment. "Yourself included?"

"For everybody." Anna saw the trace of a smile on his long face. Then he resumed, "Some day I hope to have a lot of children of my own."

Enjoying herself more than ever, Eugenia pressed the Major. "I hear there's to be a marriage in town. Do you know about it?"

"Ah, Miss Morrison, if there is, we'll hear in time." Eugenia fell silent, and Anna allowed herself an inner laugh. Clearly Tom Jackson could keep a secret.

At that moment a townsman walked by, acknowledged Jackson's introduction, and asked a random question about the fall election. "Oh yes, I'll vote for him," Tom answered. "He's a good Democrat."

Anna frowned. Major Jackson a wild yahoo, a follower of that band! Like most Whigs, the Morrisons knew Democrats but not a great many of them, and Anna still remembered old Uncle William Graham's fulminations against that crew. Sensing her surprise, the Major commented quietly as they resumed their walk, "I'm not active in politics, but I *am* a Democrat." His words gave her to understand that, no matter what a North Carolina plantation female might think, he had his own opinions.

Eugenia did not let the matter drop. "Why," she murmured with a sidelong glance at each of them in turn, "I've heard sister Anna say she'd never marry anybody who was a soldier, a widower—or a Democrat!" Anna blushed but did not try to deny this; her statement still seemed sensible to her. A moment later, as they approached a corner, they nearly collided with a lean, gaunt-faced man, holding an umbrella in one hand and a heavy volume in the other. As the absent-minded stranger was about to pass them by, Tom took his arm.

"Sir, I have two friends you'll want to meet. The Misses Morrison, Dr. George Junkin."

The President of Washington College bowed gravely, and Anna felt a flash of interest. She should have recognized that marked Junkin manner, so noticeable in his daughters Maggie and Ellie.

With a visible effort, Dr. Junkin focused his attention; the deep voice had an incisive note as he expressed a hope of seeing them again. "But you understand that final exercises are on us, and nobody can be busier than a college officer at such a time." With a harried look, the elderly President asked several questions, nodding absent-mindedly at their replies. He was obviously not one to enjoy a light conversation, and Anna found him chill, austere.

As Dr. Junkin swept off, she marveled at the concentration his every movement showed—the same fixed attention she had seen in Maggie. Tom Jackson spoke in explanation: "A fine gentleman, but he's difficult to get to know . . ." Since it was evident that she and Eugenia would have scant opportunity to know the President, Anna let the matter drop. When the Major bade them good-by at the house, Isabella summoned Anna: "My dear, we have three more parties arranged—three very nice ones." Her older sister's air made Anna realize that there would be more "prospects" on hand.

The affairs were pleasant enough, but, as Anna had anticipated, nothing developed. She met nobody who interested her particularly, and that was all there was, or would be, to it. Eugenia also remained highly uncommitted, yet Isabella did not trouble her mind on that point. And now slowly Isabella submitted: "Anna, you've defeated me. You can be as quiet and sweet-mannered as anybody on earth, up to a certain point. Then you stand firm, and nobody can budge you—nobody at all."

"Thank you." Anna kissed her sister's cheek and went upstairs. At least that was settled, and she could enjoy the rest of their stay. On the next Sunday, Major Jackson knocked again to offer his services as a church escort "if I'm needed." As it turned out, then and several times later, Eugenia had already received offers, and with a gratified smile Anna accepted the "brotherly wing" that Tom Jackson presented. The following Sunday he arrived to inquire if they had plans for church meeting that evening.

"Eugenia has, of course." The words came out before she could stop them, and Anna felt annoyed at herself. But it was too late. "You really don't have to take me, and you don't want to, do you?"

"Of course I want to." Tom spoke with considerable force, as he did increasingly when they were alone. "Otherwise I wouldn't be here, Anna." At first he had called her "Miss Morrison," then "Miss Anna"; this was the first time he had omitted the "Miss."

Her mood improving, she went in to get her hat. Suddenly she found that she was humming happily, and she made herself halt, so that when she rejoined her friend her manner was sedate.

On this late Sunday afternoon, Tom Jackson was in a more relaxed mood than she had ever observed. As they strolled along he pointed to a file of trees. "Is there anything more wonderful than a sight like that?" Before them she saw a dozen tall oaks in a symmetrical line against the clouds. "And listen," he whispered. The birds were settling for the evening, and she caught distant chirps and made out a flash of wings past the glint of a brook.

For some time Major Jackson talked on almost excitedly, nodding toward the lavender distances, naming a projecting peak, a crag half-lost beyond the rolling farmlands. Anna gave him a closer scrutiny. The man had a touch of the poet in him, a warm appreciation of the scenes around him. Then he faced her, and all signs of his emotion faded. It was clear to her that Tom preferred to hide this side of himself.

Soon they passed a house whose occupants he knew, and his expression changed again. "Look," he said, indicating a window at which a middle-aged couple sat quietly together. His voice was low: "I've been on the outside for a long time watching other people. I've never known anything like that." At his touching words, Anna's heart turned.

"But you've had your own family—as a boy, anyway."

"Not for long," he replied, and now he spoke in a rush. "When I was two my father and my sister died together; he'd tried to nurse her after typhoid struck our town of Clarksburg. He was a lawyer and a good one, Anna, but he'd endorsed notes for too many friends. My mother was left with three little ones, a house they took from us, and debts. The people of the town gave us a cottage, and Ma sewed and started teaching . . ."

Anna saw his eyes darken as he hesitated. "We managed, and when I got to be six Ma married again. Another lawyer and not a successful one, and she got sick and they had to send us children to different relatives. I didn't want to leave; I begged them to let me stay, but . . ." His voice broke, and then he resumed, "We saw her once more, when they called us back to her deathbed. I'll never forget her last prayers to God, appealing to Him to look after her children, and the blessing she gave us."

During the silence that followed, pity grew within Anna: "None of it was anybody's fault, I guess, and after that I had a good enough time at my grandma's farm. They let my sister Laura and me stay together for about five years. I love Laura as much as anybody or anything on earth. . . . But Grandma died, and they sent my sister to another aunt's." Even after the passage of years, Tom's hurt remained. "Whenever I can, I go to see Laura and her husband and children over in Beverly."

Now there was a flash of bitterness in his voice. "For a little while I boarded with an uncle who didn't—didn't treat me right. I decided that, no matter what happened to me, I wouldn't stay. I ran away and said I'd never go back, and I didn't." During the next few years, Anna gathered, Tom lived with a group of uncles at the big farm his grandmother had left them. "They were fine men," he smiled gently. "Lively fellows who liked racing and sporting things, and for a while I did farm work and even rode as a jockey for them."

It was hard for Anna to visualize the serious Jackson in a jockey's role. After a moment he shook his head. "But I wanted to make a real place for myself. Our family had standing in the old days, with judges and congressmen and men in the legislature, and one of my great-uncles married Dolly Madison's sister."

Once more Anna was surprised; until now she had heard nothing about Jackson's family status. He smiled, this time ruefully. "I'm the only one left with our name. My older brother died of consumption, the same thing Ma had." Tom sighed. "Well, I managed to get some schooling and took small jobs on a railroad. When I was seventeen I was a constable, and I did other things. Then came the chance of my life—West Point.

"A fellow who had an appointment from our section went there and didn't like his first look. The minute I heard he'd returned, I snapped to attention, got letters from county friends, and didn't lose a day in riding off to try for his place. Somehow I passed a test, and now it was up to me."

As Tom spoke he touched a handkerchief to his eye, which was inflamed. "I strained them at West Point," he explained. "There was so much to make up that I had to study five times as hard as anybody else, just to hold my own. After the lamps went out, I'd sit at the fire, holding my books and papers close to the coals, and I'd work till the last light was gone."

In the dusk Anna inclined her head. Such determination and such ambition . . . His earlier words returned to her—"We can do anything we want in life"—and she told herself once more that

Tom Jackson was proving it. Ahead, the church awaited them, and they entered in silence. Taking her seat, Anna repeated the pathetic phrase: he had been so long "on the outside, looking in." Clasping her hands, she prayed that Tom Jackson would get the things he wanted so badly.

Several times again, Anna met Maggie and Elinor Junkin. The two seemed inseparable, and Anna watched the spinster Maggie's eyes follow her younger sister in almost worshipful fashion. Isabella observed, "They've always been that way. Ellie's far less brilliant than her sister, but she has a quiet common sense that Maggie lacks. Anyway, when Tom marries Ellie, he may be marrying the rest of the Junkins as well." When Major Jackson was present, the woman writer gave him an attention that had no less warmth, and Anna asked herself what the situation would be between Maggie and Tom if Ellie were not there.

She learned that, like her college president father, Margaret struggled endlessly with her duties. Mrs. Junkin had been ill and was not yet fully recovered, and her oldest girl had taken over more and more of the household management. The narrow face often appeared tired, and Anna saw lines of concentration between the small eyes. "I can't stay," she once told the Hills. "I have a thousand things to do, and time won't wait. Come on, Ellie and Tom." Tom and Ellie went.

After the three disappeared, Isabella told Anna more about Maggie. "She's very impulsive and as generous as they come—and also, I'm afraid, as imaginative. Maggie builds a picture in her mind of a person or a situation, and she won't change it, no matter what. Poor Maggie, she's as stubborn as she's sensitive. And when she sets out to do something, or have it done—watch out!" Although Maggie always treated her with bright good will, Anna still remained in awe of the precise little woman.

She also had several encounters with Major John T. L. Preston, and found him a man of varying moods. The first time he arrived at the Hills' home he was in jovial spirits; he beamed and drew her into a long talk, during which he mentioned Lexington's Franklin Society. "We had a session to debate divorce—a warm meeting and a warm topic," John Preston laughed. "I won." His manner almost added "Of course," and Anna's nerves grated. She thought of something her father had once said about a guest:

wherever the man sat was, he felt sure, the head of the table.
Certainly Major Preston had the same conviction.

Afterward, however, as the smiling man continued, Anna noted
his quick turn of phrase, his command of many subjects. Here was
an individualist, a man with a good mind who took joy in using it.
But the next time the Major entered in petulant mood, lower lip
protruding, and behind her Anna heard Isabella groan. "The Major's in one of his anti-society tempers." At his side was Mrs. Preston, as before, placating, smoothing the way. Annoyed, Anna
decided that she did not intend to bend her spirit to his, and she
spoke only briefly to him. John Preston was lucky to have a wife
like that!

A few days later the Junkins announced Elinor's engagement
to Tom Jackson, the wedding to take place by fall. The surprise
in Lexington was greater than Anna had expected it to be. There
were several remarks about Tom's great fortune in getting a college president's daughter. Hearing them, Anna's anger simmered.
And now she caught other echoes:

"He's a real peculiar one . . . One day he came tromping along
like a wooden soldier, and I swear he passed an inch from us and
never batted an eye."

"Old Square Box." The speaker was a derisive young cadet
whose companion muttered bitterly, "Fool Tom, Fool Jackson!"

Anna sought out Harvey Hill, and as she repeated the comments he rubbed his chin reflectively. "'Square Box' means his
big feet—and they *are* enormous. You see, some folks don't think
Tom's very smart. Oh, they're wrong; it's just that he's slow in taking hold of things at the beginning, and he plods along, paying no
heed to anything except what's ahead of him. Anyway, we know
he's no fool, so what do the remarks matter?"

As Anna reflected on her brother-in-law's words, she nodded.
But it did matter. If only the man acted a bit differently, were
more aware of the impression he made on others! . . . She caught
herself, and again one of Dr. Morrison's remarks came to her:
"Honor, simplicity—they mean more than all the arts of pleasing
the world." Let her try to remember that. . . . She did not remember it, however, when one vapid miss drawled to her about
the new engagement. "All I can say is," the girl sniffed, "Old Jack's
a lot brighter than he seems. Jack's going right up!"

Anna spun around. "Why don't you credit Miss Junkin with
some brightness, too?"

The drawling one's eyebrows rose almost to the roots of her hair. "Well!" Saying nothing more, she left, and Anna knew that this item would be chewed over from one end of Lexington to the other. Well, let them chew.

The school ceremonies ended, and most of the college and Institute staffs left for the summer. The town seemed almost empty. Anna spent more and more time with her sister and brother-in-law and young Morrison; spoiled though he was, she had come to like the boy a great deal. Early one evening a figure in blue military dress walked up the path, and the two Morrison sisters descended to see Major Jackson in the doorway. "I'm leaving tomorrow, and this is good-by," he told them.

"Won't we be seeing you?" Morrison demanded.

"*You* will," the boy's father replied, "but your aunts will be gone by the time Major Jackson gets back."

"Well, we'll all be meeting again, up here or down in Carolina," Tom Jackson murmured. Although she answered brightly, Anna somehow felt that a long time would pass before she and Eugenia would meet the Major again, and then, she knew, things would be different. She had seen more of this kind, stumbling fellow than almost any other Lexingtonian, and he had done a great deal to make these weeks happy ones.

A constraint fell upon them, and now, standing in the door with her brother-in-law, Tom reached out and caught Harvey's hand in a grip that made the older man wince. "I—I may not have done this properly before"—the voice was muffled—"but I must be sure to thank you for all your kindnesses, my good friend, this year and —and those other years."

Anna saw that Major Jackson was deeply stirred. Harvey Hill, greatly moved, could only nod.

"Well, good night, everybody." Touching his chin in an embarrassed way, their friend marched down the steps almost as if moving to unseen band music. Behind him Harvey spoke softly, "Now who'd have expected that? You're never sure *what* Tom Jackson will do next. He's a man of—well, surprises."

His wife took his arm. "I'm glad he did it. As I've said to you before, Harvey, I like that Major Jackson of yours."

The rest of the summer passed uneventfully, and the two sisters were preparing to return to North Carolina when, sitting by the

window on an August morning, Anna glanced up and jumped to
her feet. There was Tom Jackson.

She greeted him with a quick smile. "You're back earlier than
you expected, aren't you?" His response was a bright yet enigmatic
glance. He had a rested air, a calm that she had not observed
before, and he responded lightly to her surprise. Eugenia joined
them, demanding, "Tell us exactly what the wedding schedule is.
The Junkins haven't given out the date, so you've got to do it."

"How do you know *I* know it?" Several times Tom evaded an
answer, and each time his merriment increased. Harvey gave him
an inquiring look: "I've never known you like this before." For
once the Major did not draw back from such a comment, but continued to grin. "I'd like to hear the Morrison girls sing again," he
announced, and they gathered at the piano. Heretofore, Tom had
contented himself with listening; today, after some prodding by
Anna, he agreed to join in.

A moment later Anna, hiding her amusement, could see that in
Jackson's silence there had been wisdom. He had no voice whatever, no pitch, no memory for a tune; what issued was half groan,
half birdlike lament. Once started, however, Tom gained confidence, called for several favorites, and sang every chorus. Anna,
who always enjoyed music, played on until Eugenia, sighing,
asked them to stop. Finally, giving them a cheerful wave, their
guest left.

About noon the next day Major Hill darted in with a lively
smile: "News! The Major and Ellie got married last night. A very
private affair, and they left this morning on a tour to the North."

The three women stared at one another, and it was Eugenia
who spoke first, and ironically: "Didn't somebody say that the Major was a man of surprises?" Anna and Isabella started to talk at
the same time, to be stopped by Harvey Hill. "You haven't let
me tell the rest of it. Somebody else went along with the couple.
Maggie Junkin!"

Anna gaped: "I wonder whose idea that was?" At this point her
oldest sister asserted herself: "Now it's no concern of ours. I'm sure
they'll be happy, all three of them." A moment later, as if she had
said the wrong thing, Isabella changed the subject, and her
assistant-mother air returned. "Anyway, it's time to finish your
packing, Anna." And, with Harvey's sardonic eyes upon them,
Anna and Eugenia complied.

CHAPTER 3

Tom Jackson's blithe prediction that all of them would soon meet again was not fulfilled, for Anna's one direct link with Lexington was broken during the year after her visit, when Harvey Hill decided to move down to Carolina. Offered a good post on the faculty of Davidson College, the school Dr. Morrison had founded, Harvey accepted, and happily Anna welcomed back Isabella and her brother-in-law.

Davidson lay only twenty miles from Cottage Home; the Hills would now be near-neighbors, and it was mainly through them that Anna heard occasional news of Tom and Ellie Jackson. If she had expected messages from the earnest Major Jackson or his new wife, she was disappointed. Several years were to pass before she would receive her first direct word from Tom. The Major, as she might have realized, was not one for airy social notes.

Meanwhile she and Eugenia returned to the tall white house that stood like a welcoming friend among its sheltering trees. Wherever she went, Anna told herself as her eyes blurred at the sight, Cottage Home would be ready for her return. At the circular path before the porch was a cluster of Morrisons, young ones and older ones, the long, black-suited form of Dr. Morrison and the quick-moving figure of her mother at the front.

"Daughters, are you all right? I trust there were no accidents on the way?" Her father, Anna knew, must always reassure himself that they had suffered no physical injury. Mary Morrison's lightly lined face brightened as she beheld her daughters, and she pulled Anna and Eugenia into the hall. "I have to see for myself what you look like!" Her soft, low voice was both quick and calm.

Before she could see a great deal, however, the junior Morrisons crowded in, and with them a file of servants who had hurried over from the quarters. "What did you bring for me?" Anna's eleven-year-old brother Joe called out, grinning broadly as he reached up to kiss her.

"An' you got somethin' for me, too?" When a tiny kitchen helper shrieked the same question, Anna knew they were truly home again.

In their room, tubs of warm water awaited them. "And now, a good scrubbing for both of you, and don't forget anything that you have to tell us." Leaving with a brisk nod, Mrs. Morrison slipped off to supervise preparations for the homecoming supper.

Within the hour the family was gathered at the table, and Anna gazed fondly from face to face—Susan, her precocious younger sister, not yet fifteen; the earnest Laura, next in line; the ever-smiling Joe; Robert, eighteen months his junior; and the baby of the family, Alfred, just approaching four. She turned with loving eyes to her father as he nodded toward the butler and lowered his head.

"Dear Lord, we ask Thy blessings . . ." Although some people thought Dr. Morrison a gloomy individual, he was actually, as Anna knew, a man of reserve. When he first met people, he said little; only after a time did he speak with ease. To the delegations that so often called on him at his home, he talked firmly; he was not a man to waste words. Toward those of whose principles he disapproved, he turned a chilling look.

A memory returned to Anna of an incident still vivid in her mind, even though it had occurred eighteen years earlier. One afternoon she had been playing outside the house and had washed out her dolls' clothes and hung them to dry over the nearest objects—the tombstones in the adjoining cemetery. Suddenly her father had descended on her like an avenging figure out of the Old Testament: "Anna, Anna, whatever possessed you? To desecrate a holy place!" The spanking that followed, she often said, "made an honest woman of me," and she never did such a heedless thing again.

Her father's prayer continued: "Heavenly Father, Thy will be done . . ." The Morrisons were stern Calvinists, descendants of Scottish Covenanters, who had defied all the hostile forces around them to assert and maintain their beliefs. As Dr. Morrison neared the end of the blessing, Anna's eyes strayed to his ink-stained fingers. He must have been working over his Sabbath sermon or preparing a paper. Four times each year her father read through the Bible; daily he went over the Psalms.

She saw the bearded man's lip tremble as he gave thanks for his daughters' safe return. Anna and the other members of his family saw in Robert Hall Morrison qualities the rest of the world seldom met; he was warmly loving and demonstrative. When he was finished with his day's duties, and had left the pulpit or his plantation rounds, he spent his hours with his family, the affection he felt for all of them apparent in his gentle expression. Both of Anna's older sisters had been married in the Morrison parlor, and in each case Dr. Morrison had decided he could not conduct the ceremony. "I'm afraid I'll break down," he had explained, and Anna had seen that he was several times close to tears.

Tonight's blessing completed, a murmur rose from the children. Dr. Morrison began to carve the roast, and Mary Morrison took charge. "Joe, you can't have so much. Well, a bit more, then . . ." "Robert, Susan likes it better done than that . . ." With each such direction Anna saw "Miss Mary's" sharp eyes move about the table, and a flood of affection arose inside her.

With a smile and a quiet glance, Mary Morrison could calm a ruffled household in a moment. The wide mouth, which seemed shaped for good humor, issued five directions in as many seconds in such a calm manner that none could take offense, and, nodding gently, Mrs. Morrison would go on to her next task.

"Mother, can't I have my dessert?" Tonight it was the young Laura who called out the question, and Anna's mind went back to a day a few years earlier when some of the Davidson College officials had gathered at Cottage Home with their wives for an important meeting. That afternoon Laura had decided to take a walk alongside the brook. Mrs. Morrison had just finished greeting the women when a Negro cried from the hall, "Miss Laura done fell in de water!"

Miss Mary had whitened, but while the other women were jumping up and asking a dozen questions, she had quietly slipped into the hall and then re-entered promptly. "They've fished her out, and she's already up in bed." Her voice was so calm one might have thought she was settling a choice of dessert. A half-hour later, matters in hand downstairs, Mrs. Morrison had gone up to hold the frightened child to her.

It was only recently that Anna had begun to realize how different were her father and mother. "You two look like the last pair to have gotten married," a round-faced, round-bodied lady had observed between mouthfuls of cake at Cottage Home, and Anna had been outraged. "The doctor's all duty, and, Mary, you're all—easy adjustment." Later Anna had perceived that there was some truth in the observation. Yet it was not the whole truth. Mrs. Morrison adjusted, but she also made certain that the needed things were done.

Abruptly a voice intruded into Anna's musings. "Child, just what occupies you so much tonight?" At her father's question, Anna flushed and talked of Lexington, the Hills, the Prestons, the

Junkins—and also of Tom Jackson. Eugenia bent forward eagerly:
"Major Jackson's just about the funniest fellow *I* ever saw"—and
the girl mimicked the man's quick, tumbling speech and his
western-country accent. All at once Anna's face flamed, and before she could stop herself she snapped, "That's not kind, and it's
uncharitable, too. There are things, miss, that you don't know, that
you can't understand . . ."

As she spoke she became aware of the silence that had settled
around her. All eyes were upon her, and her father and mother—
Mrs. Morrison especially—were staring curiously. Embarrassed,
Anna dropped the subject. "Oh, well, it really doesn't matter." The
meal ended on a note of constraint, and she asked herself why she
could not have been less heated, or have spoken less emphatically.

As they left the table they heard the sound of a heavy dish
crashing in the hall, and Dr. Morrison sighed, "Old Matty gets
more careless every day." Settling in the library between Anna
and his wife, he frowned: "And poor Mike died when you were in
Virginia. The people in the quarters get older and older. I was
startled when I looked over my books today. Do you know that
more than half of them are sixty-five or more? It's a strange thing,
this slavery."

Here was one of her father's favorite themes, over which he
often pondered, and Anna listened with interest. "We could do
better if we sold some of the people and got younger ones. But
how could I see them go down to the hot places along the Mississippi, where they'd die in a season?" The gray eyes grew troubled. "It's far from efficient, the whole bondage system, and it's
helped weld one crop, cotton, on us." For years, Anna knew, her
father had been trying to mix and rotate crops, only to return repeatedly, like most of his neighbors, to the old staple.

"King Cotton." Dr. Morrison shrugged. "All the grief he's caus-
ing the country, with so many hotheads on both sides. The bel-
ligerent ones shouting around the South, and then the wild people
in the North who won't return runaways and keep holding meetings to stir up trouble . . ." His sigh was ironic. "The abolitionists
don't realize that if we freed the slaves we have at Cottage Home,
overnight, it would ruin us—and where would they go to support
themselves?"

Ruefully Anna nodded: "No matter what we start talking about
these days, we end up as we are now—talking about slavery. If

they'd only keep the screamers silent for a while and try to work things out. But those Democrats . . ."

Her own words made Anna halt. Tom Jackson was a Democrat. Did she include him? She made an effort to concentrate on what her father was saying, but although she listened intently, the long trip had taken its toll. She missed a phrase, then a sentence, and soon she was dozing on the sofa. When she had fallen asleep, her mother turned to Eugenia: "Child, who *is* this Major Jackson that Anna got so disturbed over?"

Now began a satisfying return to her favorite spots around the seven or eight hundred acres of Cottage Home—the rear garden where she could be by herself, away from the sometimes pressing younger children; the picnic spot down the road; the quiet third-floor retreat in the house itself; the kitchen and smokehouse, separated from the main building for safety.

Her first news of Tom came through the Hills, who reported that the bride and bridegroom had returned from their trip north. After hunting vainly for a small house in overcrowded Lexington, the couple had taken up quarters with the Junkins. Anna recalled Tom's earnest words—above all, he wished for his own home. Instead, it appeared, he would be surrounded by Junkins, old and young, and would be a guest in someone else's house. What was it Isabella had said? Tom was marrying not only Ellie but the entire Junkin family. Then she reminded herself of another comment her oldest sister had made: such matters were not their concern. And they weren't.

At first Anna did not think of Tom for days, then weeks at a time. One morning, however, a stranger with a long face drove up to the house, and as he approached she found herself reliving the hour when Tom had come to visit them on the day of his marriage. That night she dreamed she was attending the wedding. Tom had changed into a glittering, debonair gentleman whose pungent observations made the company applaud. During the ceremony, his bride turned around, and Anna saw that she was not the handsome Ellie, but Maggie the poet, who recited a lyrical stanza about love from the altar itself. At that highly un-Presbyterian climax, Anna woke. Usually she described her dreams to Eugenia, but she kept this one to herself.

Soon afterward her sister had her own confidence to entrust, and Anna found she had been right in a prediction she had made to herself. Eugenia would be going to the altar first. From the time of their return, Anna had begun to notice how frequently Rufus Barringer, a slim, energetic young lawyer from Concord in North Carolina, visited the family, and how close to Eugenia's side he stayed.

"How much do you like him?" Anna asked one day as she and Eugenia stood together on the porch, watching Rufus stride toward the hitching post. Eugenia's stare, followed by an uncertain smile, provided the answer. Anna suffered a sudden hurt, a feeling of injury so deep that it astonished her. Was she jealous of her own sister? Perhaps, she had to admit, but there was more to the subject than that. She would be losing this girl who had been at her side for most of her life, and she would be very much alone.

Forcing back her confused emotions, Anna pressed Eugenia's arm. "Everything's going to be fine, you'll see." As if to make up for her first impulsive reaction, she went to work to help affairs along for the couple. Rufus would be a good match; for all of his youth, he was already winning a reputation as an attorney. She took care to let him see her good will, and whenever he called she discovered excuses to leave the couple alone.

"I have to look at the butter in the spring house . . ." "There's some sewing on the top floor to get ready for the servants. Do you mind if I leave?" Clearly, Rufus and Eugenia did not mind, and one day, coming in to rejoin them after an hour, she found the girl alone and wide-eyed, her hands clasped in her lap.

"He's seeing Father right now. Do you think it will be—be all right?" When Anna took Eugenia's hands, they were cold to her touch. "Of course it will be all right. Why should anybody object?"

Eugenia paused, apparently debating with herself. After a long silence she explained, with a look of apology, "I mean . . . Anna, *you're* not engaged, and sometimes people expect the older sister to get married first and the next one to wait."

The words hurt Anna more than she had expected. She tried to carry the matter with a light air: "Why, that's ridiculous. I'll take a husband when I want to, and if I want to." Yet as she tossed her head, she realized that from now on a lot of people would use the phrase "old maid" to describe her, just as she had used it to describe Maggie Junkin. A twinge of anxiety, almost of panic, moved inside her. Had a gate been slammed against her?

The Morrisons agreed promptly to Rufus Barringer's proposal, and that spring the clan descended from several counties for the wedding. Isabella and Major Hill rode over from Davidson College, the high-strung young Morrison beside them. From Charlotte came Anna's other older sister, Harriet, with her husband James Irwin, the landowner and businessman. Their urbane brother William made the trip from Washington City.

As Eugenia took her place beside Rufus in the big parlor, Dr. Morrison and his wife stood close to the minister friend who was to conduct the ceremony, and Anna served as maid of honor. Would she one day take the role Eugenia was now playing in this same room, with the family assembled around her? Even now it seemed to her that several of her cousins were eyeing her with cold speculation. A moment later, as the solemn Eugenia responded to the minister's question, Anna had a sickening sense of deprivation. Years later she declared, "The loss of her sweet companionship was, up to that time, the greatest trial of my life."

During the hours that followed, Anna tried to hold back any sign of her sadness. She must be happy for Eugenia, she must think only of the good life that lay ahead for her sister. For the most part, she believed she succeeded. The following morning, with the others beside her, she stood next to the carriage that was to take the couple away. She reached out to the flushed girl for a final embrace. "Promise you'll write and keep in touch with me?" As the carriage rocked off, Mrs. Morrison drew Anna to her and led her to the house. "Now, miss, both of us have to get right to work. Think of all the things there are to do—clearing out the rooms, sending letters, packing . . ." With an affectionate pat, Mary Morrison started her daughter on her duties.

In this and other ways, Anna's mother let her know she understood something of her feeling. Gradually the pain lessened. Eugenia sent frequent word by post and by friendly messengers, and when fall came it was the younger sister who forwarded the next definite news about Ellie and Thomas Jackson. "A man from Lexington said the marriage is going very well, and they expect their first child before long."

Anna reread the note. Then Major Jackson *was* enjoying something of the home life for which he had yearned. On impulse, she went upstairs to gather cotton cloth and colored threads; she would make a doll of the kind she had learned to fashion at the Moravian school at Salem, and send it to the Jacksons for their baby. As her fingers worked over the familiar pattern, she hummed to herself.

Hearing her daughter's light voice, her mother, who was passing in the hallway, the plantation keys hanging at her waist, entered Anna's room. She gave the girl an inquiring glance, and Anna explained, "For a couple I met in Lexington."

"Oh, yes, the Jacksons, I suppose. Both Eugenia and Isabella have told me about them." Miss Mary's face was noncommittal, but the penetrating eyes focused on Anna. "You've thought a lot about—about them, haven't you?"

"I suppose so. Shouldn't I have?" As she spoke, Anna wondered what her sisters had been saying—Isabella in particular.

"There's no reason why you shouldn't, my dear." Mary Morrison took a seat, and Anna saw a new perpendicular line between her gray eyebrows. "Only . . . Well, your father and I think it's finally time for you to be considering your own future."

A retort rose to Anna's lips, but she repressed it. Instead, she remained silent and shrugged, and Mary Morrison reached out to stop Anna's sewing with a gesture. "Child, let's not hide our thoughts from each other. Tell me, do you want to be like that Miss Phillips from New Orleans?"

Miss Phillips was the ridiculous, faded little sparrow of a woman who had visited them recently. She had corkscrew curls, wore finger mittens, and repeated skittish tales of the many men she had chosen to reject. Anna's mother went on, "Strange as it may sound, I've been told she *could* have been married once. But she waited too long."

"I don't know what this has to do with me." As she replied, Anna felt the beads of perspiration on her upper lip.

"Child, child." Mary Morrison's voice had a pleading note. "Don't let any—any impossible ideas and regrets keep you from seeing what's close to you, and possible. After you reach a certain age, men won't come around."

Anna became more and more disturbed as her mother continued. It was her duty to listen and to respond, yet she found it very difficult. She did not want to discuss these matters with anybody, even Miss Mary. At last she got up. "All right, I'll try to be a little more . . . a little more the way you want." Mrs. Morrison was somewhat relieved, though not entirely convinced. She left, sighing, and her place was taken by the round, husky brown form of Hetty, Anna's onetime nurse, now her maid and also general household helper. Hetty was high-spirited, and about fifteen years

Anna's senior. She was energetic, identified herself firmly with the Morrisons' concerns, and had a fierce interest in Anna's affairs.

Obviously Hetty had been listening outside, and equally obviously she agreed with Mrs. Morrison. Her black eyes raked over the girl, and her silence was heavy with meaning. Only after a few minutes did she speak in a high-pitched voice: "Miss Eugenia's lef' a fine piece o' lace, and I might could fix it fer a nice low-neck dress. Low as the Doctor allow it." Anna shook her head wryly; whatever plans Mrs. Morrison had in mind for potential suitors, Hetty would do her best to make them succeed.

As her maid talked on, Anna reflected. No one in the house had a stronger concern than Hetty for Morrison or Graham family standards. A guest of whom she did not approve drew scalding comment: "Thas' a half-strainer. Maybe he's not from Georgy, but he's a cracker anyhow." Hetty graded other callers in her own special fashion. The house had its show room, the parlor with paneled walls, a huge fireplace, and some excellent pre-Revolutionary sofas and chairs, originally Graham property. The family, however, generally preferred the book-lined, map-hung library, cozier (and also better warmed) than the parlor. In her mind, Hetty separated the sheep from the goats:

"He a nice 'un for the lib'ary." "Them, they belong to the front parlor." Or, in some cases, "That sort ain' worth our kitchen, I say." In any event, as Hetty folded her arms before her this morning, Anna could almost feel the pressures tightening upon her from backstairs as well as front.

The doll on which she was working never went to the Jacksons. On a visit to Davidson College, Anna had a long talk with Harvey Hill. Almost at once he asked, "You haven't heard what happened to Ellie Jackson?"

"No, except that the baby was about due."

Anna's brother-in-law paused. "It came, a girl, but she never breathed. And Ellie—she died at almost the same time."

Anna stared at Harvey. Such a harsh double blow, and so sudden. Poor Tom Jackson! To have everything taken from him in a day or two . . . She could think of nothing to say as Major Hill added, "They don't seem to know the cause, except that a little before it—it happened, poor Ellie made a long, hard trip by carriage over the mountains to visit Tom's sister Laura. The two women got along very well, and he was mighty happy about that; you know how much Laura always meant to him. And then . . ."

Harvey's next words escaped her. Under those circumstances, how much worse it must all seem to their friend. Swallowing, she asked Harvey, "Tom himself, how is he now?"

"It's been a grim thing for Old Jack." Harvey spoke very slowly. "Far more than for most husbands. I've never seen anybody who missed much more in life and realized it, too. Getting married like that was the best thing that ever happened to him." Harvey let out a long breath. "Major Preston says Jackson told him he'd be more than willing to follow Ellie right now, if God wished it. He goes to the grave every day and stands there for at least an hour. And poor Maggie . . ."

"What's happened to her?"

"You remember how devoted she was to her sister, almost worshipful? Their mother died just a short time before Ellie, and the two losses were too much for Maggie. She took sick right after Ellie's funeral, just broke down, and they sent her up to Pennsylvania to stay with some of the family for a change of scene and a complete rest. And Maggie's still there."

On her way home Anna pondered the dark words. The older sister, grieving so terribly . . . Suppose something like that happened to Eugenia? After a time her thoughts went to Tom. Those long visits to the grave, and his bleak talk of his own death . . . Would it all affect him permanently? The question remained with her for a long time.

As she stepped from the carriage, Anna spied a dark figure on the porch. "You real late," the shrill Hetty chided her, "and your ma and that fella been sittin' a long time."

"Which fellow?" Handing over her straw hat and light coat, Anna hesitated before she entered the house.

"Don' know." Hetty's evasive answer left Anna in no doubt that she knew quite well but would say nothing more. The girl's curiosity rose, to be tempered quickly by a hint of foreboding. On the sofa, next to her mother, sat a young, slightly plump man, impeccably dressed in broadcloth, with a shock of yellow hair and a pink complexion that made his face look as if permanently outlined in a shaft of light. At the sight of Anna he bounded to his feet and gave a wide smile.

"Dear, Reverend Conrad. He's here to talk to your father." In Mary Morrison's almost buoyant manner there was a trace of anxiety. "He's going to stay for supper, and isn't that nice?"

As Anna nodded, the guest burst into speech. "It seems a long time since we met. Oh, yes, excuse me. We did, Miss Anna, but it was a big crowd, and I can understand, of course, how you . . ." Reverend Conrad continued at length, explaining, apologizing. He was nice enough looking, she told herself, with his narrow nose and greenish eyes. If he would only stop being so tentative, so uncertain. "Miss Anna," he resumed, "I envy you your traveling so much. Oh, not really envy, I mean I . . ."

The newcomer went on and on, saying little or nothing. Anna had only to nod. She did, at intervals, and meanwhile her mind reverted to a lonely figure beside a distant grave. If she met Tom now, she would remind him, "Not my will, but Thine." She would——

"Anna, Reverend Conrad is asking a question." Her mother's words carried a reproof.

"I'm sorry." Anna faced the embarrassed man. "It's just that I had bad news today about—a friend. What did you say?"

The evening continued in much the same way, as she made replies which she hoped concealed her preoccupation. Reverend Conrad beamed as expansively as ever when Mrs. Morrison and Anna said good-by at the door. "Now you'll write before you get back month after next? We'd all like to see you again." As she spoke, Mary Morrison nodded several times, and Anna jumped when her mother's fingers pressed against her back. "Yes, Reverend Conrad, we certainly would," she murmured, and waved at him from the door.

When their visitor had left, Mrs. Morrison led her daughter into the house. "Now, young lady, what were you saying about bad news?"

It was on the day the new caller was to return that Anna had an answer to some of her own questions, from her sister Isabella, who was making a visit in the vicinity and had stopped at Cottage Home for an hour. While the servants watered her horses, the older sister talked of the flurry over a supposed slave uprising, then of the heavily rounded new skirts, which both agreed were foolish. "Still, we'll all be wearing them within a year," Anna shrugged. (Six months later, they were.) After that, to her relief, Isabella brought up the subject uppermost in Anna's mind.

"Oh, our friend Jackson's less disturbed now, though he's still sad. And he's staying with the Junkins, you know." About to start off, Isabella looked back. "Maggie's home, too, and we hear that

she and Tom are helping each other a lot, studying Spanish together every evening. Of course, there may be nothing serious in
any of it. Maggie's always been the mental type, hasn't she?"

Anna raised her hand in a silent good-by. Long after the carriage disappeared she watched the plume of dust that trailed
behind it. Clearly Isabella had told her these things with a purpose in mind; almost certainly her sister and mother had been
conferring. If only Isabella would stop interfering, stop playing
assistant mother as she'd done before. And now, in spite of her
effort, Anna's mind went to the two cases in this neighborhood in
which sisters of a woman who died eventually married the widower. A fragment of one of Isabella's conversations during her stay
in Lexington echoed in her ear. "When Maggie Junkin sets out to
do something—watch out." However "mental" the woman poet
might be, when two people who had so many common ties were
thrown together so much——

"Miss Anna, you sure thinkin' hard 'bout somethin'." Hetty's
high soprano, a few inches from her ear, made Anna start. "Mr.
Conrad soon be here, and I cut yer some fine roses fo' yer neck."
As if she had not heard, Anna walked slowly inside.

Through that winter and the next summer Anna alternated between two concerns: the regular visits of Reverend Conrad and
scraps of news from Lexington. She received no direct message
from Tom, but her mood lifted when her brother-in-law informed
her with a warm smile, "Our friend McIntyre had a long session
with Old Jack, and Mac says he's beginning to go around the town
a little. The doctors keep recommending a real change for Tom,
and trying to push him into making the trip to Europe he's always
talked of."

About to turn from the subject, Harvey added casually, "Oh,
Jack wanted to pass on his respects to us, and to you too, and to
say he thinks now and then of your visit up there." Anna gave her
brother-in-law a long look and stifled the temptation to ask for
more information; she must not play the fool, she told herself earnestly. Yet she could not thrust away the reflection. So Tom Jackson remembered her. Perhaps she could write a pleasant note,
explain that she had been wondering how . . . But as the thought
formed, she realized she could not do it. Even in this modern
year of 1855, a thing of that sort would be questionable.

"Reverend Conrad due mighty soon." At Hetty's prodding,

Anna began a desultory toilet. Accepting a pink skirt from the
maid, she told herself that the young minister was a good man, so
well-intentioned—and so extremely dull. He had yet to say anything she could not have predicted well in advance. Was it her
education, the training her father had given her, that made her so
unimpressed? Even if it was, she would prefer to keep the education and pass the Reverend Conrad by.

With a sigh Anna joined him downstairs to go to a party at a
nearby estate. There she noticed that none of the eighteen- or
nineteen-year-old girls were missing her escort's bland words and
gestures. An idea suggested itself; why not? Bringing several of
the girls over to him, she made an excuse to leave, and watched
from a distance as they assumed poses of breathless interest. Now,
however, it was Reverend Conrad who stood half-yawning, peering over their heads. Like many before and after her, Anna
pondered: why must the one you hope for be unconcerned, or
concerned with someone else?

Rejoining her, Reverend Conrad let her know that he had understood the incident. "Miss Anna," he whispered, "I'm a patient
man, very patient." When he left her with a touch of sadness,
Anna shook her head. She was afraid he would have full opportunity to prove he had that virtue.

Still other eyes had apparently witnessed the episode. Before
the week ended, Anna learned that both her mother and Isabella
had been giving considerable thought to the matter of her caller.
The older sister paid a seemingly unplanned visit and, approaching Anna in the garden, began without preamble. "Do you really
feel strongly against Reverend Conrad?"

"I do! Nothing's going to happen there, and you can tell Mother
that." This time she could not restrain her anger. During the pause
that followed, Anna heard the steady drone of a wasp among the
flowering bushes. "So it's as bad as that?" Isabella's voice had lost
its usual crisp decision. For a moment she remained silent, then
began again:

"Girl, I hope you're not building up something in your mind,
something without any hope or any—any basis. Sometimes you
can be so stubborn that you hurt yourself . . ." Anna looked away
and said nothing at all. Whatever she might be building or not
building was her own concern.

"Well, we'll have to try another way . . ." Moving off, Isabella
spoke as if to herself. Anna started to call after her. She didn't

want them trying "ways" for her; why didn't they simply let her alone? Miserably she stared down at the cut flowers in the basket before her, and let them slip to the ground.

Almost at once Anna discovered what the new way was to be. Her father talked twice of a Reverend Eagan from the Charlotte area, and mentioned that young man's plan to accept a temporary pastorate in their vicinity. Another minister . . .

Now, unexpectedly, she received a reprieve from the situation. It had been a long time since she saw Eugenia, and for a good reason. Months earlier, the girl had confided shyly that she was to have a baby. Anna had replied in delight, and she and Eugenia had exchanged a series of happy notes. Then, with the baby's birth only a few weeks off, Rufus Barringer dispatched a carriage to Cottage Home with a message. He thought his wife would be much easier in her mind if Anna was with her when her time came.

At once Anna wanted to be there. "I can go, can't I?" Nervously she thrust the note into her mother's hand. Mrs. Morrison's concern matched her daughter's. "You surely can. If only I didn't have everything to watch over here . . ." Miss Mary gave one order after another, and by early afternoon Anna was off, Hetty at her side in the carriage. Sitting forward, she tried not to think of the other birth—Ellie and Tom Jackson's child.

Her first probing look at her sister, and Eugenia's smiling greeting, reassured her to a degree. "It's just that I've been edgy," the girl told her. "And I'm tired, more tired than I've ever known myself." From then on Anna and the young husband stayed in Eugenia's room for hours at a time.

Two weeks passed, and the baby was overdue. "Nothing to concern us much," the doctor said. "It's mainly her emotional state. We have to make her relax as best she can." Eugenia seemed to Anna much too wan; as she lay in bed her fingers plucked anxiously at the sheets. To occupy her, Anna told of Cottage Home events, of Hetty's pungent comments on several Alabama callers. But although the girl nodded and laughed briefly, she relapsed quickly into a listless silence.

As Anna's uneasiness increased, there flashed through her mind the picture of Ellie Jackson and the child who was born dead. Biting her lip, she turned aside, and when she glanced up again, she caught her breath. Eugenia's face was contorted, and she was twisting from left to right on her bed. "Quick," Anna directed the

alarmed Hetty, "get word to the doctor, and Mr. Barringer too."
As the maid sped off, Anna took Eugenia's hands and tried to
quiet her whimpers. God, be kind to the girl . . .

The next hour was a growing agony. Eugenia suffered badly,
sweating, grimacing, her head rising and falling. Her screams
came every few minutes, and still the doctor did not arrive. Anna
had been present at several childbirths at the plantation, but
never under such conditions. All at once her sister gave a cry that
was almost a screech; as it pierced the air of the overheated room,
Anna ran to the window and sank to her knees. Please, let Eugenia
be spared this, and she would do whatever her father and mother
wanted; only let the torment stop . . .

Anna lifted her head. Silence had fallen, and she discovered
Hetty working intently over her sister. The brown arms reached
far down, and she saw a pinkish form in the light from the street.
A smack at its bottom, and a shrill complaint rang across the
chamber . . . For the next hour (the doctor and Rufus came when
they were no longer so urgently needed) Anna was so busy with
the little girl and Eugenia that she forgot everything else. Only
when she was able to sit down, breathing heavily, and wipe her
wet face, did she remember the pledge she had made as she
prayed at the window.

That night Anna dreamed of a strange mass wedding, the sort
about which she had read in a book of ancient history. With her
appeared her own groom, a shadowy individual whose name
someone muttered—"Reverend Eagan." When she moved toward
him, he ignored her. Angrily, she looked about to see dozens of
other couples in a circle about her, and suddenly she spotted one
face, that of Tom Jackson. Who was the woman beside him, the
small figure in white? She had to know, and she touched the
bride's shoulder. The woman swung around, but before Anna
could discover who she was, she woke. Could it have been Maggie
Junkin, or was it someone entirely new to her? The scene disturbed her and she could not get it out of her mind.

The new child was plump and pert, and Eugenia told Anna,
"I've picked her name—Anna, after you." Anna was so greatly
touched that when she tried to speak she could not.

She was alone when, soon afterward, Harvey Hill appeared at
the Barringer door, on a week-end visit to inspect his niece. Without waiting for Anna to bring up the matter, her brother-in-law
addressed her brightly: "They've talked Jack into making his

European trip. Leaving right soon, and everybody says it's what
he needs most of all." Though they spoke for some time, these
were the words that Anna carried with her when, after her long
good-bys, she set off again for Cottage Home. Harvey had made
no mention of Maggie Junkin, nor had she. In any case her
thoughts were of Tom. In this change of scene, this interlude of
rest and travel, God grant that he receive the benefit he needed so
badly.

Mrs. Morrison greeted her with a warm embrace, a dozen inquiries about the baby, and, as she and Hetty unpacked, information of the kind that Anna had expected. "Dear, Reverend Eagan
will be here in a few weeks." Her mother studied Anna's expres-
sionless face. "Won't you be glad to meet somebody else, somebody new?"

"Oh, that will be very nice, very nice!" Forcing a pretense
of interest, Anna asked several questions, and Mary Morrison
nodded gratefully. With each day the Morrisons managed to drop
a word about the approaching visitor until, as Anna told Hetty in
some amusement, "This time they're making me really curious
about the man."

Soon Reverend Eagan arrived, and when Anna entered the library one afternoon she found a young man in a black suit, with
dark hair and swarthy skin, standing motionless before the fireplace. His face was interesting in an irregular way, Anna decided
at once. His eyes appeared opaque in their blackness, and his skin,
though closely shaven, gleamed slightly blue at the jowls.

From the first Reverend Eagan demonstrated a marked reserve,
an unchanging solemnity. He bowed, and his voice boomed out
from a point deep in his stomach. "Miss Anna, a pleasure." Both
Dr. Morrison and his wife began to talk, and Anna added several
sentences of her own. Then the visitor took a breath, fixed his gaze
upon her, and responded, "Yes." All three Morrisons picked up
the conversational thread, and a few minutes later Reverend
Eagan breathed deeply again and intoned, "Why, no."

Over supper Dr. Morrison worked to sketch in the newcomer's
background, his training, the rare record he had made in a few
years. At intervals the young minister nodded, and that was all.
As she was telling him good-by at the door, it occurred to Anna
that he had not said more than five or six consecutive words during
the entire evening, and as they went back into the house, her

mother had an absorbed air: "I'm sure he'll be more—well, articulate after we know him better."

Anna doubted it, but said nothing. When the dark youth came back for a second visit, she discovered that she had been right; at the end of this evening both of her parents were close to exhaustion with the long effort they had made. Now, a new surprise— Reverend Conrad again. As the pink-blond applicant bounded up one afternoon, Anna gaped. Couldn't he realize how she felt?

It seemed that he could not, and for the next few months Anna had one caller, then the other, and sometimes both. Glancing from the first to the second, she told herself sadly that she had to take one of them. Both Dr. Morrison and her mother wore fixed expressions, and there was an ever more persistent note in their hintings.

Fall arrived, and on the first cold week end her brother-in-law walked in, beat his hands together in the chilly hallway, and turned toward her with an appraising stare. "Young lady, you can guess I've heard from Lexington again. Yes, Jack's home from Europe and starting everything again with a vim. Oh, that's a new word they're using in Charlotte, though I'm not sure what it means . . ." As Harvey, his eyes gleaming mischievously, rambled off into this triviality, Anna had an impulse to snap at him, "Get back to the subject, please, and stop the foolishness." Nevertheless, she remained silent until he returned to Tom. "By the way, Anna, I wouldn't be surprised if Old Jack didn't begin to—er, look around the world again."

"Look around the world . . ." She wondered if Harvey Hill sensed the thumping of her heart. Precisely what did he mean by that? In any case, she thought more and more of Tom Jackson. Would they meet again soon—or ever again? He still had not sent a single note to her, or indicated anything other than a vague memory of her.

In early winter Eugenia visited Cottage Home with the baby, and Anna gave her namesake unending attention. On a chilly December morning she sat on the floor of her room beside the little girl, who was crawling determinedly about. The junior Anna had wide eyes and light hair, and she laughed almost constantly.

"What a fine child!" Talking partly to the baby, partly to Eugenia, Anna held the tiny form at arm's length to admire her. From her place across the room the child's mother laughed to herself. "Wait till you have one of your own."

The two girls looked up as Hetty approached with a neat envelope. "Jes' come by pos', f'om a Major Jackson."

Anna's breath quickened. Eugenia stared inquiringly, and her eyes went from the letter to her sister's face. Anna felt a swift embarrassment, then an emotion that was half happiness, half fear. Suppose it was only a casual message, or one that meant nothing at all? A moment later her composure and her confidence returned. It was the letter for which she had been waiting a long, long time.

CHAPTER 4

Like Tom Jackson himself, this letter was ungraceful. Sitting beside Eugenia that morning, Anna read hastily and without paying heed to her curious sister. He had been thinking a great deal of late, he wrote, of their meetings in Lexington, their walks and the evenings he had spent with her and the Hills. As Anna might have heard, God had shown His will by taking his wife and child, and for a time he had allowed the tragedy to overwhelm him. Now, however, he wanted to let her know he remembered his "old friend, Miss Anna Morrison." He finished "with kindest regards . . ."

More slowly she reread the message, balancing the words. Some people might consider it strange that Major Jackson should write her after so long a time, and in a way it *was* strange. Then she assured herself that thus far, at least, there seemed to be nothing definite or settled between him and Maggie Junkin. The surge of relief that went through her made her realize for the first time how deeply the question of the older woman had been etched in her mind. And now she could admit to herself all the things she had never been willing to face about her feelings for Tom Jackson.

In the confusion of her emotions, she wished suddenly that she were alone. Nevertheless she forced herself to face her sister, who extended her hand for the note. As the girl read it, she smiled, and when she had finished, she asked, "Hm, what do you make of it?"

Anna picked up her sewing. "Nothing. It's just a greeting."

Eugenia gave a dry laugh. "If you believe that, Anna, you know less about men than I think. You're going to have a visit from Old Jack, and right soon, I can tell you." As a married woman, Eugenia automatically had begun to assume a superiority over Anna in all matters involving men.

At the words Anna's heart quickened again. Perhaps she should reply to him, say that she also recalled the summer, that she was glad he had returned . . .

Her sister guessed her thoughts. "I hope you aren't going to answer him."

"Why, of course not."

"It's up to him to make the next move, and don't you anticipate it." The dinner gong rang a moment later, and Anna accepted her release with unspoken thanks. At the table, when he had finished reciting the grace, her father exchanged glances with Mary Morrison. "Child, I understand a Virginia friend has written you."

"That's true." Anna felt a brief dart of anger, then reflected that, in a place like Cottage Home, few secrets were ever possible. Gingerly she spoke of Tom, and Dr. Morrison went on, his voice deeper than ever, "How old is Major Jackson?"

"About thirty-three, I think." As she answered, Anna fumed to herself. Why couldn't she speak less nervously? She had nothing to apologize for.

"And I take it he isn't from one of the old Virginia families?"

Anna lowered her fork, repressing the answer that had come immediately to her tongue. Neither were the Morrisons, nor her father's own candidates, Reverend Eagan and Reverend Conrad. To say that, however, would have been to break with the habits of a lifetime and to cause a bitter scene. Already Sue and Laura were listening with interest. And so, instead, she responded quietly, "I don't think he is; he's from the western section, but his family's had a good position in its time."

"I see, but no great position now."

A dull sense of uneasiness settled over Anna, and she applied herself silently to her chicken. If—if things worked out with Tom, did her duty still require her to accept someone whom her father preferred? Her eyes darkening with worry, she looked around the table. Eugenia sat with lowered head; the younger sister, never one for a fight, would be neutral. But now Mary Morrison faced Anna with a hint of a shrug which only Anna noted—a shrug that had its own meaning. While Mrs. Morrison would not commit herself, she was letting her daughter know that she was not yet firmly against her. "We shall see," Mary Morrison was saying . . . Suddenly Anna felt almost bouyant.

Christmas approached, and during the next ten days or so of family parties no one mentioned the name of Thomas Jonathan Jackson. Dr. Morrison's attitude was clear; several times he spoke of Reverend Eagan, and his remarks were so pointed that Anna judged he had made his choice. The dark, mute Reverend Eagan . . . The prospect of a lifetime at his side made her quiver.

In an uncertain mood Anna went one afternoon to her room to resume work on some dresses she had started the day she received Tom's note. First she sewed a line of extra buttons which matched the brown of her eyes on a reddish afternoon gown. From the wardrobe she took up a blue evening dress with comparatively short sleeves. Holding it critically against her, she found it lacking. Simplicity was nice, but this had all too much simplicity. After a hunt through her closet she drew out a piece of creamy lace. "We'll hold that for a real occasion," Mrs. Morrison had once said. Well, Anna might have an occasion before long, and she wanted to be ready.

A heavy step pounded down the hall, and Hetty was in the doorway, her black eyes missing nothing. "Exter buttons, bes' lace . . . Mus' be de Pres'dent hisself comin'." Hetty regarded the out-lander Jackson from Virginia, of whom she had heard several things by now, with open suspicion. When Anna made no response, the maid asked a pointed question. Then she halted abruptly to go forward and squint through the window.

Joining her there, Anna saw a horseman tying his mount to the hitching post. While she could not be certain, it might be . . . it was. There he came, walking firmly, deliberately, his eyes fixed as on a distant point. As she saw his neat uniform—white trousers, dark blue frock coat, with shoulder straps, closed up to his chin with brass buttons—a pulse beat in Anna's throat. Tom Jackson's face was leaner, his frame lighter; he must have lost weight in the past few years. Yet his color was good and his air bright. When he disappeared on the porch below, she was caught by a swift, joyful tenderness.

Hetty grunted. "Don' 'pear like much to *me*."

The words brought Anna back to the immediate situation. "That's enough. Now get me some warm water, and hurry, please!" Not too quickly, Hetty left the room. By the time she reappeared Anna had completed the new lace collar and thrown off her plainer attire.

Splashing the water over her, Anna called out, "You're sure Miss

Mary is talking to him, and Miss Eugenia, too, and they've sent to the back fields for Dr. Morrison?" Meanwhile she told herself that Tom must have left Lexington only a few days after he sent the letter, and that was a good sign.

Almost at once a doubt suggested itself: Suppose he was only passing through on an errand, say a conference about a teaching position in another college? Thrusting back the speculation, she went over the things she would say to him and how she would say them. After a final touch to her tightly combed hair, a quick running of her tongue over her full lips, a rub of her hand over her cheeks to give them color, Anna slipped to the hall and descended, the wide skirts of her dress brushing against the stairs.

The gown might be too light for such a day, and too festive; she would wear it nevertheless. A look told her that the guest had been taken to the library. As she approached, she heard Tom's voice and his usual quick sentences: "I can be here only a couple of days, ma'am. My leave is a short one, and I had to promise I'd be back on Monday."

From the doorway Anna saw her mother's surprise at the new dress. Dr. Morrison himself had not yet arrived, but her brothers and sisters formed a circle around the Major, who stood as if holding off a hostile force. When she entered he seemed startled, and he flushed and stammered. His assurance of only a few minutes ago was, alas, deserting him.

"Miss—Miss Anna! It's good to—to see you again. I've thought about you all this week . . ." With that, as if he had confessed to some indiscretion, Tom's tight voice trailed off, and he stood still, hands stiffly at his sides. At the same time that his words stirred and delighted Anna, she felt a quick start of compassion for the awkward fellow. Mercifully her mother intervened, "Major, I wish you'd tell us about your trip here. The roads are bad now, aren't they?" This subject occupied him for a few minutes, and from then on, Jackson managed well enough.

"What was Europe like?" He echoed Anna's question. "It was everything I ever imagined it would be, and more, too. But I always ask my friends not to mention the subject to me." A rare touch of humor lighted his long face. "Just name it, and I'm off on a lecture."

Mrs. Morrison murmured a light comment, and Anna relaxed a little; her mother was not unpleased. A moment later, however, Jackson made some awkward statement, and Anna's sister Sue

snickered with all the sophistication of the teen-age girl, young
Joe snorted, and Eugenia's merriment was only half-suppressed.
Tom lowered his eyes in embarrassment, and Anna struggled
against the impulse to lash out at her sisters and brother. Instead,
she plunged into another topic.

"Maggie Junkin," she asked, "is she back at her writing?"

At the question Tom assumed an amused smile, tinged with
affection. He gave her a sidelong glance: "I'd say that Maggie is
busy at other things now, romantic things."

"Oh." Anna asked herself if he meant Maggie—and him. All the
thoughts she had tried to dismiss returned in a rush: the widower,
the same house, the sister of the dead wife. Her face must have
mirrored something of her confused feelings, for her mother
quietly took over the conversation.

The next half-hour, Anna decided in retrospect, was among the
darkest of her life. Words drifted aimlessly past her; did any of it
matter? Even when a firm step signaled her father's arrival and
she greeted him, she saw the scene through a gray haze of misery.

"Father, Major Jackson has come to see us." Her voice sounded
flat in her ears, and she paid scant heed as the two men spoke
with marked restraint. A few minutes later she discovered that
Mrs. Morrison was addressing her husband: "Robert, Anna and
the Major haven't had a moment to talk together." Mary Morrison's expression became more purposeful: "Don't you think they
could go to the parlor for a while before we have supper?" Giving
Dr. Morrison no chance to reply, she issued directions to two
servants: "Make a good fire in the library, Joseph, and you, Henry,
take the Major's bag to the room upstairs."

In the hall Mrs. Morrison had an opportunity to whisper to
Anna, "Don't be so upset, but go in there and smile!" Anna could
only nod; even had she wished, she could not have explained what
was in her mind. With Tom at her side, she followed the dark attendant into the big, paneled room, which was even chillier than
she had expected. The couple sat down together on the couch.

"Well, Anna." Tom's gaze moved quickly over her, and at last
he sensed her downcast spirit. She lowered her eyes, and his hesitant words dropped like pebbles into a distant lake. A heavy silence followed, and she faced him; in spite of herself she had to
bring up the question that hovered over her. "What about Maggie
and—the romance?"

A surprised frown appeared between his eyes. "I'm not sure I

should tell any more, because neither of them says much about
it."

"Neither of *them?*"

"Why, no." Tom had still not perceived her meaning, and she
was happy that he had not. Unable to speak for a moment, she
felt a rush of overwhelming delight. How foolish she had been . . .

"Well, I guess I *can* tell you." Now his smile reflected her own
widening one. "The man is Major Preston. Maybe you hadn't
heard that his wife died last year, and——"

"But Maggie and the Major! They're the last two I'd ever imagine getting married. The first time I met them they were practically at snarling point, and he certainly doesn't have a high
opinion of lady writers."

Tom shook his head: "That's all true, and still . . . Well, after
Miss Sally died, they began to see each other a little. Maggie's
always had a fine hand with young people; she helped raise so
many of the Junkins. And the way it turned out, I suppose I was
a sort of agent, bringing the two of them together. They've had
some stormy arguments, but now it's all set—I think," he ended
cautiously.

Anna's eyes shone with relief and her amusement at the picture
of the two oddly matched lovers. After a moment she forgot everything else as Tom leaned toward her. His hand went out, then
he drew it back, and when he spoke it was in a muffled voice.
"Anna, for a time I was sure my life had reached a dark place,
that everything worked against me. I couldn't accept what——"

Suddenly he coughed, and so did she. From the fireplace a
swirl of brown smoke spiraled through the room. Her eyes smart-
ing, Anna groaned to herself; what would happen to them next?
"Let me attend to it," he murmured, and poked at the meager
blue flame that flickered from the kindling. She watched help-
lessly as he worked, until, red with exertion and embarrassment,
he gave up: "I just can't do it, Anna."

Trying to conceal her chagrin, she called into the hall. One of
the house servants came in and struggled with the fire, but he
had no better luck. By now the room was acrid with smoke, and
Anna, surrendering to the situation, led Tom back to the library,
where they explained what had happened as good-humoredly as
they could. Then followed a long effort at conversation-making
with Dr. and Mrs. Morrison: the newest arguments over extension
of slavery to the territories, last week's steamboat explosion on the

Mississippi near Natchez. Close to exasperation, Anna wondered
when and where she and Tom could be alone.

Once again Mary Morrison acted. Taking her husband's hand,
she gave him a significant stare: "My dear, you're the only one in
this house who really knows about that fireplace." Reluctantly, the
minister left accompanied by his wife, and the couple sat awkwardly with the giggling younger Morrisons until Anna's parents
returned. Both were flushed with smoke, but Mrs. Morrison had
an air of triumph. "Fallen bricks that cut off the draft—that's all.
And now you young people can go back." She smiled them away,
and Dr. Morrison peered less happily after them.

This time a log glowed in the fireplace. When Tom drew Anna
forward, his fingers remained on her arm and his touch stirred
her. On the sofa next to her he spoke even more quickly than
usual, his words pouring out: "Anna, you may know what—what
I'm going to say. It was odd, the way we met when things were
so different for us." She listened, her color rising. His eyes did not
leave hers, and his look was one of petition and appeal. "But I
believe everything's happened for us the way it was meant to."

Anna's breath caught in her throat. Pausing, he asked more
slowly, "Don't you think so, too?"

Anna reflected. She knew that Eugenia would tell her to act
uncertain, to answer that she did not know. She could almost hear
her younger sister's voice: "Don't be too eager or you'll lose the
advantage." Her lips tightened. She didn't want any "advantage";
what she wanted was the man beside her.

"Yes," she told him. "Yes, I think it was meant this way." A moment later he reached out clumsily to her; she inclined her head
and he kissed her tentatively, inexpertly.

A wry suggestion crossed her mind; for a man who had been
married a year or more, Tom Jackson did not demonstrate any
great skill at this art. Then, however, he held her more firmly and
gave her a warm and exploratory second kiss. Her arms tightened
around him; he paused to murmur to her, and his lips went over
her cheeks and throat . . . Afterward they settled back, Anna still
in his arms, and sat gazing into the fire.

"The room's a lot warmer now." She smiled and reddened, and
they laughed together. Tom grew serious, and after a long hesitation he spoke. His voice was tense; it was as if he had to force
out his words. "Anna, I don't have the fine ways of a lot of people,
you know, and I suppose I can be difficult. I have to tell you some-

thing more, too. You may not have heard it, but I haven't been really well for a long time."

With an effort, Tom continued. "For a while I felt sure I was in danger of consumption, and I've had—well, nervous complaints. I've managed to control my health, but I've had to struggle over these troubles for a long time, and still do. I'm never sure . . ."

This was surprising, and yet it did not matter. "My father's had sickness for half his life, and he's survived," she assured him. Now, like her mother, she could be working at her husband's side to safeguard his health.

"Still, Anna . . ." He spoke as if he had memorized everything he meant to tell her. "I've been afraid several times that I was going blind. I've overused my eyes, and I've had to make hard rules for myself, so that even today I never use them after dark."

Though he obviously wanted to say more, she put her fingers over his lips. He had had so many things to fight against, and how well he had fought. Footsteps sounded in the hall, and she talked nervously, "Tom, about my father . . . I'm not sure. He's had other plans, and we'll have to see what we can do."

Clearly Tom was disappointed, and yet, she gathered, he was not entirely surprised, for Dr. Morrison's reserve had been evident. As he nodded, an emotion that was part anger, part anxiety welled within her. She was twenty-five now, and her father couldn't really forbid them in a showdown. But she prayed that matters should not reach that state. Her face tightened at the prospect of the harsh hours that might be ahead for her and Tom.

A few minutes later Hetty appeared in the doorway. "Supper right soon, and Mike, he here to show Major to his room." The maid took the opportunity to give Tom a long, close scrutiny. When he disappeared with a last whispered word to Anna, she and her mother had a few minutes for a private exchange.

"You're sure of the way you feel about him?" Pushing Anna back at arm's length, Mary Morrison stared into the rapt face. "You are," she answered her own question, and sighed slowly. "One thing, then, though I hesitate to bring it up, child. Your situation, your entire life will be a lot different if you marry the Major. As a teacher's wife you won't have the servants you're used to, or the easy, casual ways."

"I don't care about any of it, any of it."

Although she gave her daughter a somewhat dubious look, Mary Morrison nodded: "I suspected you'd say that. Very well, we'll see how we can manage." After a few questions about Tom, she left.

Through supper Anna made little effort to conceal the glowing happiness that enveloped her. Eugenia cast puzzled glances at her and at the erect figure seated opposite them, while Dr. Morrison continued in a stony mood, making only brief replies to his wife's remarks.

"Anna tells me Major Jackson is a deacon of his church," Mrs. Morrison said hopefully.

When Dr. Morrison inclined his head, the Major took up the theme. "Yes, several of us give evenings regularly to church meetings, and I've never stayed away from one of them. A member once told me he missed some because he lacked time. I replied that I didn't see how that could be, or how he could have time for anything else during the hour set aside for this important business." As Tom explained, Anna saw the deep sincerity in his eyes. These words were not spoken to please the man at the head of the table, but because Tom Jackson truly believed them.

"Well put, sir." Dr. Morrison nodded, and before long described some of his own experiences with congregations. His interest growing, he put a question. "Major, are you of the new church or the old?"

Anna's spoon halted in midair, for her father had strong feelings on this point.

"The old. I don't hold with a lot of those people who'd temper doctrine to meet the shifting world."

"Indeed." Dr. Morrison said nothing more, but Anna knew that Tom Jackson had answered him well. A few minutes later her father brought up a subject of his own: "Major, you know something of farming, I hear. I wonder what your opinion is of cotton?"

The younger man frowned: "Cotton's done harm to the South in a lot of ways. We'd be better off if we'd develop a balance and save our soil . . ."

As Tom responded, Anna realized that he had again struck a favorite note of her father's, and now the two traded experiences.

"I've always said that a good soil renewer is . . ."

"In Western Virginia we start late in spring, and . . ."

Although the dinner ended on a pleasant note, Anna understood all too well that matters had not been settled. "I must leave not later than the morning after next," the Major observed quietly, and from the set of his heavy jaw she knew he meant what he said. What to do next? She could only follow the lead of her mother, who sat quietly, smiling and waiting.

Before long Dr. Morrison rose. "Time for all of us to be going up." After a family prayer, he inclined his head. "Good night, sir." Sadly Anna started away, and as she did Mary Morrison murmured, "Don't rush things, child, don't rush . . ."

The next day Dr. Morrison appeared somewhat more friendly, but it was evident that he had not yet been won over. Breakfast passed without incident, except that the minister noticed how little Tom ate. In Lexington, Anna had become accustomed to her friend's careful food habits; she knew that he took no gravies, no rich or spicy dishes.

"A fine ham is a good way to start the day," Dr. Morrison observed as he held out a plate.

"Thank you, sir, but I haven't been able to eat it in years. Only a bit of milk and bread—no butter, ma'am—and some of the fruit, if I may have it." Though Anna's father nodded, the words had not impressed him greatly. After breakfast, Dr. Morrison left for a trip around his acreage, his dogs yelping around him and his horse; he would not interrupt his usual routine for Tom Jackson. Taking her guest on a walk about the plantation, Anna showed him the spinning room with the "summer kitchen" below. He inspected the looms before which the elderly women worked, and then the cabins of the Negro quarters, the dairy, and the smokehouse. While he asked several alert questions, she soon realized that something was hovering over him.

"Will you tell me what's disturbing you?" she asked as they rested beside a wooden fence near the garden.

"It's just this," Tom began, and his eyes had a look of pain. "Anna, I didn't say much about—Ellie, and I want you to understand. She did so much for me, gave me a—a stronger belief in myself, and helped me move more easily among people. She . . ." As he continued Anna felt a hurt she could not force away. Did Tom have to tell her all this about the other girl? Nevertheless, she made herself listen: "I'll never forget her, Anna, and I—I hope you'll realize it."

"Of course, Tom." Though it cost her an effort, she smiled and hoped to end the subject lightly. "Just don't forget me either!" He grinned, and they started back. On the way Anna mused: try as she might, she would remember that other woman for a long time—the one Tom had first chosen, who had been with him that full year or more. She could see Ellie in his arms, resting beside him . . .

At supper Mrs. Morrison set a tone of casual, easygoing ex-

change. Nervously Anna watched the others. Wouldn't her father
give some hint that his approval was growing? As she sat playing
with her food, her anger broke. He had raised no objections
two years ago when Eugenia wanted to marry Rufus, or when
Harriet had Mr. Irwin's proposal, or Isabella Major Hill's. Across
the table Eugenia remained noncommittal, and Anna suffered a
stab of irritation.

Perhaps she should speak out now and tell her father precisely
how she felt about Tom. Then, if he wanted to, let him try to stop
them! But she remembered a neighbor, a girl who had done something of that sort four years ago and had still to be reconciled with
her family. The thought of so sharp a break was too painful, and
slowly her resentment slipped away. Forcing her attention back
to the table, she found that the topic of slavery was under discussion and that Tom was speaking.

"I've seen nothing in the Bible to forbid it, and yet I'm not one to
go around crying out for the system. I don't believe I'll ever go and
hunt for somebody to own. But there are two slaves in my name in
Lexington."

Anna was surprised; no one had mentioned this to her. Where
were the two? He told them as he resumed: "Both asked me to
take them from their owners. One's old and not well, and she felt
sure they'd sell her far south. The other—I agreed to let him earn
his freedom, and he's doing it."

Her father nodded, and Anna was profoundly touched. The
more she learned of this good man, the greater grew her admiration for him. "And now let's have some music." Mary Morrison
spoke up as they left the table. Anna went to the piano, and there
Tom joined Eugenia and Sue. When the highly unmusical voice
rang out, Dr. Morrison glanced up sharply, then managed to conceal his amusement. Anna had forgotten how badly Tom sang,
and how exuberantly. As if entirely unconscious of her father's
reaction, Tom went on as serenely and loudly as ever.

After a time, Dr. Morrison got to his feet, called for them all
to retire, gave the blessing, and stamped upstairs. With an uncertain look at her mother, Anna told Tom good night. What
would happen in the morning? Tom had to leave then, and the
whole matter was still up in the air. She spent a restless night,
and, waking at six-thirty, gazed out of the window. What she
saw made her sit up, transfixed. The Harvey Hills' carriage
waited at the side; it must have just arrived. Sipping at the warm
milk Hetty had brought, she asked the maid for an explanation.

"Didn't you hear your Ma sen' a message to the Major and Miss Isabella yestiddy?" The girl frowned, for whatever Miss Mary's opinion of Tom Jackson, Hetty still reserved her approval.

Anna jumped to her feet. Harvey Hill liked and admired Tom, and he also had considerable influence with her father. For all his occasionally quizzical remarks, Harvey was on her side! As for Isabella . . . Anna's face fell. Her oldest sister, she feared, had been using her authority against her in conferences with Mrs. Morrison. But now that their mother was on Anna's side, surely Isabella would not oppose the match, would she?

As Anna dressed, Hetty entered with a bulletin: Major Hill was having an early breakfast with Dr. Morrison and Major Jackson, and Miss Isabella had just joined them. At the news, Anna slowed her own preparations; it would be best to leave the group alone as long as possible. But even though she took her time, the meal was still being served when she descended, and she hesitated at the bottom of the stairs. Her mother met her there, and they stood for a time, tensely silent.

"Oh, they're coming out now." Anna found herself whispering as if she were a conspirator as the four emerged, single file, from the dining room, a stern Dr. Morrison in the lead, Tom Jackson bringing up the rear. He seemed to be tired; perhaps uncertainty had kept him from sleeping well. By unspoken consent they all went to the library, and there, after a pause, Harvey Hill laughed nervously, "Well, Father, we're waiting."

Dr. Morrison's eyes moved from face to face, and slowly his manner softened. "After some consideration, I can make no objection to an engagement between Anna and the Major. I would have preferred a longer wait, but I understand that Major Jackson must return, and in these days of rush and informality . . ."

Anna heard the rest in a joyous confusion. Tom hoped for a June or July wedding, after the Institute had closed, and he promised that if possible he would visit again before then. Now they were all exclaiming, shaking hands, exchanging kisses, and Sue, Laura, and the other young Morrisons ran in to share in the excitement. During a lull in the congratulations, Isabella caught Anna's eye and they went together to the end of the hall. "My dear," her sister whispered, "I want you to know how glad I am, after all. For a long time you worried me, and so did—the whole situation." For once the competent Mrs. Hill showed a marked embarrassment. "I thought you were foolish and that it couldn't work out, or wouldn't . . . Well, I'm happy I was so wrong!" Isabella took her in her arms, Anna cried a little, and then they returned to the others.

Suddenly she realized that Tom looked anxious, and he told her, "Anna, I have less than twenty minutes left, and I've had them saddle my horse." Even at a time like this, he must live by schedule! Drawing her aside, he talked for a few minutes, and she sensed that a last worry nagged him. "Darling," he said, "I'm doing cadet training at the Institute, and if a new war starts, you understand they could call me right away?"

Relieved that the subject was no more serious, she shrugged: "This country hasn't had a war in years. We'll deal with that problem when it comes up." Not until a day or two later did she realize that Tom had not meant a foreign conflict but another kind. Meanwhile, as she kissed him a warm good-by, a random memory touched her. She had once sworn she would never marry a man who was a widower, a Democrat, or a soldier, and now she was to be the wife of all three in one! And it did not matter at all, at all . . .

Exactly twenty minutes after his warning of his time limit, Tom Jackson jumped on his horse and rode away. The family waved at him from the doorway, and then returned to the library. "Nothing in this house will go as usual today, I'm afraid," Dr. Morrison said as they settled around the fire. Deep in conversation, no one paid much heed to outside sounds until the butler bowed at the minister's elbow.

"Beggin' pardon, sir, Major Jackson outside and pray kin he talk to you private." Everyone stared and Anna half-rose, to be pulled back by her mother. Could something have gone wrong? From the hall they heard the Major's voice. "Dr. Morrison, I believe I told you my salary was $1500 or a little more. I was so preoccupied, sir, I wasn't precise."

"That's not important, my boy." Dr. Morrison's tone was soothing, and Anna sighed in relief. Nevertheless she lowered her eyes and wondered what her family would think of this.

"I'm afraid it is important, Doctor. I earn only $1485, and I didn't want to mislead you." The conversation continued for several minutes, and once more the Major started off, this time more quickly to make up for the time he had lost. As the hoofbeats fell away, Harvey turned to the Morrisons: "A thing like that may not matter to us. To Old Jack it does. You know, to be correct in everything you say—that isn't a bad thing."

At her brother-in-law's words, Anna smiled, all her love for Tom Jackson in her eyes. Let others call him peculiar; she admired him all the more for what he had just done. Then hastily she swung around: "Oh, I just remembered something; Reverend Eagan is supposed to come over tonight!"

During the next few months Tom and Anna corresponded once a week, and she soon learned the depth of the man's feelings, his regard for her and also for his religion. He wrote more easily than he spoke, though he would never be an easy stylist, and many times she was to reread his words:

It is a great comfort to me to know that although I am not with you, yet you are in the hands of One who will not permit any evil to come nigh you. . . . I have been sorely disappointed at not hearing from you this morning, but these disappointments are all designed for our good.

Frequently Tom described his trips through the Virginia countryside, and she recalled her first surprise on discovering how much he savored the richnesses of the land. He declared:

In my daily walks I think much of you. I love to stroll abroad after the labors of the day are over, and indulge feelings of gratitude to God for all the sources of natural beauty with which He has adorned the earth. . . . In the morning, all animated nature (man excepted) appears to join in expressions of gratitude to God; in the evening, all is hushing into silent slumber. . . . And as my mind dwells on you, I love to give it a devotional turn, by thinking of you as a gift from our Heavenly Father.

With each note Anna learned more of his strong religious convictions. He never sent a letter if he knew that, to reach her, it must travel on a Sunday, and he asked her to follow the same rule. When one of her notes arrived after dark on a Saturday, when he could not risk eye injury by reading it immediately, he waited until Monday. When his friends discovered this, several of them guyed him and one asked, "Now that you have the letter in your pocket here at church, won't your curiosity distract you from worship even more than if you were to open it now?"

To this, Tom told her, he shook his head. Since he followed his course from a sense of duty, he felt that no such distraction would occur, and it did not. Anna read the note to her father and nodded. Although she was a minister's daughter, she was getting instruction from Tom Jackson!

The month of April brought the Morrisons a hard blow. One afternoon while she was in the garden, Anna caught sight of one of Harvey Hill's servants jumping down from the saddle. Drawing up her skirts, she intercepted him. "Lil' Masta Morrison, he taken down real hard, and dey wan' you-all dere!"

A few minutes later Anna and her mother, their faces white, started for Davidson College. On the way Anna thought lovingly of the tense boy; overindulged as he was, she found him ever dearer to her. By the time they pushed open the Hills' door it was too late. Isabella greeted them with a low groan, "I wish it had been me," and sank against Mrs. Morrison. Anna stood crying to herself as she recalled the boy, so quick-witted, so bright-mannered. She was still with the Hills when Tom wrote her, and his first words made her start. He had prayed that the heavy affliction might "be sanctified to them," he said, and added:

I was not surprised that little Morrison was taken away, as I have long regarded his father's attachment to him as too strong; that is, so strong that he would be unwilling to give him up, though God should call him for His own. I do not believe that an attachment ever is, or can be, absolutely too strong for any object of our affections; but our love to God may not be strong enough. We may not love Him so intensely as to have no will but His. . . . Is there not a comfort in prayer which is nowhere else to be found?

Anna read over the letter again. There were those who would consider some of its phrases harsh, and yet she believed she could understand Tom's meaning, his emphasis on God's will. After a time she took solace in his final words.

By now it became evident that his work would not permit him to return to Cottage Home before the wedding, and Dr. Morrison agreed to a July date. Alone, Anna reflected how strange some might think it that the marriage had been arranged so promptly. But she felt certain that Providence had planned it all in this way, and she was satisfied. In mid-May she slowly reread the newest of his messages:

When in prayer for you last Sabbath, the tears came to my eyes, and I realized an unusual degree of emotional tenderness. I have not yet fully analyzed my feelings to my satisfaction, so as to arrive at the cause of such emotions; but I am disposed to think that it consisted in the idea of the intimate relation existing between you, as the object of my tender affection, and God, to whom I looked up as my Heavenly Father.

She remained alone for a long time with this letter. How often Tom thought of God, and how earnestly he hunted for meanings. For years he had groped for his way, and now that he had discovered it he clung strongly to the faith he had chosen. Was she half so devout? She had the answer to that; she was not.

As July approached, Mrs. Morrison devoted part of each day to preparations for the wedding and the trip East that would follow. Weeks earlier they had ordered Anna's trousseau from New York— a trailing white dress and traveling costumes in four colors. "I've never had anything like these," Anna told her mother in gratitude.

Several times Tom had written of his sister Laura, now Mrs. Jonathan Arnold of Western Virginia. Remembering his special attachment, Anna wrote Laura, urging her to attend the wedding. But, as Tom had anticipated, the retiring Mrs. Arnold explained that she could not make the long trip. Anna was deeply disappointed. She felt that she had to meet this woman who meant so much to Tom, of whom he spoke so often.

With some surprise, Anna learned that one of the groomsmen would be Reverend Eben Junkin, brother of Maggie and Ellie. His first wife's brother an attendant at the groom's wedding to the second . . . And another groomsman was to be Tom Preston, oldest son of the Major, who would soon marry Maggie. Her fate was curiously connected with the Junkins and the Prestons.

The days of early July passed nervously for Anna. When Tom rode in, forty-eight hours before the ceremony, she kissed him, then drew back with a look of anxiety. "My things haven't arrived from New York! And it's too late to do anything more about them."

"Why not simply wait?" He laughed as he said it, and his amusement made Anna frown in anger. "They'll be here, you'll see," he added, gently.

"Oh, will they?" She turned away so that he would not witness her flare of bitterness. Only a man could be so smugly certain of something about which nobody could be sure. After a moment she felt his hand on her sleeve, and she spun around to receive a package. "My wedding gift," he told her with a slight smile, and she opened it to find a gold watch and a set of seed pearls.

As she kissed him, Anna was ashamed of her muttered words a few minutes earlier. But before the evening was over, her frustra-

tion had returned. Her sisters and the early guests milled around
her, and she struggled through greetings, questions from the servants, instructions from her mother. When the trousseau had not
arrived by noon of the day before the wedding, her lips became
a thin line. With a shrug, Mary Morrison started to search
through the clothes closet: "I'll change the neck of this white one
and attach some lace. These other two, with a few alterations . . ."

Anna was weeping, and Mrs. Morrison dropped the garments.
"Please, child, this isn't like you, and it's not really Christian to
place such value on possessions." Anna's only answer was to sink
against her mother and cry harder than ever. Let Tom be the
forbearing one; she wanted the wedding dresses she had been
promised. Why couldn't people be relied upon?

The household retired early, and for Anna the night was a
long, disturbing one. She woke well before dawn on this day of
July 16, 1857, to lie staring at the canopy above her. In her dreams
figures had loomed before her, and she had been fleeing through
gray-black landscapes—fleeing from something she could not de-
fine. And now she could not hold back the fears which pressed
upon her, the speculations which, until now, she had stubbornly
avoided.

She would be a substitute for another woman; when Ellie
Junkin had died, Tom hoped to go to his own grave. How could
his feeling for *her* match what he had felt for his first wife? Even
as she named Elinor to herself, Anna had a sensation of sickening
hurt.

Still other doubts suggested themselves. After all, what did she
know about this man? Perhaps there were harsh things, facts he
had hidden; perhaps he would turn out to be a cruel, twisted
character of some kind . . . As Anna rolled from side to side, a
groan escaped her. She wanted to stay here at Cottage Home,
where she had always been happy; she did not want to go off to
a life of which she understood nothing!

A creak sounded, and Hetty paused in the doorway, a jug of
steaming water in her arms. "You all right, Miss Anna?" The high
voice, gentler than she had ever heard it, was like a calming hand,
and the phantoms were gone. Anna sat up, hugging her knees,
and opened her eyes wider as Hetty carried in something else
with an air of high achievement—a white box. "Four more downstairs, jus' arrive by messenger from town."

Anna jumped up, pulling at the papers that held her wedding

gown, calling to Hetty to bring the other boxes. She was interrupted by a knock, and there entered an unexpected figure—her
father. Did he have doubts about the marriage, or was she imagining it? He hesitated! "Now, my dear, don't upset yourself
about this . . ." At his words a new concern dug at her. "About
what? What is it?"

"Only that somebody made a mistake and didn't pick up the
wedding papers in town." At the sight of Anna's face he hastened
on: "One of the men has just gone for them, and he'll be back in
time. If he's a little late, we'll delay things."

A wedding with all of them waiting foolishly, and perhaps even
then the papers might not be ready . . . Though Anna realized
that she was being ridiculous, the tears would not stop. For the
next few hours, as Mrs. Morrison and Eugenia worked at the
trousseau, altering a sleeve length, refitting a waist, the brides-
maids hovering around them, her sense of foreboding did not
leave.

The tense afternoon grew warmer, and she thought of Tom sitting with the other men of the wedding party in that stifling upper
room. The ceremony was to be at "early candlelighting," as the
North Carolina phrase had it, and by the time she stood before the
full-length mirror in her wedding gown, the papers had still not
arrived. Her sister Sue darted in: "Major Jackson wants you not
to worry, 'cause he's sure they'll be here." Anna groaned. It was
well enough for him to say that; she'd be the one they'd whisper
about when the wedding was held up.

Then a sound reached her—a horseman sweeping along the
road, and from the window she saw a familiar figure, waving a
document. Smiling, she discovered that her last fear had gone;
everything would be all right after all. She touched her temple,
from which Hetty had drawn back the dark, almost glistening hair
with the braided coronet at the top. Her usually pale cheeks had a
flush which did not leave, and she knew that she had seldom appeared as well as she did this evening. Her "French look," her
full lips and wide brown eyes—they stood out against the soft
white of her gown and the gauzy veil that Hetty dropped over her
head.

At the mirror Anna ran her tongue over her lips, and lifted
her fingers to her large, new earrings. She wondered if Tom would
like them; about to take them off, she dropped her hand. This was

one matter in which a husband's preferences would not change her
mind!

A whisper from the hall, a stir and chatter among the brides-
maids, and with a tilt of her head Anna stepped forth. Her father
waited gravely at the head of the stairs, and together they went
with slow steps down the long flight. Once more he had explained
that he could not trust his emotions on such an evening, and he
had asked Dr. Lacy, president of Davidson College, to officiate.

Ceremoniously Anna and Dr. Morrison advanced with the
music to the parlor, where her mother, a handkerchief rolled
tightly in one palm, looked toward them with a small, affectionate
smile. As their eyes met, she read in Mrs. Morrison's a warm love
and also a certain hesitation, as if her mother had a last few reser-
vations of her own. As for her sister Harriet and the well-to-do
Mr. Irwin, her businessman brother-in-law, and even the subdued
Isabella Hill—did their faces hold signs of a final doubt or two?
Let them doubt; she'd show them how wrong they were!

Nearby, Tom himself stared fixedly at her; she saw the beads
of perspiration on his forehead. His gloved hand shook slightly
at his side. By contrast with Anna, he had become very anxious,
and for a moment she wanted to reach out and reassure him.

Dr. Lacy cleared his throat, the music died away, and Tom's
manner changed to one of grim determination. When the minister
approached the climax of the rites, he turned to the bridegroom;
whether or not it was Tom's unbending expression, Anna thought
that Dr. Lacy spoke with heavy stress when he asked him to be an
"indulgent" husband. A moment later, however, the minister used
similar emphasis in requiring her to be an "indulgent" mate. In
both instances, she eventually told herself, the point was a wise
one.

For what seemed hours, people clustered around them for endless questions, predictions, and repeated good wishes. At last the
carriages rolled off one by one. The younger Morrisons slipped
away, and after final words with her mother and father, sisters
and brothers-in-law, Anna and her husband walked quietly up the
stairs. The clock ticked steadily on the landing, and from below
came a muffled sound as someone closed the piano. Her hand
trembled against Tom's for a moment, then steadied. At the end
of the shadowed hallway their room waited, and with it another
life.

PART II

The Wife

. . . everything in perfect order—every door 'on golden hinges softly turning' . . .

—Thomas Jonathan Jackson,
as quoted by Mary Anna Morrison Jackson

CHAPTER 5

"*Mía esposa* . . ." The hand that caressed her was tender, and Tom Jackson's low words had a warming quality. Sitting beside Anna as she brushed her hair at the dressing table on this morning six weeks after their wedding, he touched the long strands that reached to the bench. Since their marriage, he had seldom failed to take his place near her at this hour. Today at Saratoga Springs was no exception to the rule.

"*Esposita*. Little wife . . ." When Anna turned to him, she saw that her husband was looking at her with a gentle possessiveness. She remembered how surprised she had been when Tom first began to use phrases from his Mexican War days. He was her happy *hombre*, she was *muy querida*, very dear to him. Those two years in the Latin country had influenced his life more than she had realized. She had soon discovered that Spanish was his language of affection; in it Tom told of his love far more readily than in his own tongue. Was that the effect of his years as an orphan, a habit of repression or shyness acquired in his youth? Whatever the reason, his speech, which was guarded at most times, was easy and free in playful Spanish.

These weeks went more happily than any Anna had ever known, and today she felt a serene contentment. She had something to tell Tom, news that she had learned with certainty only the previous morning. Several times since then she had prepared to say it, but somehow the proper moment had not come. Sometimes others were at their elbows, sometimes . . . Even today she suffered a sudden diffidence.

"Tom, do we really have to go out now?" she began. He wrapped his lean arms around her, and her words were lost as his lips went slowly over her mouth and cheek and throat. She sighed; here was a man who wanted her as she had never been wanted in her life, and the knowledge was good. She would have liked to stay here for most of the day, and so, she suspected, would

he. "Anna, little one . . ." Tom's voice was husky; she smiled up
at him, and then saw his eyes change, his face become set in firm
lines.

"But we can't stay," he said. "Don't you remember, we have to
join that couple from Boston at nine-thirty?" In a second he had
become again the determinedly methodical Thomas Jonathan
Jackson.

Anna's mood lingered, and she spoke drowsily: "Couldn't we
see them a little later and explain?"

Even before she had finished her question, she realized that
Tom would hardly agree. "Dear, we told them we'd meet them,
and unless we're really sick . . ." As his voice trailed off he gave
her an indulgent glance that annoyed her. Sometimes he treated
her like a child.

A moment later Tom rose, to take up his shaving at the other
side of the room. In the mirror Anna watched his dark, well-
muscled shoulders moving as he performed his task. He worked
quickly and precisely. Her anger left her, and, returning her attention to the brush in her hand, she mused affectionately. She
still found it fascinating to see how different he was from the Tom
Jackson others knew. In place of his stern, usually humorless air,
she found a tenderness, a love that enveloped her.

Three days after the wedding they had set out on their trip,
beginning by coach and transferring to the train for Richmond,
where they spent a week. The stately city, with its tall residences
on the hills, their pillared porches dominating the vistas, and with
its unbroken avenues of small iron-decorated houses, had charmed
her. Solicitously, Tom had led Anna in and out of the homes at
which they called to meet friends and connections of her Uncle
Graham and others to whom they had letters. He watched her
almost anxiously: "You're feeling well, *esposa*? Is everything all
right?"

Finally, smiling to herself, she had confronted him: "You're
spoiling me. I may expect this all the time." At her words he
looked at her long and steadily: "My dear, it's the way you're
always going to be treated." Since then she had realized that her
husband meant precisely what he said.

Anna had discovered, too, how much he delighted in varying
scenes, in travel itself, and how carefully he prepared for their
small trips. From Virginia they had gone to Baltimore, then to
Philadelphia, and then to New York. In this last city he had stud-

ied guidebooks and handbills, and they had followed a careful
schedule, taking steamers that glided along the Hudson, riding
through the parks, climbing to that much-talked-about place, the
spire of Trinity Church.

There, with Tom's military coat protecting her from the wind,
Anna had stared at the sparkling river, the bay alive with vessels,
the green country stretching in every direction. "If I could," Tom
exclaimed, "I'd want to do nothing more than this kind of thing."
He had told her of Europe: the vineyards and battlements along
the Rhine, the craggy Scottish highlands, the "sea of ice" in
Switzerland. As Anna's eyes glistened in response, he faced her
impulsively. "Anna, we'll go back there together, I promise it!"

Tom's hand had tightened over hers, and she nodded in delight.
Several times since then he had mentioned the subject and they
had spoken of the places Anna wanted most to see. Now and
then she found herself thinking with a rising pleasure: perhaps
they could make the trip in, say, three years from now . . .

First, however, they must give full attention to other matters.
When they were packing to leave Cottage Home he had turned
to her in a rush of feeling: "Anna, I'm going to make something
of my life. Something you and my family and—and everybody
else will understand. We Jacksons have had a place in the world,
and if I can manage it we will again!"

His words had startled her, and for the first time she had sensed
how deep was Tom's ambition, even though he did not reveal it
to others. As he continued, his intensity, his frowning absorption,
had made Anna's flesh tingle. Her husband had a part, and a good
part, to play in the world around them, and she was going to give
him every assistance within her means, do everything possible to
make his way easier. Solemnly she had promised herself. Then
immediately she pledged something else: she was going to help
him show his abilities to any doubters in her own family!

Every day or so she learned something new about Tom: things
he had done, people he knew. Several times she had been irked,
and had demanded, "Why haven't you told me that?" Generally
he shrugged or looked sheepish or merely blank: "You didn't ask
me." Once or twice Anna laughed, and yet she reflected that although Tom did not seem to hide things deliberately, it was almost
as if he lived behind a series of curtains. As each lifted, more of
the man was revealed. But she felt that several last curtains still
remained.

From New York they had moved toward Saratoga through Niagara, and for days she had followed patiently as Tom plodded along walks and up and down steps. If she had considered him an untiring walker before, she was now learning how indefatigable he really was. Together they rode for hours on small boats and stood on the banks of the Niagara, staring at the white majesty of the surging falls, the rapids, and the foaming current. In a low voice, Tom had murmured, "How can anybody who sees wonders like these doubt the Creator?" Silently Anna inclined her head and let him lead her away.

But today at Saratoga an oblique memory struck her. Tom had already come to this watering place—indeed, he had made much this same trip with Elinor Junkin. She felt the twinge that she sometimes suffered at the thought of the first wife; there were so many things she wanted to ask about their life together, and yet she could not bring herself to it. Tom had told her, at the time he proposed to her, that he would never forget Ellie. Had his love for the other woman been different from his feeling for her, and since Ellie was the first, was his love for *her* stronger and more lasting? Now and then, when she saw him deep in thought, she wondered if he had Ellie in his mind.

And soon they would be going to the town in which he had lived with this first wife, seeing people who had known and liked her, visiting her family. And all of them, Anna told herself, would be comparing the stranger with the handsome girl who had been one of them. She could almost hear their words: "She's all right, maybe, but do you remember how Ellie . . . ?" "I can't think what made poor Jack . . ."

Now, as Anna sighed on this morning at Saratoga, Tom's voice boomed almost in her ear, and again he sat beside her at the dressing table. "Dear, what's the matter? Is it the trouble you've been having with your throat?"

Anna flushed at his concern. "Oh, no, Tom, that's practically gone." The recurring pains of the past week had all but disappeared, she assured him truthfully, and changed the subject. Relieved, he pointed to his watch. "Anna, we don't want to be late for our meeting." As she adjusted her bonnet and gathered together her purse, shawl, and umbrella, Anna reflected that some of their fellow Carolinians might fume if they knew of Tom's spontaneous friendship with the New England couple. But he got along well with people of many different beliefs, didn't he?

On their way from the hotel room, Tom looked her over and whispered, "Beautiful! The most beautiful woman at Saratoga." He kissed her quickly and held her against him. Happy as Anna was at the tribute, she chuckled at its absurdity. Then she paused. Perhaps this was the moment to tell him her news. "Tom, please . . ."

Before she could speak the first words, her husband had started purposefully down the hall. Shrugging, Anna hurried with him across the crowded lobby, past the high, two-storied porch with its ornamented columns, to the tree-lined walks. Porters shouted, coachmen in brass-buttoned coats cracked whips as they rode by, and women twirled parasols of a dozen colors . . . Here was the shiny stage of the country's great watering place—high life and mixed life, silks and laces, tall hats and strange faces.

Anna and Tom went unnoticed in the throng, and although Tom appeared entirely unconscious of it, Anna had to admit she felt temporarily nettled. The Morrisons were somebodies in North Carolina, and after all—her head tilted at the thought—she had been a guest at the White House and at Washington mansions. Even to herself, she could not deny that Tom had a certain "country" air. True, he had seen more of the world than she, but he did not show it. At that Anna stopped herself; she had been disloyal, and she had also been thinking like a provincial.

Past them went two women whose shimmering ornaments bespoke Paris. They were accompanied by a couple of effete young men who chattered with a bored air. For a moment Anna wondered why there were so many mincing youths about the resort. Just as the group passed the Jacksons, one of the women halted a foot or so from Anna, languidly surveyed her and the rest of the crowd, and drawled in an icy voice, "Clarice, who are these people? There's really nobody here this year."

Anna's face went white with resentment. As she stiffened, Tom sensed her reaction. Whether she would have retorted she was never sure, but before she could, Tom's fingers tightened on her arm and he led her quietly on. After a moment he said, "*Esposa,* people like that aren't worth losing your temper over. Let it go by you."

"Hm." She wished she could be that forbearing. Or did she? There might be such a thing as too much forbearance! Gradually, however, her annoyance evaporated, and by the time they had passed the last of the rows of cottages and had taken seats on a bench to await the Bostonians, she had returned to her usual calm. From his pocket, Tom drew out a letter from his sister, and Anna saw the love that often filled his eyes when he thought of Laura Arnold.

"She's mighty pleased that we'll be visiting her next week," he smiled. Then, after a moment's silence, he shook his head. "Laura doesn't have too much excitement in her life, and you'll be an event for her. Long before we were married, you remember, she hoped to meet you." As Tom continued, Anna recalled that Laura had grown very fond of Ellie during the girl's visit shortly before the baby's birth. And by now perhaps his sister was as curious about Anna as she had been about Ellie.

Tom went on, "I think she's worrying a little about me, my health, and everything else." In his face Anna read devotion and the brooding sadness she sometimes found when he talked of this sister.

"Tell me," she ventured, "Laura worries a lot, doesn't she?"

"She's had a lot to worry her." Tom was troubled. "When they took us from Ma, she was very upset, and I suppose we clung together more than most brothers and sisters. Later, they separated the two of us, and I didn't see her for a long time. I don't believe Laura ever really got over those years."

A hint of tears glistened in her husband's eyes, and Anna, greatly moved, placed her hand on his arm. "I want to see her very much, more than ever." Tom's gratitude softened his face, and he pressed her hand to his mouth. "Good, good," he added with a slight movement of his head from left to right—a mannerism of his to which she had grown accustomed. When he did that, she knew he was very much pleased.

The next few minutes passed in silence, a silence Anna enjoyed. Just to be here with Tom, with the world far away and the lake shining before them . . . Slowly, however, she sensed that Tom had become irritated. "Those people are nearly fifteen minutes late. Let's go for another row on the lake." He had reddened; she saw his nostrils flare and his face tighten as he struggled for control. She had long since realized that at times Tom Jackson had a temper, although he usually controlled it.

"Maybe they've been delayed, and are on their way now." She spoke softly and persuasively, but Tom gave no sign that he had heard her. Instead, he jumped to his feet and started toward the water. Anna's own temper rose, and she called to him, "Tom, you can go alone if you like. I'm going to wait a little longer."

With an astonished air he turned back and rejoined her on the bench. As they sat silently, Anna asked herself which of them was being arbitrary. Perhaps it was she, but she had no intention of giving way. At the moment she really did not look forward to a session on the water; her throat was beginning to ache again, and the nearby pavilion was cool and inviting.

The minutes went by. Tom remained calm, staring at his big hands. Anna meanwhile became more and more edgy. At last she stood up and looked around. The couple had still not materialized, and she faced him with a wry glance. "I'm sorry, Tom."

Instead of showing signs of self-vindication, as she might have expected, he shrugged good-naturedly, and he talked of other matters as he took her to the landing. "Visiting springs like these always helps me, Anna. The waters, the air, or whatever it is— I feel better than I have in a long time." Anna nodded happily; he had an air of ease and relaxation, a calm look of well-being.

Within a few minutes he was piloting the rowboat with hard strokes toward the middle of the quiet lake. "Isn't this fine?" he asked as they glided among the floating cups of the water lilies. "It's pleasant, very pleasant," she answered, leaning back against her pillow, and soon she was conscious of little except the ripple of the waves, the fresh smell of the green plants, and the way her husband watched her.

Now, finally, the time had come. "I have news—something that's important." Anna started to speak, but her voice failed her.

He glanced indulgently at her. "My allowance wasn't big enough this week?"

"That's not it at all." She replied more crisply than she had intended. "Tom, it's—I'm going to have a baby."

There was a long silence, during which Anna heard only the splash of the water and a distant cry from the shore. Tom's mouth opened; she saw him swallow, and then a swift joy changed his features.

"Anna, Anna." Lowering the oars, he leaned toward her. "I'd hoped, but I never thought—I mean so soon . . ." As he stared she realized that he seemed at least as happy as she that his child was within her, and she thought again of the way he had assured Eugenia, on the Morrison girls' first visit to Lexington, that in time he expected to have a great many children. Now they had made a beginning.

"Anna, it's what I—what I've wanted more than any . . ." He did not finish, and she smiled at his excitement and confusion. Taking her hands, he managed to bend forward to kiss her. He almost upset the boat by his quick motion, and as she cried out, he caught at both sides to balance it.

She felt a sudden thrust of pain in her cheek and throat, and winced involuntarily. Tom became instantly solicitous. "It's the same thing, but worse than ever," she told him through tightened lips.

With a series of heavy strokes of the oars, he headed toward shore. "We'll see the doctor right away, as soon as we can get to his office. Do you think you can stand the walk over there?" Anna nodded, and in spite of her suffering, she felt a faint flicker of amusement; already she had become a more precious object to him. But the agony pressed upon her again, and it continued all the way to the physician's quarters.

There they discovered promptly that the pompous, bull-necked doctor had scant time for such an unglittering patient. Before he even examined Anna, he explained with a hurried look, "The commodore's on his way. He made his appointment yesterday."

"But this is an emergency," Tom insisted, and as he spoke Anna saw his long jaw set in resentment. "I'm not a commodore, but my wife's in real pain." After an examination that appeared all too brief to Anna, the doctor sighed. "An enlarged gland, I'd say. Treatment? Why, more of the waters and hours of simple rest, ma'am, and a bottle of this to give you relief in the meantime."

Through a haze of throbbing agony, Anna took Tom's arm. "We're leaving here today," he told her tensely; and a few hours later, pressing a saturated cloth to her face, she let him hoist her to a carriage. As she lay with her head against his shoulder, he talked soothingly: "I have a friend near here, a good doctor. He'll give you the proper attention."

Anna shuddered as the new doctor probed at her throat and pressed at her jaw. He shook his head. "A gland, all right, but what's caused the trouble I can't honestly say." When he recommended a Philadelphia authority, they headed for a new destination. Only then did Anna realize something: "Tom, we won't be able to get to your sister's place after all. There won't be enough time before school starts." He nodded slowly.

In Philadelphia they called on one medical expert, then another, and gradually Anna improved. The second one recommended a short stay at a place Tom had visited before—Rockbridge Alum Springs, only eighteen miles from Lexington, and they welcomed the suggestion. There they spent hours in and about the waters. By degrees the inflammation disappeared, and now for the first time they could speak serenely and happily of the baby and of the prospects before them.

One day soon after their arrival at the Rockbridge spring, following a walk through the uneven, overgrown terrain, Anna found Tom at work over a letter. He was rereading it with such care that she became curious. "Are you afraid you've said something wrong?"

"No." He looked at her frankly. "It's just that I have to check my spelling. I never learned it well."

"Oh, a great many people don't spell perfectly," she shrugged.

He responded with an air of earnestness. "But I've studied enough to be able to do it, and it's my fault that I don't." Thereafter, Anna noted, he kept a dictionary close at hand and consulted it regularly. A day or two later, as he was writing to a fellow Virginian, she leaned against the table and read:

I hope that in the course of time we shall be able to call some house our home, where we may have the pleasure of receiving a long visit from you. . . . I shall never be content until I am at the head of an establishment in which my friends can feel at home in Lexington. I have taken the first important step by securing a wife capable of making a proper home. And the next thing is to give her an opportunity.

Anna smiled at Tom's words, then grew serious. As much as he, she wished for a residence in which to start their life in Lexington. "You know I've never had my own home," he explained, looking up at her. Already, however, she realized that there would be problems. "I searched and searched before I left," he reminded her, "but I couldn't find a single place that I could afford." Housing continued at a premium in the college town; she remembered that he and Ellie had failed to locate anything. As before, the shadow of the other wife lay in front of her . . .

"So, to start with, we'll have to stay at the hotel I told you about," he finished. Though she nodded, Anna could not rid herself of her disappointment. She had never lived in a hotel, and now she thought of tales she had heard about the discomfort one

suffered in such places. She recalled the pathetic yearning in
Tom's voice that night he had told her of his feeling that he was
always "on the outside, looking in." More than ever, she wanted
them to have their own house.

She tried to joke: "Anyway, you've promised me one," she told
him, "and I'm going to hold you to it!" Smilingly he agreed.

As he turned away, Anna's gaze went to the collection of books
Tom had brought with them on their trip: a history of England,
a small set of Shakespeare, a French grammar with a bent cover.
Picking up the history, she found it marked on page after page—
"important," "note,"—or merely underlined here and there. She
inspected another volume and another, and each was heavily
penciled.

Noticing her interest, Tom explained. "Anna, for years I've studied things by subject—first a general history of the world, then
modern times, country by country. For a while I tried to look into
politics and also art . . ." She marveled at the way he had divided
the world of knowledge into distinct subdivisions. Had she ever
known anyone who yearned so for information? During the past
few weeks Anna had watched him as he read for a half-hour,
dozed against his will, and woke to push determinedly ahead.
"Why don't you stop and sleep for a while?" she had asked several
times, but he always shook his head and resumed his work. Once
or twice, as he nodded and his grip loosened, Anna had taken the
book out of his hand. But when, each time, he opened his eyes
again, he had calmly retrieved it.

This morning she realized that for the fifth consecutive day her
husband was going over a much-thumbed volume of Napoleon's
maxims. When she glanced over curiously, he nodded: "Every
time I pick up this book I learn something." Tom often quoted
the Corsican: "Bonaparte always tells you . . ." "As Napoleon said
in his Italian campaign . . ."

His interest warmed. "Anna, he was the greatest soldier of all.
None of this defense and letting the other fellow hit. Attack and
attack, hit 'em and hit 'em again. That's what fighting a war
means!" His eyes had a fierce glint, and she began to understand
what Harvey Hill had meant when he said that Tom "enjoyed
war." But before long he closed the book and became his quiet
self again.

A knock sounded, and a servant entered with a letter from Major Preston containing information about the reopening of the In-

stitute. When Tom put it aside, Anna asked, "What about Maggie and the Major? You think it's—working well?" For some time she had been wondering about that marriage.

"I'm sure it is," he answered quickly. "They're both sensible people." She smiled to herself. In his male naïveté Tom believed that things were as simple as that. "They may be sensible, Tom, but they're both set in their ways, aren't they?"

He smiled, and told her more about the Preston courtship. "Anna, the wedding was almost called off. Maggie's impulsive and excitable, and the Major wants things the way he wants them. Well, after she accepted him he said he'd like the wedding to be August 2. That was about five months less than two years after his first wife died—and some people think at least that much time should pass between marriages—and Maggie said no."

Tom frowned at the recollection. "John argued and argued, and announced she'd marry him August third or not at all. Maggie jumped up. Very well, she'd never marry him! Days went by, and neither made a move. Her father appealed to her, but that didn't help. Then I stepped in, saw the Major and Maggie, and argued hard, let me tell you. Since they were in love, I said, a few months didn't matter. Each of them sighed, and one morning I arranged a meeting, and the Major gave way—by one day! The wedding was August fourth."

Anna laughed, then fell silent. Soon she would be meeting both of Tom's friends again; the closer the day came, the more uncertain she grew about the prospect. To so many of the Lexington people she might be an intruder, especially to those who had been close to Ellie and Maggie. And the new Mrs. Preston could sting if she wished . . .

On their last day at the springs, as Tom pushed Anna back and forth in a swing, he glimpsed her face and stopped: "What is it, child?"

She tried to explain, until he put his hand tenderly over her lips. "Everybody has fears, and then we find they amount to nothing. Just be your own good self, and if some people don't think well of you, it will be their loss. If I worried about the way people were going to take me or not take me, I'd spend all my time in a fret." As he talked, she reminded herself of Tom's hard beginnings and his endless efforts, and she felt ashamed of herself. When he took a seat beside her, she put her hand over his and lifted her face. No one was going to intimidate her now, neither the Prestons nor the Junkins nor anybody else . . .

The stagecoach rocked around one of the last curves before Lexington, and Anna gazed at the outlines of the high mountains she remembered. How different this was from her last trip! That morning Tom had told her they would be staying at the town's best hotel, "but don't expect too much." She wanted to remain cheerful, and so she did not dwell on the prospect. A dour chamber, bare, probably undusted, yet reeking of cleaning fluid . . . In the early autumn dusk a cold wind roared past them, and she shivered.

The unseasonably chill day had been overcast for hours, and now, without warning, rain splattered into the stage. Before Tom could shut the window, Anna's sleeve and skirt were well soaked. "Here, let me put this over you," he said as he draped her in his military coat. Through a steady downpour they rolled into the dim town, and she waited on a wind-swept corner while Tom superintended the removal of their baggage.

"Nobody to meet us, because they weren't sure when we'd arrive," he murmured. Smiling, Anna tried to forget the contrast with her many returns to Cottage Home, and tried not to think of her mother's words: her life here would be far different from the one she had known. A wave of longing for North Carolina and the Morrisons swept over her. To be back with the family for a little while—with Tom along, of course . . . Only at moments like this did the yearning come to her, and today it was stronger than ever.

"Here, the hotel's right ahead." Directing the attendant, Tom led her beneath a balcony to a bleak entrance way. There she discovered a slight, gaunt-faced Negro, in an ancient coat and white trousers, who stared earnestly toward them. "Evenin', Major."

"Ah, it's Albert." Tom's tone was very friendly. "Anna, Albert works as a waiter at the other hotel, and I'm helping him earn his freedom."

Anna looked at the man with a new interest; her husband had spoken of him several times. Albert bowed and inquired politely about Anna's health in a voice that showed some education. "I hope you'll be real happy here, ma'am," he said. His good will warmed her, and she thanked him in a somewhat improved mood.

Albert faced Tom again. "Major, Miz Preston send to say can you all come over to the house for supper? They hope you can, 'specially because Mr. Lyle's not so well lately."

Tom gave Anna an inquiring glance. She was wet, chilled, and badly tired, and wanted nothing so much as a long, soaking bath and a warm bed. But the invitation seemed important to Tom. "Of course," she made herself smile. "We'll be there as quickly as we can get into dry clothes."

Reaching their door, Tom thrust it open. A round green lamp beside the window sent a softening glow over a neatly furnished chamber. She saw a wide table, several chairs and pictures, a rug with a light pattern. Although the furnishings were undistinguished, they were clean, and the entire room had an air of welcome. Beyond waited a bedroom, far smaller than her room at Cottage Home, yet neat and airy. Her eyes filling, she turned to her husband. "Thank you. It's a good start."

When they settled in the carriage Major Preston had sent, Anna asked about Mr. Lyle. Tom responded, "I suppose he was my first Lexington friend. An old bachelor, and he had a little bookstore that was famous around here."

Chuckling, Tom continued, "Nobody ever ran a shop like Mr. Lyle's. He liked to walk around the town, and left the place whenever the mood hit. If you found a book you liked, you took it and left the money. The store was more of a club than anything else; people dropped in for talks and meetings with friends or just to pass the time of day with Mr. Lyle." After a pause, Tom added, "And he's the best Christian I ever met."

Anna felt a stir of interest; this older friend clearly meant a great deal to Tom: "A Christian—in what way?"

"He had a little money, not much, and he used up most of it, giving families 'loans' for a new start." Tom spoke softly, yet fervently; she had to bend forward to catch all his words. "When I arrived here, Anna, I was worried over my future and I had—spiritual troubles, too. Mr. Lyle gave me books and told me about faith and prayer. As much as anybody, he helped change my life."

The carriage passed a lighted corner, and Anna saw that Tom was staring ahead, as if at a distant point. "What's happened to Mr. Lyle now?" she asked him.

"He had a stroke. It happened in church one Sunday, and Major Preston's taken him in." He glanced up: "We're here, and

there's the Major on the porch." At this Anna forgot everything
except the hours that lay ahead. In spite of Tom's reassurances,
she was slightly uneasy; suppose this meeting proved unpleasant?
The rain had stopped, and she saw the outlines of the big, ram-
bling house. As they stepped from the carriage the imposing form
of Major Preston rose before them, bowing and calling directions.
He was in a happy humor tonight, Anna noted with relief.

"The new Madame Jackson. And welcome to our home!" As the
rich voice rang out, one Preston after another poured forward,
and she and Tom ascended the curving stair to the accompani-
ment of good wishes, handshakes, and smiles from several gen-
erations of the family. In the doorway, outlined against the yellow
light, was a small figure.

"Anna Morrison . . ." While Maggie Preston's face remained in
the dark, two cool hands reached out to hers. "Anna, I'm glad
you're going to be in Lexington, taking the place my sister had."
At these words the newcomer had a chill. "And so you'll be a
sister to *me*." The sentence, spoken in an intense tone, ended
dramatically, and Maggie drew Anna inside so that both stood
in the light. The little hostess smiled happily, and her blue eyes
searched the face before her, much as they had when the two
women had first met.

Relief swept through Anna, and with it a sudden gratitude.
Though Maggie's first remark had embarrassed her, she was now
certain that her hostess had spoken out of a wish to be friendly.
"My child"—the older woman leaned closer—"you and I will have
a lot to talk about later."

Maggie swung around toward Tom Jackson, and her light eyes
took on a glow in which interest and admiration were unhidden.
"Brother, brother Tom. It's like old times again, isn't it?" Anna
watched, resentment rising suddenly in spite of her effort. It
would not be quite like those old times! Her gaze shifted to Major
Preston, and she saw that he was regarding Tom and Maggie with
a happy look. Anna was ashamed; she should be glad that both
these people thought so well of her husband.

As Maggie talked on with enthusiasm, Anna saw her turn repeatedly to Major Preston, drawing him into the conversation,
smiling, appealing to him for his opinions. Beyond any question,
Maggie was in love with the man she had married. Had she ever
had more than affection and high respect for Tom Jackson, as
Anna had first believed? Here was something that she would

never know. Nevertheless Anna felt a new ease. As for Ellie Junkin . . . Tom's first wife's name came up casually three or four times. No one lingered over the matter, and for this Anna was grateful.

"Why, look who's standing over there!" It was Tom, putting his arms around a young Preston who had arrived late. A little girl entered; he kissed her, then pummeled the boy. Once again Anna realized how attached Tom was to children, and how much they liked him. This was good to know, for she intended to have a lot of them.

Maggie's voice drew her attention. "Anna, I suppose you're going to join Tom in his classes for the colored?"

Classes for the Negroes . . . Here was another matter of which she still knew nothing. Before she could reply, Tom intervened, "I'm hoping she will, as soon as we get around to it, sister Maggie. We haven't even unpacked yet." The subject was dropped, but Anna made a mental note: it must be added to her list of topics for further exploration.

A sound of rolling reached them, and through the doorway came a servant pushing a wheel chair. In it was a smiling, stout-faced man whose skin seemed drained of blood. "Mr. John Lyle." Major Preston made the introduction with a flourish, and Anna moved quickly toward the invalid. While Mr. Lyle could never have been handsome, he had a homely goodness in his counte-nance. His small dark eyes traveled from one member of the party to the other, and a somewhat reedy voice addressed Anna: "My dear Mrs. Jackson, there's never been a more welcome arrival in our town."

The words and the smile that accompanied them made her feel suddenly much less an interloper. As Mr. Lyle remained motion-less before her, she realized that he was badly paralyzed. Taking a seat beside him, she listened as he spoke about the town, his earlier days, the Lexingtonians they both knew. He never referred to his illness, nor did any of the others, and Anna marveled at his bright humor and his lightness of heart.

Meanwhile Anna glanced to left and right at the great, gloomy oil paintings, the chairs like thrones, the heavy furniture, the doz-ens of ornaments. The place, which Maggie apparently found in this state when she arrived, had the cluttered air that Anna's mother described as "a wonderful magnet for dust." Nevertheless the newcomer recognized the look of a home, of a much lived-in

home, and she reminded herself that before long she wanted her
own place—smaller, but comfortable and filled with people in this
same way.

Even as she did so, she had a thought: a house like that with
so many rooms, halls, and servants to manage! She did not envy
Maggie her task, and yet it was clear that the onetime old maid
had fitted herself well into what might have been a thorny role.
Major Preston nodded and smiled beside Anna, and the stepchildren had a happy, casual manner. To win the hearts of these
children had been no small feat, perhaps the hardest Maggie had
to accomplish.

Two maids, opening the folding doors, announced supper, and
Anna and Maggie entered the dining room beside the invalid.
Anna found herself seated between their host and Mr. Lyle. Apparently the paralyzed man had already been served; he merely
sat there, talking with the others. From her place of vantage,
Anna noted how skillfully the new Mrs. Preston managed a table
set for fifteen or sixteen, and how tactfully she handled two of
the younger stepchildren while she kept the conversation going
without interruption.

Eventually Mr. Lyle referred to one of Maggie's "new poems,"
and the hostess corrected him with what Anna thought was her
first sign of sharpness. "Oh, no. I haven't written anything lately.
I've been much too busy." Maggie's bright eyes met her husband's,
as if to seek approval or confirmation. The Major, however, maintained a noncommittal look and went on to other matters, and
Anna caught a slightly discordant note.

As Maggie and Tom chatted, Mr. Lyle bent toward Anna, addressing her in a low, confidential tone: "My child, I hope you
won't mind my saying this to you. You're what Tom has needed
for a long time. Don't ever underestimate that husband of yours.
I've known him from his first days here, and I've watched him
grow with every year." He dropped his voice even lower, and
added with a hint of urgency, "There's very little this man can't
do. Almost nothing, Mrs. Jackson, almost nothing."

So someone else believed in Tom, and believed in him warmly.
Deeply stirred, Anna missed none of the words that followed:
"My child, he can reach great heights, if he develops more—more
confidence in himself." She had promised herself to do everything
she could to help Tom Jackson realize his capacities, to make the

world recognize him. Mr. Lyle was now telling her what her task was . . .

"He must believe in himself, and you must help him do it—no matter what some people may say about him." At that point they were interrupted, but Anna's mind would not leave their friend's final comment. "No matter what some people may say." He had tried to caution her—about what, precisely? It would be wise not to prod Mr. Lyle, and yet she was to ponder the question for a long time to come.

The meal was ample and tasteful—a thick chicken and vegetable soup followed by roast and chops, light cream and cake, a platter of fresh fruit and nuts. Maggie's quick eyes ranged over the table, losing no detail: the passing of a salt shaker, the distribution of items among the smaller children. The older woman was almost too alert, and Anna wondered why she could not relax a bit more.

Toward the end of dinner, two of the boys reached for the cake at the same time. They began to argue, and Maggie leaned over to quiet them. Simultaneously their father clapped his hands: "Both of you, leave the table right now, and no cake for either!" When they retreated tearfully, their stepmother appeared about to intervene. Then she tightened her lips and tried to cover the breach with a casual observation. As she did, Anna noticed that her hand was trembling so hard that she had to steady it against the table. The new wife still had some difficult moments.

Supper over, the Prestons, the Jacksons, and Mr. Lyle talked quietly in the parlor until Tom signaled to Anna. He had already told her that he must be up at six. On the porch Maggie took her hand: "We will be friends, won't we?" Touched, Anna gave her emphatic assurance, and a few minutes later the coachman opened the carriage door.

"Is Mr. Lyle a family connection of the Major's?" Anna asked Tom. "Why no," he answered. "The Major's known him for a long time, and he took him in when he had his stroke. Mr. Lyle will be there as—as long as it's necessary." At this moment the light from a store shone into the vehicle, and Anna saw that Tom's face was sad. Suddenly he spoke again.

"One of the older town people told me that as a young man Mr. Lyle was in love with Sally Carruthers, who later became Mrs. Preston. But Mr. Lyle wasn't—well, wasn't a prize catch; he didn't have any great prospects. Then John Preston came into the picture, and Mr. Lyle fell in his shadow. Preston was wealthy and good-looking, and he had a bright future ahead of him. They say that Mr. Lyle never let Sally know just how he felt about her, and when the wedding took place, he suddenly left Lexington."

Tom continued, "After a while Major Preston found out that Mr. Lyle wasn't doing well in the other town, and John sent for him and helped him get started with the bookstore. Now and then he secretly wrote off the store's losses, and brought Mr. Lyle back into the family circle."

Thoughtfully Anna nodded. Here was another John Preston, and from then on she would think differently of her husband's sometimes lordly friend. Softly she asked, "The Major's first wife, did she know the reason for all this?"

"I don't think she ever did."

At the door the coachman bowed, and Tom Jackson led Anna across the brick sidewalk. Tonight she had learned a great deal about her husband and his friends.

CHAPTER 6

"Ah, Anna, that's not the way to be happy." During the first few months of their marriage she heard Tom say this a hundred times. Indeed, it seemed to be a kind of motif of their life together. He used the words so regularly that as soon as he started to speak them she would stop frowning and turn to him with a smile or a shrug of agreement.

Adjustment, discovery, discovery, adjustment . . . Daily she made changes to fit herself into a regime far different from anything she had known. More frequently than she liked to remember, she lost her composure or her temper and blinked back her tears while Tom appealed gently to her.

"The way to be happy . . ." Of the many things her husband taught her, one of the most important was, she thought, the calm approach to life. In time, Anna decided that she was beginning to master this way to happiness. But days came when, she feared, serenity was far away. There was, for instance, that week end a month or so after her arrival. It was late October, and a steady wind swept across Lexington from the mountains that rose in the distance. Anna slept heavily through Friday night, dreaming as she often did of her childhood in North Carolina, when she played with Eugenia and Isabella near the dairy, with Hetty watching

from the door. Dr. and Mrs. Morrison materialized and walked
toward them, and . . .

She woke as Tom stirred, sat up, and put his feet over the edge
of the bed. It must be six or a minute or two before—his invariable
hour for rising. He touched her shoulder and whispered, "Sh,
esposa, go back to sleep." While she lay half-dozing, she heard
him kneel for several minutes of prayer beside the bed. Not
once since he joined the church, he had explained, had he neglected this first of the many appeals he made to God each day. A
moment or so later the door closed, and from down the hotel
hallway there came the sound of splashing water. No matter how
icy the day, Tom always took a cold bath.

A little later he tiptoed back, reached for the heavy boots and
army overcoat he had laid out the night before, and slipped from
the room. A fifteen-minute walk before breakfast lay ahead of
him, and meanwhile Anna rose with an effort, yawned, and looked
up as the maid entered with a bowl of warm water. "Good morning, Ellen. The Major must be halfway through his walk by now."

She lost no time in dressing and supervising the light breakfast
the maid set on the small table in their sitting room. As she did,
she smiled to herself; by now she knew how important it was to
Tom that everything take place on time. A few days earlier Anna
had delayed their arrival at prayer meeting by going back to the
hotel to get her handkerchief. When they had reached the
church, they discovered that services had been under way for
perhaps five minutes.

"No, dear." Tom had taken Anna's hand as she reached out to
turn the knob. "We have no right to disturb other people's devo-
tion." Astonished, she protested, "But it's only a very few minutes."
He nodded: "Napoleon once said that the reason he beat the
Austrians was that they didn't know the value of five minutes.
He did."

"Yes, but—*we're* not invading Austria; we're going to church."

"Time is always important." Giving Anna his arm, he had led
her away. "I suppose the fault is all mine," she observed tartly.

"No." Her husband answered in a quiet voice. "It was partly
mine, because I should have explained matters beforehand."

His calm acceptance had made Anna suddenly furious. "Why,
even my father doesn't insist that someone who comes a little late
to his service . . ." She had been unable to go on.

"Each to his own way, Anna."

The remark had seemed unfair to her. "You have no right to criticize my father!"

"Please, my dear. I'm not criticizing anybody." They entered the lobby and ascended the stairs in silence. Upstairs, Anna flung her hat on the bed and turned her back to her husband. After a moment, Tom came over to her, a cheerful smile on his face. Soon her irritation disappeared, and she kissed him apologetically. It was their first quarrel, and a foolish one, and she had to see that it did not happen again.

Since then Anna had discovered that Tom's day was carefully divided into segments, organized more thoroughly than she would ever have thought possible. He knew what he would be doing every hour, every half-hour, every fifteen minutes. When he first described his routine to her, she had stared in disbelief, and at first she chafed under its restraints. "Can't you stop a bit earlier?" she had asked. Or, "Tom, I want to talk to you, and it's practically time."

In each case he answered smilingly but firmly, "No, I can't stop yet." Or, "Practically time, but *not* time." One day he had gone to her with a solemn look: "Anna, please understand. I've tried to set regulations for my life, and one of them is—*govern yourself*." Unconsciously he pointed a finger. "One lapse invites another; if you slough off once, you set a precedent for the next time. Don't you see?"

She was beginning to see. That week she had picked up one of the blankbooks in which he had set down his early rules of conduct. She read:

"Through life let your principal object be the discharge of duty. . . . Disregard public opinion when it interferes with your duty. . . . Endeavor to be at peace with all men. . . . Never speak disrespectfully of anyone without a cause. . . . Be truthful in all things. . . . *You may be whatever you resolve to be.*"

More than anyone she had ever met, Tom Jackson tried to live by the principles he had adopted, including that of exact truthfulness. One day she said casually, "Mr. Lyle has a fine Swiss watch, you know." Tom looked at her: "My dear, you *don't* know that, and I don't either. Neither of us has had any experience with Swiss watches." "Why—why, everybody says it." He remained firm: "It still isn't good to say something when you're not sure of it."

And in the matter of treating others with respect . . . Major

Preston had had a bitter dispute at the Franklin Literary Society, and the town echoed with stories of the other man's harsh tongue. When Anna burst into resentment at the Major's opponent, Tom shook his head: "There's no need to speak as you're doing, Anna. I won't have anything further to do with him. I'll simply leave him alone, and that's enough. He's a deceived man."

A "deceived man" . . . Anna wished she could maintain so even a tone, but she feared it would take her some time to acquire the art. Nevertheless, Tom was neither chill nor oversolemn in their lighter hours together. On the contrary, there was something almost childlike in his gay laughter, his winks across the room, the way he caught her in his arms. On their first day in Lexington Anna had gone down the hall and, returning, opened the door to discover an empty room. Where was he? As she entered, she was seized from behind the door in an overpowering embrace. She sighed and smiled happily with him, reflecting how surprised the townspeople would be to see him so buoyant in his love.

"Everything fix' right, Miss Anna?" The hotel maid's inquiry brought her out of her musing, and hastily she poured the milk and inspected the table: plain bread, boiled eggs, fruit. The clock struck seven, and less than a second later the door opened, as she had been certain it would. She lifted her lips for a brief kiss, and Tom took his place and bowed his head in prayer. One day the previous week, Anna had entered the room several minutes late, to find that her husband had finished praying and had begun his meal without her.

"And how are you, Ellen?" Tom asked the maid. Anna had become accustomed to the courtesy with which he addressed the black people, bowing and speaking to each one who passed. This morning she thought that Tom had a more serious manner than usual, and in a moment she learned why. "There was a note downstairs from my sister Laura," he told her. "Our explanations of why we couldn't get to visit her haven't done much good. She's upset, and thinks we didn't go because we didn't want to make the effort."

His voice was thick with emotion, and Anna, too, was disturbed. Now all at once Tom was telling her things he had never previously revealed about his sister: "Matters like that affect her more than they do most of us. She's a shy woman, and sensitive—very sensitive. Laura has a strong conscience, a sympathy for people, and she's ready to help anybody or strike out for anything she thinks is right. At the same time, Anna, she feels she has her own rights."

Intrigued, Anna listened. "From time to time Laura's worried me. Moved around as we children were, she hasn't always been strong in her faith. She joined our church for a while, but now I'm afraid she doesn't go often. I pray for her and appeal to her whenever I write." Tom spoke haltingly, and he seemed profoundly upset. Knowing his strong feelings about religion, Anna could sympathize with him. "When she comes back to the church, it will be my happiest day in years."

As moved as he, Anna told him, "No matter what happens, we'll go to them next summer. And can't we invite Laura and the family to come here as soon as we get our place?"

"Yes, as soon as we do." Tom's tone of voice and eyes revealed his disappointment; in the past month they had inspected more than a dozen houses, all meager, drab, and costly. One place seemed promising but altogether too big, and in addition the owner had not yet made up his mind to sell. Anna glanced around the hotel room; she had added pictures and changed the curtains and mantel scarves to give the two rooms more brightness and comfort, and yet the Jacksons remained cramped, their belongings piled in the corners and under the bed. They could have only four or five friends visit at a time, and even then they seemed to bump elbows whenever they turned.

Anna missed the ease of movement she had always known, the great spaces of Cottage Home, and, not least, the piano. She told herself that once they had their own house, that was the first thing she would insist upon—a good piano! . . . When her mood brightened, so did her husband's. "There," he faced her with a lighter air. "It won't do any good to disturb ourselves. All things work together for those who love God . . . We'll see." It was something he said again and again.

As breakfast approached an end, Anna offered him a pear. "I'd like nothing more," he nodded, "but that's one of the things I just can't have." She was still learning about his troubles with food and the way he had to guard against digestive upsets. "Tom," she asked, "what causes all this?"

He shook his head. "If any doctor knows, I've yet to meet him. I believe I'd be gone now if I hadn't set out years ago to save myself—exercise, the right foods, regular habits." A rueful look crossed his face. "If I like anything, I've almost always got to give it up." Anna frowned; Tom had mentioned one diagnosis: nervous stomach. Did his condition grow out of his tense application, the unrelenting way he drove himself?

Weeks earlier, another ailment had struck him. She had seen him put his hand gingerly to his ear and his neck. "Oh, it's nothing," he had answered her immediate question, "only a little pain." But he had evaded her scrutiny, and she had noticed that he was breathing heavily. Finally he admitted he was suffering. "Tom, your eyes are inflamed, too," she had exclaimed, insisting that he visit the doctor.

He had returned with a parcel—drops for the eyes, chloroform liniment for his neck, an ammonia preparation for his throat. "You won't be able to bear me," he said with a shamed face. "I'll try," she laughed. A bit later, however, she became alarmed when she spoke to him and he seemed not to hear. "It's my right ear," he had explained. "It gets this way now and then." Anna said a prayer: God grant that the trouble go away. She made it her business to see that he dosed himself properly and followed the doctor's instructions.

Doggedly Tom rose every morning; at night he retired close to exhaustion, his voice hoarse, his eyes swollen, his hearing still impaired. He improved only slowly, but since each day brought him closer to health, Anna gave thanks and prayed again, this time that he be spared another such trial.

As she mused today Tom swallowed his second glass of buttermilk. Years earlier, during a treatment in upstate New York, he had discovered that the sour milk helped him, and now he drank it regularly. After some practice Anna decided that she liked buttermilk—within a reasonable limit. But she had yet to acquire Tom's taste for lemons, squeezed into water or sucked through a hole in the end!

"Ah, time to go." From the way he jumped up, Anna realized he must be a minute or so late. Affectionately she said good-by, and went to the window to see him swing off down the street. The morning was foggy; the dark figure became smaller and finally disappeared into the mist. Long after he was gone from view, she could still hear the faint sound of his military step. The Institute was atop a hill three-quarters of a mile away, and Anna was growing used to the sight of marches and reviews, the

steady tramp of feet, the distant booming of cannon, and the uniformed cadets' casual strolls around the town.

The two schools, the Institute and Washington College, dominated Lexington, and Anna had found life in this community
rather different from that of her North Carolina home. Lexington
was less expansive, more self-contained. The Morrisons had
shared the easy style of their planter friends; they had, she now
realized, a certain contact with the bigger cities, North and South.
But Rockbridge County, where Lexington lay behind its mountain barriers, remained quite isolated. In spite of this, Anna had
come to like the town and its people, and many of them, she felt,
were beginning to like her.

A businesslike rap sounded, and Anna opened the door. At once
she recognized a man whom she had met several times before:
Superintendent Francis Smith of the Institute. The lean, gray-
bearded individual stared at her through the tiny square glasses,
low on his long nose, that diverted attention from his small dark
eyes. "Old Specs," the boys called him, and Anna could not put
aside the nickname.

She greeted Superintendent Smith with some uncertainty, and
he appeared as surprised to see her as she was to see him. Immediately on her arrival she had sensed a certain restraint between him and her husband. Tom did not speak often of the
Superintendent, and when he did it was in formal terms. What
was the reason for this distance between them? She had never
brought herself to ask.

"Oh, Mrs. Jackson, your pardon. This is only a routine matter."
Superintendent Smith addressed her with polished ease and a
calm appraisal. "I happened to be in town and presumed that
the Major hadn't left yet. I should have known otherwise; he's always at the Institute on the dot." Anna read a suggestion of amusement in his eyes, and this piqued her curiosity. "Won't you come
in for a moment?" she asked. "We see each other so seldom."

After a brief hesitation the caller took a seat, his long legs set
carefully before him. "A pleasant place you have, madame," he
observed.

"Yes, we think it's nice enough," she replied, her mind working
ahead of her tongue. Her family had always claimed she could
"draw out anybody," and today she wanted to learn just what
this man thought of her husband and his work. Quickly she went
on. "My husband works here every day and night, and very, very

hard, so it's practically his second office." That should bring some comment!

It did not. "Indeed." Francis Smith, as composed as ever, merely nodded. "And you're from North Carolina, they tell me, Mrs. Jackson." As they talked, she reflected. The superintendent had come to Lexington when the Institute was founded and had remained uninterruptedly in command through many clashes; he had the reputation of being a man who could deal successfully with many elements, balancing them with skill. And today he proved himself the discreet diplomat. He said nothing to indicate the way he felt about Tom Jackson.

Several minutes later, with a polite bow and a good-by, Superintendent Smith left, and Anna remained for a time at the door, pondering. Then, shrugging, she went downstairs to ask the manager about a service problem. There, a high-pitched voice reached her from the entrance hall. "Why, Anna Jackson, this is the first time I've set eyes on you in weeks! Let's have a good *folksy* chat over a cup of tea."

The lady, a globular one in red taffeta and trailing ornaments, was Mrs. Petry, whom Anna recalled, and not entirely happily, from a recent Institute gathering. Since it was the only place for tea and the folksy chat, Anna invited Mrs. Petry to her room. When they arrived, Mrs. Petry was huffing after her ascent. She carefully removed her gloves and patted them out. "My, the fall gets mistier and mistier here. I can remember when . . ."

Anna politely nodded, thinking to herself that her caller had not sought her out to talk of the weather. Now it came. Bending forward confidentially, Mrs. Petry breathed peppermint, and her bright green eyes probed. "I couldn't *help* see the Superintendent as he left. No new trouble for the Major, I hope?"

"Why, why—there's no trouble. What do you mean?"

"Don't you *know?*" Mrs. Petry's manner became more genteel and more wasplike by the minute. "We don't have to mince words, my dear. I was afraid, *so* afraid, that it might be those parents or alumni, demanding again that the school get rid of the Major. Or it might even be another duel with a student." With each sentence Mrs. Petry concentrated her blows.

Anna gaped, conscious that her face had lost its color, yet unable to cover her shock. "I don't understand any of this."

Mrs. Petry proved eager to explain. "Surely, child, you've heard that every term or so some of the students have *troubles* with

poor Tom, and there are court-martials of the boys and investiga-
tions and that kind of thing. And just a year ago the alumni
presented a resolution saying that he was *mismanaging* his department."

The lady went on, embroidering her story: "I thought you'd
like to know the real situation. You're so young and new here . . .
You see, so many people think Tom just can't teach. You and I
know better of course. But the boys make fun of him, practically
to his face, hooting and calling him a *hayseed*. They do lots worse
things than that. Once two of them waited as he passed and
dropped a brick from the top story of a building. That was a
murderous trick; they missed killing him by an inch."

Anna wished desperately that she could shut out the caustic
words. Mismanagement, inability to teach, contempt of her husband, an act that might have brought his death . . . And now
Mrs. Petry had still more to say. "Then there was that student, Jim
Walker, who challenged him to a duel. Well, the Major didn't accept, though a lot of people believed he should have in *honor*, and
some don't think so much of the Major since then . . ."

More followed, but Anna remembered only bits and phrases.
Though the tea had not arrived, she could stand no more of this
flow of pink malice, and she got up: "You'll have to excuse me." At
the door she nodded a firm good-by, and Mrs. Petry left in a
flutter: "You must realize that I only have Tom's interests at
heart . . ."

Anna closed the door with a bang and stood trembling in
the middle of the room. She had to find out about this, and at
once. Whom could she ask? Suddenly the answer came to her—
Maggie Preston. But perhaps that would not be wise, perhaps it
would be best to wait until her thoughts were composed. Then
she reached for her hat. She would go to the Preston home because
she had to.

On her arrival, a surprised maid led Anna to the kitchen, where
she found Maggie almost hidden behind an enormous apron. Her
fingers were tinted a bright red, and she was surrounded by four
dark helpers and jars of fragrant-sticky preserves. "Anna, just a
few minutes," the housewife called out casually. "Two things
won't wait—a husband's supper and a batch of plums." Then a
second look at her guest's set face made Maggie change her plans:
"Oh, I'll come now, and you girls finish this for me."

In a blur, Anna let her friend escort her to the privacy of the library; and there, without preamble, she told her story. Finishing, she stared directly at Maggie and spoke emphatically: "I wish you'd tell me the truth—just what's happened." Maggie rubbed her hands together, and her voice was hesitant. "Anna, I was afraid you might hear something like this, and you've heard it the worst way."

Maggie paused as if debating how to proceed, and Anna continued to regard her firmly. "Well," Maggie resumed, "I have to say that Tom's really not a very good teacher, not even a good one. It may be something he isn't precisely fitted for, Anna. When he came here, he wasn't prepared for the work, and I remember how nervous he was, and unsure of himself. Several of his courses involve science and computations. Those aren't easy subjects, and Tom's never learned how to explain things simply, and—well—divert the boys. He's deadly serious, and"—the little woman sighed—"with all his good qualities, Tom hasn't much humor."

Instinctively, Anna objected: "We laugh together a lot, and he's always bright and lively." Then slowly she subsided. "That isn't the same thing, though." A moment later her mind caught at another of Mrs. Petry's statements: "What about the complaints to the board?"

Maggie moved from her chair to a place beside her friend. "Tom's gotten into furious arguments with some of the boys. To him, there's one way to do a thing, the textbook way, and his students have to do it that way. The cadets say Tom's too stiff and unbending and unreasonable. Still, child"—Maggie took her hands—"the Superintendent and the board didn't accept the alumni complaint. They just put the matter aside, and the whole thing simmered down. Tom demanded a full investigation, but the board said no."

While all this brought her a certain comfort, Anna was not completely reassured. "And Superintendent Smith?" she asked.

"Well, he and Tom aren't close friends. I'm afraid the Superintendent doesn't think the Major's any great shakes as a teacher. But he didn't give way, and Tom has stayed on."

Anna stared at her fingers, which were clenched in her lap. "Those terrible stories about the way the boys jibe at him?"

Maggie faced her with an almost pleading look: "Child, the cadets aren't easy to handle; you should hear some of the things Major Preston tells me. They do laugh at Tom because he's 'odd' and different. That's true about the brick, and it was dangerous,

though I hardly think they meant to hurt him. But, my dear"—
once again Maggie pressed her hands—"a lot of others in the town,
including many of the cadets, like Tom and admire him, and don't
ever forget that."

Anna lowered her head. "And that duel?"

"Jim Walker's from Western Virginia. He's a hotheaded boy,
and he got into an argument with Tom about talking in class.
There was a court-martial and Jim was dismissed. He wouldn't
leave town and sent a formal challenge. Oh, Anna, don't believe
that Tom ignored the thing." Maggie's face reddened with her
emotion. "It hung over him for days, and he talked to Major
Preston and a lot of others. They had a hard time persuading him
not to accept."

Now Anna's friend spoke in a burst of anger: "Let me tell you
it took courage for Tom to make his decision! He reasoned that
he was a good shot, and with his long army training and experience he'd probably kill the boy. Also, as a Christian he said he
couldn't do it. But if Jim Walker attacked him, he'd simply have
to defend himself. He took this stand in a place where a lot of
people are still wrapped up in that crazy code of 'honor'." For the
first time the former Pennsylvanian's background came out.

Before Anna could respond, Maggie grew reflective. "Still,
Anna, I sometimes think . . . It might be better if Tom went to
another place, another atmosphere, to start over again. A while
back he did apply when he heard of a vacancy at the University
of Virginia, and Colonel Robert Lee, the superintendent at West
Point, gave him a strong recommendation. He didn't get the position, but it's the kind of thing that he may keep in mind."

Robert Lee. Hadn't Tom mentioned fighting in Mexican War
battles with a Virginian of that name? A moment later Anna's
mind returned to Maggie's suggestion. After all, perhaps a new
school or even a complete change of work . . . It was a subject
to be considered.

Now Maggie was speaking again: "Wherever Tom goes,
though, he mustn't change too much. It's best if we—Tom or anybody else—stay ourselves, and not try to fit the mold that others
want for us."

What did this mean? Maggie continued, "I've had problems of
my own here. When I married Major Preston I was somebody
with a 'Yankee' background, and his family was old Virginia, with

estates and traditions and manner. Worse, I wrote!" All at once
the poet was speaking of herself as she never had before.

"My hands shook when I walked in to see the assembled
Prestons. They stood like an army against me; even the pictures
on the wall seemed to be staring me down. Everything was so
different. They gave me my own maid to help me dress, run my
errands, and do everything else she could. Anna, I was scared
pale." Maggie shrugged. "Well, I made up my mind that, strange
as I was among them, I'd be myself and try not to worry what I
said or did or how best to behave. And before long the barriers
came down. Not all at once, and some still stand. But I've managed, and Tom Jackson's got to manage too—by remaining true
to himself. It's up to you to encourage him, give him more confidence, deep inside, than he has now."

As the words faded, Anna remembered another conversation in
this house. Here was much the same thing Mr. Lyle had said: she
must see that her husband developed a greater confidence in his
abilities . . . Strongly moved, Anna rose to leave. When she bade
her friend good-by, she kissed Maggie Preston's cheek. This hour
had meant a great deal to her. And how good a friend Maggie,
whom she had once feared, had proved to be.

On the way home, however, she could not blot from her mind
the things Mrs. Petry had said. Over her hung the harsh jibes at
Tom, the feeling that he did a poor job as a teacher, and the
threatened duel. Jim Walker . . . That name was to return in
her dreams. And yet Maggie had lifted some of her burden.

At that she thought again of her friend's almost pathetic con-
fession of her own difficulties. Suddenly Anna realized a strange
thing. She and Maggie had switched roles, in a way. She had
been used to a great deal and now did with less, in two small
hotel rooms, while Maggie, accustomed to a more austere household as the daughter of a college president, had had to readjust
herself to more expansive ways.

Anna reached the hotel in time to greet Tom on his regular
eleven o'clock return. She knew she must say nothing about the
morning's incidents, but the effort was wretchedly difficult. The
next two hours were to be devoted to a "silent period," during
which her husband studied. His work must not be interrupted.
After a quick kiss Tom went to the window, where he had a
high desk, made to order by a carpenter so that he could stand
as he worked.

"I sometimes feel drowsy, and this keeps me awake," he had explained. "And it keeps my digestive organs in good alignment." At those words Anna had looked questioningly at him. "In proper position . . . Anyway, that's how it's best for me." Here was a small mystery she never fathomed. Today he reached out for the Bible and the Commentary that lay on his desk. Both were, Anna knew, heavily marked. As he labored over them, she sewed and answered letters. Even though she could not speak to him, it was good to be here with her husband, and slowly her composure returned.

After his Bible reading Tom took up his schoolbooks and technical reading. As she watched him grimace in his concentration, a sudden pity rushed over her. Until now she had never understood the full extent of his troubles and the way they must almost have overwhelmed him at times. To know that so many doubted his capacities and sneered at his efforts . . . She had to fight the impulse to reach out to Tom, to talk to him of what she had learned. Sternly she restrained herself; she could never tell him of the day's disclosures.

As the study hour drew to a close, Tom took out a paper and began to figure carefully. Sensing her curiosity, he murmured, "My tithing for the church." She realized that he had set aside a precise tenth of everything, and she halted. She had forgotten this duty in her own calculations, and now she would have to cut out several purchases she had intended to make! A moment later he showed her some items in his accounts—a small investment in a building association, a share in a town business. By Cottage Home standards, the figures were meager, but they revealed a regular increase in recent years, a saving here, a slight gain there. Some would say the Jacksons lived frugally, and yet, she assured herself, they had enough, and they were preparing for their future and their children's.

One o'clock, and the maid knocked with their dinner. Replacing his book, Tom smiled and Anna nodded warmly; this was the time for which she had been waiting. At once he introduced a topic which must have been in his thoughts for some time: "Tomorrow I'm reopening my Sunday school classes for the Negroes, and I hope you'll come with me." He had already told her something about the classes. He had begun them a few years earlier, and she gathered that they had had a certain success.

"I'd certainly like to go," she told him. "I've held Sunday

school classes in Carolina, and couldn't I do the same thing here?
There are dozens of children among the people we know."

After a little thought he replied. "That's fine, *esposa*. Still,
. . . Would you mind holding them for the colored? It's so much
harder for them to get teaching of that sort." To Anna the suggestion was a new one, and she hesitated. "I've never done anything like it, and I'm not sure how I could manage."

"What you make up your mind to do, you can do." As she heard
him repeat this favorite principle, Anna frowned. It might be far
more difficult for her than it was for him. Nevertheless she looked
up with a resolute air: "All right, I'll try it if you'd like." The decision made her feel much better.

After dinner came a half-hour of rest and conversation—another
set part of his schedule. Then he turned with a bright glance:
"A surprise. I've borrowed a carriage and we're going for a ride
outside town." Welcoming the change, Anna hurried into her coat,
and as they drove along the mountain edges they found themselves in a land of painted clouds. Few other vehicles passed, and
they seemed alone in a vast blue-white serenity. Anna sighed contentedly as they reached one of her favorite stretches, from which
opened a vista of unending distance. "Let's get out," she urged
him, and together they stood at the edge of a high crag, the wind
whipping against them as they watched a panorama of fading
blue and green and gray.

"The Valley of Virginia," Tom whispered. "Anna, I think this is
the most beautiful place in the world." Slowly she agreed, but
then an uneasy thought suggested itself. Perhaps Tom liked this
part of the state too much for his own good. Remembering
Maggie's words that morning, she asked, "Haven't you thought
that you might like to go elsewhere, or do some other work?"

Her husband remained silent for a time, then frowned. "My
dear, the Lord will decide. If it's intended that I should change,
His will will be shown to us." Drawing her up, he started back to
the carriage, and on their way she pondered. Perhaps Tom was
right, but when would they know, and how would they know what
was right for them?

After supper came the last phase of Tom's day, and a vital one,
his hour or so of application without the use of his eyes. Although
he never read after dark, he had trained himself to take full advantage of this period. During the day he went over his school-
work and other studies carefully, memorizing facts, dates, topics.

"Now," he had explained to her, "I'll review them without a book or any other help." And tonight, as on many other nights, she watched him tighten his eyes and murmur to himself. Several times he rubbed his cheek and ran a handkerchief over his perspiring forehead.

Once she had asked, "Tom, can't I get the information for you?" Startled, he had given her a look almost of disbelief, then slowly shaken his head. A moment later his mind had gone far from the room. He had developed this power of concentration to a phenomenal degree, as he computed long mathematical problems and repeated pages at a time to himself . . . A rustle of movement, and now at last Tom turned to her, his face creased in lines of happy greeting. She had her husband again.

The next day started early, like all their Sundays; for Tom and Anna Jackson the Sabbath was, in a way, the busiest day of the week, with services, devotions, and duties. And this Sunday had a special meaning: it marked the reopening of Tom's classes for the Negroes. They went promptly to church, but en route she stopped for a brief chat with a friend until Tom cleared his throat and they left hastily, to arrive in a rush.

In church, Anna might have enjoyed a small revenge had she been so inclined. The earnest pastor, Dr. William White, stepped forward, and Tom listened intently for several minutes. Then drowsiness settled over him, and he began a long fight to resist it. His head sank to his chest, and she nudged him: "Tom, wake up, wake up." The head rose swiftly and the sleepy eyes opened, but only a short time later they closed again. For a long minute his chin remained against his cravat, and to her dismay Anna heard a snore. "Tom, please." Pushing his arm, she awakened him again, and once more the process started. Around them several people watched, among them the amused Maggie and John Preston.

This was nothing new; it happened almost every Sunday. As resolute as Tom was in his religious interests, he could not stay alert in church. Was this sleepiness connected in some way with his health, or did he simply push himself so hard that when he had a quiet hour his fatigue caught up with him? Yet, oddly enough, he could generally repeat most of what Dr. White had said. During his waking moments he concentrated hard!

Through the midday meal Anna found her mind returning to the afternoon class for the slaves; she would observe Tom's work today and take up her own the following Sunday. But could she manage it? . . . At two o'clock they left the hotel for the meeting hall. In the doorway Dr. White smiled benevolently upon them, and Anna had never seen the easy-mannered man so animated.

Major Preston, a strong supporter of the classes, bowed, and as Tom took their friend aside, the minister addressed Anna warmly: "For years after I came here I tried to reach the dark people in one way or another and failed—until Tom suggested this, and then did it. He planned the classes, organized them, and drew in other people to help with the teaching. Do you know he talks to the colored people's owners, sends out letters, and makes report forms? No schoolwork in Virginia gets closer attention."

Anna showed her surprise. Her husband had never revealed how much he did; he had not even indicated his full role in launching it. "Here come our first recruits." Dr. White inclined his head, and she looked up in eager interest. Toward them moved an uncertain file of men and women of various ages and various kinds of garb. Near the front, in his waiter's dress, walked the lean Albert, whom Tom was helping earn his freedom. Behind him were six or seven Preston slaves, the two Junkin servants, a tiny woman with eight children, and many others new to Anna.

"Evenin', ma'am."

"How do, Major, and you, too, Doctor?"

In each case Tom nodded solemnly. At the end of the line was an elderly Negro woman, plump and beaming. "This is Amy," he informed Anna. Several times she had heard him mention the good-humored Negro woman who "did a few things" for him in Lexington. Today, as Amy went inside, it was Dr. White who explained more to her.

"Poor Amy came to me," the minister said. "Her owner had gone bankrupt, and she was going to be sold for debt. She'd seen Major Jackson at her old house, and asked me if he could help her. It was a pitiful scene; Amy cried when she told how they would take the whole lot of them down to Louisiana or Mississippi, and she felt sure she wouldn't survive it. And I can't forget the way she asked Tom: 'Please take me, please take me. . . .' He had no real work for her, and at her age she couldn't be very active anyway. Still, he bought her and found a home for her with a family on the outskirts of town. Every month he pays them a little for her lodging."

As Anna looked across the entranceway to her husband, deep

in conversation with Major Preston, she was caught by a new feeling of love and admiration. More than ever she had to do something, whatever she could, to help him and to advance his efforts, and again she reminded herself: Maggie and Mr. Lyle had indicated the way to her.

Tom pulled out his watch. "One minute before three," he announced, and though no one else was in sight, he waited until that minute had passed before he led Anna and the two men inside and locked the door. "No late arrivals," he smiled. She saw Dr. White and John Preston glance over in surprise. To her, however, this brought no wonder at all.

Dr. White delivered a short invocation, and then Tom stepped forward, to talk awkwardly. She realized that he had worked for a long time over his remarks, but he uttered them in halting words. "You know why you're—you're here today. You will be here—er, every week to—to place yourself in touch with—with God. How many—how many believe in God?"

All except one of the right hands lifted, and after a moment that one followed.

"How many wish to be in a state of grace?"

The final word proved a puzzle, and one hand lifted slowly, another, and then all the rest. "Remember the Sabbath to keep it—keep it holy," Tom went on. "Do you understand?"

"Sure do."

"You right *there*, Major!"

From then on Tom spoke with greater conviction, and to her relief the class progressed easily. After a time he called for a hymn, and most of the slaves joined in a harmony which grew with each stanza. Taking up the Bible, Tom read a passage and went through its meaning and applications. There followed instructions from a catechism and hymnbook, and he announced awards of Bibles and Testaments for those who made good records.

Anna missed not a word of what he said, or of the reactions. As Tom asked for the final hymn, she took part in the singing, as did Major Preston and Dr. White, and her voice rose happily to the ceiling. Tom had done very well, succeeding better than she had anticipated he would. Outside, the minister seized his hand. "Whatever you do, my boy, here or anywhere else, this will be one of your finest works."

Flushing, Tom nodded. As the gathering broke up, Anna saw

Major Preston watching her husband with a warm look. When they had left and she and Tom were walking home, he spoke at last, his voice husky: "I hope Dr. White's right, and this will have some effect." All at once he seemed to remember her suggestion of yesterday in the mountains. "For the present, Anna, I think I'm where I should be." Silently she inclined her head.

CHAPTER 7

The next six months had a single focal point for Tom and Anna: the baby that grew slowly within her. For both of them, it was a daily concern. Each evening, as he returned to their rooms, Tom's first question was, "My dear, is everything all right? You're sure?" When she nodded, he generally patted her hand in gratitude.

One day, before he could inquire, she called out gaily, "Tom, I'm fine and the little one is, too, as far as I know." At his hurt expression, her manner changed. "Oh, I'm sorry," she smiled ruefully. "It's only that you're so anxious about him." That the child would be a boy she took for granted, and she found herself speculating on his future. Perhaps he would be a planter or a lawyer or a minister. A soldier or a teacher? Tom was both the latter, of course, but Anna did not know just how much she favored those professions. Whenever she had trouble with her budget, she decided that her son should not be a teacher!

Meanwhile, there had been an important change in their living arrangements. First of all, the hotel would not be a good place for the baby's arrival, and when Anna discovered the amount of their monthly rent she asked, "Why can't we board somewhere and save some money?" At first Tom was hesitant. Then, several times within ten days, bands of drunken roisterers at the front of the hotel waked them after midnight. This convinced him, and he set out to hunt new quarters.

In his absence Anna reflected smilingly over an exchange between her husband and the hotel manager. Didn't Major Jackson ever drink? that dignitary had asked. "I did when I was younger," Tom had replied, "but I gave it up, because I liked it too much." For him the decision had been as simple as that . . .

After several inquiries they located two rooms, larger than their present ones, in the neat home of a teacher, Mr. McFarland. A widower, the teacher had a Negro housekeeper and a maid who would help serve the Jacksons. "It isn't an ideal arrangement, but it will be an improvement at least until we have a place of our own," Anna assured Tom. "Good, good," he agreed, with a characteristic movement of his head. But when would they have their home? They still had not been able to find one. Firmly Anna put the question aside; she must not brood over that disappointment.

Settled in their temporary quarters, Anna discovered that the baby overshadowed all her plans, all her conversations. His name would be Tom, she had decided. Whenever she watched her husband with the young Prestons, she sensed his yearning for his own child. Her pregnancy was not far advanced, and because they had more space they were able to have a few more friends in for evening visits.

"Tom, I'd like to ask Superintendent Smith and his family," she suggested one day. His face clouded, and for a moment Anna believed he would say no. "Very well, if you think you should," he answered. Her own feelings toward the Superintendent were mixed, and yet, as Maggie had pointed out, that gentleman had refused to give in to the hue and cry against her husband. And surely he would be a good man to have on their side . . . The event went pleasantly enough, and thereafter, it seemed to her, Tom spoke somewhat less guardedly of his superior.

In that instance, as in others, Anna felt that she was helping Tom, advancing his interests, giving him something of the increased confidence Maggie and Mr. Lyle had told her he needed. More and more this was to be her role, and she looked forward to it with heightening satisfaction. Several times the Prestons came to visit them, bringing with them Mr. Lyle who, despite his illness, kept up his end of the conversation.

Soon, however, neither Maggie nor Anna would be calling on many people for a time. Not long after her friend learned that Anna was pregnant, she announced that her own baby was on the way. "You know," Anna said to Tom, "when she gave me the news she looked embarrassed but also—well, almost triumphant." The little woman of thirty-seven, whom the town (and also Anna) had written off as a spinster, had fooled them all. As she talked with Tom, Anna's happiness at Maggie's news matched his.

One morning when she left the boarding house on an errand, she was seized by a sudden pain, and was compelled to halt when she reached the corner. The scene swam around her, and she caught at a picket fence to support herself. A moment later she

saw Dr. White hastening toward her; with him was a middle-
aged woman, her pepper-and-salt hair drawn up under a plain
black bonnet. "My child," the clergyman murmured, and added
discreetly, "you shouldn't be out now."

"Poppycock," Dr. White's companion retorted in a brisk tone
that helped restore Anna's spirit. "I'm Mrs. William Page from
down the street—just back from a long trip. Mrs. Jackson, let's go
inside for a few minutes." Mrs. Page's eyes had a glint that said
"no nonsense" to anyone from a stage driver to a governor, and
she had the simplicity of a woman who had reached the age at
which she spoke and acted as she pleased. Toward Anna, however, her manner was kind, almost maternal.

Leaving the minister on the street, the two women entered the
house. Anna's answers to her sharply worded questions satisfied
Mrs. Page, and the older woman fetched a glass of water and
gave Anna a pill from her purse. Then she offered several bits of
sage advice and finished by asking, "Child, isn't there some older
woman around to help you?" Anna shook her head, sensing that
Mrs. Page would take precisely that role. And she was right.
Thereafter her neighbor called frequently with broth and expert
counsel. Tom welcomed her enthusiastically, and the three spent
hours together before the fire. One evening, Mrs. Page was to sit
with Anna while Tom attended a short meeting of the Institute
faculty. It was a night which, for all its quiet beginning, had more
drama than Anna could have anticipated.

As the servant removed the supper plates, Tom sat back with
an air of deep satisfaction and drew out a letter. "I wrote it to
sister Laura—within an hour after I got *her* note this morning.
She's come back to the church." Anna's eyes went quickly over
Tom's letter: "I thank our heavenly Father for having given you
that peace which passeth all understanding, and which the world
can neither give nor take away. . . . You may expect dark hours,
but never for one moment permit yourself to despond . . ."

Anna looked up happily. She read the joy in Tom's eyes and
remembered what he had once said: the day Laura rejoined the
church would be his happiest in years. They talked together about
his sister, and he spoke warmly: "It should help her a lot." The
more Anna heard of the conscientious, troubled woman, the more
interested she grew, and the more she wanted to meet her as
soon as she could. "This summer, no matter what happens, we
have to be with Laura," she declared, and Tom smiled.

A few minutes later he went to his upright desk for a period of final study. While she watched, his eyes opened wide and his lips moved. He lowered his head; apparently he was going over some computation, and then he turned: "I've just realized I made a mistake today with a cadet, and I'll have to rectify matters."

She smiled. "You can correct it tomorrow, whatever it is."

Tom continued to mull over the subject as if he had not heard her. A few minutes later Mrs. Page appeared in the doorway, shaking the rain drops from her shawl. "Major, I'll warrant you'll be one of the few people at the meeting tonight." Still absorbed, Tom answered their neighbor only perfunctorily and left.

For the next hour Anna chatted with her friend. "No, I'm afraid neither my mother nor Eugenia can get here when the baby comes. Eugenia has her second child now, and Mother's tied down by a hundred things. If she left, Cottage Home would practically collapse. But I'll have one familiar face with me—Hetty." Several times her former maid had asked if she could join Miss Anna, and the Morrisons would soon be sending her on.

"That will mean a lot to you, won't it?"

Anna nodded. Only during the past few weeks, when Hetty's arrival had become a definite possibility, had she understood how much she missed the dark woman who had been at her side during most of her life. "And you do miss the plantation," the older woman commented.

"Well . . ." Instinctively Anna began to deny the statement, then admitted it. "If only Tom and I could be with them now and then," she sighed. "I'd like to take him home with me . . . Oh, I don't mean that. Tom's place is here, and so is mine." As she spoke, a gust of rain splashed against the window, and Mrs. Page got up to look out. "That meeting's been going on a right long time."

Suddenly Anna remembered Tom's earlier words: he had to "rectify matters" with a cadet whom he had "treated unfairly." She thought of Mrs. Petry's story of James Walker of Western Virginia, and the near-duel. Suppose—suppose Tom were with the cadet now, in a bloody dispute! Why hadn't she sensed his meaning when he first brought up the subject?

All at once her forehead was wet with perspiration, and her face took on a waxy color. To Mrs. Page's questions she shook her head. "I'm all right, just a little upset. Well, if you believe I should lie down . . ." As she rested on the sofa, her mind worked swiftly. She had to be alone, to think this through. She forced herself up: "They must be expecting you at home now, mustn't they?"

At last the kind-faced matron left, with some misgivings. Anna arose from the couch and paced up and down the room. The only sounds were the padding of her feet across the rug and the pouring of the rain outside. She knew what she had to do—get a carriage and go in search of Tom, from one place to another until she found him. People might talk; if so, she'd let them. Anna threw on a coat, pulled open the door, and almost fell against a tall figure, glistening and dripping in the hallway.

"Tom, thank God, thank God . . ." She was crying, and he took her back inside, to rub her hands and ask several questions. After a time Anna was able to bring herself under control.

"You're all right? Nothing's happened?"

"What could have happened?" He blinked foolishly. Reassured, Anna's practical nature asserted itself. "Change your clothes, right now, and then tell me exactly what took place."

A few minutes later Tom stood before the fire, a blanket draped around his shoulders. "Anna, I'd held up that boy as having made an error, and I couldn't have slept comfortably tonight until I told him I was wrong. I was already obligated to attend the meeting, and I did; the moment it ended I went to the barracks."

"In all that rain? Three-quarters of a mile each way!" For a moment Anna could not believe her husband.

"Why, yes. Nobody at the meeting had a carriage, and it was my responsibility." He was insistent on his point.

"Tom, the cadets must all have been in bed."

"They were." He addressed her with a greater calm than ever. "I had him waked, and we talked it over."

Anna's mouth fell open. What a story the boys would have! And it would be twisted to even more fantastic lengths by gossipers like Mrs. Petry. "Oh, couldn't you realize . . ." She was so disturbed that she had to stop for a moment, and Tom intervened. "My dear, this really isn't the way——"

"'The way to be happy.' I'm sure it isn't, but look, Tom——"

As he looked and listened, his head jerked suddenly back and he sneezed lustily several times. Anna moved into immediate action: "Where's the cough medicine, and those throat pills?" For the next few minutes she dosed him, then got him into bed and covered him with extra blankets. "But—but, Anna," he protested, "we have another twenty minutes left before bedtime."

Her answer was to lower the wick and blow out the lamp. This was one night they would not follow a schedule! As she lay beside Tom, with the smell of camphor and ammonia thick around them, she thought of the way their discussion had ended, and chuckled. "Tom, dear," she began. "Tom . . ." When she touched him she found he was deep in slumber.

The next morning he insisted on rising as usual, and he had just returned from his walk when the maid entered with their food. The girl had a subdued air. "Message jus' come f'um Miss Maggie. It's Mistah Lyle—happen jus' a lil while back."

The maid went out, and Anna and Tom stared at each other. He started to reach for a piece of bread, but his hand dropped to his side. "We knew it wouldn't be long . . ." Anna murmured in a low, broken voice, and then fell silent. Tom rose, his food untouched. "Why, it's like one of my own kin. If—if it hadn't been for Mr. Lyle, things might be very different for me."

Uncertainly he started for the door, but Anna led him back, forced him to swallow something and to take his cough medicine. With a worried sigh she watched him leave for the Preston home, and prepared herself for the sad event that was to follow. The next day they walked together up the wide stairs to the Preston parlor, where more than a hundred people had gathered to pay their last respects to the old bookseller.

Tom's face was badly inflamed, and Anna had asked him if he had to attend the services. She herself felt unwell, and he in turn tried to persuade her to remain home. "In your condition, Anna, people might wonder," he said. She lifted her head to him: "I *want* to be there, and I'm going with you." As they paused near the coffin, Dr. White began, speaking through pale lips: "Dear Lord, one of our best, one of our finest of spirits . . ."

Across the room Maggie Preston put her hand in the Major's, and Anna saw the lift and fall of her own husband's heavy shoulders. A moment later Tom put his handkerchief to his face. Once again she recalled his story of Mr. Lyle's renunciation of his love— the first Mrs. Preston. Now both of them were dead; the Major and his new wife stood beside Mr. Lyle's casket. God's workings were unfathomable; and yet, His will be done.

Dr. White's voice dropped, and the crowd moved toward the

door. As the men took places beside the coffin, Maggie whispered to Anna, "Tell brother Tom I know exactly how he feels today." Nodding, Anna reflected that until recently she would have been jarred at hearing Maggie call Tom "brother," but today she accepted it without question.

Since Mr. Lyle had no burial place in Lexington, Major Preston had arranged for him to be laid to rest in the Preston family plot. At the cemetery Maggie took Anna aside. "The Major and I decided on these lines for the tombstone: 'He was the truest friend, the bravest man, and the best Christian ever known to him who erects this stone to his memory.'" Anna whispered her approval; while the feeling was Major Preston's, she suspected that his wife had much to do with the wording.

Although she had decided not to tell Tom about her encounter with Mrs. Petry, the subject rankled, and one day when they were out walking they passed the lady. Anna started to ignore her, but thought better of it and nodded. "What has Mrs. Petry done to you?" Tom inquired with a hint of amusement in his voice.

For a moment Anna was tempted to make a direct answer. Instead, she contented herself with a brief reply: "A little trouble you wouldn't understand. She's what you'd call a 'deceived woman,' and as you've said in such cases, I'll simply let her alone."

"Still"—the quizzical air continued—"I sometimes keep on speaking a little, even to 'deceived' ones."

"Very well, I'll speak a little." Thereafter Anna did, but she also managed to keep the woman at a distance . . . That same day brought an encounter which showed her that other townsmen had a far higher opinion of Tom than did the lady critic. On their walk, Tom hailed a handsome, middle-aged man of vigorous manner accompanied by a slim youth of seventeen or eighteen with a diffident, boyish air. Anna recognized the former as Dr. William N. Pendleton, pastor of the Episcopal church, whom she had met only casually, and now she acknowledged Tom's introduction to the light-haired young man. "Anna, this is Dr. Pendleton's son, Sandie, and I think we'll all be hearing from him in the future."

Tom proceeded to address the youth and his father. "Sandie, since you've gone to higher college, you've had to give up the boarding school you run, haven't you?" As the boy nodded, his timidity left him, and he and Tom spoke on with authority about courses, costs of instruction, and maintenance.

Now the impressive-looking minister faced Tom. "What's the report on those new guns they've been testing?" Dr. Pendleton and Tom debated fluently on gun emplacements and firing distances, and Anna was amused to discover that, despite his clerical collar, Dr. Pendleton talked exactly like a soldier. Meanwhile she turned to Sandie: "You have been managing a school?"

Embarrassed at her air of surprise, the youth answered: "Yes, ma'am. I finished here at Washington College when I was seventeen, and now I'm working for a higher degree at the University at Charlottesville." Again his manner altered; this time there was a certain pride in his voice: "I've been earning my living for some years now." His look was bright and winning, and his vocabulary unusually good. Anna's eyes went from the young man to his father; each obviously regarded Tom with high respect. She liked these Pendletons, she thought to herself, and then added with a smile, she would have liked them even if they did not feel as they did about her husband!

When the friends parted, Anna asked Tom several questions. "They're fine people," he agreed with her. "Dr. Pendleton hasn't had an easy time in Lexington. There aren't many Episcopalians here, and for years he had to make do with a shabby rectory and seven hundred dollars a year when he had a large family to raise. Sandie turned the upper story into a school and helped keep the Pendletons going."

Tom shook his head in fond, almost fatherly fashion. "Poor Sandie was a tiny, delicate child, and Dr. Pendleton sent him to Washington College at thirteen. Think of confronting a board of professors at that age and taking examinations in Greek, mathematics, and the like! Well, Sandie came through, and graduated last June with highest honors."

"But the father," Anna went on. "He's so much like a military man."

Tom chuckled. "He should be. He's a West Point graduate with three full years in the artillery, who eventually turned to the ministry." Anna's astonishment increased; these Pendletons were even more prodigious people than she had suspected. She made up her mind to see more of them from then on.

Soon afterward, when she and Tom were crossing the walk before the house, she grasped his arm. "Help me in," she whispered as she fought against her faintness. But she had to give up the effort, and she woke to discover herself in bed. Tom was kneeling beside her. "Don't exert yourself, *esposita*," he told her. "The doctor's on the way."

After his examination the medical man shrugged. "Your condition's—all right; there's nothing that rest shouldn't take care of. From now on, you're not to leave the room, and not to worry about anything." As he and Tom brushed aside her protests, Anna settled back with a frown. She was only "all right," and still she should not worry. But what was wrong with her?

When the doctor left, Tom came in smiling. "A tonic for you, from North Carolina. Hetty's on her way by train. My, are you as happy as *that?*" During the next few days, every heavy step on the porch made Anna sit up; had Hetty arrived? The family wrote that they had sent the trusted maid alone, with tickets, pocket money, and detailed instructions. She was traveling by stagecoach and railroad to Richmond, changing there, and so on. By the end of the week Anna fretted: "Tom, she's never been anywhere without one of us, and suppose she's lost or taken sick on the way? Suppose we never hear about her . . ."

While Tom was trying to soothe her, a shrill voice reached them: "Where she at?" A moment later, as Anna forced herself up with a happy cry, the familiar figure faced her; Hetty held a carpetbag under each arm, and her eyes were wide with excitement. She ran forward to clasp Anna's arms and laugh and cry, "When they ax me where I goin', I say 'Goin' to Virginny, but the Lord know *if* I git there or not!'"

In her excitement Hetty had paid no heed to Tom. Finally, she spun around and, spying him, bowed in a stiff, self-conscious manner: "It's nice to see yer, Major, and we glad we all made it."

Faintly Anna responded, "*All* of you?"

"Yes'm. Didn' they tell yer I bring my young 'uns, Cy and George? They in the hall right now." Going to the door, Hetty drew in two big-boned youths, about twelve and fifteen, who gaped around the strange room.

Tom and Anna exchanged glances. The Morrisons must have taken it for granted that they would expect the boys. But three more mouths to feed, three more people to look after . . . Before Anna could speak, Tom came forward. "That's all right, Hetty. I'll take George and Cyrus and arrange quarters in town for them, and we have something ready for you here."

An hour later, when Tom took his place beside her, Anna was apologetic: "I hadn't known about them . . ." With a smile he cut off her words and proceeded to another topic: "Tomorrow you can start teaching the boys to read, and they'll go to church and Sunday school every week." Amused, Anna settled back against her pillow. Tom and the doctor had ordered complete rest, and she had had to give up her regular Sunday teaching for a time. Nevertheless, Tom was going to put her to work in a good cause.

During the six weeks before the birth of her baby, Anna's mood fluctuated. For hours she lay placid and content, listening to Hetty chatter about Eugenia, Eugenia's two children, and the Hills, Irwins, and Morrisons. Then she would grow nervous, ordering the window up, then down. Her mind went back to the recent funeral at the Prestons' and to the death of Ellie's and Tom's baby. Two or three times she woke from a dream in which she had been staring in horror at a dim box. What did it hold, a man or a child? Each time, as she tried to reach it, the box faded away.

Once Anna sat up suddenly after a nightmare during which she saw herself back at Cottage Home, a baby in her arms. Unaccountably, Tom was not there. "Where is he?" she had asked, and her mother shook her head. Even more strangely, Mary Morrison had taken the child from her and vanished, and finally Anna seemed to be alone in a vast, billowing plain . . .

"What—what is it?" Her husband had wakened at her sobs. "The baby's going to be dead, I know it!" As Tom pleaded with her she told him, "I'm twenty-seven, and that's old to be having a first child." He insisted she was wrong, cited facts and examples, and put his arm around her: "There's a military rule that I wish you'd learn, my dear. 'Never take counsel of your fears.' It will only hurt you and whatever you want to do."

"Never take counsel . . ." Anna ran over Tom's words, and her disturbance lessened. But before she dozed away she inquired, "Suppose we were separated . . . I mean, if one of us went much before the other?" He had turned on the light, and in its reflection she read his look of hurt. "*Esposita,* don't say anything like that." After a silence he spoke again: "To have you leave me . . . I couldn't think of a worse calamity." Tom's voice had both tenderness and fervor. "Whatever trials God has for me, I hope I'm spared that."

Anna squeezed his fingers; his words had stirred her strongly.

He turned off the light, and a little later she asked herself if he died before she did, and if she had to face many years without him . . . Determinedly she closed her eyes.

In the morning Major Preston arrived with a broad grin and a well-wrapped object. "We have several to spare, and Maggie and I want you to have it for this baby and the ones that will follow." Ripping off the coverings, the Major displayed a richly carved cradle, ample enough for twins or even triplets. Before Anna could thank him properly, he had left. Soon afterward, the bell rang once more. Hetty jumped up: "This is visitin' day." She brought back a totally unexpected caller, Maggie's father, Dr. George Junkin.

"I trust you are well today, Mrs. Jackson, and the Major too." The president of Washington College spoke formally and with marked restraint. Anna had had few close meetings with the austere, usually preoccupied man, and she found herself ill at ease. For a few minutes Dr. Junkin talked on in clipped sentences, and Anna noted that his voice had lost little of its Pennsylvania edge. How truly chill he appeared, and how poorly this interview was going.

Then, reaching for a handkerchief, Anna turned suddenly, and in Dr. Junkin's eyes she saw an earnest wish to be liked, and also an edginess that matched hers. The man was trying to find a meeting place between them, and she was offering him no help at all. Touched by her discovery, she spoke quickly of Maggie and the other Junkins in Virginia and Pennsylvania.

Her words encouraged Dr. Junkin, and he went on more easily, with growing feeling: "It's hard to be separated from your young ones, or some of them," he said. "My roots are here now, and yet part of my heart seems to be far away, and beating somewhere else." Anna recalled Maggie's story of the day she was confronted with a mass of Southern Prestons, and it occurred to her that Dr. Junkin must consider such people even more alien.

Almost as if he guessed her thoughts, Dr. Junkin resumed: "Mrs. Jackson, my family and I are happy in Lexington, happier than we've ever been in our lives. We have peace here, and neighbors who are sympathetic and friendly." Anna was faintly perplexed; why did the earnest man stress so much the way he got along in the town? In any event, the president left her with smiling good will, and she felt more kindly toward him than she had since her arrival.

On Tom's return she pressed him for answers to the many questions about the older man that Dr. Junkin's visit had brought to her mind. At first he hesitated, and then he answered thoughtfully, "I've always gotten on with him, but many people don't. They say he's too dogmatic and won't make allowances for other people's failings. In the last two colleges he ran, he had fights with the townsfolk and the graduates—matters of discipline, church affairs, and also something else.

"Even though he's from the North, Anna, Dr. Junkin's always been pretty sympathetic to this section. He believes in gradual emancipation, not abolition. He's taken a middle position, and some people have raged against him for that." Tom shrugged. "But I'd say he's more at ease here than he's ever been before." Alone, Anna mulled over what Tom had said; she was glad that Maggie's father had found serenity at last. Both the Prestons and the Junkins had come to mean a great deal to her.

With her confinement ever closer, Anna's thoughts centered more and more on the baby. "More milk, please," she told Hetty. "And no pie, not even a little piece." In a New York paper which she had received she discovered several articles about children. She read them carefully and quizzed the doctor until he guffawed, "Ma'am, no mother has to be told how to hold a baby. The first time you pick it up, you'll know."

More earnestly than ever, Anna wanted this child as a symbol of their union. When she looked into the mirror, she knew she had a new beauty; in her eyes was a clear strength, and she saw in her white skin a color that had never shown itself before. Most of all, she read in her expression a deepened knowledge, a wider comprehension. Was it a realization that she had a share in life's processes, in its fullest development? For the time her fears had retreated, and she could not have concealed her happiness had she tried.

Then, three weeks before the baby was due, a sudden, staggering pain stabbed her. The clock rang midnight, and as the throbbing within Anna became worse, Tom dispatched Hetty down the street. Her husband stood by her bed and Anna stared into his haggard face. For his sake, she wished she could control the expression of her pain. Try as she would, however, she could not; she gave a harsh groan, and he winced as if he had been struck.

At last the doctor arrived. He ordered Tom out, and Hetty took

a place beside the bed. Anna's fingers tightened over Hetty's
wrists, and the dark woman whispered soothingly. Was the doctor
disturbed, or did Anna imagine it? She remembered stories of
premature babies who were defective, crippled. After a moment
she was seized by a succession of wrenching agonies. Though the
window had been lifted to admit the cool spring air, she was
drenched in sweat; it ran into her eyes and down her breasts.
For a few minutes the pain lessened, and she breathed slowly with
closed eyes. Then she rose to her elbow and tried to fight a new
twisting inside her.

"Doctor, how much longer? Can't you tell me, please?" For
months she would see in her sleep the monotonous shaking of his
head, the doleful look as he sat beside her. She prayed, asking
deliverance from this travail. God's will be done, but need she
go through all this? At one point she opened her eyes to discover
a new face, that of Mrs. Page.

"There, Anna, try not to struggle." The two women, Negro and
white, were twin comforts. In her groaning, she must have voiced
some of her fears, for Mrs. Page murmured to her, "It does no
good to hurt yourself with such thoughts, child . . ." A fresh agony, worse than ever, tore at her, and then she had a sense of
swift depletion, as if she were sinking into a dark, subterranean
land. From a point that appeared far off she heard a thin screech
like that of a small animal. After a flurry of movement, a clatter
of basins, her senses revived, and a smell of blood and sweat rose
about her. From above there peered down the lined countenance
of Mrs. Page, and she saw hands holding a brown-red form that
moved faintly within its wrappings.

"Is he"—Anna's voice sank—"all right?"

"Yes, child. It's not a boy, though."

"Oh." She had not thought of that possibility. Numbly Anna let
her head drop, and she could not have said how she felt. After
that a haze swam around her until Tom's face materialized, and
he rubbed his cheek against hers and smiled and smiled. Though
he said something she could not understand, she did not need his
words to tell her of his happiness.

For several hours she slept, and when she awoke she found her
husband there again. Tom whispered almost shyly, "See, she's
been waiting for you to open your eyes," and held the baby out
to her. "Keep her here for a while," Anna murmured, "and let

me just look." She did, until Hetty with a determined gesture removed the child to the cradle the Prestons had given them.

One worry persisted in Anna's mind. The baby was so very small, its frame so meager. "Is it because the birth was premature, and will she be sickly and weak?" she eventually asked the doctor. "She *is* tiny, like most of them born that way," he nodded. "But don't concern yourself; we'll just give her extra care." Though Anna's spirit improved, she was not completely reassured.

A few callers arrived to congratulate Tom, among them Major Preston, Dr. Junkin, and Dr. White. When would they leave? After what seemed hours the visitors departed, and Tom bent down in a half-tearful, half-laughing outburst. "Anna, Anna dear . . ." He reached for her tenderly. All his Spanish phrases came back, and her eyes filled. "You've made me a happier *hombre* than I've ever been," he told her. After further endearments he gave her a long look. "What name would you want for her?"

"I haven't thought of any."

"I have. Mary Graham, after your mother."

Anna's gratitude welled up as she thanked him. After a time he drew away with a boyish smile that had something of mischief in it. "What are you holding back?" she asked.

"You may not like it, at first anyway," he grinned. "I thought matters over and I've had several talks . . ." Seeing her impatience, he blurted out the rest. "I've arranged to buy the house on Washington Street and take it in six months."

"That big one, with all the rooms and passages?" It was the old structure which had appeared too cavernous for their purposes. "Why, just to heat it, and the servants we'd need to keep it up!"

"We'll have a lot of hands now," Tom chuckled, and Anna remembered their extra supply of help. Still, could the two boys do very much? But Tom argued away all her misgivings. During the next two weeks, as her strength gradually returned, her last fears about the baby began to slip away. Though she was still very small, the child looked lively and had a lusty voice. The new Mary waked Anna each morning with a soft cry. When the little one seemed to stare from one of her parents to the other, Anna felt a glow of heightened happiness. Had life ever been so full for her? Her good will extended to all of Lexington—even, she assured herself, to Mrs. Petry!

She glanced through the window, and, for the first time in days, she was aware of the world outside. Spring had broken over the

Valley, covering it with a carpet of soft green and trailing lines of blossoms. Returning to the baby, Anna took her up, and a rush of tenderness came over her. This tiny life, which had grown out of their joy together, was her pledge, and Tom's, to the future.

As she studied the round face, with its air of complete trust, Anna promised that she would give Mary a full life, a happy one. The years stretched happily ahead, years in which she would work at her husband's side. Whatever they did or wherever they went, they would have this core of private delight. She herself had not entirely recovered; the premature birth had caused internal complications—"female troubles," as the doctor put it. For the moment, however, that was unimportant.

Tom smiled: "She has your eyes, and your 'French look,' and something, well, elflike about her."

"And that nose, it's as strong as yours," Anna replied, and both laughed. Tom listened to Anna's plans: "She'll have a good education, like the one they gave me at the Moravian school, and trips to Washington City and New York to see what the world's like. I want her to be tall, not tiny like me; she's going to marry early and have a big family." With these blithe observations Anna halted; first let *her* raise her own large family.

After a moment Tom spoke in deep earnest. "More important than any of that, Anna, we'll bring her up with care. Love and affection, yes, but also the best rules for developing proper habits —discipline, rewards for good behavior, and firmness when she's bad." With inward amusement Anna agreed; this was Tom Jackson's way!

When he left she sorted out the small hill of gifts—a doll from Maggie, a stuffed animal from Mrs. Page, boxes of presents from North Carolina sent on with a half-dozen excited notes from Cottage Home, and a special treasure in an ornamented rattle, a Junkin family possession given Mary Graham by the president of Washington College. She glanced up; Tom was here again, much earlier than usual.

"I couldn't help coming back, because I wanted to be with you," he laughed. "When I walked past Washington Street just now, the family invited me in and showed me from room to room." As he explained, his manner became slightly sheepish. "I picked a fine big one and a smaller one behind it, both for nurseries. For Mary and her brothers and sisters."

Anna smiled. She longed, as did Tom, to move into their house immediately. After a time he took up the dark-haired baby, lifting her gently to his face, and Anna watched in quiet joy. She had seldom found Tom so relaxed or looking so well. He glanced toward her and spoke in a low voice: "We're a family now, a real family at last." Then they talked once more of the coming summer, when they would take the child to his sister Laura. In a mood of peaceful happiness they blew out the lights.

Dawn had not yet lightened the sky when Anna's eyes opened. Usually the child wakened shortly before Tom; today she lay silent. Pushing herself up on one elbow, Anna heard a delicate breathing from the cradle, and lay back relieved. A moment later an impulse she could not have named made her tiptoe across the room.

Little Mary was awake, round eyes staring at the ceiling, but oddly listless. The round mouth was wide open, as if the baby had trouble breathing. When Anna touched her, she felt a burning skin. "Tom, Tom, get up!" As she cried to him, a spasm of fear seized her. In a moment he stood beside her, then dressed quickly, throwing a coat over his tieless shirt, and ran out of the house for the doctor.

Roused by their voices, Hetty put her head into the room. "Hetty, she's *so* quiet, and I don't know what to think." Anna's voice broke, and she let the maid hold the child. When the doctor arrived he took Mary aside, and Hetty built up the fire as Anna and Tom waited tensely. When the doctor faced them again he frowned: "I'm not sure yet, but it may be—jaundice."

"Isn't that very serious?" Anna knew little of the disease, but the word had a frightening sound. Still noncommittal, the doctor gave them instructions, ending, "Try not to disturb yourself, Mrs. Jackson; that isn't good for your own condition. We can only wait for time to tell us more, and do all we can."

Anna stared at him, and a bitter retort came to her lips. She should not disturb herself, she should "wait for time to tell . . ." Swinging about, she stopped at the sight of her husband. Tom had gone to the window; hands clenched, eyes closed, he was praying. Ashamed of her own reaction, she walked to the child's cradle and sent up a desperate appeal. Then, against every effort, she began to cry. Tom put his arm around her waist, and they stood there together, looking down at the silent baby.

A day passed, a new week opened, and Anna and Tom alternated at the cradle. Mary showed some signs of improvement; for several hours she would rest easily, and then the fever would rise and she would lie back, voiceless, more subdued than ever. The urine that colored her diapers was a deep yellow that frightened Anna. The child would not nurse at her breast, and rejected water when Anna pressed it to her lips.

Mrs. Page moved in and out, and one morning Major Preston appeared with Dr. Junkin. Soon afterward came Dr. White. As the group took places beside the cradle, Anna's eyes went from one to the other, and all at once she read what was in their minds. No, it couldn't be; Mary had to live! She would prefer to die in the child's place. Harshly she remembered Tom's words of a few evenings ago; they had become a family at last . . . Anna's grief overwhelmed her, and as she started toward her husband she sank to the floor.

Together he and Major Preston helped her to the bed in the next room. Tom sat on the edge, talking softly, trying to soothe her. Later she recalled only parts of his anguished sentences. "God's will be done, Anna . . . If it pleases Him to take her, we can only accept." As he spoke she thought of the new house and the rooms he had selected for this baby and the others to follow, and she turned away.

Lying there, Anna grew slowly aware of a silence from the next room. "Tom!" She got up, and although he tried to stop her she shook him off and ran to the door. At the first sight of the circle about the darkened cradle, she knew that it had happened.

They had no plot of land for the burial, and Tom bought one in the town cemetery, which lay above the valley and was framed by gray mountains. In a blur Anna rode there with him and clung to his arm when the minister spoke. "Suffer the little children to come unto me . . ." As from a great distance other sentences reached her. "This child will not be alone . . . Most of the people who have died on earth and gone to heaven are little children." The minister's words hardly touched her; numbly she listened and let Tom take her back.

On the way their carriage brushed against the bursting green of the spring bushes, the peaches and blue-whites of the dogwood blossoms, the spread of wild growths along the mountainside. Now the sight came to her like a blow. Less than a week ago she had

watched it all in joy as she thought of a widening future for her
and Tom.

In their room Hetty presented a letter. "Miss Maggie say give
it to you when you come in. And here somethin' for you to drink."
Their friend, about to have her own child, had not been able to
attend the funeral. Tom opened the note, and Anna took a single
sip of the tea. She could not drink it. She replaced the cup and
took the paper her husband held out. She read:

And so, Anna dear, you are represented in Heaven! . . . Go
when *you* may, a little angel-child will be there to welcome the
mother she never learned to know on Earth. Is not there something like sweet comfort in this? . . . It was hard to give up your
baby. I know you had it almost a month, and every day would
necessarily endear it to you, but you are willing (and I am perfectly sure my dear Brother is fully so) to put the darling into the
Savior's arms. *He will take care of it for you.*

Their child waited for them in that gentler place . . . "He will
take care of it for you." The poet's words were like a quiet hand
upon hers, and Anna's head went up slowly. After a moment her
gaze shifted to the next room and a small mound of toys that
Hetty had gathered in the corner. At the top sat the doll that was
Maggie's present and the ornamented rattle, the gift of Dr. Junkin
. . . She looked away.

CHAPTER 8

The months that followed were in some ways the bleakest of
Anna's life. Tom's quiet words, his example, the appeals of those
around her—all of them helped, but not for very long. She would
nod; she found a certain consolation in the warm sympathy she
received, yet soon she would find herself staring at her hands
and thinking of her dead baby.

"God has taken her, but He has taken her in love . . ." As
Anna repeated the comforting sentence, she would remind herself that the child was happy, that she had gone to a better place
than any of them knew. Then, however, Anna's mind would turn
to the future, to Tom's plans and hers, and she would recall her
pledge to give the little girl the best kind of life. She had had no
chance to keep that promise . . . It was especially hurtful to remember Tom's program for Mary's training: love and affection,

firmness in developing good habits. She could not continue with
the thought.

Her husband moved about quietly, accepting the situation with
a calm she wished she possessed. Several times Anna reminded
herself that for him the death had been even harsher; he had
already lost his first wife and the earlier child, and before that he
had lost his parents and his brother and sister. But although her
heart went out to him, her burden still oppressed her.

Then one afternoon she received a letter from Eugenia in Charlotte. The younger sister sent her sympathy and love, and, too,
the love of her children—the boy, and the girl named for Anna.
In the note Eugenia talked hopefully of a reunion with Anna before the year ended. This part of the message lifted her spirit.
So she would be seeing her sister again, and before very long.
The news made her days brighten a little.

Within a week a second and hastily scrawled note brought
grim news. A few hours after writing her, Eugenia had caught
typhoid fever, and was the victim of a sudden June epidemic that
had swept the Charlotte area. She had already been buried.
Anna's mouth opened in disbelief . . . She read on: the pestilence
continued, and for her own protection she must not consider a
trip to North Carolina under any circumstances. With a broken
cry, she let the paper fall from her fingers.

In the arms of Hetty, who had been close to Eugenia for more
than twenty years, Anna wept hoarsely, and she asked herself
why her sister, with two small children, should have been taken
while she, Anna, was spared. The maid sobbed with her, "It a
curse, a curse on us. Somethin' we done, somethin' we bein' punish'
for!"

At these words, Anna drew back: "Please, Hetty, don't say that.
If you do, I'll believe it. We're being tried, that's all." And as she
prayed she sought to make herself accept. When Tom arrived
and read the note, he laid it on the mantel with an unsteady hand.
For an hour he remained beside her, reasoning, consoling; and
memories rushed back to Anna. She had been with Eugenia, of
course, when she met Tom Jackson. And now the youngest of
the three had gone first.

After a time Tom took her into the next room. "Little one, we
should think about leaving here for the summer. The doctor says
both of us need a rest, and badly, and he believes my health
might benefit from a visit to a specialist in the East." As Anna

inspected her husband's face she realized that it was gaunt and
pasty. He had grown haggard in the tensions of these weeks, and
his throat and ears obviously bothered him again.

Nevertheless, she was so distraught and abstracted that she
could find no words with which to answer. "You'll keep it in
mind?" he asked. She nodded, but the last thing she wanted was
a trip or a jaunt. Hastily Tom assured her, "It will be quiet, I
promise, as quiet as anybody could wish." He said nothing about
the matter for another week, and then he introduced a subject
to which she gave swift attention.

"*Esposita,* I've talked to the doctor about—about our prospects
for a family." Ever since the recent dark days Anna had been
wondering, and now she listened intently. "He says there's no
reason we shouldn't have other children, and good healthy ones."
The last few words made her wince, but the news was welcome.
"Thank you, Tom. It's fine to know that."

At once her conscience prodded her; how could she refuse him
the summer vacation he needed so badly? She asked him when
they could leave, and gratefully he went on to arrange with Mrs.
Page for the supervision of Hetty and the two boys. Anna paid a
final call on her doctor, who examined her and shook a finger:
"Just relax while you're gone. Lead a simple, easy life and let
nothing upset you, nothing whatever."

As she told the doctor good-by, she asked herself if matters
could be worked out as easily as that. Nevertheless the two months
that followed were far better than Anna had expected. She and
Tom went North by gradual stages, beginning with Fortress Monroe on the Virginia coast, a point of special interest to Tom. "As a
military man, I owe it to myself to see the place," he explained
briskly. They were there for three days, and Anna spent hours
under a parasol, luxuriating in the sun, drinking in the fresh
scenes, gazing out over the green water.

Nearby Tom talked with fellow officers, walked with binoculars
along the parapets, and made pages of sketches. Returning to her,
he spoke with enthusiasm: "Seven bastions for cross and flank fire,
and beautifully constructed—by one of Napoleon's aides." If there
was a Napoleonic connection in anything, Tom quickly found it.
"And Colonel Robert Lee was stationed here for a while." Several
times of late, Anna reflected, Tom had referred to the fellow
Virginian who had recommended him for the University of
Virginia post, an act of approval for which her husband was

clearly grateful. A moment later he entered upon a long explanation of the way the fort commanded the locale.

Anna smiled as she faced him: "When you turn to anything that's military, you practically glow. Tom, the way your eyes light up . . . You're almost a new man." Then, spontaneously, she asked, "Would you want to go back into the service?"

He pondered the subject for nearly a minute and then he shrugged: "Anna, you have no idea of the nomad's life an officer leads, shunted from post to post, sent away on short notice, ordered from one end of the country to the other, Florida or Texas, Illinois or the Canadian border or even out to California." His emotion darkened his blue-gray eyes: "For a man with a wife and family, it's very bad. I've lived it and I know. And the daily routine, the monotonous life, the poor chances for advancement——"

"Yes, Tom, but . . ." She could not say that, in spite of all this, the army might still be best for a man with capacities in one field and—she hesitated—lesser ones in another. At that moment a child's ball sailed past their heads, and two boys darted toward them. Laughing, Tom tossed the ball back, and simultaneously a nurse with a baby in her arms rounded a bend in the walk.

"Oh, those children are into everything." As the woman apologized for her charges, Anna reached out to the baby. He smiled tentatively, and when her finger came within reach, grasped it. He had a round face, an almost elfin manner; he looked much like their Mary. The same dark hair, the same buttonlike eyes . . .

"How old is he?" Tom asked.

"Two months," the nurse replied, and hurried off after the boys.

Anna fought to keep from crying as she stood there in the sunlight. If Mary had lived, that would have been her age. All at once the day had lost its meaning, and Anna took Tom's arm to return to their boarding place. That night in the dark of their room he comforted her.

From the Fortress they boarded a steamer for Cape May. Slowly Anna's mood improved. She stood at the rail swallowing the bracing air, and sat with Tom for hours on the deck. From the Cape they traveled, again by boat, to New York. On this leg of the journey he drew out the first of a set of books he had brought with him. "Dear, this summer will be for Shakespeare."

Anna laughed to herself; even the Bard had his allotted place in the Jackson time schedule. In any case the prospect was pleasant, and she read to him to save his eyes. After some discussion they decided to start with *Macbeth*, and, though the witches' scene left Tom dubious, he became alert with the first mention of Scottish military affairs. "I can well understand that campaign," he said once. Again he murmured, with his old gesture of agreement, "Fine, very fine." And he lifted himself in his chair: "Mark that, please." Soon afterward: "I want to go back to her speech; will you be sure to put a note there?"

They were still concentrating on Shakespeare when New York Harbor came into view one foggy morning. It reminded Tom of the day he first beheld England from the sea, and now he talked of the high bridges and the grim Tower of London from the Thames. As he went on steadily, excitedly, Anna observed, "You're enjoying this, aren't you?"

"Yes," he answered. "Aren't you?" She nodded, and they settled back in contentment. After the bustle and confusion at the New York docks they rode to a small boarding place near Twentieth Street, and that same afternoon Tom launched a program of trips that would keep him occupied during most of his waking hours. Anna was to rest at least half the day. In the mornings he went forth on what he termed "exploring expeditions," walking from one section of the city to another. He would join her for midday dinner, and then take her to the places he thought would interest her most.

"Don't you like this?" he would ask. "Isn't that as fine as they've said?" Nearly always, Anna decided, he was right. A point along the Hudson made him relive his ride down the Rhine, an ancient building near the Battery recalled a smoky façade in Amsterdam . . . Suddenly he caught her hand: "Anna, next year let's try to make the trip to Europe we've talked about." His face lighted with his enthusiasm. "With you, I'll enjoy it even more than I did the first time."

Her heart quickening, Anna agreed. At last she would see the spots she had thought about so often, and her mind jumped to the English moors, to the south of France . . . Meanwhile Tom had gone to see the doctor, who was also a professor in one of the medical colleges. After several visits he returned to her one day with an uncertain stare, and his manner made her go to him at once.

"I—I don't know what to think about this, Anna. He didn't say anything at first, but now he's concerned about my hearing. And he believes one of my tonsils is inflamed and the trouble may extend toward the lungs."

Anna tried to hide her disturbance: "Anyway, it's a good thing we've found somebody who understands about such things," she told him, "and everyone says he's a very fine doctor, don't they?" To herself she speculated that her husband might be in serious difficulty. He had helped her through her troubles, and now it was her turn to buoy up his spirit. Her head lifted, and she went to work with a new purpose, which occupied her from then on.

She joked, hunted for unusual stories in the New York journals, and insisted that they go to several band concerts in the park. After a time it seemed to her that Tom's mood was easier; she nevertheless kept up her efforts with a steady zeal. He returned from his visits to the doctor in varying tempers. "It's certainly a new treatment for me," he would say. "I'm feeling somewhat better, but . . ."

Though she tired more quickly than she would have liked, Anna made Tom take her on his morning as well as his afternoon jaunts. They rode the horse cars for long distances, strolled for an hour or so at a time, or hired a carriage for rides through the park. Tom developed a fondness for the Düsseldorf Art Gallery, and they wandered through its halls for several days. "Here's one like a scene at the Prado in Madrid . . ." "Anna, only in the British Museum did I see such a big one . . ." Tom did not know a great deal about art, yet it was clear to Anna that he had a natural appreciation; she listened with respect to what he had to say, and generally she agreed with his judgments.

From Lexington they received a brief, excited message. Maggie and Major Preston's first child had been born—a son, and a plump one. Anna took up her pen to send congratulations: it was so good to realize that their two close friends . . . Her hand faltered, and she stared at the half-blank sheet. Maggie had her own baby, in addition to the other children in that crowded household, while she and Tom . . . Somehow Anna made herself finish her note, but the bitter reflection continued.

"Anna." Tom stood in the doorway, and again she quickly sensed his disturbance. "He's going to perform a small operation on me tomorrow, in his office," he began, "and pare off part of my tonsil to check the pulmonary trouble." At once she arose and went to him. That was frightening. For her, as for most people, the word "operation" had an alarming ring. She wanted to be with her husband the next day, and she asked, "When do we go?"

Tom shook his head: "The doctor wouldn't want you there. Darling, this won't take long, and I'll come directly back." From his tone Anna knew there was no possibility of a change in his decision, and she submitted, then worked to brighten their evening. They retired early, and she spent a sleepless night. When he left the next morning she remained in their room trying to push away her growing alarm. Why was it taking so long? And if anything—anything serious happened, did the doctor know that he should call her?

At the window, Anna watched every carriage that passed below. Finally one halted, and Tom stepped out, pale and unsteady on his feet. Running to the door, she met him in the downstairs hall and tenderly led him upstairs. "I'm all right," he insisted, but she hurried him into bed and assembled the medicines around him. For several days he lay back, propped up with pillows, or sat in the easy chair, swallowing gingerly, rubbing at his ear and throat.

Gradually his condition improved. He smiled at her stories, he moved casually about the room, and, over her protests, he went for a short walk with her at his side. His hearing seemed better, though he had not entirely recovered. "Still, it's something to be grateful for," he said with a smile. At this she wondered, even if Tom eventually wished to go back to the army, would there be a place for an officer who could not hear perfectly?

As they were talking together the landlady knocked, bringing them a note addressed in a handwriting Anna recognized. Reading it, Tom frowned: "Poor Laura. She's a bit upset, this time about her son Thomas, the one she named for me. He's a bright boy, I think, but the settlement at Beverly is so small and so isolated that his chance for an education is mighty poor." While he spoke, Anna thought of Laura's note to her, after the baby's death. It had been touching, and had given her encouragement and solace. And this summer, in spite of all their intentions, they had still not been able to join the Arnolds.

After a moment's hesitation Tom faced her: "Anna, if the boy can't get away from Beverly for at least a short time, there's no chance that he'll ever move in the sphere I'd like him to know. I've been asking myself . . ." As he searched for words to continue, Anna bent forward:

"I'd be happy to have him with us in the new place, Tom. Why didn't you bring this up before?" A boy around the house would be good for them. Taking her hand, her husband thanked her, and within the hour she sent a warm invitation to his nephew, adding to it the hope that Laura and her husband would come to visit the Jacksons whenever they found it possible.

That night, as she combed her dark hair before the mirror, Anna decided that the trip had been of benefit to both of them. Tom had a rested air and a calm composure, and her own cheeks showed a slight flush. Her brown eyes gleamed back at her from the glass; she would be able to face the year ahead with something of her old serenity.

They gave their final days in New York to the selection of furniture for the new house. At the first place they visited the prices made Tom frown, but after considerable thought they bought a few special pieces there: a graceful dining table, a sofa, and two big chairs. After that they called at a less expensive establishment, whose offerings had good, simple lines that Anna approved, and there they filled out their list: carpets, rosewood bureaus, a bathing tub, a rosewood bedstead, rocking chairs, a marble-top side table, a parlor carpet . . .

When they counted the money left in Tom's pocket, Anna faced him: "We've been without a piano for a long time. Could we possibly afford one?" Whether she knew it or not, her eyes held a warm appeal. "You want it badly, don't you?" he smiled. "Well, I want it if it isn't too much to hope for," she answered. Her mind went back to the many evenings at Cottage Home, when the Morrison family had gathered around the piano . . . With a quiet nod he led her to a music house, and there, after considerable inspection, they settled on a moderate-priced instrument. Now they could go back to Virginia! For a time, of course, they would not play it, but later . . .

The sight of their boarding house, reviving so many memories, made Anna's hurt return for a time. Then, however, she busied herself with her tasks, and the dark memories slipped away. She was quickly welcomed by the Prestons, Mrs. Page, Dr. Junkin, and others. Maggie cried out a fervent greeting and held up her baby, a pudgy infant with a direct look which, Anna thought, held a hint of his father's command. Taking the boy in her arms, Anna felt a brief twinge, but the excitement gave her little opportunity for sad reflections.

Maggie and Anna talked of the future and in particular of the new residence. "We're giving you a big sofa that was redone a year ago," Maggie announced. She was making many changes in the Preston household, removing dozens of heavy items, old pictures, and ornaments. "They've always had twice too many things over here," the poet smiled, and to Anna's surprise, Major Preston nodded agreement. Mrs. Page would contribute an arm chair, Dr. White a collection of books, and President Junkin presented them with a small desk from Philadelphia, once used by his father. "Now all you have to do is fill two stories and a half with other things," Major Preston boomed, and Anna's mind returned to that problem.

During the weeks of school opening, first drills, and faculty affairs, Anna made several visits to the house on Washington Street to measure windows and floors. When they first approached it together, she and Tom halted and he murmured, "Our house, our *home*." She reminded herself again that this would be the first he had ever owned. As they stood in the narrow street in the winter dusk, they studied the tall structure, with its high, narrow roof, its rows of windows at each of the two upper levels, and the graceful latticed stoop that extended over the sidewalk. The sight stirred Anna more than she had expected. How comfortable it looked, and how ready to welcome them.

Tom had brought with him a list of necessary changes, and as they went through the house he added to it: "These hinges have to be replaced, and I'm going to put in a new door downstairs. And wouldn't you want more pantries? . . ." The list grew longer and longer, and Anna smiled, "You won't get half those things done." Later, however, she learned that he had accomplished every one, and more.

When they returned to the boarding house that evening, they were greeted by an excited Hetty. "Young Master Tom, he got in and I don' know what to do, so I feed 'im." Her heart stirring, Anna hurried in. As she entered, a freckled youth with a shock of light hair dropped his fork and rose with an anxious look. About twelve, Tom's nephew was obviously a country boy; Anna found a resemblance to her husband in his nose and the set of his eyes. Though the new arrival might have a lot to learn, he made a good first impression.

"Uncle, I'm real glad to see you, and—and Aunt Anna, too." As Tom shook the boy's hand, his namesake became red with embarrassment, and Anna tried to restore his ease. Joining him at the supper table, they talked family affairs. "Oh, Ma's fine enough, though she still has the frets about a lot of things." "Yes, Pa's well, and busy as all get-out this time of year." A little later she saw young Tom stare on hearing a remark of his uncle's: "I start school-work *tonight?*"

"You do," Tom repeated forcefully. "I've arranged for you to study English and Latin under Mr. McFarland, but I'm going to coach you myself in Spanish and other things, and your Aunt Anna may be willing to help you in catechism and Sunday school. And everything has to be done thoroughly, son. Don't go past anything till you understand it. You see?" With a look that approached awe, Tom's nephew inclined his head.

Tonight Anna listened while Tom, tapping a pencil, addressed his nephew. "Spelling and reading—they're the most important of all; if you're defective there, you'll be in trouble in every other subject. Now, how do you spell 'character'?" On and on went the questions, the observations on methods of learning, and Anna began to wonder whether it was wise to start so strenuously. Suppose the youth lacked Tom's dogged will . . . Shifting her glance to him, she discovered that he had a dazed, almost glazed expression. "I'm afraid he's worn out," she told her husband. Young Tom shot her a warm look, Tom agreed reluctantly, and three very tired people went to bed that evening.

In the following weeks the youth got up as early as his uncle, applied himself steadily to his private classes, accompanied Tom on walks, and watched drills and other events. Young Tom was hard-working and likable; by degrees he opened his heart to Anna, and she enjoyed being with him. Yet he still seemed uncertain of himself, and Anna sensed that he was a bit in awe of the endlessly systematic Major Jackson.

One day she saw the boy gape as Tom snapped out a succession of orders and, before his nephew could get out a word, left the room. Young Tom's dismay was evident, and now Anna acted. "Let me sit with you a few minutes," she suggested, and his gratitude was profound. "I think he meant . . ." After a few minutes the youth had solved his first difficulty. "I can handle the others," he informed her, "and I sure do thank you for what you've done."

Happily Anna nodded: "I'll be right over here if anything else isn't clear." Young Tom was proud, however, and he declined to ask for further aid that day. But thereafter he approached her from time to time, and she was glad that she could do something to make the boy's tasks less overpowering.

A little later Anna watched young Tom gaze dully at a long page of notes; for the past day or so she had seen him struggle under the increasing load of work. When Tom returned, she drew him into the hall. "The boy needs a few hours off, to walk around the town and rest." Her husband gave her an astonished stare: "If he does that, he'll fall behind schedule."

"Tom, let him fall behind, for today anyway." She pressed his arm. "He needs some relaxation, and you haven't realized it. I'm with him more than you are, and I know what's happening."

Once more Tom gave her an uncomprehending look: "Being here is a fine opportunity for him, and I'm sure he understands it. Every hour he loses means that much less time to advance himself."

"That's true, and still . . ." She argued and appealed, and at last she won. Young Tom was delighted when they told him he could spend the rest of the afternoon as he liked. "Just enjoy myself?" he gaped. A moment later he had darted into the hall and down the street. Returning with a happy, relaxed air, he resumed work with spirit, and Anna exchanged a knowing glance with her husband.

Through Christmas and the holidays the three of them gave their time to readying the new house for occupancy, and soon after the New Year they watched their helpers put the newly arrived furniture in place. The piano Anna and Tom had purchased in New York had a position of honor, and, as she looked at it shining in the parlor, Anna felt a swift satisfaction. Did it mean more to her than anything else in the house? She had to admit that it did, and that it made the place seem like home to her.

But she had a harsh moment when she opened a door to the chamber that Tom had originally chosen for the nursery. There he had placed the Prestons' cradle, and Mary's toys were piled in it. She turned her back and walked nervously to another part of the house. When would the room be used? There were still no signs of a second child. The disturbing thought stayed with her until she drifted off to sleep that evening.

In the morning, just as she awoke in the strange, curtainless room, Tom jumped up with a vigorous gesture. The preceding

evening he had given minute directions to Hetty, who was installed in an upper room near Cy and George, and even now Anna
could make out vague noises in the kitchen. Soon she heard the
sound of water and quick, thumping movements, and then Tom
left for his early walk.

Arriving with a pitcher of hot water, Hetty shrilled, "Happy
mornin', Miss Anna." After her bedside prayer Anna sent the maid
back to the kitchen: "Be sure breakfast's ready in time, because
I want to start things properly in this house." Finishing her bath,
she dressed quickly and thrust up her hair with a hasty gesture.
There was no time to braid it, and she rolled the long brown
strands into a loose knot. Even so she was late, reaching the dining
room just as Tom entered. Two or three seconds afterward their
nephew stumbled in.

Anna's first glance told her it had been a mistake not to have
inspected things in advance. Hetty had set out dishes as in-
structed, but that was all the table contained. There was no milk
or bread, nor forks or knives. From the kitchen her ear caught the
breaking of eggs; obviously the maid had fallen well behind
schedule. Slipping to the door, she called to Hetty, who replied,
"Jes' a minute. The eggs cookin' right this minute."

Before Anna could speak again Tom stood behind her: "Hetty,
you and the boys are supposed to be in the dining room now, for
prayers. We always begin the day that way."

"But Major, the eggs git too done ef I leave 'em."

"Nevertheless, prayers come first, right now."

Complaining to herself, Hetty removed the eggs from the top
of the stove and with heavy steps followed Tom to the dining
room. There the Major recited the prayer in a deep voice. Back
in the kitchen, Hetty labored on with a clatter—somewhat louder
than Anna judged necessary—and when the eggs arrived they
were even drier than she had expected. Hetty was older than
either of the Jacksons; she had watched Anna grow up, and she
clearly felt her importance.

From now on, Anna told herself reluctantly, they would have
to use a firmer hand in Hetty's management. Before the day ended
she realized that Tom had the same thought. Returning from several calls, he brought with him Amy, the quiet older woman whom
he had purchased several years earlier. She would live with them
and work for them, although her age would keep her from heavy
duties.

"We'll give Amy the room next to Hetty's," Tom announced, and the friendly, plump servant smiled her agreement. "Now." Going to the door, he summoned Hetty and her sons. "I want everyone to understand," he said, with his eyes on the younger woman, "that Hetty will do the housework, and Amy the cooking and some of the laundry, and all of you take instructions from Mrs. Jackson. Is that clear?"

It was. Hetty inclined her head with what seemed to be a touch of sharpness and turned with an angry rustle of her cotton skirts. She was the last to leave the room; when she walked out she failed to close the door behind her. Standing beside her husband, Anna wondered what he would do. She almost held her breath as Hetty's steps sounded along the hall, down a flight of stairs, and to the kitchen. Only when the maid had reached her destination did Tom go to the door and call to her.

Hetty returned, and Tom spoke crisply to her: "You left the door wide open, and it's part of your duty to shut it every time you leave."

Hetty looked from one to the other, and Anna returned her gaze with a troubled frown. Would there be an outburst, or a sullen stare? "Yes, sir," Hetty addressed Tom, and her face was a study when she drew the door behind her. Tom nodded to Anna: "I think those extra steps may make her remember the next time." Anna found that they did; Hetty had caught the point.

Within a few days Tom summoned his nephew and set to work with evident delight to "patch up this place and make it really ours." He acquired a set of tools—plane, saw, hammer—nails, and a supply of lumber. As Anna, Hetty, and Amy sorted over piles of clothing and lined shelves with paper, Tom tested windows and doors and took out the rotting end of a banister.

Anna heard him speaking while he labored: "Son, hold the bolt tight." "Now hit it hard, as hard as you can!" As usual her husband drew a lesson from each task: "Whenever you see a piece of wood in this condition, get rid of it . . ." His nephew seemed to enjoy this work even more than Tom; clearly he considered it better than classes. A moment later Anna lifted her head as her husband gave another direction: "Make a large shelf for my lemons. Lemons are good for you, boy, good for anybody. Nobody can have too many of them." The youth's wide eyes made Anna chuckle to herself.

Tom went past her with an armful of books, and when he

dumped them on the chair she picked up several for inspection. "You still don't have a single novel," she remarked casually. "Don't you like them at all?"

"I do," he assured her with a serious look, "and that's why I don't read them. I get interested and they take too much of my time. Our time, Anna, that's the most important thing we have."

She touched the books before her. Tom was right, of course; they must not squander time. And yet, wouldn't he some day reach a stage at which he could enjoy some of the lighter things he had the capacity to appreciate? Surely Tom would not always need to struggle so hard.

He had left her, and now his voice came from the hallway, where he stood beside his nephew: "You'll get along much better if you remember—'A place for everything, and everything in its place.'" For her husband, Anna reflected, this was one of the major rules of life. For her, alas, it remained largely a goal. By now she knew she had a great deal to learn about housekeeping. While her mother had tried to train her, this was the first time she had taken over the management of a home. She made mistakes in cleaning methods, mixed supplies, and forgot where she set things down. Several times, defeated, she sank wearily to her chair, wondering where she had put a lost article. "A place for everything," yes; but where *was* the place for this one?

Her husband put a room aside for his study. "You'll want the living room for the young ones, and I'd be in their way and they'd be in mine," he told her with a businesslike air. At the words Anna felt a pang of regret. Thus far Tom had always studied beside her, and though the hours were silent ones, she had looked forward to them. Now he would be alone, and so would she.

On a winter evening two months after their arrival at the new house, Tom walked slowly from room to room and joined her at the parlor entrance. In the steady light from the fire, his sharp features had a new contentment: "Well, ma'am, your house is in order for you."

She smiled at his use of the pronoun "your." It was a recent quirk; when he began it she had been so much amused that he had extended it to other things: "Your salary," "your servants," "your furniture." Glancing around at the spotless woodwork, the painted floors, the draperies hanging neatly in the lamplight, she knew that they had achieved at last the home they wanted. Here they would create their own small world. She still had worries about maintaining the building, and problems arose every day or so. But this was not the time to fret over such things.

Behind her Tom spoke quietly, almost to himself: "Anna, this is a place for happiness." All his deep feeling was in his words as he added, "Every door 'on golden hinges softly turning.'"

Gazing up from the sofa, Anna nodded happily: "Sit down, and let's talk a little longer."

"I can't think of anything I would like better, my dove," he said. For a few seconds he appeared about to agree. Then he frowned: "But it's my regular study hour." As if to prevent himself from changing his mind, he left her. No matter how softly those golden hinges turned, Tom had his duties! Left to herself, Anna took up her sewing with a sigh.

In the morning she learned one of the reasons for his recent spurt of industry. Clearing his throat, he announced in a voice from which he could not keep his excitement: "Anna, we're going to have a farm. Oh, a little one, about twenty acres on a high stretch not far from the Institute."

At her glance of inquiry, he grinned. "Yes, I *can* afford it. Figured everything out in the budget." Relieved, Anna settled back to hear the rest. "I know something about farming, but now we're going to find out how much of a farmer I really am." He called in Tom and their four Negro helpers. "All of us have had some experience in growing crops, and each of us will have something to do on our new farm."

Anna felt a quickening interest. She could read the pleasure in Hetty's face. The maid, she recalled, had always enjoyed the farming operations in North Carolina, and her boys had worked in the vegetable gardens at Cottage Home.

But a few days later, when she first saw Tom's property, Anna's mouth dropped. It was hilly land, and Dr. Morrison would have considered it highly unpromising. As she hinted this, Tom shrugged: "We'll see. As a boy I put in many a day on places far worse than this." Doubtfully she nodded.

For weeks she inspected the boxes of seeds he had bought, and watched him study a yellowed copy of Buist's well-known book on crops. "A fellow officer in the army gave this to me years ago, and I've never lost it," he explained. Now Tom was drawing up careful schedules, so that he had only to glance at his calendar to know how he and his forces would be operating at a given time.

One day he asked, "Wouldn't you like to spend the afternoon out there with us?" Anna did not even bother to reply; she seized her hat and almost ran down the stairs with him. On their way in a borrowed carriage, Tom addressed her with strong emotion. "You don't quite know what this means to me. My early years taught me to love farm life. The smell of fresh-plowed earth, the satisfaction of a fine day of planting, the sight of your first crop . . ." Listening, she told herself that this was another phase of her husband's life of which she had never learned. A second surprise awaited her a few minutes later, as they stopped before a gray wooden workhouse at the edge of the plantings.

She blinked at the long, deep furrows and the stretches of early green between the fences. She saw young fruit trees in a line, one row of vegetables after the other, and several mules. Before her she was amazed to see the lean and thoughtful Albert, the hotel waiter who was buying his freedom from Tom. "Whenever Albert has a free hour he's out here," her husband explained.

For nearly two hours Anna read in the shadow of the work-house, looking up occasionally as the others passed. Toward the end, Tom, breathing heavily, dropped beside her, and she wiped his gleaming face with her handkerchief. He sighed deeply: "Good, hard labor . . . I feel better every time I put in work like this, away from my classes, from my desk, from the town." At once the suggestion occurred to Anna: Might this be an answer for them, a new, happier occupation for Tom, for which he was better fitted than teaching or the army?

She put the question: "Tom, suppose we could make a start in real farming. Would you—mightn't you like that?"

Getting to his feet, Tom stood with arms folded, his face outlined against the sun, with the nearest mountain as a background. His eyes passed over the fields before returning to her, and unconsciously he grimaced: "Anna, we'd have to see. It would depend on so many things. And whatever way we're to follow, it will be shown to us." Quietly Anna nodded; it would be shown . . .

And now they could open their doors to their friends as they had never been able to do before. They saw the Prestons and the Junkins, especially the President, who showed less and less of his old reserve when he called on Anna; the Whites came to visit, as did Mrs. Page and the Pendletons. Regularly they received the graying Episcopal minister, Dr. Pendleton, the man of stalwart figure and crisp military carriage, who arrived with his good-humored wife and, once or twice, young Sandie. The scholarly boy seemed to Anna to become taller and more personable every time they met.

She watched in appreciation as Sandie used part of each visit to take the younger Tom to one side and talk with him. And she told herself now, as she had done before, that these months were doing the freckled youth from Beverly a great deal of good. The more she learned about the likable Tom Arnold, the more curious she became about his mother.

In early spring Anna received a message that one of her cousins who lived not far away, Dr. Samuel B. Morrison, would be passing through Lexington with his young daughter. Promptly Tom suggested an invitation: "They could stay overnight, or as long as they liked." Anna wrote Dr. Morrison, and when he arrived she went to the door to greet him and the tiny girl who was clinging to his coattail.

"She's only four, and still somewhat frightened, I'm afraid," the father explained. "This is the first time she's been separated from her mother. Now say good evening to Cousin Anna, Mary." As the small figure in bright blue bent her knee in a curtsy, Anna's heart went out to her . . . Mary Morrison, the same name as her mother and also that other Mary, their own. But when Anna tried to take the child to her, Mary pulled back; clearly she felt that safety lay with her father.

During supper and the hour that followed, Anna managed to establish guarded relations with the younger guest. It remained for Tom to draw her out. He romped with her, rolled on the floor, and had her smiling at him with excited eyes.

At bedtime Anna turned to Dr. Morrison: "Since she isn't used to being away from her mother, perhaps she'd like to go to bed with me in one of the side rooms." Mary's reaction was immediate. Seizing her father's hand, she let it be known that she had no intention of giving him up. Smiling, Anna took them to the guest chamber opposite her room and Tom's.

An hour later, after Tom had settled in bed beside her, Anna discovered that he was moving restlessly. "What is it?" she asked. "Oh, nothing," he told her at first, only to add: "Well . . . I'm worried about the little one over there." After a moment he jumped up and tiptoed across the hall. When he came back he settled down again with a sigh of contentment. "I went in to make sure things were all right, and I accidentally woke up the doctor," he whispered. "But I'm not sorry. Mary had kicked off the covers in her sleep, and I put them back."

In the silence that followed Anna wondered if her husband understood the pang she felt at the picture of the girl so serenely asleep a few yards from them. Had matters worked out differently, tonight their Mary might be under the same roof . . . As she tried to erase the thought from her mind, Tom's hand reached out to hers, and she clung to it in the dark.

One evening not long afterward, as his study hour approached, Tom went to Anna: "I don't know why I have to go all the way to the other room when I can do the work with you here." She gave him a glance of appreciation, and then suddenly she recalled what he had said when they moved here: he was going to use the other chamber so that she could have this one for the children . . .

From then on, the living room became more and more Tom's study quarters, until one night, without further word, he brought in his upright desk. As he did, Anna bent her head to her sewing. She welcomed him here with her, of course; as always, his presence made her evening far happier. But did this mean he accepted the prospect that there would not be another child? *She* did not, and she would not!

PART III

Shadowings

. . . the storm was gathering.

—*Mary Anna Morrison Jackson*

CHAPTER 9

"Anna, what is it that's disturbing you?"

Maggie Preston gave her friend an apprehensive glance as Anna paced back and forth in her sitting room a month later. "I've never seen you so—so tense and agitated." At these words Anna started nervously and stared from the window into the street below.

"I don't know, Maggie, or at least I'm not sure. I've been asking myself the same thing for weeks." Anna's voice was low and hoarse. "I suppose I've never been quite so tired in my life. Part of it may be my physical condition, ever since the baby's birth. You know I've been seeing the doctor again . . . But Tom thinks it's also that I've been working too hard on the house."

As she spoke Anna faced Maggie with a look of apology: "Oh, it's a fine place, and it means so much to Tom and me. Still," she sighed, "I'd never realized how much there was to a place like this; upstairs, downstairs, back, and front—the last week we had trouble with the roof, too." She jumped as a crash sounded from the rear. "That's the second pile of dishes to fall today. I guess it's those boys, skylarking around the kitchen."

With a groan she started toward the hall, then returned. "It doesn't matter now." Although young Cy and George could lift and pull heavy objects, they had proved of little help in other directions. The good-humored Amy worked when she could, but her age set a limit to her capacity. "Hetty and I are the ones who take most of the burdens——" Anna stopped with a feeling of self-reproach. "This is foolish, isn't it? So many people have far worse things to contend with."

Maggie Preston had listened in silence for several minutes, and now, gently, she drew Anna to the sofa beside her. "Anna, I'm older than you are and I can talk frankly. I've wanted to say some of this for a long time. My dear, you have a fine marriage, and you're good for Tom, very good for him." Anna listened with growing interest. Maggie's comments meant a great deal; she stood, after all, in a special relation to the Jacksons.

"But you're making yourself sick, because you're struggling for perfection, and in this world that's hardly possible." As the conversation took this turn Anna stiffened with momentary resentment, and Maggie, realizing her reaction, continued almost fervently: "I know what I'm talking about, because I'm pretty much the same as you. Today John lost his temper and told me to stop throwing myself into needless things, things that somebody else could do. He called it 'yearning for the impossible.'"

Maggie went on, her words tumbling over one another, and Anna was stirred and touched. Then all at once the tension left Maggie's face and she smiled: "Anna, try to rest for several hours a day. If everything isn't scrubbed and rubbed, well, it isn't." With a kindly pat, the older woman left, and Anna lay back on the sofa.

She was grateful for Maggie's interest, her sensible advice. But there was something else in Anna's mind, something that she had thus far admitted to nobody. She had been thinking more and more about the dead child. Within a few weeks a year would have passed since they had lost Mary, and the anniversary date loomed ahead like a black signpost . . . She reproached herself. To let her grief hang over her so long was unwise, harmful to Tom and to herself, yet she could not help it.

Anna's mind returned to Maggie's statement about herself. "A yearning for the impossible," her friend had said. Was her wish for another child an impossible one? Surely God could not mean to deny them the baby they wanted badly, so badly . . .

For days Tom had been noticing her edginess, her worn look, and that night he talked quietly with her: "Why don't you go to bed early? You'll feel better if you do." Reluctantly Anna agreed. The rest helped her; she began the next day more calmly. After a few hours, however, she became very tired again, and her nerves seemed to quiver. When Cy and George, playing on the street in front of the house, started to yell out at one another, she jumped up, then sank to the sofa, hands clenched and mouth working.

She was still there when a familiar step sounded from the hallway. Back from a military drill, Tom strode up the stairs in full regimentals. She gazed in admiration at his crisply pressed uniform, shining buttons, and newly polished sword. "You look right imposing today, sir," she smiled at him.

In a second his playfulness asserted itself. Hand on the hilt of

his sword, he struck a pose and drew out the blade. "My dove,
aren't you afraid of this old warrior?" When Anna shook her head,
he brandished the sword over her, and as the blade swung daz-
zlingly on all sides she suddenly quailed.

At the first sign of her fright Tom threw the sword to the floor
and seized her in his arms. They clung together, laughing and
sighing, and he kissed her cheeks and neck. She sank back and
then, without warning, began to gasp for breath. As her hand went
to her throat, Tom stared in alarm: "Anna, you're really ill. You're
so weak . . ."

"No, I'll be myself in a minute."

Soon afterward Tom brought the doctor to the house. That
gentleman examined her and shook his head: "Perhaps a few
weeks' trip, a change of scene, would be best. At the same time
I'd suggest a consultation with city doctors . . ." Even before he
finished Tom began to plan: "Anna, I'll take you to the man who
helped me in New York. Yes, it *is* the middle of the term, but
I can get a little time off and settle you up there for treatment,
no matter what it means or how long it takes. As soon as you're
better I'll bring you back."

His words disturbed her. They had never been separated before, and she would be alone in the strange city, so loud and so
careless. And how could they afford the extra costs, added unexpectedly to their budget? When she raised the question Tom
shook his head: "I've always kept something in reserve for
emergencies, and, *esposita*, this is a real emergency for both of
us."

Hastily Anna made other objections: "But—but who'll take over
my Sunday school classes? And Hetty can't handle everything at
the house." He rejected each excuse she offered, and her weakness
kept her from making further resistance.

On a gray morning they started on the trip, first by stage, then
by railroad. As Tom helped her into the coach, a determined
figure bustled up, that of Mrs. Petry. Sighing, Anna told herself
that the lady must indeed have risen early for this occasion. "Ah,
Mrs. Jackson," she breathed at them, "I'd *heard* you might be
leaving. Will you be gone long?"

Anna struggled with the impulse to lash back, but Tom intervened: "Just a little while, we hope. And thank you for being
so neighborly." Beside him Anna groaned: "I wish good news

traveled half so fast." During the long, cindery trip she rested against Tom's shoulder, and eventually took a chair beside him in the New York doctor's office and listened intently. "We'll have to keep you under observation for several weeks, and try one treatment after another," the specialist said. "We can't promise anything, madame, and a great deal will depend on you."

These remarks gave Anna little definite promise, and her heart dropped lower as they returned to her lodgings at the boarding house where they had stayed during their previous trip. Tom had to leave the same day, although he offered to change his plans. "If you think it's important, Anna, I might remain a day longer." To this she shook her head. "No, your work is in Lexington, and I have to—to start mine up here." Forcing a smile, she repeated the doctor's phrases.

Fighting back the impulse to cry out to him to return, Anna waved good-by to her husband from the window of her second-story room. The next few days were bleak, and she missed Tom even more than she had expected. She lay for hours in her room, sipping milk drinks prepared by Mrs. McGivney, the landlady, and swallowing harsh brews prescribed by the doctor. Hearing that she would be in New York for treatment, her Uncle Graham had sent notes of introduction to several influential connections, but Anna decided not to use any of them.

She went to the doctor nearly every day, and his words were somewhat encouraging: "You're responding a bit, physically at least, Mrs. Jackson. But you'll have to fight this thing harder, and not give up, no matter how dispirited you are." She listened, nodding. New York irritated her as it had never done before. The drone of traffic, the clattering horses and the shouts that filled the air from dawn until late evening, the smell of dust that lay over everything . . . She longed for the clear mountain air, the fresh look of Lexington, the sight of the Prestons, the Whites, the Junkins, and their new friends, the Pendletons.

And several nights she half-waked and reached out to find only a chill sheet beside her . . . Meanwhile Tom wrote every day, making sure he sent his letters so they would not have to travel on a Sunday. He had penned his first note as soon as he arrived in Lexington. After that he wrote repeatedly. She kept the messages near her for rereading.

Hetty and Amy came to the door when I rang, but would not

open until I gave my name. They made much ado about my not bringing you home. Your husband has a sad heart. Our house looks so deserted without my *esposa*. Home is not home without my little dove. I love to talk to you, little one, as though you were here, and tell you how much I love you. . . . You must be cheerful and happy, remembering that you are somebody's sunshine.

All your fruit trees are yielding fruit this year. When George brought home your cow this morning, she was accompanied by one fine little representative of his sire, and it would do your heart good to see your big cow and your little calf. . . . Take care of my little dove, and remember that the day of miracles is past, and that God works by means, and He punishes us for violating His physical as well as His moral laws. . . . You are very precious to one somebody's heart, if you are away off in New York. . . . You have the greatest show of flowers I have ever seen this year. Enclosed are a few specimens.

As Anna sat with the crushed flowers in her hand, a great longing welled up in her. He had sat talking "as though you were there." She found herself remembering little things about him: the way his hair stood up at the back when he combed it hastily, his slow step when he was disturbed, his air of forebearance when he had to spend time with people he did not like. Her wish to be at her husband's side reached the intensity of a physical hurt, and she promised herself that they would never again be apart in this way.

Meanwhile he continued to write her affectionately:

You must not be discouraged. . . . We are sometimes suffered to be in a state of perplexity, that our faith may be tried and grow stronger. . . . See if you cannot spend a short time after dark in looking out of your window into space, and meditating upon heaven, with all its joys unspeakable and full of glory. . . . Try to look up and be cheerful. . . . You have your husband's prayers, sympathy and love.

After she had read this message, she lowered the page. Dusk was near, and she followed Tom's suggestion. She sat down near the window and stared toward the sky. At first she could not concentrate on the small area of clouds and brightening stars, but slowly she succeeded. Putting from her mind the worries that had accumulated, she gained a gradual composure that allowed her to spend a serene two hours before she went to bed.

Every day thereafter Anna went to the window and looked out

at the heavens, and a new resolution formed within her. The
doctor's admonition returned to her mind: she had to "fight this
thing" harder, and she would. Tom had shown her what simple
determination could do. The next day, though her head and side
ached, she bathed, dressed, then reached for her brightest earrings. For a moment her hand hesitated; these might be all right
for evening wear, but for the afternoon . . . With a lift of her head,
she put them on.

For an hour Anna rode around the park, as she had done at
Tom's side, and visited the art gallery he liked so much. There
she felt a pang; how much more enjoyable it would be if Tom
were with her talking of the pictures. Where was he this afternoon,
and what was he doing? Forcing back the questions, she applied
herself to the scenes on the damask-hung walls.

When she turned the key at the boarding house, Mrs. McGivney
met her with a grin: "Ma'am, you're looking real well today, with
that fine color and the brightness in your eyes . . ." Flushing,
Anna darted upstairs, and that night she slept long and well. In
the morning she set out early, to stroll along Broadway and over
to Fifth Avenue for an inspection of the grounds and exteriors
of the elite homes. She had picked up a newspaper and discovered there was to be a band concert that evening. She invited
the landlady to accompany her, and Mrs. McGivney agreed with
evident pleasure.

For the next week Anna followed much the same schedule,
varying it with side trips and visits to the older sections of New
York. She remembered Tom's interest in Napoleon and sought
out a bookstore, where she bought a life of the Emperor. When
they met again she would have things to tell her husband about
his favorite subject. As she moved about New York it appeared
brighter, more stirring than it had since—since when? she asked
herself, and smiled. Since she had seen it at his side, of course.

At the next concert a handsome fellow with an appraising stare
tried to talk to her during an intermission. A day later a heavy-
jowled individual, flushed with brandy, stopped her and claimed
they had met. Both times Anna walked away, and on her return
from the latter incident she went to the mirror.

Those two men had thought her attractive, and no woman
could be completely outraged at such a compliment, could she?
Then, as she studied her face in the mirror, examining the luminous color of the brown eyes and the cheeks that had regained

much of their former roundness, she realized suddenly that she had practically recovered.

When the doctor saw her again he nodded: "While I wouldn't say that all your troubles are over, we've done everything we can up here. You can go home, but don't do as much as before, and keep a cheerful . . ." Anna lost the rest as she sped toward the postal office to scratch out a letter. Tom made hasty arrangements, and ten days or so later she arrived as directed in the Virginia town of Goshen, where he was to meet her "in a private conveyance and bring my little one gently over the rough roads."

When the stage slowed up, she recognized him standing on a corner, arms folded. Eagerly her eyes went over him, noting the color of his skin, the set of his narrow lips. As she stepped down Tom kissed her excitedly and called to her: "Anna, I thought you'd never arrive! I didn't bring young Tom, because I wanted that much more time alone with you." The last news made her smile, and then, caught in a glow of affection, she put her handkerchief to her face.

A few minutes later he led her to a trim new buggy with shining sides, and soon they rode off in quiet content. She said almost nothing; it was enough for her simply to be here with her husband again. Then she cried out: "Who loaned us the beautiful horse and buggy?" He grinned: "I'm glad you like them. They're your property now, and we can ride around like anybody else in town." Anna was delighted, but she had to ask: "Can we afford it, with my doctor's bills and everything else?" Reassuring her, he turned to give her further news:

"Sister Laura's coming with the children for a few weeks, around graduation time." At this Anna had a slight start. Could she manage smoothly with three extra people in the house? Tom patted her knee. "Laura never gives anybody any trouble, and things are going to be fine between you and her."

Anna gave him a side glance. Did his voice hold a hint of uncertainty, or was she imagining it? In any case she had made up her mind to make every effort to get along with Tom's beloved Laura. If the sister proved difficult, then Anna would give way in any matter that came up . . . With that she settled back to enjoy the soaring panorama of mountain and distant valley. To be here again, and with this man . . . It was enough for her.

As they reached their corner in Lexington, Anna peered out at the narrow stoop, the well-remembered white doorway, the shades that hung unevenly in the big front windows. The door swung open, and five figures tumbled out: Hetty waving her arms, Amy beaming at them, Hetty's two boys fighting to get the baggage down, and Tom's nephew smiling diffidently at them. Anna's sight blurred, and then she was in the hall with all of them clustered around her.

"Why, who? . . ." Her mouth fell open. Alone at the end of the passage stood a tiny figure, a Negro girl hardly more than a baby, who seemed ready for instant flight. Anna stared at the child, and Tom took the youngster's hand and brought her forward. "This is another addition to the household. Emma's going to be a nice little maid for you." As if he realized the absurdity of his words, he added, "After she grows up a bit, I mean."

The girl gaped up at Anna, eyes wide with uncertainty and alarm. She looked so forlorn that Anna went to her, smiled, and touched her shoulder. Instantly Emma dropped a deep curtsy.

"How—how old are you, Emma?" Anna asked.

"Four, almost," Tom explained. "Her father's gone, and her mother died a few weeks back. Mrs. Masterson—the lady down the road—is in her eighties and couldn't care for her. Emma's mother was in my Sunday school, and when Mrs. Masterson asked me . . . I hope it's all right, Anna."

All eyes, including little Emma's frightened ones, turned toward her. If only Tom would consult her about such things, or at least tell her about them in advance . . . Anna saw half a dozen problems ahead of her, and yet how could she say no? "Of course it's all right," she assured them. Again Emma dropped her knee, so low that she had trouble in rising, and Hetty swept her up and to the end of the hall. There Emma, still silent, made a third curtsy!

During the next few weeks Anna became increasingly fond of Emma and looked forward to seeing her walking at Hetty's side or trailing behind Amy. The moment Emma spied Tom or Anna, she still curtsied; Mrs. Masterson must have drilled her in this. "I wish you wouldn't do that," Anna told her repeatedly, but Emma never lost the habit.

Though at first the little girl seldom spoke, Anna succeeded in coaxing out a few answers in a cracked, piping voice. Watching Emma dart down the steps, she sighed: how sad for any child to lose both parents. Was Tom so moved by the girl's plight because of the memory of his own boyhood as an orphan? However, Anna discovered before long that Emma was far from intelligent, that she learned very, very slowly, and only after steady repetition, explanation after explanation.

"I gits it," the child would whisper, and then proceed to make precisely the same error. Anxiously, nerves straining, she would try to follow instructions, only to confess, "I jist mix' up." In spite of all this, Tom had determined that Emma would go to Sunday school like the others, and he drilled her at home in a child's catechism. Anna heard their voices:

"What is God?"

"God is—God is . . ." Emma's voice faded. Nevertheless Tom persisted, and before the year ended the child was able to give him the correct answers. Long before then Anna had settled into a new routine, husbanding her strength and resting at frequent intervals. Though Tom wondered if it was wise, she resumed her own Sunday classes, and the welcome she received buoyed her spirits.

"Sure bin missin' you, Miss Anna." "You look right peart, an' you jist keep right on doin' what*ever* you do in New York!" But soon they would lose one of their other students, Tom's nephew, who was to return with his mother to Beverly. "He's had a good foundation this year, and he can go on from there," Tom said, and Anna could agree. The boy had improved enormously during his time with them, and no one could say that he had not labored. She wondered if, for the rest of his life, Tom Arnold would ever work so hard!

On a warm morning Anna walked hurriedly from her kitchen, where she had been supervising preparations for a special mid-day dinner. She had heard the sound of Tom's buggy wheels on this day of Laura's long-anticipated arrival, and she hastened to the front door. Opening it, she found a small, brisk-mannered woman whose face seemed mainly eyes—wide, limpid, sensitive. Before Anna could speak, Laura reached out and kissed her cheek: "Sister, it's taken quite a time, but we've finally met." The older woman fell back to inspect her a second time: "You're as nice-looking as I've heard, and I can say one thing right off. You have common sense and a will of your own. The chin tells me that. Always look at somebody's chin, Anna, and you'll learn a lot."

As they spoke Anna studied the long, lined face, the strong nose so much like Tom's, the fine gray hair parted precisely in the center, and the deep, almost sad eyes. Here was a woman of quick mind and also of strong emotions. Anna was drawn by her sister-in-law's affectionate spirit. Now, however, Laura turned abruptly and half-pulled, half-shook off her light cape. Then she gazed nervously toward the street:

"Now, where's brother Tom gone, and young Tommy, too?" When both objects of her search hailed her, Laura's eyes darted again to left and right. "And the others? I hope they aren't wandering down the street already."

Only after making certain that the younger Arnolds had been distributed properly did Laura settle down beside Tom and Anna. Even then the older woman had several matters on her mind or at the edge of it, and Tom remarked affectionately, "Laura worries by the hour—every hour brings a new trouble for her."

Smiling briefly, Laura waved her brother aside and spoke directly to Anna: "Child, everything I've found since I reached town proves one thing. This marriage has worked well for both of you." Deeply moved, Anna thanked Laura. A moment later a faint memory came to her: Ellie Junkin had been a great favorite of Laura's, and so this tribute had a real meaning.

"Now I want to hear all about Tom's health, and just how he's caring for himself." Laura put a dozen questions, minute and precise: did he safeguard his sight; was he getting his special foods, from buttermilk to butterless bread; what was his daily regimen? Tom protested in good-humored embarrassment, "Laura, there must be something more interesting than me to talk about." At that Laura frowned him into silence: "Hush, Tom, this interests Anna and me, even if it bores you."

Those matters disposed of, Laura Arnold went on to the next topic, and Anna concluded that this sister had a great deal of Tom in her. She, too, had a quality of intense absorption in the subject before her; she was able to exclude every other interest from her mind.

After a time Tom edged away. "I'm expected at the school," he explained, and left. The moment the door closed behind him, his sister caught Anna's hand: "Please tell me if he's doing well here, really. Do these people appreciate him yet?"

This time it was Anna's turn to be self-conscious. "Yes, they like Tom, most of them," she began cautiously.

"They still don't call him 'Fool Tom' and things like that? Oh,

yes, I've heard of it." As Laura used the term, Anna could see
the pain in her face.

She hesitated: "No, I don't think they say it so much. I've heard
it only once or twice, and not in some time." Yet even while she
tried to reassure Laura, Anna sensed that she had not quite succeeded. Clearly Laura understood something of Tom's difficulties
in teaching. For a moment Anna wondered if she should go further into the matter, and it was with relief that she heard Laura
take up another subject: "I hear his classes for the colored are
going well." As Anna offered details, Laura nodded slowly, happily: "I'm so very glad, Anna, so very glad." The older woman
spoke with strong emotion, and gave her a direct and solemn look:
"Does brother Tom understand that this will eventually open the
road—to freedom?"

The question came as a complete surprise to Anna. "Why, I'm
not sure he considers his work in exactly that way," she murmured,
and could think of nothing to add.

Laura herself had more to say: "It *will* open the way, and it
should! That's been one of the troubles in this country, oppression
of people. Injustice to any man or woman because he's poor or
sick or in trouble, or because his skin is darker." In her sister-in-
law's large eyes Anna read a deep pity, a sympathy for human
suffering. Clearly Laura felt differently about many matters, including slavery, from most of the people around them.

Anna thought about Tom's own attitude. He had found nothing
in the Bible that forbade human bondage; and yet she knew that
the matter sometimes troubled him, and that he shook his head
over tales of harsh masters and mistreatment of the Negroes. He
had shown great kindness toward Amy and Albert, and his feeling
for little Emma was warm . . .

"Ah, now, where could those children have gone?" Laura rose,
brushed her skirts, and slipped off in nervous pursuit of the young
Arnolds. Alone, Anna reflected that both Tom and Laura were
from a part of Virginia that had few slaves, a region largely out
of sympathy with the institution. Emancipation with compensa-
tion for the owners, or outright abolition—would either change be
made, or would slavery not only continue but expand to the new
territories, as some demanded?

Anna recalled the day her father had told her that more than
half the slaves at Cottage Home were sixty-five or older. But he
would not sell them and bring in younger ones. Dr. Morrison had

called it a "strange system," and often an unprofitable one in the long run. Anna shook her head . . . Yet those who talked against it in other parts of the country imagined all plantation people to be luxuriating in wealth. At the same time, she knew of abuses. Could there be any protection against harshness in some human natures, or against greed that sought a huge return from human property? She sighed to herself. How much turmoil, how much bitterness the whole troubled issue had caused. And, to judge by the papers, the raging fights were far from over!

Laura's stay was a happy one. She fitted herself easily into the household, and the Jacksons took her and the children to graduation events, receptions, marches, and drills. Mrs. Page and the Pendletons gave several parties which Laura attended, and the Prestons had her as a guest for two evenings. For most such occasions Laura put aside her worries, and Tom told Anna that she was enjoying her visit enormously.

Searching for her sister-in-law's essential quality, Anna remarked to Tom, "It's her—well, her goodness. I can't think that Laura would do a single act without considering whether it would hurt somebody else." As for Laura's views about slavery, Anna would not press Tom about them.

Once again all of them were invited to Dr. Pendleton's home, where they spent a calm and cheerful evening until the closing moments. While Sandie, home for the summer from his university classes, took young Tom about the house, the older Lexingtonians formed groups in the living room. In one corner Laura was speaking energetically with Dr. Junkin, and Anna judged that they were in warm agreement.

A phrase or two reached her: "These Deep Southern fire-eaters . . ." "Yes, they'll break up the Union yet." As she listened Anna paused in surprise. Hadn't Dr. Junkin come here after having troubles in Northern colleges because he had sided with Southern groups? Her curiosity growing, she moved toward Dr. Junkin and her sister-in-law, and as she did, discovered that someone else was doing the same thing—a minor local official with the reputation of being a windbag, one of the very fire-eating type the two were discussing.

A moment later the politician addressed Dr. Junkin: "Did I hear you talking against our Southern *patriots?*"

The man's loud voice carried across the room, and several people, among them Maggie Preston, glanced up sharply. In the si-

lence that followed Anna wondered what would happen next. Dr.
Junkin faced his inquisitor: "We were speaking, sir, of the hotheads who may end up by destroying the entire Union." Though
his words had an edge, the college president kept his tone calm.

Across the room Anna saw Maggie's face darken in anger and
concern for her father. Laura Arnold had begun to tremble, and
in a moment the windbag would puff up again. Anna decided that
someone had to act without delay. "It's a little late tonight for
debating, isn't it?" With an effort, she smiled from one to the other
as she spoke: "I'm sure they'll be taking this up at the Franklin
Society."

When she shrugged, Anna could feel the tension slowly subside;
her reference to the much-respected town organization had its effect. Before the politician, always a slow thinker, could reassem-
ble his thoughts, Anna drew Dr. Junkin and her sister-in-law
toward the door and thanked Mrs. Pendleton for their happy evening. A few minutes later the party broke up, and her last sight
was of the angry officeholder, his lips moving as he walked off
alone.

On the way home in the carriage Tom's sister talked excitedly
of the incident. Tom sat in silence, until at last he turned: "So
many people are crying out about guns and cannons, when they
have no idea what war is—the worst evil that can happen to any
country!"

For the first time Anna realized how profoundly the incident
had upset her husband. Seriously, he went on, "There may yet
be trouble between the North and South. So far, I'm for the Union;
I think Virginia can get her rights in it more easily than outside
it."

Anna saw Laura nod in agreement. She herself was pleased to
hear Tom's remark; like her father, she had always been a be-
liever in a firmly united nation. Nevertheless, for the first time
in several years, she thought of what Tom had said to her on the
day they became engaged: war might eventually break upon
them. Clearly he had meant a war between the two sections . . .

Sighing deeply, he spoke again: "We can only trust in God to
stop the madness of the extremists, North and South both." After
a moment's silence he astonished Anna with a casual observation:
"I've been hearing mumbling these past few weeks against my
Sunday classes. Some claim they come under the heading of 'unlawful assemblies' for blacks."

Before Anna could reply Laura cried out, "'Unlawful assemblies'—to teach religion!"

Tom retorted ironically, "They claim the classes may put 'ideas' in the slaves' heads."

"Ideas that would be good for people of any color!" Laura snapped out her answer, and she had much more to say until Tom quieted her with his hand. "Sister, don't be so upset. Everything will work out, as it always does." But long afterward Anna's mind struggled over the subject. Threats of war between North and South, attacks on her husband's classes . . . Where were they all heading? The night had left an unpleasant aftertaste.

That taste was quickly heightened. An evening or two later, as Anna and Laura sat sewing in the parlor, Tom's step sounded unexpectedly in the hall. He had arrived earlier than usual, and Anna's first glance told her that something had disturbed him greatly. His color was high, his lips tense. Following him upstairs, she found him standing at the window, eyes on the sidewalk.

"Tom, what's happened?" For a minute she thought he would not reply. Then he began to speak in a husky voice: "It's my Sunday school, Anna, and something I've just said to one of our friends. I—I let my anger carry me away."

Her heart thumped heavily, and once again she recalled the student Jim Walker and the challenge to a duel. Was it something of that sort?

She forced herself to be calm as he resumed: "You know James Davidson? I was walking home past the courthouse, and Colonel Reid, the Clerk of Court, was standing with Jim and a few others. The Colonel said he'd met the Commonwealth Attorney and believed our school was against state law. James went further, and claimed that the grand jury should take up the subject."

With a look of self-reproach Tom added, "This threw me off guard, I suppose, and I told him: 'If you were a Christian, you wouldn't say things like that!' He answered pretty sharply, too, and I turned away and came home. Both of us lost control, but still I shouldn't have talked that way."

Surprisingly enough, Anna realized, her husband was more disturbed over the last phase of the affair than over any implications of trouble that might follow for him. Her own anxiety took a different direction. Suppose the encounter led to a meeting with pistols or a street shooting? She cried out shrilly, "Tom, you've got to clear this up, somehow. Go see him, talk it over . . ."

Anna felt as if a spur were pressing into her flesh. After a moment Tom frowned: "Anna, I'm not sure I should do that. It's a matter of honor, and as a woman you can't quite see . . ." As a woman, she assured herself, she saw some things more clearly than he and other foolish men did!

Remaining calm, Anna continued to talk until Tom's self-command had returned. "Very well," he said, "after supper I'll go over."

"Thank God." Whispering the words, she led him downstairs. She drew Laura aside and explained the matter hastily. At first a spark of hot anger brightened her sister-in-law's eye, but then, as Anna took her hand, she subsided. "I won't say anything to upset him or the situation," Laura promised, her face solemn. The meal was strained; young Tom and the other Arnolds did most of the talking.

As soon as supper was finished, Tom left them. Anna and Laura sat together nervously in the parlor, where they passed the next hour in torment. "Suppose Mr. Davidson turns out to be hostile, and they have worse words than before?" Anna's question hung in the air, and Laura sighed. "We can only wait, sister, and pray."

Anna lowered her head, but she could not put aside the threat that hung over them. "I—I wish I'd never heard of those classes!" she cried suddenly, almost to herself.

"Anna, you don't believe that, really." Laura's voice had a quiet reproach, and Anna shook her head, chagrined at what she had been thinking. Tom was doing a great work, and the classes meant something to all of them, and to the town as well.

She looked at the clock; an hour and twenty minutes had gone by already. All at once she jumped to her feet. Suppose somebody were to bring word that her husband lay dead, or bleeding to death on the street . . .

The outer door opened, and Tom was there in the hall. She saw a glint of perspiration on his forehead, and he was very tired; yet she recognized signs that his tension was relaxed. A vast relief ran through her, but before she could ask a question he addressed them: "I went to Davidson's house, and his wife said he'd gone to his office. When I got there I started to tell him I regretted wounding his feelings."

Tom smiled briefly: "With that he stopped me. He was writing an apology, and he showed it to me." Tom looked from Anna to his sister: "I stayed there, going over the whole affair, and by the time we said good-by we had gotten to know each other better than ever before."

Anna caught his hands: "Tom, I'm glad, so very glad." Laura nodded silently, her eyes filled with tears. Nevertheless a doubt persisted in Anna's mind: "About that business of 'unlawful meetings' and the grand jury——"

Slowly Tom shook his head: "I don't think anything will come of it now. Major Preston is in favor of our classes, and Dr. White, Dr. Pendleton, and a lot of others. We'll wait and see." Already Tom had begun to put the subject behind him.

During the next few days Anna listened carefully for repercussions. When her husband volunteered nothing more, she pressed him: "Hasn't anybody mentioned the Sunday classes?" After some hesitation, he replied, "Only one man has—Major Preston, and he says we'll go on as we've done all along, without a change." That settled the matter, for the town's leading citizen had put his full weight behind Tom's project. Anna felt a greater gratitude than ever for their old friend: at the time of testing the man stood hard and well.

The time arrived for Laura's departure. Shaking Tom Arnold's hand, Anna told him, "You'll let us know if you'd like to come back here, won't you?" The boy thanked her and Tom, and Laura took her sister-in-law in her arms. "Ever since I met you," she murmured to Anna, her voice thickening, "I'm happier about Tom and his future." A warming affection swept over Anna. "We'll meet again, sister," she whispered. "And soon, soon," Laura answered. "From now on I'm going to be thinking a lot about you, Anna."

Wiping her eyes, the brisk woman hurried to the carriage. Hetty, Amy, and the Negro boys called out good-bys, little Emma bobbed up and down with her curtsies, and as the vehicle rolled down Washington Street, Anna slowly closed the door.

CHAPTER 10

Anna could not be sure when it was she first understood the full meaning of the shadow that moved ever closer to them during the fall of 1859 and the winter of 1860. But almost certainly she saw something of the shape of the future on the morning a stranger's name reached her out of the chill air. John Brown . . . The man and the incident he provoked would be one of the milestones of her life.

First, however, came their summer. From time to time Anna had talked with Tom about the trip to Europe, a prospect that stirred both of them. But now it appeared too difficult to undertake: the uncertainty of her health and the recent expenses made the jaunt impossible. "We'll make it next year, definitely," Tom promised. No matter what happened they would go, and meanwhile in the evenings they read about the Italian hill villages, the vineyards of Germany, and the Scottish highlands.

This summer they traveled instead to the Virginia Springs, returning in time for the opening of school. Back in Lexington, Anna welcomed the sights and sounds that had become part of her daily existence: the files of marching students, the sound of distant drums, the boom of cannon at the Institute. She watched her health, and the early autumn started well, but one morning as she hurried downstairs her heel caught in the carpet, and she felt herself slipping.

Opening her eyes, Anna found herself in her bed, with Tom and the doctor bending over her. "Nothing broken or even cracked," her husband told her with an attempt at lightness. The doctor was less easy: "You've had a bad shock, and you'll have to rest completely for some weeks. You'll follow my orders, Mrs. Jackson?"

Weakly, Anna nodded, and Tom brought her a glass of water and a powder the doctor had left. Only later, after she waked from a long slumber and reached toward the table, did she realize how thoroughly she had been shaken. Her fingers trembled, and the room seemed to be quivering in an irregular motion.

"Jes' lay still, honey. Jes' lay there." The soft-voiced Amy pressed her gently back onto the pillows, straightened the covers, and went off to fetch things Anna would need. From then on, Hetty looked after the house, stopping her work every few hours to inquire about her mistress, and Amy stayed with Anna most of the day. During this time, she came to know better than before the earnest woman whom Tom had befriended.

"No, I don' min' goin' the exter way." "You res', and ol' Amy stay right here tell the Major git back." As they talked together, Anna realized that life had hardly been good to Amy. She had lost her husband and her children, one by one, and she had appealed to Tom only when she faced a harsh uprooting, transfer to a hostile climate. Yet Amy held no resentments, asked no questions of fate, and several times Anna wondered if, subjected to such successive shifts of fortune, she would have been able to carry on so philosophically.

"Now don' worry yer head," Amy whispered to her repeatedly. "You jes' feel shook, and you got to sleep flat and collect yourself." Without Amy, Anna was not sure if she could have gotten through those weeks. One evening, she praised the aging woman to Tom, and he smiled slowly. "The sainted Amy," he said, and she nodded in agreement.

For hours Tom stayed at Anna's side, reading to her, trying to brighten her spirit. Yet she recovered only slowly, and in these days of forced idleness her mind returned against her will to the disturbing subject of a second child. There were still no signs; perhaps there would never be any. After hesitation she put the question to the doctor once more: "Is it just that I can't have another?"

He studied Anna's face: "Why, no, but these are things we can't be sure about. Your internal troubles have cleared up, and at the moment there's no physical reason you shouldn't be able to become a mother. All I can say is, take care of your general health, go back to your usual way of living, and stop being so—concerned."

She must not be concerned . . . He could be Olympian, while she and Tom yearned for the baby that was denied to them! After the doctor left, Anna turned her face to the wall. Hetty needed Amy for an errand, and Anna was alone in her room when the tiny Emma thrust in her head: "Big man downstairs an' say he leavin' town right off. Is hit right to bring 'im?"

Puzzled, Anna sat up, threw a heavy robe over her shoulders, and, with Emma beside her, received the caller. It turned out that the "big man" was the tall young Sandie Pendleton, hurried and embarrassed. "I shouldn't have come, ma'am," the slender youth apologized, "but I'm leaving for the University today and I wanted to see how you were getting along and—well, to leave you this." The boy flushed as he handed her a book of poems.

Anna was moved; as always, the personable Sandie had struck a graceful note. After she thanked him she inquired about his future. "When you get your master's degree, what are you going to do?"

Sandie thought for a moment and his reply was uncertain: "I haven't given much heed to that, ma'am. Some profession, teaching maybe. But not the army."

"No, I wouldn't believe so." The military was the last thing she had visualized for the scholarly boy. They chatted for a time, and as Sandie left with a happy smile, Anna asked herself what the next few years would hold for someone like him. Sandie had almost too much learning for his age; his adept mind was almost overtrained. How to bring up a child, how to direct him . . . Once more she reverted to the matter that hung over her. Trying to put aside the speculation, she repeated to herself: God's will be done, God's will be done.

That evening Tom entered with a smile. "We're going to try a new prescription, Anna, a trip over to Hampden-Sydney to see a doctor who specializes in cases like yours." Though she had several friends and connections in the pretty Virginia college town, her husband's words left her unmoved until he added: "If that's not enough, another remedy. Would you like to go on to North Carolina for a few weeks?"

"Would I *like* it?" Anna was speechless with confusion and delight. It was—she estimated swiftly—nearly two years and three months since she had seen Cottage Home. "And, Tom, if you could only go with me . . ." She stopped; with the school term just getting under way, she should have known better.

The days at Hampden-Sydney were beneficial, and she improved bit by bit. But was it the new doctor's remedies or her approaching return to North Carolina that accounted for her gains? In any case, when her carriage rolled up the long approach to her old home, joy surged through her. She recognized a cluster of figures on the steps, and as she reached the house they crowded forward.

"Anna, it's been too long—years too long." Her bearded father lifted his hands to her.

"Child, you don't look altogether well to me. Still, you're here and that's wonderful," her mother exclaimed as she kissed Anna. Her remarks were much the same as those a dozen others made during the week that followed. The servants moved in, and the next hour was a flurry of exclamations, directions, and questions. Mary Morrison assigned a new light-skinned girl to be Anna's close attendant. "We've put a small extra bed in your old room," she explained, "and she'll be with you at night in case you want anything."

Anna sighed in appreciation of that luxury. It had been a long time since Hetty could do more than the general household work in Lexington. Going upstairs for the first time, Anna felt a quick pang. Here she and the dead Eugenia had enjoyed their years together; here she had whispered with her sister after their return from Lexington and their meeting with Tom Jackson. Her thoughts shifted: and it was from the window of this room that she had first seen Tom when he rode up that day.

"Come, child." Her father took her arm in an affectionate gesture. "We're all waiting downstairs, and there'll be time for memories later." Happily Anna followed him, her hand in his. To be enveloped once more in the old cocoon of love and sheltering attention, with no directions to give, no schedules to follow, no decisions to make . . . The family clustered around her: among them were her older sisters, Isabella and Harriet, and her brother William, home on a visit from Washington City.

With the bright-faced Isabella Hill, Anna had a long, warm conversation punctuated by a dozen questions about Lexington friends, including Major Preston, Maggie, and President Junkin, for whom Isabella cherished a firm admiration. "I don't know any of the people you're talking about," the urbane William drawled. "Can one town have all those interesting folks?" For all his sophistication, however, William was clearly happy to see her and to learn what she and Tom had been doing.

As she laughed with him, Anna's eyes went to Susan, now a handsome, composed twenty-one-year-old, and to the alert Laura, two years Susan's junior. The biggest surprises, however, were the sixteen-year-old Robert and the family's "baby," Alfred, ten and seemingly much older. Anna's eyes misted for a moment. When she left they had been children; now the children had gone.

"Well, Anna." Her oldest sister, Harriet Irwin, asked a smiling question: "What's it *really* like up there in Lexington?" From her tone Anna sensed that the well-to-do Irwins regarded her as a sort of exile in the mountains. "Kindly" was the word for Harriet's manner, and suddenly Anna resented the patronage. Nevertheless she checked her tongue and gave a casual reply: "It's a beautiful place, as you'll agree when you visit us some day."

With that a cousin from Greensboro, who had arrived unexpectedly the same day, leaned forward with an amused light in her eyes. "And Major Jackson—he's the same as ever, I suppose?" The question was tipped with malice, and Anna glared at her, fighting the impulse to hit back. "Why, yes," she murmured. "He's just the same, and I'm very happy about that."

Her cousin's unkind words depressed her, and she managed to make an exit. Alone in her room, she struggled to understand why so many people were unimpressed with Tom's abilities, the things that set him apart. As she stood with hands clenched at the window sill, a rap sounded and her mother entered, a compassionate look on her face.

"Sit down with me," Mary Morrison directed. "Anna, I couldn't miss what happened just now, but I don't know why you're taking it this way. Tom's a fine man, and we know it, you and I and a lot of others. You're happy with him and you have a good, rich life together. Even if he isn't as—as successful as some, that isn't what counts. Now is it?"

Slowly Anna nodded: "No, I don't think it is, at least not the way some people believe." Though her mother's observations were meant to comfort her, they did not. Even Mary Morrison went on assuming that Tom would never make a name for himself. Obviously, of all the sisters who had married to date, the family believed that Anna had done least well. Yet what could she say?

The door burst open, and in ran young Joe, who had been away when Anna arrived. Her eyes widened at the husky seventeen-year-old, broad-chested and big-fisted, who beamed at her, kissed her heartily, and went directly to the matter uppermost on his mind: "Sister Anna! Will brother Tom help get me in the Institute when I'm ready? In just another two years . . ." With a smile Anna promised to do what she could.

Contentedly she settled back to enjoy this interlude. Neighbors called; she spent pleasant afternoons with them in the parlor; the Morrisons took her on picnics at the edge of the creek. Daily she strolled about the estate, climbing the fences she had known since childhood, meeting the field hands who had been at Cottage Home even before she was born, stopping at the smokehouse redolent of well-cured ham.

When the family gathered after dark around the piano, Anna counted fifteen to twenty in the room. She joined the singers, her voice rising above the others. The music was cheering, evocative of many earlier evenings. But slowly she became aware that she missed something, until after a day or so she realized what it was—Tom's almost growling voice. She had come to expect his dissonance as part of the music.

The sharp-spoken Harvey Hill rode over for a week end, and

Anna spent several bright hours at his side. They talked at length about Tom; while her brother-in-law chuckled over Tom's tastes in food and his excessive punctuality, he had a high respect for her husband, evident in whatever he said. Anna had a surprise, however, when they sat together the next night beside her brother William, and Harvey spoke suddenly and angrily of "the war that's on its way now."

Both Anna and William stared as Harvey waved his hand. "Of course it's coming, as surely as you have noses on your faces!" He almost bit out the words. "The North's conducting a systematic campaign to cheat us of our rights, keep us out of the new territories, hold our runaways, and undermine us in other ways. I tell you, they're destroying the Union, and we Southerners will be better off out of it!"

William Morrison shook his head. "Harvey, our best hope—our only hope—is in the Union. Believe me, all we have to do, North and South, is obey the law and hold our country together and our differences will be worked out. If we're not fools we can do it."

Confused, disturbed, Anna looked from one to the other. Surely Harvey could not mean the things he was saying. And now from the side Dr. Morrison addressed them slowly, a strong note of perplexity in his voice: "I don't know what will happen, but I simply can't believe we should leave the Union. I never thought feelings would be agitated this way. Everywhere you turn there's excitement, and with a national election next year . . ."

As Dr. Morrison paused, young Joe pounded the table with all the force of his seventeen years: "Well, let those dirty Yankees put one hand on the South and we'll knock 'em from here to . . ." At his father's stern stare Joe subsided, and Dr. Morrison ended the conversation: "Everybody's shouting too much nowadays. I hope we can agree on that, anyway." Only Harvey Hill appeared to disagree, and as she turned away Anna reminded herself that Harvey was an intelligent man and a shrewd one. Yet those sentiments of his . . . Did many other Carolinians hold them?

Her health was much better. Each day she trudged a longer distance over the family acres, and her color returned as her spirits lifted. But now, overnight, she felt restless. There seemed to be so little to do—empty hours, afternoons during which she could only sit, chat, and sew. All at once she realized that she missed the schedule to which Tom had accustomed her: out of bed daily at the same hour, a morning session with Hetty and Amy, fixed periods when she read to him.

Anna found herself longing for the sound of her husband's voice, for his touch as he took her into his arms after a half-day's absence . . . From the corner of the room Mrs. Morrison glanced up: "Anna, you want to go home, don't you?"

She flushed. "It isn't that I don't like to be here with all of you——"

"Of course not," her mother broke in with a laugh. "It's only that you'd like even more to be with Tom Jackson."

That settled it. Nevertheless Anna suffered a final pang as she took her place in the carriage, the Morrisons gathered smilingly about her. She wondered how long it would be before she saw them again. Just before the carriage left, the sturdy Joe jumped to the window: "You'll ask brother Tom for me—about the Institute, you remember?" Dr. Morrison pulled the boy away, the driver snapped his whip, and Anna waved until the house was lost behind her.

Stopping off for a half-day in Charlotte with the Hills, Anna had a shock when Harvey walked in with a grim look. "Anna, the telegraph just brought word about some trouble in Virginia—a slave uprising at Harper's Ferry, with white men mixed in the affair. Some of the whites rode in from Maryland, grabbed the armory, and sent out raiding parties . . ." It sounded almost incredible, and when Harvey and Isabella bade her good-by at the railroad station she asked herself if her strong-minded brother-in-law could be exaggerating.

For the next few days, as she moved from stage to train, Anna heard conflicting stories: "Things quietin' down at Harper's Ferry." "Oh, no, they're worse. Insurrectionists caught a bunch of hostages and locked 'em in an engine house." A woman next to her added a detail: "The U. S. Army ordered Colonel Robert E. Lee to put down the rising, and he's sending a charge of men against that engine house."

At Lee's name Anna felt a stir of recognition, but she shuddered at the next news, yelled from a railroad station: "The leader of thet-there risin' is John Brown, a God-damned abolitioner from the slavery fightin' in Kansas. Been in the papers afore, knifin' and murderin' people!" Insurrection, hostages, armed assaults

. . . When she stepped down at Lexington and caught sight of her husband, Anna almost cried in relief.

As she kissed him in a burst of happiness, she could not keep back her questions: "Tom, are we safe here? That trouble at Harper's——"

"Anna, please." Soberly Tom took her aside. "I'm sorry you've heard that wild talk. The slaves never rose up behind Brown, and I don't think there ever was a real risk. Anyway, Colonel Lee and his men subdued things. A few people were killed, and Brown and several others will go on trial."

His succinct words calmed her, and Anna followed him into the house, where Hetty, Amy, Emma, and the boys hurried up to them. With every nerve she longed to be alone with the man she loved, but first she must go through the duties that awaited her—distributing the gifts she had brought back with her, settling household affairs that had accumulated in her absence. As she did, she saw Tom beside her, cheeks flushed with emotion, as impatient for the reunion as she. At last they left the servants and Tom drew her up to their room.

Later that evening, as she lay beside her husband, Anna told herself that they must never be separated again. God willing, let them have long and happy years together, let all those outside troubles remain at a distance. Tonight the only sounds from beyond the house were the roll of carriage wheels, an occasional echo of street sounds. From across their chamber came the crackle of wood, the slight hiss of flames in the fireplace. The world waited somewhere beyond their drawn curtains.

But the world would not stay where she wished it. In the morning Mrs. Page arrived with an expression of concentrated anger such as Anna had never seen in the kindly face. Greetings over, the older woman pointed to the newspaper: "Just look. These New England editors are calling Brown a hero, a 'martyr'!" The same day, meeting Tom and Anna on the street, Minister White shook his head: "Some good people up there are pouring out letters asking for the man's release, praying for it, and they say even respectable elements backed Brown in his scheme."

Tom frowned: "Only a few are doing such things, Doctor. And still, so many down here think all Northerners feel the same way. If only people would stop agitating the affair!" Sadly Anna left the minister with her husband. That night she saw Tom at his desk staring fixedly before him, and realized he was going over the matter in his mind. A few days later he brought a new report: "Well, John Brown's been found guilty, and he'll hang in a week or two."

"At least the matter's going to end now," she sighed. But it did not end, and as she went about the street she caught rumors: "Gonna be more raids like that first one—Harper's Ferry and other places, too. Wait and see." The journals gave headlines to reports that were no less unnerving. "Vigilance committees" had been formed in many parts of Virginia, and people were being urged to look under houses and barns for "incendiary wretches" who were plotting to burn down farms and settlements. And one day the frightened Amy carried a tale closer to home: "White folk sayin' the soldiers from school goin' to the place where they's been fightin', and Major Jackson with 'em."

Anna saw her face pale in the mirror before which she sat. When Tom arrived she met him with her question. "Anna, that isn't definite. The governor's thinking of sending the cadet corps to prevent any threat of trouble when they hang John Brown. Now don't . . ." Nevertheless she did concern herself, and her fears grew for two more days until, shortly after eight o'clock on a late November evening, she heard a staccato rap.

Tom answered the door, and when he returned to her he spoke coolly: "We leave by ten tonight. I'm to be in charge of the artillery unit." As she listened Anna tried to quiet the thumping of her heart, and she worked swiftly to help pack his clothes. When she said good-by at the door she made herself smile. Then she settled down to the agony of waiting.

Suppose another mad band poured upon the scene with guns, as people were predicting? For two days she heard nothing. Major Preston and other Institute officers had also gone with the cadets, and when Anna saw Maggie, her friend assured her, "There's nothing to worry about. The Major's sure of it." Yet as she spoke, Maggie's face showed that she too was under a strain.

A day later Anna made a special trip to the post office, to receive only a shake of the head: "No'm, no letter at all." She was about to get into the buggy to return home when she heard a high-pitched voice: Mrs. Petry was talking to several women at the corner. Anna started to signal to drive off; why should she pay heed to that ladybird of ill omen? Then her hand dropped and she listened.

"Those Yankees are riding right now into Harper's Ferry, and

they outnumber our boys three to one! I have it straight from an
army officer." Mrs. Petry puffed with each emphatic phrase: "Real
civil war, at this very *moment*."

The scene dimmed before Anna, and when she arrived home
she descended from the carriage in a haze of pain. Somehow she
made her way up the stairs, to sit at her window for most of the
day, struggling against panic and dejection. She might be foolish,
paying attention to someone like that. But she could still hear
Harvey Hill's emphatic prediction that fighting would break out
at any time.

Was Tom already dead, had he and the cadets been wiped
out by the marauders? When dusk came she remembered his advice to her in New York. She stared out of the window at the
heavens, trying to will herself the peace for which she yearned.
Closing her eyes, she prayed: God spare Tom, spare him . . .

At a rustle, she turned around to see Hetty with a lamp: "Miss
Anna, a letter f'om the Major." Tearing open the envelope, Anna
read in a rush, and a cry of relief escaped her lips. Everything
was over, and Tom had already started home! Years later she
could repeat much of his message:

John Brown was hung today at about half-past eleven a.m. He
behaved with unflinching firmness. . . . Brown rode on the head
of his coffin from his prison to the place of execution. . . . The
rope was cut by a single blow, and Brown fell through about five
inches, his knees falling on a level with the position occupied by
his feet before the rope was cut. With the fall his arms, below the
elbows, flew out horizontally, his hands clinched; and his arms
gradually fell, but by spasmodic motions. There was very little
motion of his person for several moments, and soon the wind blew
his lifeless body to and fro . . . altogether it was an imposing but
very solemn scene.

I was much impressed with the thought that before me stood
a man in the full vigor of health, who must in a few minutes enter
eternity. I sent up a petition that he might be saved. Awful was
the thought that he might in a few minutes receive the sentence
'Depart, ye wicked, into everlasting fire.' I hope that he was prepared to die, but I am doubtful. He refused to have a minister
with him. His wife visited him last evening. His body was taken
back to the jail, and at six o'clock p.m. was sent to his wife at
Harper's Ferry. When it arrived, the coffin was opened, and his
wife saw the remains . . .

Anna winced at the grim scene spread before her. All eyes in the United States had been turned toward this spot, and toward the death of a half-crazed old man. Her mind went to Tom's account of John Brown's widow. What a terrible hour it must have been for the wretched woman—to be taken to her husband just before the hanging, and then to be shown his twisted body in the casket.

Anna's mood was solemn when her husband returned. As soon as he had kissed her Tom spoke softly, persuasively: "Now, my dove, let's put the affair behind us. It was certainly disturbing, and it shows that we'll have to be on guard. Still, that doesn't mean war, Anna—not at all. If we're all careful, and reasonable, and keep our heads, mind our tongues . . ."

Anna nodded, but as she did she asked herself how many others were doing that. Tom, who had been at the scene, talked of it far less than those whose only information came from the newspapers, often in twisted form! John Brown's name was still yelled on the streets, and there were rumors of fresh raids, protests, mass meetings.

Sadly Tom handed her a newspaper. "Some people are talking of embargoing Northern goods, cutting off contact with the whole section." And together they stared at a journal which declared: "More and more our South Carolina friends are pressing a shining remedy, one which Virginia itself must eventually face and consider—secession." At the word Anna winced.

Through the winter and spring of '59 and '60 Tom held aloof from the agitations around them. "This county is still for the Union," he told her one morning, "and I think it's going to stay that way. We can only keep our trust in God." Meanwhile it appeared that the state of Virginia was not relying entirely on God; the legislature voted to increase the state's military forces and appropriated $500,000 to organize and equip the militia.

As she read this news to him one evening, Anna watched Tom shake his head: "It's a long time since so much money was voted for a thing of this sort." It would affect them directly. Under the new measure, Institute officers, including her husband, became part of the state's military system. The governor named Superintendent Smith a member of a small commission to handle the expanded operations, and Tom remained at the Institute for extra hours, inspecting new guns, ordering and checking supplies. Sometimes she saw him for only an hour or so during the day.

In April the Democrats held their national convention, and Tom assured her with a quickening interest: "I believe we can accomplish something. After all, we're the majority party, if we can stick together." For days they followed reports of wrangling among the Democrats, and now he came in with a clouded look: "Anna, the convention's split wide open, and there'll be two separate tickets in November."

Anna frowned with him, then suddenly smiled as she reminded herself that once she had announced she would never marry a man who belonged to the Democratic party. Nevertheless she now considered herself more or less one of the band, and was ready to admit it! Within the month, as their vacation approached, the Republicans nominated a man whose name meant little to her —Abraham Lincoln. Her eyes halted at a grim paragraph: "If the fellow wins, one course is open to the South, to quit the Union." With that sentiment, she knew, Tom did not concur. Nor did she.

And now, with June, Anna felt somewhat happier as she saw a respite from military affairs. This time again it would not be Europe for them. "Things are so uncertain in this country," Tom murmured, and she nodded understandingly. "By next June they should be calmer," she assured him, "and we'll have that much more of a chance to save for a real trip." As he agreed, however, Anna asked herself whether they would see the continent the following year, or even the next. Then she reproached herself for this gloomy view. Someday, and somehow, they would go there together . . .

Before leaving Lexington, Anna sent another letter to Laura Arnold. Since the previous year her mind had gone many times to Tom's earnest sister. How Laura, with her strong convictions on matters of slavery and freedom, must be reacting to the burning debates! She recalled the older woman's hurt air and her anger as she spoke of injustice and unfairness. But Anna could not raise the issue in her notes to her sister-in-law.

For their vacation this summer Tom had picked a place of which he had heard, Northampton, Massachusetts, where the Connecticut River flowed along a green valley. As he described it, Anna's interest quickened, and when he added, "It has a fine hydropathic establishment—good for both of us," she smiled discreetly; she might have guessed that Tom would want more than simple enjoyment.

Just before they left, Anna met Maggie at Dr. Pendleton's home. With an eager look her friend took her aside and, after several preliminaries, informed her, "Maybe you've guessed . . . Well, I'm going to have another baby." Happily Anna grasped Maggie's hands: "That's fine news. I'm so very glad." As the woman poet stood there, her thin face had a radiance that stayed in Anna's mind until after she and Tom had returned home. Gradually her mood became pensive. Her husband talked happily of young Sandie and the record he was making at the University, but Anna heard little of what he said . . . Maggie was about forty, the Major was closer to fifty, and they were having a second child, while she and Tom . . .

At Northampton, in spite of her skepticism, Anna went through the prescribed routine, taking long walks, exercising, experimenting with the baths. Tom did the same things, and added a treatment of his own, one he had tried on other occasions: lying on his back with cold towels on his stomach. "It relaxes me wonderfully," he told her. "I'm sure it does," she answered, but she did not attempt it herself. She liked the atmosphere at Northampton, and they spent most of every day outdoors, strolling about in a large grove of trees. Tom gained weight, his color brightened, and her mirror made it clear that she, too, was improving.

Meanwhile Anna thought she detected a hint of coolness in the manner of certain of the resort visitors from the North. "You're imagining things," Tom chided her, "and every time you do you help the wild people everywhere. We have to behave as we've always done, as though these differences were not in our minds at all." And Tom, she decided, acted precisely as he recommended.

After this talk, Anna took care to exchange friendly greetings with couples whose accents proclaimed them Northerners. One day, trudging along a path about the hills, they met a serious-faced man who proved to be a Baptist minister from Connecticut. As usual Tom talked about faith; without referring to dogma, he and the minister had several long conversations which ended in general agreement. "A remarkable man," was Tom's comment.

That night, as they left a band concert with an acquaintance of theirs, the wife of a South Carolinian, their Connecticut friend passed. Anna and Tom addressed him cordially, but the woman beside them stared pointedly ahead. "I'm astonished that you would speak to such a man," she fumed after his departure. "He's nothing but an abolitionist, and last night he and my husband had real words. He's a person you should refuse to be seen with, Major."

Anna watched Tom stiffen. Looking straight ahead, he answered quietly, "I've found him intelligent and courteous. We may not have the same views on some things, but both of us believe in the Union."

"Indeed." The word had a coating of ice, and the lady promptly excused herself. When she and her husband reappeared her manner was still more frigid, and Tom murmured: "There are two friends we've lost." Anna was discouraged; although the country might settle its troubles if more people tried to get along as did Tom and the Connecticut man, she doubted that others would be so reasonable.

The same thought rose when, after their return to Lexington, they heard a shout from the street: "Abe Lincoln won." A moment later Anna caught the echo of a raging argument.

"That Lincoln . . . a cheap politician, a dirty-mouthed country yap. God help us, with an abolitionist like that!"

"Well, I still ain' fer lettin' them cotton-country screamers take us out'n the Union. Lincoln's a good man and he'll keep this country in one piece and——"

The dispute ended in a slap, a curse, and a confused shuffling. Closing the window with a sigh, Tom led Anna to their room . . . The following weeks brought calm to the Lexington area, but there were reports of ominous acts in the lower South. "South Car'lina's seceded—right out of the Union!" The cry, coming to them from the courthouse, made Anna speak somberly. "Tom, is it beginning to happen?"

Her husband remained comparatively undisturbed: "No, there's hope yet. Too many people want peace, and want this nation to continue. We've got to pray that they act with faith and good sense." That night Anna knelt longer than usual; surely the Almighty Father would intercede. She was trying to shake off her depression a day or so later when one of the Preston staff knocked with a note. Maggie and the Major were planning a family Christmas celebration next week, and couldn't the Jacksons join them? After a consultation with Tom, Anna accepted happily. She volunteered to assist Maggie with the arrangements, and early the day of the party she rode over to the big house to help hang silver

ornaments on the tree and wrap the dozens of presents. Maggie's
baby was due in January, but she superintended operations from
a cushioned chair, working no less steadily, no less energetically
than usual.

"Anna, what color would Tom like?" Before she had her answer, Maggie looked in another direction: "That's wonderful,
George, but what *is* it?" A moment later: "Willy, don't let the
epergne drop!" Grinning, Maggie's stepson relinquished the
fragile item to Anna, who had just come in, as he left her to meet
his friend Willy Page. After a time Tom joined Anna, and they
drew back as dozens of Prestons and Junkins arrived. Also at the
party were the Carruthers, and the first Mrs. Preston's family, who
visited here at Christmas as they always had.

The servants moved about with platters of cakes and sweet-
meats and cups of punch. Cousins greeted one another, and above
the clink of glasses and cries of welcome Anna heard the shouts
of the children. So many young ones . . . Her mind went momentarily to her home, empty of children of their own, tonight as
always . . . She reproved herself; such thoughts came all too
readily to her, and they were especially unworthy at Christmas,
the time of good will and good cheer.

For a time Anna felt lost in the throng until Willy Preston, always her favorite among the Major's sons, came over to her and
Tom. Several others followed after him, and from then on the
Jacksons were in shifting groups of Prestons, Junkins, and Carruthers, swallowed up in waves of holiday greetings. One face
Anna had missed, but finally Dr. Junkin arrived last of all. The
college president smiled and bowed, and yet Anna quickly
realized that he was troubled. In a lull in the conversation she
heard him address one of his sons: "Everybody's in a fine humor
here, so different from practically every other place I've been this
week. If things keep on this way . . ."

A minute or two later Anna was taken to another group across
the room, and she caught the beginning of a fuming complaint
from one of the Carruthers: "I still say there's one thing for the
South to do. If those people don't give way, and fast, *shoot when
necessary!*"

Startled by the young man's vehemence, Anna glanced up to
find Dr. Junkin approaching them. Another pair of eyes noted the
same thing, and Maggie rose awkwardly from her chair to take a
place beside the angry speaker: "Please, can't we put aside the

arguments for tonight?" Although the little woman's expression was pleasant, her voice had a forlorn note. Disconcerted, the youth hesitated and fell silent.

Maggie turned toward her father, and under her management the conversation took an easier direction. Anna stepped forward to help Maggie keep the talk going, and her friend gave her a glance of gratitude. Anna was relieved, but her feeling did not last long. All over the South tonight, men and women were trying to avoid clashes that might explode in the flash of a second. Yet how long could they escape the one great explosion that hung over them?

The Christmas party had lost much of its tinsel.

CHAPTER 11

January, 1861; February, 1861 . . . In these months Anna Jackson moved between calm and deep concern, hope and growing fear. James Buchanan, outgoing President of the United States, wavered weakly. Abraham Lincoln would be inaugurated on March 4, and meanwhile the storm clouds were darkening in the lower South. After South Carolina, Florida seceded, to be followed by Alabama, Mississippi, Louisiana, Georgia, and Texas, and in Montgomery the government of the Confederate States was organized, with Jefferson Davis as provisional President.

With each news bulletin Anna's spirits fell lower. Nevertheless Tom continued hopeful: "Virginia hasn't joined them, and your own state's referendum went against a secession convention. Others are holding off too." He tapped his fingers against the latest newspaper: "Anna, Virginia's working hard for the new peace convention in Washington, trying to get both sides to concede something." For days they bent together over long accounts of the "peace" meetings, and meanwhile Tom read her statement after encouraging statement by Southern Unionists.

Anna's Uncle Graham, the former Secretary of the Navy, wrote them eloquent notes: secession was mad, and the South's hope lay in calm adjustment. "He's very convincing, isn't he?" she asked Tom, and he nodded warmly: "With so many people at work this way, and praying, I can't think it will go for nothing." His tone was earnest, and in spite of the signs around her, Anna stirred to his words. Tom couldn't be wrong; he had to be right!

These tense days had their pleasant moments. Maggie Preston's second child was born. It, too, was a boy, bigger than the first. When the Jacksons went to visit her, Maggie smiled through her weariness, and the Major almost preened as he strode about the room. Dr. Junkin looked on, his usually solemn manner softened in this time of fulfillment. "It's a good hour for all of us," he told them.

But a moment later his face resumed its stern lines, and Anna understood why. Town feeling over the secession crisis was affecting Washington College. Students were wearing blue "secesh badges" and flaunting their sympathies. "You see," Tom explained, "so many of them come from states that have already seceded." Lexington itself was still in large part Unionist; in the vote for delegates to the Virginia state convention, Rockbridge County cast 1700 ballots for Union candidates and only 300 for secessionists.

Yet every day or so Anna heard rumblings among the eighteen- and nineteen-year-old students. Her eyes darkened as she watched them shake their fists on the street and call out bitterly against some of the townspeople: "Damn Yankee!" She shuddered one day when several yelled the name at one of Lexington's oldest merchants. "Poor Mr. Bright," she said to Tom. "Everybody here has known him and liked him for years. He's from Rhode Island, but a lot of the boys who are insulting him have grandfathers in the North."

After a silence Tom gave her an unhappy look: "And I'm afraid there's new friction at Washington College. Dr. Junkin's giving talks on the Constitution and arguing against secession." A firm disciplinarian, Maggie's father kept the students fairly well under control; but Mrs. Page confided to her, "The boys are getting pretty restless out there."

A few days later she listened with a sense of shock as the gray-haired woman told her, "They've chalked 'Lincoln Junkin' on the President's door, and they're calling him a 'Pennsylvania abolitionist.'" At the last words Anna protested: "He never *was* an abolitionist. In fact, part of the reason he left the Northern college was that he defended the South. Like a lot of people in our section, he believes in gradual emancipation—a middle way." A harsh thought occurred to her; wasn't it always the people in the middle who suffered?

A cheering letter arrived from North Carolina; her sister Susan was to be married to Alphonso Avery, a young lawyer, and could Anna possibly be at Cottage Home for the ceremony? Her immediate reaction was delight, but she doubted that the trip from Lexington would be possible. "Of course it is," Tom insisted, and after days of arrangements Anna set out, to enter happily into a series of receptions, parties, and other events. It was a rewarding interlude; she spent satisfying hours with her mother, evenings at Dr. Morrison's side; and the marriage ceremony brought Morrisons and Averys from several directions. For days the country's agitations appeared far removed. Yet even then the crisis intruded.

Though she tried to close her ears, Anna could not miss the murmurs: "North Carolina will be in the Confederacy with the others, just as she ought to be." "They couldn't keep us out!" In spite of the previous state vote, secession sentiment must have spread furiously in recent weeks. Anna succeeded in remaining aloof from the arguments until a young cousin shoved a letter before her:

"Look what those crazy Yankees are doing now."

Anna whirled around: "Some of us down here seem a little crazy to *me!*"

As silence fell upon the group, she sensed that she was almost alone in opinion. In the garden outside, her father and mother were walking with the older guests, and suddenly she realized that, for all his Union feeling, Dr. Morrison had of late talked little —and when he did, he had an air of discouragement.

The matter hung over Anna during the rest of her stay, and again when she rejoined her husband in Lexington. There she felt the tensions crackling all around her. In front of the courthouse, at the stores, along the narrow streets, men talked intently, while women whispered in their parlors. Repeatedly she heard a familiar name, that of "Bull" Paxton, a handsome young businessman-planter of Thorn Hill estate. Frank Paxton had been an attorney until eye trouble led him to turn to other interests; Anna and Tom had met the serious fellow a number of times, and once her husband had remarked on Paxton's combination of skills.

But now Bull Paxton was a subject of daily conversation. He had come forth as Lexington's leading secessionist, and he was a highly vocal one. On her first day home Anna caught sight of him. The stocky young man was pushing ahead with a scowl, eyes almost closed in his concentration. Behind her she heard a snicker:

"Bull's taking this here thing real hard, ain't he? Just hint you don't agree with everything he's a-sayin' and he'll grab you like a preacher snatchin' at Beelzebub hisself!" Walking on, Anna shook her head; the raging purpose in the man's eyes had unnerved her for a moment.

That same week Tom attended a discussion of Virginia's stand on secession at the Franklin Literary Society. Anna had paid little heed to the announcement of the meeting, but on her husband's return his face told her immediately that there had been trouble.

"What happened, please?" She took his arm.

"Nothing that should disturb you, Anna." Tom avoided her eye.

"It involves you, and I have a right to know."

After a moment he glanced up. "Well, you've heard about Bull Paxton's agitations?" At the name her throat tightened. Tom continued: "Tonight Dr. Junkin spoke for the Union, and Paxton jumped up and said a lot of wild things, calling the doctor an enemy of the South. There was a lot of feeling. I told Paxton he'd gone pretty far, and he answered back—and neither of us acted very calmly."

Anna's grip tightened on his arm: "Tom, there's no more to it?" She could feel the violence in the situation—a violence that might snap at any moment.

"No, the matter's ended," he informed her crisply. "From now on, though, I don't think 'Bull' Paxton and I will have much to do with each other."

Anna sank to her chair. She was sorry that Tom had lost a friend, but she gave thanks that nothing worse had happened. A few days later Mrs. Page, after marked hesitation, broached the subject: "They say Tom and Frank Paxton simply pass each other on the street. Isn't there something we can do?"

"Nothing, I'm afraid." Anna looked away. For Tom, Frank Paxton fell under the heading of a "deceived man," and this was the way it had to be. Thinking about Mrs. Paxton, of whom she had several pleasant memories, she felt a certain regret. When she met the younger woman on the street, Anna was careful to address her as usual, and Elizabeth Paxton responded to her warmly. Nevertheless the breach disturbed her.

Harsher hours were coming. In Washington the peace convention collapsed, and Anna realized the failure had shaken her husband badly. Discouraged, he took a place before her: "The Union people won't give the South any pledges to protect its rights. I'm for making still more efforts to get commitments from them, but the situation has gotten steadily worse." She had never seen him so pessimistic, and she listened anxiously. "Now some of the Union people are talking of using force against the South. If they ever do—if they ever invade a foot of our land, the whole South will be united overnight."

He paused, and ended, more solemnly than ever, "In that case Virginia would join the other states, and I'd be at my state's service. Anna, I'd have no choice."

"No, I'm afraid you wouldn't." Yet even as she repeated the words, Anna told herself that it must not happen . . . For days Lexington had reverberated to stories of rival movements. Frank Paxton and his friends raised a tall pole with a secession banner; the Unionists set up a larger one and planned to fly the American flag the next day. After Tom left that morning, Mrs. Page knocked and entered with a tense face: "Somebody took off the top of the Union pole, and people blame the cadets. And Bull Paxton's stationed himself in front of the secession pole and told the Union side—if anybody touches *it*, it will be over his dead body!"

Bloodshed had come closer. It was Saturday, a market day that brought townsmen, farmers, and cadets into Lexington, and Anna and Mrs. Page remained apprehensively together. Suddenly a man ran by: "New trouble in town, a bad fight between cadets and townspeople!" They heard a pounding of feet and confused shouts:

"Kill the slavocrats!"

"Don't let them nigger lovers beat the boys!"

From the center of town rose a dull roar, and Anna fought the impulse to run out. A neighbor cried to her and Mrs. Page as they stood at the window, "They say the cadets are going for their guns to fight it out!"

The words left Anna chill, and her hands caught at the window sill. She heard a report that sounded like gunfire. Afterward there was a long silence. Where was Tom? Were he and the other Institute officers involved in the fighting? The next hour and a half was a time of steadily increasing fear, of conflicting stories and alarms. Finally Anna made out a distant figure, and cried in relief as her husband strode into view.

"Anna, everything's turned out all right," he assured her, speaking nervously. "Superintendent Smith was sick in bed, but when he found the boys starting out with arms, he headed them off, led them back, and made a speech."

She whispered a prayer of thanks. Though they had been at the edge of disaster, the danger had ended. After Mrs. Page left, Tom stayed with her for some hours, and for this she was additionally grateful. Not until dusk, when Willy Preston arrived with a message, did Anna learn the whole story of what had happened at the Institute.

"Ma'am, Major Jackson made the best talk of anybody when they were trying to quiet the boys. He got up and said military men gave short speeches and he wasn't any hand at such things. Then he told us the time for war hadn't come, but if it ever did —to draw the sword and throw away the scabbard!"

After the boy left, Anna sat reflecting. How strange it was to find Tom making a rousing address of any kind. And his words were frightening. Had he ever before gone so far? A little later she asked him about the incident, and he replied, "I'm still in favor of trying for peace, up to the final moment. But more and more you hear threats of military action against us—attack, invasion. If the North ever does that, I'm for a hard fight, as hard as we can give them!"

His eyes blazed: "And if war does start, I don't hold with those who want to fight only by defense and with a fine caution; I'd hit the enemy and hit whenever he moved in reach. That's the way to wage war, the way of Napoleon and the other great soldiers."

Anna was deeply troubled; she had seldom seen Tom so provoked. The recent events had carried him farther than she realized . . . In silence they retired for the night, and although Tom slept soundly, for Anna there was scant rest. The shadows had grown very black.

For days they had talked over the alarming stories that drifted in from Charleston, where Union elements, holding the harbor forts, faced new Confederate forces. The Federal garrison at Fort Sumter required reinforcement, and before long a decision would have to come.

The next morning Tom left at his usual hour. Almost at once he darted back up the stairs, his face red with emotion: "Anna, a courier's just in from Staunton, and he says the Union decided to provision Fort Sumter—and the Confederates under Beauregard have fired on it!" He added, his voice rising, "That's the end of

talk, and war is right upon us . . ." With that he hurried out again
to the Institute.

Alone again, Anna clenched her hands and tried vainly to return to her duties and to supervise Hetty and Amy. A long silence,
and a horseman brought the town electrifying word: President
Lincoln had called for 75,000 volunteers to defend the Union
against armed rebellion! A roar went through the streets, and as
Anna peered out the window, men shook fists and fresh secession
flags waved on the corners. If any Union sentiment remained in
town, it could not be found today.

"Everything's changed now," Tom told her in a low voice on
his return. "When they decided to use force, the entire issue became different. Virginia will be going out of the Union, and I'll
be following my state." The old beliefs, the old convictions were
crumbling. At the hour of showdown, his loyalty to home had
won . . . Anna lowered her head against her husband's shoulder,
and they clung together silently in the dusk.

Riding down the street the next day, she discovered Maggie
Preston in the vehicle opposite her. Her friend had a woebegone
air, and she called out, "Will you follow me to the house?" There
the tiny woman sank weakly to her chair. Her face was sallow,
and she appeared physically ill.

"Anna," she began, her voice hardly audible, "there's been new
trouble at the College, the worst yet, and I—I'm not sure what
Father's going to do." A moment later they heard a man speak
out in anger from a nearby room, and Anna recognized the deep
tones of Dr. Junkin himself: "It's treason! You people are bringing
ruin to your country and yourselves. To try to destroy a government that's brought good to so many . . ."

A second voice reached them. Major Preston was talking, and
he sounded amazingly calm and patient: "Sir, you know I've been
a Union man all along—till the other night when Lincoln made
that proclamation. Now my first duty's to my state. I'd prefer to
have Virginia stay in the Union, but once it leaves . . ." Anna felt
a confusion of emotions; Major Preston's words had a deep pathos
and also a disturbing note. Though John Preston's temper broke
easily, he must have made up his mind not to lose it with his
father-in-law. The rift between them was wide, and yet Major
Preston was trying to prevent it from growing.

As the words went on in the next room, Anna turned anxiously to Maggie: "I think I should go." Her friend's look asked her to remain: "Anna, please . . . I don't know what's going to happen next." A door slammed; Major Preston had left the house. With a slow step the college president approached. For a moment Dr. Junkin seemed like a sleepwalker, unaware of their presence. In his face Anna read a sorrow close to despair.

Lowering himself into a chair next to her, the elderly man clenched his trembling hands, and his head sank. Then slowly it rose, and he addressed Anna: "Mrs. Jackson, you'll soon hear what's just happened at the school. For a long time I've watched the influences at work on these young men. Yesterday they put up still another of those disunion flags, and I told them it must go down."

Anna was afraid that Dr. Junkin would collapse before her. Maggie listened intently, her eyes tight with pain. "Today," he continued, "the faculty sided with the students, and I've just called the trustees—to give my resignation." Each sentence, Anna sensed, was harder for him to speak.

"As I said to you once, I've been happier these past thirteen years than at any time in my life. I'm seventy, and my roots have sunk deep in Lexington. My wife and two of my children are buried here. Others of my children have married in Virginia, and I always expected to work here to the end."

Dr. Junkin forced himself to his feet: "But now I'm going to leave the state." At his words Maggie cried out, and her father moved toward her: "Child, I'll wind up my affairs and take a carriage back to Pennsylvania tomorrow." His earnest eyes searched his daughter's face: "At least one of your sisters is ready to leave with me."

Maggie sat speechless in her chair. Anna remembered the special bond that had existed between father and daughter; Dr. Junkin had begun the girl's training at six with lessons in foreign languages, and they had spent long years in study and discussion. Maggie caught her father's hand, and Anna heard a long sob. George Junkin seemed visibly to weaken, and then, after clasping Anna's hand, he left the house.

As his footsteps died away, Maggie wiped her eyes and seated herself next to Anna: "I don't know who's right, Father or John. All my life I've looked up to Father; he was always the wise one, the one who understood things, who pointed the way for us." Maggie's voice was husky: "But when I married John I threw in my lot with him, and I became a part of this place, this house, with our children around us. And now, when will I see Father again, or my sister or my brothers in Pennsylvania?"

Lowering her head, Maggie Preston wept to herself, and her sobs shook her narrow shoulders. Anna took her hand and tried to reason with her: "Maggie, you couldn't do anything else. And when this is all over, Dr. Junkin will understand."

"When it's all over . . ." Maggie lifted her swollen eyes. "When will that be, and will he still be alive?" At those bitter words, Anna caught her friend in her arms. When she slipped out of the house, she asked herself in despair, How many other families were being split in this way?

Her trip home showed her a town maddened with excitement. Men screamed on the streets, secession banners waved from windows and stores, and in front of the newspaper office an orator was haranguing a crowd:

"We've won before we start! I tell you Yankees can't fight. Nothing but a bunch of grabbing shopkeepers. Whoever heard of a Yank that could ride a horse or fire a gun?"

On and on the boasts went, flamboyant, exultant. When she reached the house Anna repeated some of them to Tom, and he rubbed at his chin: "Hm. A lot of people are saying the same things. But, my dear, you and I know a lot of Northerners who won't be afraid to fight." As Tom spoke, she thought of the dozens of Northern friends that they had made. Now these people would be their enemies, citizens of another country.

She had to tell her husband of Dr. Junkin's decision, and Tom received the news with a look of pain. "I wish he could have felt differently," he said huskily. "But I would have guessed he would do it. I lived in his house for several years," he reminded her, "and I'll always respect and admire him . . ." Tom let out a long breath. "You realize, don't you, that his sons in Pennsylvania will certainly join the Union forces? And the two Junkin boys in Virginia—they'll go with the Confederacy." So it would be brother against brother, a sister in one camp, another with the enemy . . .

A little later, as she and Tom started for the supper table, Anna's mind went back to a question that had been nudging her for several days: "Tom, what will the army want you to do? Surely they can use you best to teach other people, train men, since you've had ten years in classes here and——" His penetrating stare made her stop, and her voice trailed away.

"Anna, they'll want me in the fighting, if any comes, and that's where I'd want to be." With a sense of impending disaster she heard him continue, "We expect they'll summon the cadets into service at any time, and some of the officers will go along." He read her thought: "Yes, I'll be one of them."

His words sent a chill through her. He would go "at any time . . ."

The next days were a period of suspense and foreboding; newspaper bulletins told of swift enlistments, there were reports from Richmond of mounting military preparations. A letter from Cottage Home informed her that her Uncle Graham was returning to North Carolina. He had stood hard against secession, but now that his state was leaving the Union he would go with it.

Suddenly Anna heard a drum boom nearby, a blare of music, the tramp of hundreds of feet and a long cheer, followed by dozens of others. Hetty darted in: "They's young soldiers, a lot of 'em." Her voice was higher-pitched than ever. She and Anna went to the stoop to catch a glimpse of the quick-moving files.

As she stood there Anna felt a stir, the beginning of a new emotion. This was a nation they were forming, under a new flag, and she was part of it! Perhaps, after all, the Confederates might proceed in peace, under their own government, their own regulations . . . That would be for the future to settle. But from now on, whenever a line of men marched down the road, whenever a band blared from the corner, she would come to attention. Her country, her new country . . .

A moment later Anna thought of Bull Paxton and his followers, of the cries and countercries that had rung out between the elements on Lexington's streets. She reminded herself that they would all be together now—even Bull Paxton. That might be hard for her to accept; for weeks she had considered the man a hateful symbol of dissension. Nevertheless, many things would be different from now on, and she must try to forget some of the furies of those recent weeks.

Anna's mind shifted to her own family. Her brother in Washington—what would he do? Her father and her brother-in-law, James Irwin, were too old to be actively involved, and Joe and Robert were too young, she told herself. As for the others . . . From home came one message, then another: Harvey Hill had volunteered in the service of North Carolina, as had Rufus Barringer, Eugenia's widower, and Alphonso Avery, young Susan's husband.

And there would be others, members of the family and friends, who would march off. She sighed to herself. Nevertheless she would accept, because she had to accept; she would work for the Confederacy in any way that suggested itself. What could she do? She began to think of sewing, of donations. As she did a small smile played at the corner of her mouth. How quickly her whole outlook had shifted, and how completely!

It was a Saturday evening, the end of a week that had left Anna spent and worn. Tom faced her wearily: "The thing I'd like most is a quiet Sunday, without talk of politics or fighting. And no conferences at the Institute. I want only the privilege of communicating with God." A few minutes later, throwing off all the pressures that were weighing on him, he was asleep. Anna tried vainly to doze. What was going to happen next?

After an uneasy, broken rest, she suddenly woke up. The clock showed only five-thirty, and Tom was still resting peacefully. As she sank back, she asked herself, had she imagined it, or had someone rung the doorbell? The sound came again, with a peremptory firmness. Going to the stairway, her heart beating heavily, she met the alarmed Hetty. "Some soldier, say it right important."

Anna turned to find Tom beside her, a heavy coat thrown over his nightshirt. "I'll be right down," he called. Numbly she returned to her room, to wait motionless in her chair, and when he faced her again she knew what he was going to say: "I'm to take the cadets to Richmond today." Before she could speak he added: "No time for breakfast, but I'll manage to get back before we go."

Anna's hands trembled; it was only a matter of a few hours now. Hetty and Amy awaited orders, and she turned mechanically to them: "Let's fix a good, substantial meal, and . . ." Her voice broke, and she forced herself to go on to other preparations. From the medicine box she took several bottles, Tom's many remedies for his illnesses. As she lifted them to the light to make sure each one was full, she wondered what would happen to his health if he had to march long distances and spend the nights in drafty tents or in the open. By great effort her husband had conquered most of his ailments, at least for the time. But Tom was still a far less sturdy man than most. The thought was not comforting.

By eleven that morning she heard quick steps, and he reappeared: "We have just an hour or so before I leave the house. We're starting the march from the Institute at one o'clock, and I

ought to be there well ahead of time." After some persuasion he
sat down to the meal she had prepared, made up of the dishes
he had trained himself to eat. Would he be able to get such food
in the army? Meanwhile Tom addressed her in nervous sentences:
"Anna, I've had no chance to write sister Laura, and I wish you'd
do it tomorrow." "You'll know how to send my mail?" Then,
guiltily, he added, "But this is the Sabbath, and we must talk of
less worldly things."

Although a dozen questions were on her tongue, she could not
bring herself to ask anything more. All at once neither of them
could speak, and they did not finish their food. "Please, come up
with me." He went to their room, and Anna followed, her heart
hurting as she did. There he took out his Bible and chose the
chapter in Corinthians dealing with the hope of resurrection. His
words began slowly:

For we know that if our earthly house of this tabernacle be dis-
solved, we have a building of God, a house not made with hands,
eternal in the heavens . . .

When he finished, he dropped to his knees, and she sank down
beside him. Lowering his head, Tom Jackson prayed to his God:
"Father in Heaven, on this day of trial, we place ourselves under
your protection . . ." Anna had never heard him speak with such
conviction and intensity. "And we ask, even now, for peace. If it
is consistent with Thy will, may Thou avert the danger that hangs
low . . ." His voice was choked, and Anna covered her face with
her hands.

"And now, *esposa*." The hour had arrived, and they would be
separated for some time to come. In the doorway Tom took her
hands and explained: "Stay here until we see what happens. If it
doesn't look as if I'll be back soon, you may want to go to North
Carolina. But we can always hope, Anna, that it won't be too
long . . ." As he talked, Tom's eyes went over the house as if he
were trying to memorize the rugs, the furniture, the windows, the
door. Then he kissed her again, and started to say something more.
Evidently he changed his mind, for he ran down the stairs, to
ride quickly toward the Institute. Her eyes dimmed, and she felt
as if someone had put out a light.

At the Institute the cadets, having finished their meal, stood
impatiently in loose files. Tom had asked Dr. White to offer a

final prayer, and the minister, knowing the Major's punctuality, took care to finish in time. Everything had been readied, and presently the men and officers grew restless. Although many pairs of eyes focused on Tom, he remained seated on a stool, staring absent-mindedly ahead.

Mutters began in the ranks: "Let's get going." "When do we get started?" Finally a subordinate officer sought Major Jackson: "Mayn't we set out now, sir?"

Tom Jackson's light eyes passed over the other man's face, and he pointed to the barracks clock, which showed ten minutes before the time. "When the clock strikes, we'll go," he remarked quietly. Only when the signal sounded did he call out: "Right face! By file, left march!"

From the stoop Anna saw a cloud of dust, and her hands clenched. About this time last year, she and Tom had promised themselves that they would go to Europe for the coming summer. Only a few months ago, after her illness, she had insisted to herself that they must never be separated again. Never be separated . . . "Please, Miss Anna . . ." Hetty took her arm and led her inside.

The next weeks were tense and restless, and Anna worked steadily in an effort to distract her mind. The letter Tom asked her to send Laura proved hard to write. She tried to be reassuring, to tell her sister-in-law that the troubles might end soon, perhaps even without any fighting; she said, too, that Tom had acted in the way he thought he had to. Yet as her pen moved over the paper, Anna remembered Laura's anxious face, her concern with matters of conscience, her feelings about slavery. What was happening now in Western Virginia, and how was Laura taking all this?

When she went to post her letter, Anna saw a file of marching men, the volunteer Rockbridge Rifles, Lexington's first such troops to leave for the front. Crowds were cheering, children waving flags, and her eyes halted at the sight of a familiar face, that of young Elizabeth Paxton, Bull Paxton's wife. She caught a quick glimpse of a husky first lieutenant moving off down the street.

And now Elizabeth Paxton broke into sobs. The two children at her side, who had been staring excitedly around them, looked up in anxiety. Anna went over to the younger woman, and drew her to her: "He used to get into such rages, such fights . . ." Eliza-

beth cried. "But I never thought that he'd go off as soon as this."
Anna walked her to the carriage, trying to comfort the stricken
wife, and waved an unhappy good-by. As they disappeared, a
question touched her mind. Tom and Frank Paxton would be under the same banner; she had talked no more with her husband
about his differences with Frank. Surely they could make up the
quarrel now . . . But would they?

Anna asked several Institute friends another question, one that
would not leave her. What kind of role would the officials give
Tom in the war? Neither Major Preston nor anyone else could
answer her query, and she began to worry. But then, she smiled
bitterly. Only a few days earlier she had hoped her husband would
be a teacher and would not have to see direct service. Now she
was ambitious for his advancement.

Was she being illogically feminine? Perhaps she was; nevertheless Anna assured herself that she wanted her husband to advance, and she intended to do whatever she could to help him.
With what she hoped was delicacy, she mentioned Tom's Mexican
War record, only to receive a dismaying response.

"Yes, ma'am," a young officer replied, "he had a good record."
Was there a slight stress on the word "had"? An older man gave
her a kind look as he commented, "You know, it's too bad Major
Jackson didn't stay in the army after the war. He'd be right in
line now, and people in Richmond would remember better." With
each conversation Anna's mood declined until one evening at the
Prestons, when she spoke with the most youthful of the lot.
"The Major's the hardest-working man I've ever met," he said,
"but . . . but strangers mayn't appreciate him as we do here."
At those words Anna's spirit dropped still lower.

Every day or so she received a letter from Tom in Richmond.
Arriving there, he had seen his cadets encamped at the Fair
Grounds, where they set to work to drill raw volunteers. But what
of Tom himself? He told Anna he had no definite assignment,
and at once she answered: if he were going to stay there for a
time, she wanted to join him. She had heard of a dozen women
who had done this. His reply was not reassuring: "I would very
much like to see my sweet little face, but my darling had better
remain at her own home, as my continuance here is very
uncertain."

Her "sweet little face . . ." Anna fumed to herself. No matter
what Tom said, if he stayed there much longer, she intended to

take that little face to Richmond. A day later her mood improved when Hetty brought in a paper. Colonel Robert E. Lee now headed Virginia's state forces, and the story added that, to join these state troops, Lee had rejected an offer to command all the Union forces. Lee was, Anna remembered, Tom's Mexican War associate; he knew Tom's abilities . . .

Her husband's next note brought news, but of someone else. Anna's oldest brother William had passed through Richmond on his way to join the North Carolina forces after quitting his government post. And so the Morrisons would have still another hostage to fortune.

A day or so later came an answer to her repeated queries, an answer that made her fret. Tom had received an assignment— a desk in the engineers' department. He had little experience in this field, and did not consider himself fitted for it. At once Anna sought out Major Preston: "Is Tom going to be wasted for the whole war in an office like that?" Their friend frowned: "Anna, everything's in a rush there, and muddled up. Still, I've heard that several people we know—our state convention delegate among them—are going to Governor Letcher to correct the mistake. You'll see."

And within forty-eight hours Major Preston was proved correct. The Governor recommended Tom for appointment as colonel of the Virginia Infantry, in command of the strategic point, Harper's Ferry. A promotion and an important assignment . . . Her eyes brightened, and she felt a thrill of happiness. At long last, some recognition for her husband! She was momentarily less elated when she learned what had happened in the convention which passed on his name. A member stood up: "Who is this Major Jackson, that we're asked to commit him to so responsible a position?" To that the delegate from Rockbridge County had replied: "He's a man we can tell to hold a post, and he'll never leave it alive!"

Tom received the appointment, and Anna's delight rose higher than ever. Around her she saw a new interest in Tom and a heightened respect for him. She mused over the name Harper's Ferry. Tom had gone there in the John Brown case; his fortunes seemed curiously wrapped up in the spot.

When Major Preston called with Maggie, who was greatly subdued in these days of trial, he told Anna warmly, "Harper's Ferry may decide a great many things for us, and both sides see its

importance." She listened eagerly as he explained that the handsome settlement, on a tongue of land between the Shenandoah
and the Potomac, had been an important munitions and supply
base for the United States. "When our troops first moved on it,
the Union set fire to the armory and withdrew. Now there may
be a clash there at any time."

Munitions, gunfire between heavy forces . . . The prospect left
Anna in an uncertain mood. Nevertheless, she tried to remind herself, Harper's Ferry might give Tom his great chance. And now for
days she and Maggie thumbed over reports from the scene. Tom
had gone swiftly to work, ordering heavy drilling, furious preparations—so furious that even here in Lexington one could catch the
rumble of complaints from volunteer officers. The two women
pored over an exciting dispatch: using a careful scheme for jug-
gling regular B. & O. railroad movements through Harper's Ferry,
Tom had trapped about fifty-five locomotives and three hundred cars at the spot, thus adding to the South's badly needed
equipment!

The feat stirred the state, and as Lexington cheered, Anna's
eyes met Maggie's. There she read a reflection of her own high
satisfaction. Virginia had begun to hear about this man whose
skills these two had appreciated for so long. No matter how torn
Maggie's emotions about the war, she could not hide her delight
in Tom's rise.

His latest letters were quick, joyous ones. His post, he said, was
one "which I prefer above all others . . . an independent command." "Little one, you must not expect to hear from me very
often, as I expect to have more work than I have ever had in the
same length of time . . ." One letter was only a line in Spanish, in
which he poured out his love. Again: "I am strengthening my
position, and if attacked shall, with the blessing of Providence,
repel the enemy. . . . Oh, how I would love to see your precious
face!"

His earlier words came back to Anna: he had no sympathy with
people who fought only defensively, all care and caution; he
would strike hard if and when the enemy moved within reach.
She remembered his long study, the way he bent over Napoleon's
maxims, his analysis of the Corsican's campaigns. Perhaps all his
life had been a preparation for this hour . . .

Under the tensions of war, it became increasingly hard for Anna
to handle her domestic duties, to manage the big house with its

many rooms and hallways. Until now she had never been there
without Tom, and he had made many of the decisions about re-
pairs and supplies. Her friend Mrs. Page spoke to her with a
serious air: "Anna, you're overtaxing yourself again. Remember
what happened to you last time. Why don't you close up this
place and stay with me till things settle down?"

For a time she hesitated, but finally she accepted the offer
gratefully. With the help of Maggie and her motherly friend, she
located a place for Hetty's growing boys and one for Amy and
little Emma. Mrs. Page would provide quarters for Hetty at her
home. In spite of the careful arrangements she had made, Anna
still had difficulty in saying good-by to her several helpers. "We'll
be back together before long," she assured them. But as she spoke,
she asked herself, much as Maggie had done on the day her father
made his decision, Before how long? When would they come together again?

In Mrs. Page's home Anna found it easier to relax, and these
were calmer, more peaceful days. She saw a great deal of two
youths she knew well—Mrs. Page's son Willy, and his good friend,
another Willy, the son of Major Preston. She read Tom's letters to
them and talked with the boys of their futures. "I'll be in the war
the minute they let me, a few weeks from now," Willy Page announced with a lift of his head. When Anna expressed her doubts,
the boy's mother nodded sadly: "I can't stop him. Unless they
decide they don't want them so young, he'll be leaving."

Eventually Willy Page prepared to go, and Anna watched Willy
Preston, twelve months or so his junior, grow sad. "Maybe they'll
take me next year," he said in a low, hurt tone. "If the war's still
on." He made it clear that he would be disappointed if hostilities
were over before then. Anna sighed . . . If they could only be
sure the end would be so swift.

Overnight one familiar face disappeared; Major Preston had
gone to join Tom at Harper's Ferry. The development made Anna
happy; it was good to know that Tom would have his old friend
near him. She was not prepared, however, when Dr. Pendleton,
the Episcopal minister, nodded with a smile, "I'm going to the
army this week."

"That's fine," Anna had responded. "We can always use good
chaplains."

The rector's astonishment was plain: "Why, no, in active service as a captain. Remember, I graduated from West Point, and

last year some young men of the town asked me to drill the Rockbridge Artillery. Now we've all enlisted, and Tom's summoned us
to join him." Before she could absorb this, Dr. Pendleton added,
"And my son Sandie will be there too. He'll be a second lieutenant.
He's been itching to go, and finally he got a place."

Sandie, the boy of such remarkable intellect, well trained in
languages and the classics . . . Hadn't he indicated to her that
he had no interest in the army? Now Sandie, too, had been caught
by war's contagion.

As comfortable as she was with Mrs. Page, Anna's loneliness
did not end. The person whom she wanted most could not have
her with him. Ever more frequently her mind turned to Tom's
suggestion: perhaps she should go to North Carolina for a time.
She had begun to think about Cottage Home and the family, to
wonder how the war had affected them. Then one day Tom wrote
that it seemed best for Anna to go to her parents until they knew
more about the future. In a depressed mood, she set to work to
have the furniture packed and to lock up the house.

At that point a courier brought the town a message at which
Anna stared in disbelief. As she had known, the Confederate
States had voted to move their capital from Montgomery to Richmond, and heavy reorganizations had started. Now, blinking, she
read that, in taking over from state forces, the Confederate au-
thorities had named a new commander at Harper's Ferry. General Joseph E. Johnston was to take the place of Colonel Thomas
J. Jackson.

Thrusting the paper into her pocket, Anna went to her room.
Just as Tom had gained his opportunity, it had been taken from
him. He received a lesser assignment at the same post, heading
a new brigade of Virginia troops at Harper's Ferry, and he wrote
philosophically, "You must not concern yourself. . . . I hope to
have more time, as I am not in command of a post, to write longer
letters . . ." Yet he could not hide his hurt, nor could she.

A few weeks later Anna had another hard message. General
Johnston, deciding that the exposed place could not be defended
before superior Union forces, had ordered Southern troops to give
up Harper's Ferry. Perhaps the man was right, but bitterly Anna
asked herself if her husband would have done that. Soon her mood
changed. The matter was settled, and it would do no good to
agitate herself over it; it would help neither Tom nor herself. With
new resolution, she pressed ahead to finish arrangements, and

when her tall brother Joe arrived one spring day to take her to
North Carolina, she rode over to the house on Washington Street
for a last inspection.

Going from chamber to chamber, Anna could not hold back the
memories that crowded in on her. Here it was that she and Tom
had knelt to pray on the day he left. In that corner he had worked
nightly at his high desk, and over here he waited several times
to surprise her by catching her in his arms. At the opposite corner,
so empty now, had stood her prize item, the piano they had
bought in New York. How many times had she sat there with Tom,
listening to him singing in a voice whose off-key sound she had
come to enjoy. So many happy hours, so many good days together
. . . In spite of her disappointments, it had been a place, as Tom
had said, of "golden hinges softly turning."

Her final stop was at a room which had long been empty, the
one which they had planned originally for a nursery. The toys,
untouched by little Mary, were locked away in a trunk, perhaps
forever. The scene clouded, and she walked quickly down the
stairs.

PART IV

Mrs. Stonewall

. . . when the wars and troubles are all over, I trust that, through divine mercy, we shall have many happy days together.

—*Thomas J. Jackson to Mary Anna Morrison Jackson,*
July 16, 1861.

CHAPTER 12

"Father, there's *no* word by the post?"

Dr. Morrison shook his head, and with a look of regret left the house to return to his inspection of the Cottage Home acres. Anna resumed her restless walk up and down the room. On this July day of 1861, about a month after her return, life seemed to be standing still; the first great battle of the war was now being decided at a point far removed from them.

The Morrisons had greeted Anna with joy; for the first time in years they were to have her with them indefinitely. "Child, I don't like the reason that's brought you," Mary Morrison had said, "but we're happy and grateful that you're here."

Brothers and sisters, visiting cousins and servants had moved steadily around her, and for a week or two Anna had enjoyed the old comfort, the long-accustomed serenity. Then, with only slight warning, the war's new crisis had broken, and everything had faded before the black fact of Manassas. For weeks they had heard vague stories of the massive Union army concentrating in and around Washington. The Confederacy had waited, and now the Northern forces were rumbling out.

A day or two later, early details poured into Charlotte. At a point close to Washington itself, the Confederate and Union armies were lunging at each other. The two greatest military masses ever seen on the North American continent were meeting in a clash that might settle the war, end everything one way or the other . . . But for Anna, Manassas Junction had only one immediate meaning: Tom was in the midst of the harsh fighting.

"Child, you've got to stop this." Her mother came behind her, to catch her arm.

"I can't stop it." Anna shrugged off Mrs. Morrison's hand. "He may be dead right now, or dying somewhere on those fields." With a slow shake of her head Mary Morrison left, and Anna sank to the chair beside her desk. By force of habit she reached out for

the box in which she kept Tom's letters. What had happened to
his career since those first days at Harper's Ferry? The only military names heard today were General Johnston and General
Beauregard. The dramatic Creole from Louisiana had won swift
fame as a result of the firing on Fort Sumter, but Johnston—what
had he done except pull back and march around and around?

Anna frowned. Perhaps she wasn't being fair to Joe Johnston;
only last night her father reminded her that the man had found
himself heavily outnumbered. Nevertheless she had gathered
hints of her husband's opinion of Johnston as a soldier; Tom
seemed to feel that he was overcautious, unwilling by nature to
face a direct battle. Her eye picked out phrases from the letters:

General Johnston made some disposition for receiving the enemy if they should attack us, and thus we were kept until about
noon, when he gave the order to return. . . . I hope the General
will do something soon. . . . My orders from General Johnston required me to retreat in the event of the advance in force of the
enemy. . . .

His letters carried another theme—one that disturbed her:

I sleep out of doors without any covering except my bedding.
. . . I have been sleeping out in camp . . . and generally found
that it agreed with me well, except when it rained. . . . My table
is rather poor, but usually I get cornbread.

Lying on wet ground, eating food that would probably make
him ill . . . Could Tom survive under such conditions? Then she
went back a few lines. She had suggested that he write more
often, disregarding the possibility that his notes might be carried
on the Sabbath. He replied:

As to writing so as to mail letters which would travel on Sunday, when it can be avoided, I have never had occasion, after
years of experience, to regret our system. Although sister Isabella
gets letters from her husband every day, is she any happier than
my *esposita*? Look how our kind Heavenly Father has prospered
us: I feel well assured that in following our rule, which is Biblical,
I am in the path of duty, and that no evil can come nigh me. All
things work together for my good. But when my sweet one writes,
let the letters be long, and your *esposo* hopes to send you full
ones in return; and when the wars and troubles are all over, I
trust that, through divine mercy, we shall have many happy days
together.

At the final sentence Anna's face softened. It had become almost a refrain with Tom: once the war ended, they would have long, good years with each other. Repeatedly he reminded her of it, and she clung to the thought. Happy word from Richmond had recently lifted her spirits. In a period of many military promotions he had a new rank, that of a brigadier general. But meanwhile he told her far less than she wanted to know:

You say that your husband never writes you any news. I suppose you meant military news, for I have written you a great deal about your *esposo* and how much he loves you. What do you want with military news? Don't you know that it is unmilitary and unlike an officer to write news respecting one's post?

Nevertheless Anna still wished for real information. And now the comparative calm of recent weeks had been broken when the stage driver from Charlotte stopped with a message: Northern forces had pushed back Beauregard's advance guard, and the newspapers carried rumors that the Creole was appealing to Johnston to send his men in a forced march. "They says unless the two Southron armies can git together, things'll be real bad."

As Anna had stared, the driver spat out a mouthful of tobacco and went on, "Both sides supposed to be killin' lots of men. Must be a terrible thing, soldiers breakin' under cannon fire, runnin' ever which way." Sickened, Anna turned aside. She tried to remind herself that all such talk was undependable. Nevertheless, she had spent a grim evening in her room, dreaming that she saw Tom staggering across a field, being helped by a strange woman in black. A moment later the woman ran toward her, and when her face was visible she proved to be Tom's sister Laura, weeping, screaming that he was gone. Anna had wakened with a cry that brought her mother into her room.

Today, more anxious than ever, she went to the library, where the midafternoon heat attacked her in waves that sent the perspiration down her neck and along her legs. Had she ever known it to be so hot, so airless?

Hetty produced a moist cloth: "Miss Anna, lemme wipe yer face and yer wrists to cool yer off." Lowering herself on the sofa, Anna lay back for an hour. Then suddenly, at the sound of quick footsteps outside, she thrust herself up. By the time she reached the front door, her sister Harriet was hurrying across the grass. Anna braced herself; was this the bad news?

"Anna!" Harriet was gasping. "The minute I found out I rode here to tell you. We've won, and magnificently! The Union army is running back to Washington, and our men are pushing right after them. They say in Charlotte that they may be in the capital already, fighting in the streets."

Anna's breath caught in her throat. How wonderful a success! Perhaps their side had ended the war . . . For the next few days she and the other Morrisons lived in a daze of happiness, repeating those words to themselves. Her concern for Tom's safety lessened; if he had been injured she certainly would have heard by now. But only the vaguest news came from Charlotte, and as far as anyone could tell, Washington had not fallen. Then the mail brought a note in Tom's writing, and Anna almost snatched it from the driver's hand:

Yesterday we fought a great battle and gained a glorious victory. . . . Although under a heavy fire for several continuous hours, I received only one wound, the breaking of the longest finger of my left hand; but the doctor says the finger can be saved. My horse was wounded but not killed. Your coat got an ugly wound near the hip. . . . My preservation was entirely due, as was the glorious victory, to our God, to whom be all honor, praise and glory. . . . Whilst great credit is due to other parts of our gallant army, God made my brigade more influential than any other in repulsing the main attack. This is for your information only—say nothing about it.

Much stirred, Anna reread his lines. Tom *had* been in danger, then, his coat torn by a bullet, his horse injured, his finger hurt. Her thoughts shifted: her husband had had a great deal to do with the victory, and yet she was to "say nothing" of his role. How *could* she be silent? In the morning, however, she found that others had already learned something of his feats. The stage driver, dropping the day's mail, flashed a broad smile and addressed her in a loud voice: "Good morning, Mrs. Stonewall!"

Anna gave him a puzzled look, and her father and mother, standing beside her, were similarly mystified. A woman passenger, who had heard the driver's words, called out with a beaming air, "Ma'am, I'll have to tell my folks I saw Stonewall's wife."

"Stonewall?" Was it some kind of joke? Before Anna could ask a simple question, the stage had left. An hour later Harriet Irwin rode back and addressed them eagerly, her sentences tumbling together in her excitement: "Mother! Anna! The papers are just

in, and everybody—everybody's talking about Tom. During the
worst of the battle at Manassas our side was being whipped, but
he and his men held fast. General Barnard Bee of the South
Carolinians called to his men to look at Tom: *There he stands
like a stone wall. Rally behind the Virginians!* That carried the
day, and the South's gone wild over the tale."

Anna gaped; it would take her a long time to absorb this news.
Tom a hero, his name on everyone's lips, even though he now
had a new and strange nickname. It was the last kind of story
she would have expected to circulate about her reticent husband,
who showed so little of himself to the world . . . Harriet added,
"There's a lot of argument about what happened *after* the fighting.
Some of our officers were all for pushing on to Washington, but
General Johnston said we weren't ready."

The day lost some of its brightness for Anna. So the Confederates had not thrust forward, and the war would not be over.
For the rest of her life Anna would hear the matter argued from
time to time: might the conflict have been settled at that point?
Eventually she was to know, as she suspected today, that Tom
Jackson had been one of those who favored striking at the Union
capital. But now she did not worry for long. After all, she had a
great deal to be happy about.

Twenty-four hours later Tom wrote again, and Anna's hand
tightened as she read one of his lines. Among the many who had
died in the fighting was Willy Page . . . Willy, the son of her
good friend, and companion to the Preston boy. How often had
she seen the two youths together, and, only a few months earlier,
how earnestly had Mrs. Page's son told her of his future plans!
Anna's thoughts and her heart went to the motherly woman who
had made her way easier during her years in Lexington.

Trying not to cry, she wrote a long letter to the Page family.
When she finished it her eyes went to a newspaper beside her,
and halted at another name. General Bee, who had stood close
to Tom during that climactic moment at Manassas and had given
him the title of Stonewall, had died soon afterward of a bullet
wound. Anna put her hand to her face. The Lord gave, the Lord
took. There, but for the grace of God . . .

Through Maggie Preston, Anna learned of an incident which
provided Lexington with a subject of conversation for many
weeks. Soon after Manassas, Dr. White received a letter in Tom's

handwriting. He had picked it up at the post office, and when he saw it, the minister murmured to those who crowded about him, "Now we'll know all the facts." What he read was:

My dear pastor, in my tent last night, after a fatiguing day's service, I remembered that I had failed to send you my contribution for our colored Sunday school. Enclosed you will find my check for that object, which please acknowledge at your earliest convenience . . .

With a slow smile Anna told herself that to Tom those classes were no less important than the fighting in which he risked his life.

Nearly five months had passed since she had seen him. His wounded hand disturbed her. It did not seem to heal, and his reassurances did not satisfy her. A rumor reached North Carolina that made her frown: a doctor had urged that the broken finger be amputated, but Tom refused. And she heard tales of the example he had given his men at Manassas, where in the thick of battle he had held up his hand so that it would bleed the less, but had fought on, stirring the members of his brigade.

Now this band too had a name—the Stonewall Brigade. It consisted largely of Virginians from the Valley of Virginia or from the mountains on either side. They knew their region and knew it well, and Dr. Morrison talked repeatedly to Anna of their feats— quick raids, strikes that harassed the numerically stronger enemy. With each story she wondered more about the Brigade. What was it like, and what was Tom himself like in his new role?

More and more she yearned to see her husband. Several times in the late summer and early fall of 1861 she wrote him that a number of North Carolina officers had received leaves, among them Sue's husband, Alphonso Avery. Couldn't Tom get one too, and join her here at Cottage Home? With her first such letter he gave her a lesson in war and its demands:

My darling, I can't be absent from my command, as my attention is necessary in preparing my troops for hard fighting . . . and as my officers and soldiers are not permitted to go and see their wives and families, I ought not to see my *esposita,* as it might make the troops feel that they were badly treated . . .

Again, he joked:

Don't you wish your *esposo* would get sick, and have to get sick leave and go home, so that you couldn't envy Sister Sue? . . .

Still much remains undone that I desire to see effected. . . . Every officer and soldier who is able to do duty ought to be busily engaged . . .

Years later Anna was to comment proudly that "from the time he entered the army . . . he never asked or received a furlough, was never absent from duty for a single day, whether sick or well, and never slept one night outside the lines of his command." But now she frequently felt upset because he was not with her.

Others, she discovered, were complaining of Tom's firm policy in this respect. A well-meaning townsman relayed a disquieting report. About the time of Manassas, one of the brigade officers received a message that his wife lay seriously ill, and he asked for a furlough. Tom refused; the officer was compelled to remain at his post, and she went to her grave, leaving her husband bitter against his commander. But, Anna reasoned, if the officer had known Tom's character he might have understood and forgiven.

As she wrote to him, Anna puzzled over the subject of Tom's sister. Confederate fortunes had gone badly in the vicinity of Beverly, Laura's home, where the Union General McClellan wrested away a large area of Western Virginia. Beverly itself lay in Northern hands, and Anna had received no answer to her last two letters to Laura. Had they even arrived? Then one day, as she talked to a passing acquaintance from the western section, Mrs. Arnold's name came up in the conversation. "I saw her a little while ago," the woman began, and hesitated. "She—she hasn't been in touch with you?"

"Why, no. What did you start to say?"

"Well . . . there isn't any doubt among my friends that Mrs. Arnold's supporting the North. It's an odd thing for Stonewall's sister."

Anna nodded slowly. Knowing Laura's convictions on slavery and the Union, she was not too surprised. Should she feel angry or hurt? she asked herself. She thought of her sister-in-law's innate goodness, her earnest sympathies, and she could not find it in her heart to condemn her. Yet there were many in Virginia and North Carolina who would feel no such mercy. For hours Anna sat thinking unhappily of this new situation: the war's harshnesses had come closer than ever; like so many others, the Jackson household was divided by conscience.

Anna's longing to be with her husband grew stronger every day. Why couldn't she go to him? No matter how much difficulty the

trip might involve, or how uncomfortable the camp, she wanted
to be there, if only for a few days . . . a matter of hours. She
wrote him this several times. Once Tom indicated that she might
make the trip and stay with a family near camp, but unexpected
orders took him away immediately after he had written.

Still she persisted, and now her eyes widened at his newest
message. The discomforts and annoyances of wartime travel were
far greater than she realized; still, "Should there be a good escort
coming on and returning, little one can come. . . . I know not
one day what will take place the next, but I do know that I am
your doting *esposo*." It was hardly a note of emphatic encouragement; nevertheless Anna went immediately to work to make arrangements before he could change his mind.

She spoke to a family friend who was planning to go to Virginia
to seek a military appointment there, and they settled details so
that within a few days they were ready to start out together. The
train clattered; it moved by jerks and starts, stopped for hours at
a time. Their nerves were frayed when, after agonizing delays,
they arrived in Richmond. There, to their chagrin, her friend
discovered that, lacking a passport, he could not ride on to
Manassas with her.

On Saturday morning Anna stood alone, staring in dismay at
the wretchedly dirty railroad station. She had not expected this
grimness, the piles of rubbish, the smells of garbage and urine.
Men belched and gawked, a heavily painted woman rolled her
hips as she passed a circle of soldiers, and a pair of drunkards
tripped over Anna's skirt. When she pulled back one grinned:
"Ma'am, you sure smells good." Alarmed, she fought an impulse
to return home.

But she had come so far, and she was so near to Tom . . . Her
shoulders tightened; she would get to him if she had to crawl.
At the telegraph office she sent him a message, and then she
pushed into a railroad coach and hunted for a seat. She saw only
one other woman, a frowsy individual carrying a bottle of whisky
in a paper bag. All around them men sprawled, snoring or
bickering.

As Anna grew more and more alarmed, a uniformed figure went
by. He seemed familiar. "Captain White?" The man turned, and
to her relief it was a friend from Charlotte. "I have a brother in
a hospital near Manassas," he told her, "and I'll be happy to get
you to the right place over there." When they had arrived he

stepped off the train with her, and they made one inquiry after another without success.

"No word about a Miz Jackson." "Ain' no place at all to stay in this yere spot." As Anna's anxiety rose her friend suggested that they ride on to the next stop, Fairfax Station. There were no messages there either, and the settlement appeared even more crowded than Manassas, and more squalid. The only place to wait appeared to be the railroad cars, which were remaining on a siding until morning. In one of them they came upon a plain-faced woman who welcomed Anna: "Sure, miss, we'll keep each other company."

The Captain locked the doors to keep out the soldiers who were gaping at Anna, and she and her woman companion suffered through a long, wearing night. By midmorning the Captain would have to leave on his own errand; before then he went with her to the Fairfax hospital, where they had at least partial success. "There's a small room that they can let you have for a few hours," he told Anna. She thanked him profoundly and sank into a chair in the room. A wave of nervous apprehension spread within her. What would she do if Tom had not received her messages?

If Anna had hopes of a Sunday morning rest, they soon vanished. The door had no lock; soldiers pushed it open repeatedly and peered in. When she went to the window and looked out, a group of soldiers was sawing wood, and after a moment she realized they were making coffins. Close to hysteria, she turned away.

Then slowly, with an effort, she brought herself under control. She could not stay here with her face to the wall. Going to the window again, she saw groups of men, pale and bandaged, sitting in the sun or hobbling on crutches across the green. Her eyes softened. After all, the roaring drunken ones made up only part of the army, and there were many others, brave, gentle-speaking. Before her lay the victims of gunfire and cannon blast, youths and old men who had fought under their new banners.

Two hours passed, and a third. Before long Anna would have to surrender the room, and what could she do then? Her anxiety increased almost to fever pitch. Then she heard the creak of a horse-drawn ambulance, and gazed down into the yard. A tall figure stepped out, and she almost cried aloud to him across the clearing. After so many months, her husband . . . She studied his face, his figure, his manner. He looked well, far better than she had anticipated; he was much tanned, his hair was long, and he had a red-brown beard.

It seemed an hour before Tom ascended the stairs. Finding her waiting eagerly in the hallway, he started to speak, then seized her in his arms, drew her into the room, and shut the door. For a long minute they held together in silence; he kissed her several times and stroked her hair. Then he released her and stared hungrily, happily. "My darling, I got to Manassas just after the train left . . . Oh, Anna!"

She had a dozen questions to ask about him and his work, but Tom, it developed, had other plans, and he took her arm. "They're having Sunday service for my brigade—the Stonewall Brigade," he explained shyly, "and we can get back just in time." On the way she received a few of the answers she wished, and she was still making inquiries when they rolled up before a gray farmhouse. The scene which followed would be cut deep into her mind.

The simple farm building in which she was to live stood at the side of a gently rising hill, a green expanse with irregular lines of trees. The yellow-red fall leaves lay scattered in small circles, and here and there in the distance Anna saw the tops of numberless tents. On the shaded porch a dark-clad churchman awaited her, and soldiers, some on benches, others standing, covered nearly every foot of space in the yard and far beyond.

"Anna, Mrs. Utterbach." A friendly woman bowed to her, and to Anna's embarrassment Tom brought forth one person after another. She felt dusty, her face was smudged, and her eyes smarted; nonetheless she must go through with the presentations.

"Sandie Pendleton!" She spotted the face of the brilliant young man, now on Tom's staff, and a moment later she spied his father, who seemed to fit his military dress to a rare perfection. Now she gave a start: "Major—I mean Colonel Preston . . ." Her eyes sparkled at the sight of her old friends, and they were talking of Lexington when Tom whispered, "Now, Anna, we'll start the services."

The minister stepped into the yellow sunlight and lifted his hands, and Anna saw hundreds of heads bowed in prayer. "Friends, today we join our hearts, our hopes . . ." As the penetrating voice soared above the assembly, Anna watched Tom's profile against the light. Then her gaze shifted to the faces on all sides. These were her husband's men, his followers. Suddenly she remembered Laura's question of the previous summer. No, nobody was calling him Fool Tom now.

Later they rested together in a quiet upstairs room, curtains drawn against the sunlight. "Please," he asked her, "nothing about the war today. Let's turn away from that subject for a while."

In the peace of the little chamber, with its cleanly scrubbed wooden floors and its plastered walls, they closed their thoughts to the world. Tom murmured in Spanish, his lips against her cheeks as she whispered her replies. "How long can I be here?" she eventually asked, and lifted herself on her elbow to study his face.

"If I had my way," he smiled dreamily, "it would be a year, two years, the rest of our lives. But it has to be a month or so at the most, I'm afraid. By then the army will be leaving here." A few weeks, perhaps less . . . Nothing must spoil it for them.

In early morning she heard a muted bugle call and looked over happily as Tom rose. With a firm gesture he drew her up after him: "Don't be long, my darling; the staff is used to early breakfast. Oh, yes, you're going to have most of your meals with us." At his words she protested, but he smilingly pushed her into preparations, and soon she took her place, somewhat apprehensively, at a long and crowded mess table improvised under the trees.

The officers got up stiffly, and Tom mumbled a few words of introduction. Anna could see that, no matter what experience her husband had, he would never develop ease of manner in the formalities of life. A dark face bent over hers; it was Jim Lewis, Tom's Negro attendant. "Yes, ma'am, all ready for you," Jim greeted her ceremoniously. "Bes' food in the whole army." •

This observation brought forth a series of loud groans. "That still don't make it much." "Wish the Yankees had it right now." As she studied the plate Jim had set before her, Anna became aware that most of the officers were inspecting her, comparing her with their wives or other women they knew. So this was the woman Stonewall had picked. And were they asking—why? If only she were taller, grander . . . And perhaps she should have worn her best green silk instead of the untrimmed gray.

Sandie Pendleton sat near her, and he spoke suddenly: "Ma'am, you're looking mighty nice today."

"Thank you." Flushing happily, Anna told herself that the rather naïve compliment was precisely what she needed to restore her confidence; for this she would long thank the twenty-one-year-old officer. After her rest the previous night her skin had a good color, and in the mirror a few minutes earlier her eyes had had the look of—what? she asked. A woman deeply in love, who had at last been able to rejoin her man.

Sandie's voice reached her again through her musing: "And we're all thankful to you, Mrs. Jackson, for these eggs." He grinned. "If you weren't here, I don't know *what* we'd be having." The remark produced guffaws and broke the reserve; before long everyone was talking, and it became possible for Anna to connect names and faces. She missed Colonel Preston and Dr. Pendleton, absent on other duties, but opposite her sat a man whom she recognized—the small, dark-bearded Turner Ashby, the cavalry raider with a brooding, almost Arabic appearance. She recalled that Ashby had been a quiet lawyer until the war started, without military training; then almost overnight he had emerged as a warrior who thundered out of the night, leaving terror behind him.

Quickly Anna placed another figure—Jeb Stuart, an obvious gallant, flushed with merriment, flamboyantly dressed. He had a yellow sash, his hat sported a black feather, his cape was lined in red satin. Studying the striking face, Anna assured herself that, despite his gaudy raiment, he was not foppish. On the contrary, there was something strongly masculine about the officer. Obviously Stuart liked war. Hadn't Harvey Hill said the same thing about Tom? Yet Anna sensed a difference. Tom's make-up was basically more earnest; in the essentials, despite all that had happened to him in such a short time, her husband had changed very little.

On his plate were plain bread and two lemons. As he squeezed one, Jeb Stuart grinned and a moment later pointedly passed Tom a bowl of heavy gravy. "It's something you've got to try, General." With a grave air Tom declined, and several of the officers chuckled.

The badinage had a friendly, affectionate quality, and by the time breakfast ended, Anna could see signs of her husband's new standing in the deference his aides gave him, the concern with which they watched him. Yet he wore his old military garb from the Institute, and though it was newly pressed for her visit, it had none of the spit-and-polish style she noticed in many of the others. And Tom lacked the cocky air some of the men affected.

"Well, you've been asking a lot about Manassas." He turned to

her. "Let's look it over." Before Anna could decide whether or not
she really wanted to inspect the battlegrounds, he was leading
her to the ambulance. Near it she saw Dr. Pendleton, and was
happy to learn that her old friend was going to accompany them.
For the next hour they rode, halted, and rode again over an irregular, partly wooded ground. "This is Bull Run itself," Sandie's
father pointed to a meager, unimpressive stream. She could not
hide her disappointment. So this was the place that would be
remembered in the history books.

"And here's the Widow Henry's house, where the sick old
woman refused to leave." As Dr. Pendleton indicated the spot, the
area suddenly came alive for Anna. "You know this became a point
of raging battle, and a shell killed her." Anna peered through the
sunlight at the remains of a house. A moment later the minister-
soldier nodded: "And there's where the General and the Brigade
took their stand." Anna looked with eager interest; would she ever
hear the story without thrilling to it?

When the road turned, the wind brought a faint, sweetish
stench. A few feet away, half-covered with brown earth, lay the
skeletons of several horses, hide and flesh clinging to them. A vul-
ture circled lazily in the distance, and she saw a slight mound
from which one or two human bones protruded. She recalled that
hundreds of men had been shoveled into hasty graves or trenches
all around this area. She shivered; this was the terrain in which
thousands had rushed and slashed and fired, murder in their
hearts. Now there was only the silence of a great tomb.

A young officer approached and, after a few preliminaries, observed casually, "I just rode a few miles out of camp, and do you
know I could spy the dome of the Capitol in Washington?" This
information, intended to amuse them, left Tom noncommittal. But
Anna winced. It was not good to be reminded how close the two
forces lay to each other.

"I believe Mrs. Jackson has seen enough." To her relief, Dr.
Pendleton closed the inspection. Back at the house, after some
hesitation, she told Tom what she had heard of Laura's attitude
toward the war. He shook his head with feeling: "Why can't she
realize that we're acting in self-defense, protecting our homes, as
God intends men to do?" Slowly his face softened, and Anna read
the warm love that she found there whenever he thought of his
sister.

"But I suppose she has reasons for thinking as she does, just as we have." He let out a slow breath. "Anyway, whatever Laura believes, she believes with all her heart and soul."

"Tom," Anna assured him, "after all this—this ends, you and Laura will meet again, and there'll be nothing to stand between you. You'll see."

He nodded: "I hope so, *esposita*, even though it may be a long time. All that section has stayed in Union hands, you understand." As he spoke, she wondered how many months or years would have to pass before Tom could see the woman who had meant so much in his life. She put out her hand and touched his: "I'm sorry it's worked out this way."

Tom lifted her fingers and kissed them gently: "There must be some purpose in it, Anna, some reason . . ." Together they went to the window, and as they gazed out at the fields beyond the house she tried to lighten his mood: "The victory here was a mighty fine thing for us, wasn't it?"

He gave her a steady look: "It may have been the worst thing that's happened. A defeat might have helped us more." When her eyes widened at his vehement statement, he explained, "The South went crazy with pride after Manassas; our success made most people think we'd already won, or all but won. Thousands of men left the ranks, and volunteers dropped off. At the same time the battle shocked and mortified the North, stirred it up to fight harder than ever before. And don't believe the orators who tell you those people can't fight!"

Anna thought of all the friends and acquaintances who would consider such talk unpatriotic, even dangerous. Tom had more to say: "We're not taking this war seriously enough, most of us. We wear bright badges and scream against 'Yankees,' but we don't like to drill and march. A lot of our people believe a gentleman doesn't take orders; because they've been used to commanding, they don't want anyone to command them. Did you hear about the young fool who challenged a sentry to a duel because the man halted him in an 'insulting manner'?" Tom's cheeks puffed in anger: "Well, if they serve under me they'll drill—and take orders and work!"

To her still further surprise, he exclaimed again, "A lot of the trouble goes right to one place, Richmond. Everything's slowed up there, everything's late and defensive, always defensive. If Mr. Davis would let us concentrate our man power for real strikes, pounding blows—a true invasion of the North, with every ounce of our resources, Anna! But he and his friends don't give the signal, and so we sit and wait while the enemy builds and builds against us."

His face settled into lines of discouragement, and for the first time Anna realized her husband's strong feelings about Jefferson Davis, the high-strung, inflexible Mississippian who was President of the Confederacy. A former army man himself, Mr. Davis ran his War Department with a firm hand, and others, she gathered, differed with his policies.

She had to change Tom's depressed spirits. Taking his hands in hers, Anna spoke softly. "Can't we sit in the orchard over there?" she asked. At the side of the farmhouse, with the blooming bushes around them and the murmurings of hidden birds in the trees, Tom and Anna enjoyed their first such peaceful hour in many months. For a time they remained there in a happy silence. Then she faced him.

"Tom, when the war ends, what will you want to do?"

"Go right back to teaching," he answered instantly, almost defensively.

After a moment's pause Anna asked, "Wouldn't you prefer to do something else—stay in the military or go into another work?"

"I don't think so, my dear. Anyway, we'll see how the matter develops."

"Yes," she agreed, "we'll have the happiest times we've ever known." On this September day at Manassas, she had no doubt whatever of the prediction.

The days rolled on more swiftly than she would have believed possible. Although Tom had a heavy schedule—inspections, conferences, reports, map studies—he managed to give several hours a day to her. They were largely unclouded hours, and both kept away from topics that might have been disturbing. Nevertheless, as she lay beside Tom late at night or as she sat alone in the early afternoon, her thoughts reverted to the shadow in the distance. Before long the war would break upon them again . . .

One afternoon soon after her arrival, Anna caught sight of the urbane figure for which she had been searching ever since she came here, John T. L. Preston. With a bright look Colonel Preston joined her on the porch, and sighed happily, "Anna, it's fine to see you anywhere, but especially here. And isn't it wonderful that

Tom's done as well as he has?" In her friend's face she saw only good will and delight in Tom's rise.

"Oh, yes, Maggie's in a good mood," Colonel Preston answered her question, and his eyes became more serious. "At least as good a mood as any of us can be in such times."

Should she ask about the Junkin household, or was that too delicate a topic? She decided to speak the question that was on her mind.

Colonel Preston hesitated before he replied, "Yes, we hear from the family in Pennsylvania, and by a long process. Maggie and her sister up there get a letter through the lines every now and then. They're well, but that's about all we know. Except that Dr. Junkin's offered to help the Union officials in any kind of work they want him to do. And both of his sons up there have volunteered."

John Preston's mood seemed to darken, and after a word or two more he excused himself. "Good day, Mrs. Stonewall," he called to Anna with an attempt at lightness, and she colored, but not with displeasure. Of late, she had become used to the name and —why not admit it?—a bit proud. It was a tribute to her husband and his deeds, and if she shared a little in the honor, why not? A moment later she cautioned herself. She must remember that this was a reflected glory, and not her own!

Colonel Preston's conversation with her was still on Anna's mind when Tom came back a few hours later. He talked appreciatively of their friend: "I'm lucky to have him here. He knows so much more of the world than I do, and he does a lot of confidential work for me, connections with Richmond officials, politicians and people like that—and other dealings that take special skill." This was another surprise; apparently there was more to being a general than she realized.

Before Anna could ask more, Tom added, "I've been able to help him and Maggie a little by getting a few messages across the lines to Philadelphia. Not military word, but about their personal affairs." He had said enough to let her understand that his own secret agents had a part in such operations. It was satisfying to know that her husband assisted the Prestons in maintaining that thin line of contact with the other side of the war . . .

On their way to supper that night, Anna thought she detected something familiar about an officer walking ahead of her. Not quite sure, she studied the husky, bearded young man until he turned; it *was* Frank Paxton. Her eyes darted to Tom's, and she wondered if she should speak to Paxton. Though in the same camp, he and Tom might still not have ended their disagreement. As she hesitated, the young officer smiled, and she gazed up in a new uncertainty.

Frank Paxton quickened his pace, and when he had reached them offered a brisk salute and smiled a broader smile. Anna stood silent and then Tom cocked his head: "Frank, I think that new beard's fooled Mrs. Jackson completely!" Anna bowed hastily, and after a moment the awkwardness passed. She felt a sudden release, a warming relief. For nearly ten minutes they chatted on, and at the end Tom observed quietly to her, "Frank's one of my aides; I suppose you hadn't heard that, had you?"

He gave her a direct look: "He's here because I asked for him. He made a fine showing at Manassas, and I told the army I wanted him with me."

One of his own aides . . . For Tom Jackson those bitter days just before the war were entirely in the past, wiped carefully from the slate.

A day later, sitting in her room, she glanced up as a young soldier knocked: "Ma'am, the General wants to know can you come downstairs?" Surprised, she followed him to find her husband standing beside a horse. He turned to her with an almost exultant air:

"Well, what do you think of him?"

"Him? Who do you mean?"

"My mount, Sorrel, though we call him Fancy, too." Anna's incomprehension made Tom frown.

She gave her full attention to a small, drab animal which she might otherwise not have noticed, and smiled, "He's anything but 'fancy,' isn't he?"

Not entirely pleased, Tom shrugged: "I picked him first for you, when I believed the war might be over in a hurry. He'd be fine for a lady, wouldn't he? But now I've gotten attached to him." Anna inspected the sorrel with greater interest and decided that there was more to him than first appeared. He had compact, rounded lines and great soft eyes. The moment he reached forward and nudged at her arm and shoulder, she was won to the little creature.

"The endurance of a giant," Tom boasted, "and he knows the

secret of rest. Halt!" At the command the horse sank down and rolled over like a dog. "Sorrel does that every time we stop for a while."

They looked up to see an officer riding toward them with two aides, and Anna needed no long camp experience to understand that this was an important caller. "Oh, Anna, I forgot to tell you— somebody's on his way to meet you. General Johnston."

Her husband's superior, one of the South's major figures of the war . . . Once again Tom had neglected to inform her when she should have been notified long in advance. Hastily Anna patted her hair, wet her lips, and walked forward in embarrassment.

Before her stood a small, slim man with what Anna's mother would have called a "good head," round, well molded, the graying beard precisely in place. Everything about the erect Joseph E. Johnston seemed perfectly in place, composed; between him and Tom Jackson she recognized a profound contrast. All at once Anna felt herself disheveled, unprepared.

"Mrs. Jackson, no visitor was ever more welcome." The General addressed her in almost courtly style, his small eyes missing little. Leading their guests inside, Anna talked as brightly as she could. Tom, with his usual circumspection, had said only the friendliest things about Joe Johnston, who had recognized his merits on many occasions. Nonetheless, Anna was more certain than ever that her husband did not agree with much of Johnston's basic strategy.

The General was speaking: "And, madame, how do you home people think matters are going for us?" At the unexpected question Anna paused, then spoke her mind: "Well enough, General, but if the others are like me, they'd like to see a lot more men in our ranks."

Her remark had scored. General Johnston beamed: "Madame, I hope you have a chance some day to say that to—to certain people in Richmond."

Anna decided that even though her comment had been welcomed, she had said enough, and it was with relief that she heard Tom change the subject:

"There's to be a review of the General's command this afternoon, and he'd like you to be in the stand."

She hesitated, but Joe Johnston pressed her, and within the hour she took a place beside him and his aides along the crest of the nearby hill. Drums beat, officers shouted orders, and before them passed a long procession of men on foot, men on horseback, heavy guns, light equipment. As the sun glinted on the bayonets and the ground shook under the pounding feet of the marchers, Anna was seized by an emotion close to exaltation.

With such soldiers and leaders, and so much determination, how could their side lose? Then around a turn came the new Confederate banner, flying in the air, and a military band that beat out the swift, stirring notes of the South's official song, "Dixie." A high yell broke forth, a series of shouts and soaring cries, and the review ended.

Dusk had fallen, and for a last few minutes Anna paused with Tom at the top of the hill, looking down at the camp of the Stonewall Brigade, its tents luminous in the blue evening, the campfires beginning to glow among the trees. Later she would realize that at this hour she had viewed her world through a light in which all things were good. Forgotten were the snarlings, the squalor of her recent trip, and the grumbled complaints she heard on the way. Tonight she was happy, and so was Tom, and the future awaited them.

In their room he faced her: "What was that song they played just now?"

For a moment Anna thought he was joking, until she recalled how hard Tom found it to remember a tune. As she explained he nodded: "Sing it to me, so I'll recognize it the next time." She began slowly, *"Oh, I wish I was in the land . . ."*

Tom moved his head up and down with each line and smiled when Anna finished: "Again, please."

Once more she sang it for him, and as she reached the close he told her, "Now again." After that he called for a fourth rendition. Anna, out of breath, started to laugh, and he joined her. They collapsed together on the sofa, roaring aloud until she quieted him: "Tom, the people downstairs will think——"

With a warm kiss he closed off her complaint, and neither of them bothered what the people downstairs thought about them or about anything else.

Could Anna have enjoyed that day as much as she did, had she known it would be their last for months? While they were dressing the next morning a courier rode up. Tom went off to talk to him, and when he rejoined Anna his expression was serious. "I'm afraid we're going to move camp, and you have to go, *esposita*."

"How much longer do we have—until the end of the week?" He gave her a sorrowful stare: "Anna, it's today. Now."

"No, I don't believe it. I've been here less than two weeks." When he shook his head, she cried, then quickly realized that tears were useless, and rubbed her eyes with her handkerchief. "Very well, I'll be ready the minute you say." Tom went off to check at his headquarters, and returned just as Anna finished packing, to be with her for the last few minutes, while Sandie Pendleton waited outside. "He'll help you start back home," her husband told her, and his look was graver than before.

"Tom, you'll be careful, more careful than ever?" Though it sounded foolish, she had to say it. He nodded, and at that moment Sandie knocked with a new dispatch. A last word or two, an embrace, and Tom all but ran from the farmhouse.

When she went down the steps, her feet lagging, the yard before the house was crowded no longer, but bare and deserted. The last military aide had gone, the horses and wagons had disappeared, and the September wind whipped past her, blowing wisps of hair in her face. It was the sad closing of a joyous visit, and she shivered to herself.

Then, however, Anna's head lifted. Now, perhaps, she could hope again for the child that had been denied them. Firmly she clung to the possibility. Surely it would happen, surely their long yearning would be fulfilled.

"I'm ready, Sandie," she told the young soldier, and smiled as he helped her forward.

CHAPTER 13

September, October, November of 1861 . . . For Anna Jackson these were months of slow waiting, of marking time in North Carolina, of fruitless questioning. But to one of her questions she received an answer soon after her return from Virginia. There would be no child. With that realization came a sudden return of all the doubts she thought she had succeeded in putting from her.

As Anna sat in the dining room at Cottage Home, her eyes moved around the crowded table—sisters, brothers, relatives close, and relatives distant. At one side of the room Mary Morrison had set up a small table for the youngest children, and their high-pitched voices punctuated the hum of adult conversation.

One of Anna's nieces, finishing her pudding, slipped from her seat to stand beside her aunt. She reached out her soft hand tentatively; Anna smiled, took it, and held it for a moment. Then, whirling around, the piquant little brunette darted out of the room, and several of the others, excused by their parents, started after her.

So many of them, of so many ages . . . Anna's gaze followed her favorite, the black-eyed niece, and her look clouded. Almost any child with button eyes and a certain elfin air made her think of her own Mary. Forcing herself to attention again, she joined the easy conversation around her, but she found it impossible to change the direction of her thoughts. She was the only one here without children.

She had reached thirty-one and Tom thirty-seven. Were they to have only the memory of the baby who had been with them for a month? After a time she could make no sense of what was being said, and, rising, she slipped out to go to her room. She was sitting there when her mother rapped and entered. "Child, I was watching you just now," Mrs. Morrison began without preamble. "You're still thinking of little Mary, aren't you?"

Anna nodded. Then, although she realized she would regret her remark, she was compelled to add, "You just can't understand how I feel about this, Mother. You had twelve."

After a pause Mary Morrison replied, "Yes, I've had a lot of children, but don't forget, two of them died, both little girls. And with each death I thought that I'd never recover from the blow. One of them seemed dearest of all, if only because she was so tiny, so helpless. When they closed her grave I was sure they'd buried my heart."

Sighing, Mrs. Morrison took Anna's hand: "Well, I survived, and then the next one came. No, I guess I've never quite gotten over those deaths. Still, I've had other gifts from God to make it up to me, and I think you will too. Try to believe that, child."

Anna sat silently. Her mother was saying things about her own feelings that she had never before hinted. Anna's eyes filled, and she turned. "I'm sorry," she whispered, "and ashamed of myself."

"No, don't be ashamed—be hopeful. Please remember, Anna, there's always room for hope. Just . . . Just don't shut it out." Anna repeated the words, nodding. Her mother had given her a new comfort, a reassurance, and in the months that followed she held it close to her.

The early winter passed slowly. Where was Tom now, and how was he faring? A month and a half after her arrival at Cottage Home she received her first reassurance in the form of news that stirred her.

As a reward for his accomplishments, Tom had received another promotion, to major general, and now he was in charge of the new military district of the northern Virginia frontier, between the Blue Ridge and the Alleghenies. Anna's heart quickened. This was the Valley of Virginia, the region Tom had come to know and love above all others. The assignment was just the sort for which he had hoped. He warned her he would not be "altogether independent," since General Johnston would remain in over-all command. Nevertheless she replied happily to his letter, so happily that her remarks drew a quiet comment from him:

I trust that my darling little wife feels more gratitude to our kind Heavenly Father than pride or elation at my promotion. Continue to pray for me, that I may live to glorify God more and more, by serving Him and our country.

When she read this, Anna lowered her head; as usual Tom had proved far more devout than she, and she deserved the gentle reprimand. But he still could not prevent her from feeling delight at his advancement! And callers at Cottage Home told her how the Valley people themselves regarded Tom's appointment: "It's the best news they've had in a long time." "Stonewall understands that country better than anybody we have." "Now Richmond won't get *all* the attention." But one visitor made a casual observation that stunned her for a moment: "Too bad, though, isn't it," he asked, "about the Stonewall Brigade? The General having to leave it behind, I mean. I'm wondering how he'll do without it, or it without him."

So the almost legendary band with which Tom had fought thus far was to stay behind. Before long Tom verified this disquieting news, and a friend sent Anna a Richmond clipping describing her husband's farewell to the Brigade. The men had lined up before him as he sat Little Sorrel. They had followed him for months, Stonewall told them; he had never found them wanting. His old followers, these men of the mountains and valleys, listened with tears while they stood at attention in the Virginia dusk, the wind

lifting the edges of their frayed banners. Jackson himself had
shown signs of growing emotion, and finally he lifted himself in
his stirrups, tossed aside the reins and threw up his arm:

"In the army of the Shenandoah you were the First Brigade;
in the army of the Potomac you were the First Brigade; in the
second corps of this army you are the First Brigade; you are the
First Brigade in the affections of your General; and I hope by
your future deeds and bearing you will be handed down to pos-
terity as the First Brigade in our second War of Independence!
Farewell . . ."

With that he sat back on his horse, his mouth working, his eyes
gleaming, and catching up the reins, he rode away to the ear-
piercing "rebel yell." This last tribute brought the General closer
than ever to tears. He slowed his mount, he pulled off his cap,
waved it several times, and pounded off, the men's cries following
him for a long time . . . Anna put the story aside. How much these
men loved him, and how he would miss them.

Now, he wrote her, "I shall have great labor to perform. . . .
Colonel Preston and Sandie Pendleton go with me." He headed
toward Winchester, the Valley town through which he and Anna
had passed on several trips. For days she thought happily of his
prospects, until one of her father's contemporaries remarked, "I
was glad to hear about General Jackson's appointment, even
though he's going to have a lot of trouble."

"What kind of trouble?" At her sharp question their guest hesitated, as if sorry he had introduced the subject. "Well, Miss Anna,
they've made him major general without a division behind him.
He hasn't been given the men he ought to have—only a handful,
and military conditions are mighty risky around there anyway.
The Union's dug in right near Winchester, and by spring it can
pound down with some real power, maybe knock all our forces out
of the Valley."

However regretfully the comment had been made, its implications were clear, and provided Anna with something new and
frightening to contemplate. A few minutes later their caller un-
wittingly added to her burdens, for she overheard a snatch of the
older man's conversation as he mounted his horse to leave: "Dr.
Morrison, there's a feeling in certain Richmond circles that, while
the General's had some real successes, he isn't quite—prepared for
a bigger place. Some think he's a bit erratic, undependable.
They're wrong, I'm sure, but you keep hearing . . ."

That was enough, and Anna turned angrily away. But the sentences rang in her mind, and she could not sleep that night. Had Tom been given a post beyond his ability—or one doomed in advance to failure? From then on she read his letters with an uncertainty that would not leave her. Her husband let her know that he was working strenuously to build up his inadequate man power, that he was appealing for additional forces, hunting men and officers wherever he could find them.

Scores of applications were arriving, Anna saw with pleasure, and Tom told her of some of his requirements: was the man intelligent; was he faithful, industrious; did he get up early in the morning? Reading the final question, she smiled. How like Tom that was. Would he have accepted Napoleon himself if he knew him to be a late-sleeper? She doubted it.

Anna did not smile as October and November brought darkening developments for an area and a man who meant a great deal to her husband. Several times Tom had referred to the assignment of General Robert E. Lee to the extreme western area of Virginia. "It's a place we've got to hold, Anna; if it goes we'll suffer a hard blow." As for Lee, Tom had spoken with strong conviction: "He's the best soldier I know on either side."

Now, however, reports arrived of troubles in Lee's area, rivalries among Confederate subordinates, conflicting jurisdictions, and firm Union sentiment among the people, who had scant sympathy for slavery or Eastern Virginia traditions. With her mother and father Anna frowned over Confederate military disasters, repulses, withdrawals. "That whole line of villages is gone . . ." "Things are looking dark."

Each loss in Western Virginia brought more resentful words about Robert Lee. "Ninny Lee . . . as much fight in that one as our nursemaid." " 'Ol' Evacuatin' Lee—all he *kin* do!" Finally, Lee was recalled to Richmond, and that chapter of the hostilities had ended. Alone in her room with the papers before her, Anna looked desperately at the carpet. Might this some day be Tom's fate—an impossible assignment, and with it a lost reputation, a career in eclipse?

As she stood there, she thought of one of his letters over which she still worried. The chill weather had "made me feel doubtful of my capacity, humanly speaking, to endure the campaign, should we remain longer in tents." Since the war's beginning Tom had never spoken in such strong terms of his health. And surely,

general or no general, he would have to spend some of the cold
weeks ahead in a tent. Anna read on: "But God, *our God*, does
and will do all things well; and if it is His pleasure that I should
remain . . . He will give me the ability." Though she believed as
Tom did, her apprehension would not leave her.

In this mood Anna received other news which only deepened
her sadness. Their old Amy, whose care Maggie Preston had su-
pervised since Anna had left, had died. Tom wrote his wife "the
tears came to my eyes more than once" when he read their friend's
letter telling of Amy's passing. And Anna's own eyes dimmed.
"The sainted Amy," he had called her, and Anna remembered one
of the things he had said a short time back: the Negro woman
had been "ripening for heaven."

Tom had written Maggie to make certain that payment was
provided for the funeral, and he was gratified that so many of
Lexington's whites and Negroes had followed Amy's body to the
grave. He arranged for care for the retarded little Emma, and
meanwhile he continued to correspond with the Lexington man
who had charge of Hetty's boys, George and Cy. Among other
things, the man must make sure that the youths attended church
and also Tom's old Sabbath school classes.

And later Anna smiled fondly when a friend told about a Lexington youngster whom Tom had met in a tense moment during
an enforced march. Her husband had greeted the boy and asked
a question: did he know that their old Sunday school classes were
still going well? Then, with a brisk nod, Tom Jackson had returned
to the war!

For three months Anna had been asking Tom when they would
meet again. As before, he had hesitated. With winter upon them,
there might be a certain military lull; on the other hand, his duties
had grown heavier than ever, and he could not be sure how much
time he could take from his work . . . Then he told her that if
he remained in Winchester for the winter he hoped to be able
to send one of his aides for her, so that he could have her at his
side for the season. But his next message made her spirit sink:
he still did not know whether he would stay in Winchester.

Her yearning increased when Tom described his headquarters,
a six-room cottage "papered with elegant gilt paper." "If I only
had my little woman here, the room would be set off." If she came,
he was sure she would like Winchester a great deal, as he did, and
also that she would like the people, who were especially kind to

him. Two houses from his quarters lived Reverend James Graham,
the Presbyterian minister, with his wife and family, and Tom
knew she would be much at home with them. (Despite the name,
the Grahams were not family connections, Anna learned.) Then
her eyes widened: he "hoped to send for her" as soon as he could
make arrangements.

She did not wait for the arrangements; she would give him no
chance to change his mind. Members of a neighboring family
planned to go to Richmond, and she went to them a few minutes
after she received Tom's letter, to ask if she could accompany
them. By the time they packed, she had finished her own preparations and had sent a messenger to Charlotte to dispatch a telegram
to Tom. In her trunk she piled several silver-framed pictures that
had been Tom's favorites, her best brushes and combs and his as
well, and a number of other personal treasures. She was going to
make this stay as homelike as she could—and she was also going
to stretch it every possible day!

On the long December train trip she listened absently to her
friends' talk. In return for their kindness she owed them good
cheer at the least, but try as she might, she could not concentrate
on what they said. All her thoughts were of Tom and the situation
in which he found himself. Then she heard her husband's name
from the seat behind her.

"I hear grumblin' about that Stonewall fellow."

"Yeah, they say he's hard on the soldiers—makin' 'em walk the
chalk line, drillin' them like a fiend, slammin' the book at 'em for
breakin' rules, even makin' 'em git passes to go to town. They gotta
haul tail, or else."

A low chuckle reached Anna's reddening ears: "Still that's not
the way to be popular in this war."

"Sure ain't. You know, some people ain't so sure, anyhow, about
Stonewall. They claim he's mighty wild and undependable. Don't
have the judgment a general ought to have—askin' impossible
things, and pullin' odd behavior. You ever hear how he likes to
stand up to 'digest' his food, and the way he puts cold towels on
his stomach, and the crazy things he eats . . ."

Anna left her seat. The stories about Tom's personal habits an-
gered her beyond words. If only people understood how he had
to struggle against his sicknesses! Then she repeated the complaints against his drilling of the men. Didn't these Southerners

want to win the war? During the rest of the almost endless journey, she could not banish her concern.

Reaching a chill, dreary Richmond, she told her friends good-
by: "I'll be fine, and you mustn't worry . . ." The Confederate
capital appeared even more crowded and dusty than it had the
last time. She planned to stay for two days, buying new clothes
for the first time in months. After thinking over her last experiences on the grim trip to Manassas, she decided to make definite
arrangements for an escort for the last part of her journey.

Her first visit to a store showed her that she would have to cur-
tail her purchases. "Yes, ma'am, prices *are* fierce," the sallow clerk
agreed. "It's this blockade, and the way the war's interfering with
everything. I don't know what isn't scarce and getting scarcer."
Simpler dresses, fewer bonnets than she had expected to buy . . .
She would make do with less.

On her second night in Richmond a woman knocked at the
door of her hotel room: "Mrs. Jackson? The minute I heard you
were here, I rode right over." The lady had a gushing yet determined quality. "May I come in? You don't know me, but I'm
one of your cousins, originally from Greensboro, and it's wonderful you're here." For a few minutes the speaker flowed on about
distant connections of whom Anna had only the vaguest recollections, and then abruptly she became businesslike:

"I'm sure Mrs. Jefferson Davis hasn't heard you're in town, and
I want to send word to the Chesnuts of South Ca'lina and the
. . . oh, lots of others. They'll want you to go to the President's
house on Clay Street and I certainly intend to have a reception.
You haven't been fair, not telling us you'd . . ."

As she listened to the cascade of words, Anna asked herself
whether, if Tom had not achieved such victories, this flighty
stranger would be bothered about her. At once she knew the answer. Her guest had what Mary Morrison once described as an
"inventory glance"; busy as her tongue was, the lady's eyes missed
nothing: the quality of the combs, the luggage, the cut of the
dress that lay over a chair.

Anna was repelled: "I'm sorry, but I leave in the morning. I'm
simply stopping on my way to see my husband."

"Oh." These words, obviously bizarre to the woman, left no
room for debate. "Well, you'll let me know when you come back?
There are so many people here, charming families, circles of . . ."
Many sentences later the caller left, and Anna returned to more

important subjects. Through a note forwarded from Charlotte she had been put in touch with a quiet, elderly man who had to make a trip that would take him through Winchester, and she departed with him the next day.

The smiling fellow proved more than a little absent-minded, and so attentive in his care of "the little lady," as he described her, that he forgot to watch her luggage. When they left the train at the town of Strasburg, they could not find her trunk. All her clothes, old and new, her personal items, their family objects . . . what could she do about them? "Oh, they'll show up," her escort assured her. "Even in these days, railroads almost never lose things."

Glumly, Anna entered the stage for the last lap of their trip, with the aging man at her side. The two spoke together until a burly officer, overhearing their conversation, tapped her shoulder: "Begging pardon, ma'am, you won't see General Jackson in Winchester. He's on an expedition to break up a dam on the Chesapeake and Ohio Canal. He's had those fellows out for days and nights in ice water to their hips, with the Yankees potshotting at him."

Perhaps the man had intervened out of kindness; nevertheless Anna did not miss the criticism in his remarks. Her thoughts shifted: either Tom had not received her message or he had had to leave. Would this be a repetition of her first disturbing day near Manassas?

When the stage halted at Winchester she looked with an uncertain air at the hotel sign. She could barely make out the lettering in the dim lamplight. "We can try there," her companion told her, his voice revealing disappointment that he still had her on his hands. A group of soldiers stood together a few feet away from the carriage, and Anna scanned their faces. One was heavily muffled in a military overcoat, a dark cap drawn over his eyes. For a moment her heartbeat quickened. But no, it couldn't be Tom; the man remained motionless.

Anna and her escort started up the long flight of outer stairs, and she caught footsteps behind her. Just as they touched the porch a pair of firm arms seized her from behind, and Tom was chuckling and kissing her.

"Then it *was* you over there!" She tried to talk through her breathless laughter. "Tom, why didn't you let me know?"

"I had to make sure it was my own wife," he grinned. "Didn't want to kiss somebody else's *esposa*." She suspected that his shyness before strangers had won over his first impulse to show his affection. "I just got back from our work on the dam," he explained, "and I've reserved a room for us at this hotel." A few minutes later, apologetic about the missing trunk yet relieved that he had disposed of her, Anna's companion left. Alone upstairs, she and Tom clung together with joyful whispers.

"I've so much to tell, to ask . . ." As she started to speak Tom put his hand over her lips. There would be other times.

When she woke with a start at dawn, the cracked ceiling and the sharp outlines of the ugly bed frowned down at her, and Anna wondered for a moment where she was. Then she felt her husband's arm move toward her, and she lay back with a rush of happiness. After a while Tom got up and bent tenderly to kiss her throat and arms. While they dressed a slight uneasiness stole upon her. Suppose her visit here proved a mistake, the place unsympathetic and disagreeable? At breakfast Tom smiled away her doubts: "Let's go out and see." Lacking a change of costume and her usual toilet articles, she had managed as best she could. "We'll arrange something," Tom assured her, and, nodding, she told herself that her privations were small compared with those so many others were suffering these days.

"Our war home . . ." Tom murmured the words, and long afterward she was to use the term for the old-fashioned town with its red brick sidewalks bordered with silver maples, and its lines of white houses, neat-chimneyed, stretching across a level central area and rising toward the hills that encircled the settlements. Farms and apple orchards spread in the distance, and the gardens had a tidy, ordered look in contrast to the grandeur of the mountains that lifted their peaks in several directions.

"The North Mountains," he pointed to one side. "And those low ranges are the Massanuttons." During the following months Anna was to hear these names repeatedly, and she would always remember the lands they dominated. "This valley is our breadbasket," Tom nodded. "It pours out grain and cattle and foodstuff for the war, and Winchester is a really strategic spot. If we lose the Valley, we might as well give up." A moment later, putting that subject aside, he called her attention to one old home after another in the early Revolutionary town. "And here are my quarters."

The house was a pleasant one with a fine simplicity of design. A young aide awaited, and they spent an hour or so rearranging furniture. Although the place would be hard to keep warm and lacked comforts, she would be here with her husband, and that was enough. After they had finished their work at their own place, Tom took Anna to the Graham family manse, only thirty yards away. With some hesitation she stood beside him as he rang the bell near the arched door.

A small, neat young man, accompanied by three or four smiling women, greeted them. "We've been waiting for you for days," Mrs. Graham told her with an easy good will. "Your arrival is a happy event," an older woman echoed her, and then the minister addressed Anna with an earnest air: "General Jackson's here as our defender, but we've come to know him as our friend."

With that the minister's cheerful wife indicated a place for Anna on a big sofa before the crackling logs in the fireplace of the sun-splashed parlor. It was a lively household; although everyone was simple-mannered, there was an evident background of taste and education, and Anna responded quickly to the Grahams' warmth. She glanced about the well-filled room with its lines of oil paintings, its massive old furnishings and deep rugs. In the numerous bookcases she saw embossed old volumes next to new ones . . . The voices around her drew her attention. Already, it developed, the news of Anna's missing trunk had spread. "I'm sending dispatches to try to locate it," Tom explained, and a moment later Mrs. Graham and her mother, Mrs. Magill, spoke up.

"I'm about your size, and I'd be happy to lend you a few dresses," Mrs. Graham assured her. "And I can help with toilet articles and the like," Mrs. Magill volunteered. Anna thanked them; how different were these people from her Richmond lady . . . A giggle sounded, and three children thrust their heads through a curtain. Jumping up, Tom seized them and laughed with them until their grandmother led them away.

It was time for Tom and Anna to leave, and the Grahams accompanied them to their quarters. Before she left the young minister's wife whispered to her, "Please come over whenever you can, and if there's anything else you need . . ." The welcome was unfeigned, and Anna felt touched.

Taking a seat beside her a moment later, Tom spoke slowly. "Anna, this visit mayn't be altogether easy for you. I've never worked so hard in my life, and I ought to be at my desk right now. I'm getting more men though I'm not sure when they'll arrive. But when they do come I'm going to have to be away some time."

At Tom's last words, she faced him: "Away on an expedition, and in cold weather like this? When will it be?"

He gave her an intent look: "You remember one of the things we read together in Napoleon? 'An active winter's campaign is less likely to produce disease than a sedentary life by campfires in winter quarters.' More than that, we ought to be striking right now; the longer we wait, the longer we give the North to build up a strong force against us . . ." His voice trailed off, and she realized that Tom had made no direct answer to her questions, and that he would make none.

His musing ended, and he turned to her with a lighter manner: "You'll be seeing a lot of familiar faces in the next few weeks. My old Brigade is back. I asked for it, and Richmond finally agreed." His face showed his satisfaction, and her smile reflected his. This was the best news she had had in a long time.

"General Lee wanted it . . ." At his words Anna gave Tom an inquiring stare: "Lee? Where's the General now, since the bad time he had in the West?" Tom's air further brightened: "He's back in Richmond as military adviser to President Davis, and that means a steady hand over there, where it's badly needed." Tom did not have to emphasize his meaning. He preferred the hand of R. E. Lee to that of Jefferson Davis.

In the week that followed Anna divided her time between their quarters and the Graham parlor. Tom had to be away even more than he had expected, and she rejoiced in the friendliness and lively informality the Grahams showed her. Her glimpses of the town were limited for the time. Strong winds cut through the streets, and snow fell intermittently—"the coldest weather we've had in years," Mrs. Graham announced.

Several times the Jacksons were the Grahams' guests for the evening. Twice the children brought in their soldiers' games, and to Anna's surprise their grandmother, Mrs. Magill, lowered herself nimbly to the floor beside them. "General, and you too, Mrs. Jackson," she cried to them, "you're not too elderly to join us, are you?" After a moment Anna and Tom sat cross-legged on the rug. Glancing in, Mr. Graham grinned, "Let me be reinforcement for Stonewall!" By then several others stood over them, crying encouragement to the two competing sides. As Tom pushed a cannon forward and overturned it, the youngest Graham frowned, "General, you're real clumsy!"

In the laughter that followed Anna discovered that she was more relaxed than she had been in months. When they sat back, arguing over their military deeds, Mrs. Graham slipped out and in again with a plate of cakes. "If these taste sickly, that's what they are. I left out the sugar because I just didn't have any."

Taking a seat by the big fire, Anna munched happily. In this winter of '61–'62, many things were in short supply and growing steadily shorter. Nonetheless, the Grahams and Magills took deprivations as a testing. And Mrs. Graham was an observant hostess.

At their first meal a servant passed a well-seasoned dish, which Tom rejected with a firm gesture. Evidently it was one of Mrs. Graham's prize recipes, and Anna felt the impulse to whisper to her husband, "Can't you make a pretense of eating it?" But she checked herself; as he had told her long ago, he never made such pretenses. She need not have concerned herself, however. Mrs. Graham obviously was not hurt by Tom's refusal, and from then on he was served only milk and plain meat, fruit, and, as often as not—a lemon.

"Where do you get the lemons, with all our scarcities?" Anna inquired. Mrs. Graham gave her a merry glance: "I don't. The General keeps me provided with a dozen at a time, and I suspect he has people in Richmond watching for them." After that Anna noticed that Tom generally carried the fruit in his pocket or in Little Sorrel's saddlebag.

The weather continued bad, with snow falling for hours from a dim sky. That night they retired early, and less than three hours later a pounding from below sent Tom into the chill hallway. As she sat up in bed, Anna heard the moan of the wind against the roof; stumbling to the window, she discovered it had begun to snow again. Tom returned from the hall and paused beside the bed, and she asked, "Has anything happened?"

"Yes." For a moment Anna thought he would tell her nothing more, and she could barely restrain her anger. Surely he could speak freely to his own wife. Then, sensing her reaction, he turned and his voice was muffled: "*Esposita,* General William Loring's agreed to join me with his soldiers from Western Virginia, and he'll be here soon. I won't have anything like the forces I've wanted, and he's to keep command of his own men. But there'll be several thousand more here, and I guess we can do something with that number."

Her mind working quickly, Anna settled back. More soldiers, and the expedition against the Union that the town had been whispering about . . . Until tonight she had not believed the operation so close. As Tom lay down beside her she heard his quick intake of breath. He must be thinking about the problems of supply and assignment of the new forces.

"Please, Tom." She put out her hand. At her first touch he gave a slight start, but then he sighed and squeezed her fingers reassuringly. After a time a low snore told her that he was resting at last. Now, however, Anna herself found it impossible to sleep. Dawn had approached by the time she fell into slumber.

From that day on she felt the pressure tighten about her. Tom seemed edgy and preoccupied, and she saw far less of the Brigade officers than she had anticipated. The distant figure of Colonel Preston; the lithe form of Sandie Pendleton, and Turner Ashby, the celebrated raider, who swept by one day on his no less famous milk-white steed, his gray eyes fixed on a point ahead of him . . . Those were all.

But she could not hold back an exclamation when she saw an unexpected face at her door. "George Junkin! Whatever business you have with the General, I want a few minutes afterward." George was Dr. Junkin's nephew, who had been brought up in Virginia. Her eyes went over the youth's uniform; he, too, was fighting against his uncle's side. She chatted happily with him for a few minutes, but although she wanted to inquire about President Junkin, she closed her lips; it would be unfair to upset the young man with such matters.

And she must not ask Tom where the expedition was going or when. But she could not shut out the sight and sound of the hundreds of new troops moving about the town, nor the comments of many of General Loring's soldiers. One day, as Anna and Mrs. Graham were on their way to pay a call, they heard several men talking on the street corner:

"This Stonewall thinks he's cock o' the walk."

"That's what *he* says. Gen'l Loring's nobody to be ordered around, let me tell you. He outranked Jackson before this war, and he'll do it again!"

"You watch—somebody's gonna pop his balloon for 'im."

The hostility in the voices shocked Anna. At her side Mrs. Graham cleared her throat, then commented laconically, "I'm afraid the thought of serving here doesn't sit well with some of the people around General Loring." As they continued walking Anna read the shape of future trouble. When Tom joined them that night Mrs. Graham announced, "Whether or not you'll tell us if you'll be here, General, we're going to plan a fine Christmas—and keep hoping you can join Mrs. Jackson and the rest of us."

At these words Tom's eyes twinkled, and still he did not reveal his secret.

The next few days at the Graham manse were taken up with a swarm of preparations: chopping nuts, making candies (small and lumpy, yet still candies), trimming the tree, wrapping the gifts. For Anna an unexpected present arrived shortly before the great day—her long-missing trunk, which Tom's agents had located in a railroad storage room in Richmond. With a cry of delight she dug into its depths to bring out their personal things and, with special happiness, her favorite new gown, a soft blue velvet.

On Christmas night she put on the dress and a pair of small earrings of lighter blue. Atop her head she placed an ornamented comb which the Richmond clerk had informed her was "just what they're wearing right now in Paris." Anna cocked her head at her husband. "Do I look all right?" He was standing behind her, and he gave his answer by bending over and pressing his lips against the back of her neck. In the mirror her wide eyes had a new brightness, her cheeks a heightened color. This visit to Winchester, troubled in some ways though it might be, was good for her . . .

For several happy hours Anna lost herself in the Grahams' festivities. The children darted in and out, while the adults laughed, sang Christmas carols, and drank holiday punch. At the piano Tom joined the others; the results were hardly more musical than heretofore. Then came the opening of gifts. As the cries and thanks rang out, Anna's mind returned to the previous Christmas, when she and Tom had been guests of the Prestons.

Just a year ago, and now they had all been scattered—Maggie's father and sister in the North; her husband, two of her brothers, and her cousin in the Southern armies, two other brothers in the Union ranks. And Anna and Tom themselves were together for only a time. When the holidays came around again, where would they be?

For Tom Jackson the season also meant an unanticipated gift. A youthful officer appeared before him to tell of his capture the previous June, in Western Virginia. Finding him in bad condition, the Union doctors had sent the Confederate to one of their hospitals, where a quiet, earnest woman had gone about, helping to care for the cases that needed particular attention.

"She looked after everybody, Yank and reb alike," Robert Ransom went on, "and she was really kind, a fine, serious nurse. One day somebody told me she was Mrs. Laura Arnold, your sister, General." The young man had more to say: "Typhoid fever broke out in the hospital, and Mrs. Arnold decided to take me into her home to save me, sir." There she nursed the Southerner back to health, until he was exchanged . . . As Tom repeated the story to Anna, he shook his head: "That was just like Laura, wasn't it?" Greatly moved, Anna nodded slowly.

But the following day she winced when she heard another version of her sister-in-law's behavior: "Did you know that General Jackson's own sister's gone for the Yankees—traipsing around their hospitals and nursing their sick?" "Yes, and if she had any shame or loyalty or even consideration for her brother . . ." For a time Anna debated how she could explain the matter to these people. Then she tightened her lips. Nothing she could say would help; at hours such as this, in North or South, such words meant nothing.

Late December, 1861 . . . Every day found her anxiety increasing. Would Tom be leaving tonight, or would it be the next morning or the next? He spent more and more of his time away from her, and when he returned he always had an abstracted look. "Good, good," he would tell her with that characteristic shake of the head, then turn aside with a preoccupied frown. Although the weather continued cold, it had brightened, and Mrs. Graham murmured to Anna, "I think the signs point to some action."

New Year's Eve was a quiet, subdued evening, and they retired early. Once or twice Tom had seemed to be deep in thought, but Anna told herself that was nothing unusual. Hadn't he been the same way for some time?

She woke just before dawn, and with her first glance at Tom, as he stood by the washstand, she knew that the day of his departure had arrived. She sat up, her body stiffening in apprehension. He had already dressed, and his first words brought her a further surprise: "Anna, I've talked with Mr. Graham, and you're going to stay with him and his family while I'm gone. It will be best that way . . . You won't hear much from me for a while. But we're both in God's hands . . ."

As always, her husband had decided in advance precisely what he would say, yet now he hesitated: "*Esposita,* remember the old rule I've told you. Never take counsel of your fears." He spoke a few last caressing words in Spanish: she was very dear, "*muy querida,*" to him, and she must be calm and think of him. Hearing the old, loving phrases, Anna's anxiety gave way to an overwhelming despair. She must not cry, she must not . . . and only after he had embraced her and walked swiftly down the stairs did she let the tears come.

It was a long time before she could control her trembling, get dressed, and go downstairs. Shortly thereafter, the doorbell rang and both the Grahams awaited her, a servant at their side. "We'll move everything right now, so you won't have to go back and forth a dozen times," Mrs. Graham told her, and mutely Anna nodded.

An hour and a half later she stood beside the Grahams, watching the last of the thousands of men pound on their way. Once she thought she spotted the dark-skinned Turner Ashby, more Arablike than ever as he galloped off on his white steed, but she could not be sure. Where was Tom? None of them could find him.

"What a brilliant day!" Mrs. Graham was speaking, and Anna looked around her. The thermometer had risen, and it seemed more like April than January. The last bits of snow were melting, and there was a slight breeze; in the clear air Anna felt that she had only to put out her hand to touch the green-draped mountains.

"Eighty-five hundred men—five battalions and companies," Mr. Graham explained as the columns disappeared in clouds of dust. "I couldn't help hearing today that the General ordered every man to take five days' rations and keep one day's supply cooked in advance. They're heading toward Pughtown and Bath and maybe Romney, where the Union's dug in heavily. Well, the weather's cooperating beautifully."

Anna gave thanks, yet even as she listened to the minister she caught sight of a small cloud in the distance. After breakfast she excused herself and went to her new room, where she watched the cloud widen until it covered the sun. By early afternoon the skies had turned leaden, and the Massanuttons were hidden from view. A rising wind whistled against the house, and before dark snow swirled over the town. The household continued subdued, all thoughts focused on the men moving steadily away from them. When Anna apologized for her own preoccupation, Mrs. Graham patted her hand in silence. Grateful for the Grahams' tact, she went uneasily to bed, where, before she fell asleep, she heard a still more disturbing sound—heavy sleet. The weather had turned strongly against them.

Unable to close her eyes, Anna eventually lighted the lamp and sat up, hugging her knees. Those thousands of men, exposed to the elements on such a night! And over and over she repeated words that Tom had told her before: "Anna, in any military operation the great thing is speed—speed and surprise." Would this change throw all Tom's plans awry?

Breakfast was a cheerless meal; even the children did not talk. As soon as she could excuse herself, Anna climbed back to her room. Although the Grahams had done a great deal to make her quarters bright and comfortable for her, she could only sit miserably staring ahead. Several times Mrs. Graham rapped, bringing her tea, trying to draw her out of her numbed state. Each time Anna asked the same questions and each time her friend shook her head: "No, my dear, no news of any kind."

Another two days passed, and in the evening the older woman, Mrs. Magill, entered. Her manner was subdued and uncertain: "We hear there's been fighting. That's all—no word as to who won, if anybody." With a low sigh Anna sank back. Meanwhile, hour after hour, the wind ripped by and the sleet pounded against the roof and windows. In this below-freezing weather, she thought of Little Sorrel and his rider, and shivered for both.

Through that night and most of the next day, Anna alternated between despair and vague hope. Late in the afternoon an elderly friend of the Grahams knocked, and she heard him from the next room: "We've had some successes, and the Union's pulled back from two towns. But"—Anna could feel the old man's hesitation—"but I'm afraid General Jackson's having trouble with some of our own men. The suffering's been really terrible, worse than any of us can imagine."

As Anna stiffened, the grim words went on: "The weather was so good at the start that a lot of them threw their overcoats aside or tossed them into the wagons, and they didn't listen to Stonewall's orders about food. So they had no covering against the snow and sleet, and sometimes they didn't even have anything to eat. They say that thousands lay down exhausted in the open and woke in the morning to find themselves under snow."

Anna covered her face with her hands. If only she could blot out the unhappy tidings . . . But there was even worse to come: "The roads have been like soggy marshes, or as slippery as glass, and men went sliding over the sides, wagons crashing over the edges. Sometimes they claim the soldiers' feet froze to the ground. Animals died of cold or injury, and wagons were delayed with supplies . . . A nightmare. A lot of those men are inexperienced, undisciplined troops, and they're all but demoralized."

As Anna listened with whitened face, the guest lowered his voice: "General Loring and his officers are supposed to be complaining to Richmond, and folks say there's going to be an explosion over the whole thing."

After the man left, Anna remained alone, her breath coming quickly in her anguish. Tom was winning, and yet his own side, or some of those on it, were stirring against him . . . Did they blame him for the weather? That evening the Grahams retired early, as did Anna. After a night of nervous turning, she went out in the morning and stared with Mrs. Graham at the sight of scores of Loring's soldiers lolling around the town. Mutters reached them as they passed:

"The man's mad, a crazy, inhuman slave driver."

"He'll kill us all if he has his damned way. Men sprawled along the roads everywhere you look . . ."

Mr. Graham, who was walking behind the two women, took their arms and led them back. On the way he explained to Anna in a low voice, "Some of them have gotten sick leave, or even quit the campaign." Anna nodded sadly; as Tom had explained, he had only limited control over Loring's troops.

Then eagerly she picked up a letter from her husband and found better news. Romney, a town which had been the Union center and a main objective of the Confederates, had fallen to Tom's army. The Northern forces had abandoned tents, equipment, great supplies of food and properties. Anna's hand shook as she read Tom's notes describing the way Union generals had burned mills and homes, killed domestic animals, and destroyed anything else that might have been useful. For fifteen miles, he said, the retreating enemy had left a continuous spread of charred ruins, lines of dead cows and horses. But his men had reclaimed important territory, and had broken Union communication lines and established points from which to carry on future drives.

The days passed slowly until Anna counted three weeks since Tom's departure. A lull had fallen, and she waited tensely for the next developments. Considering the weather and the condition of the troops, what would he do now? Then one evening in late January, as she sat with the Grahams in their parlor, the bell rang and there he was, a new Tom. "Anna . . . Anna . . ." His face had a fresh, newly-scrubbed look, and his eyes were shining in eager love and expectation.

Despite the strain of his recent troubles, Anna sensed something else—a glow of achievement. Then, when he caught her to him, she thought only of him and this reunion. Had she ever seen him so joyous, so full of animation? Drawing back, Tom laughed, "I rode practically forty miles today through muck and slush to get here. Left one of the older staff men behind. He said he wasn't so anxious to see Mrs. Jackson that he'd break his neck keeping up." He finished with a small smile: "When I arrived I was so thick with mud that I cleaned up before I came over." With that, his hand went out to hers, and she seized it.

Now the Grahams moved closer, and for the next hour Anna and the others listened as he spoke, though guardedly, of his recent operations: "We didn't win all I'd hoped, and we've had to give up part of our plans. But my Brigade did everything I could have asked of it." A moment later he added, "And we've lifted morale for a great many miles around here. I left General Loring and his men to guard Romney and keep it as a base to push on from the next time."

Anna, her eyes sparkling with excitement, wanted to hear a great deal more. But Tom slapped his knee: "No more war to-night, if you please." He gathered the children to him, and his eyes went to the cheerful family circle. "Ah," he murmured softly, "I've been thinking of scenes like this ever since I left Winchester. This—this is the very essence of comfort."

Later that evening Mr. Graham said, "Why don't you stay here with Mrs. Jackson instead of transferring everything back to the other house?" Anna looked at Tom, and both nodded. It was a happy solution, and thereafter the Graham home was theirs. Daily Tom rose for a quick trip to headquarters to check on developments, then returned for a pleasant family breakfast.

The next few days slipped by in a rush. Anna saw the people of the town smile at Tom and call out grateful greetings to him. At the same time, however, she became aware that many gave him cold stares. Reports spread that he had treated some of the troops cruelly, inhumanly; and again Anna caught the words that had alarmed her on the train: "wild," "a peculiar man." And she could not force away the hint of the Grahams' elderly caller: there would be some kind of "explosion" over the campaign.

One morning Tom stayed longer than usual at headquarters, and then, from the pounding of his steps as he came to their room, Anna knew something was wrong. Opening the door to him, she stared. His face had reddened, and his jaw was tight with a rage such as she had never seen there. His hand clutched several tele-graph slips.

"What is it, Tom? You can tell me . . ." When he seemed not to hear her, she reached out for the papers, and mechanically he relinquished them. As he continued to stand there, eyes wide with emotion, she read the first short message:

Our news indicates that a movement is being made to cut off General Loring's command. Order him back to Winchester immediately.

It was signed by Judah P. Benjamin, the Confederate Secretary of War. Anna's gaze went to Tom's. Obviously General Loring or his friends had persuaded Richmond to issue this order. At last Tom spoke in a tense voice: "They're not comfortable enough there, and they want an easier berth. So they've undercut me, wrecked everything we've done . . . Well, we can't fight a war like that—at least I can't."

Her own bitterness flared: "Tom, it's outrageous. Without ask-ing you, or checking further into the matter, to accept what those people claim, and act this way . . ." Then she remembered the other sheets, and hastily she scanned them. The first was Tom's recall of Loring's men, as ordered. The other was addressed to Secretary Benjamin:

Sir—Your order . . . has been received and promptly complied with.

With such interference in my command, I cannot expect to be of much service in the field, and, accordingly, respectfully request to be ordered to report to duty to the Superintendent of Virginia Military Institute at Lexington, as has been done in the case of

other professors. Should this application not be granted, I respectfully request that the President will accept my resignation from
the army.

As she stared at her husband, Anna Jackson realized that his
career, and their futures, hung in the balance.

CHAPTER 14

Through the rest of the day Anna sat quietly as silence settled
over the Graham manse and over Tom's headquarters. Had her
husband acted wisely? And was there anything she could do to
help him? Unsure and confused, she could do nothing but await
developments.

After they had finished their conversation Anna and Tom went
downstairs. The atmosphere at the breakfast table was con-
strained. Tom spoke with an enforced brightness, but his flushed
look and the set of his mouth made it clear to the Grahams that
trouble was upon them. Neither the minister nor his wife asked
any questions, however, and they did not try to stop Anna when
she went quietly to her room after the meal.

Within the hour Mr. Graham stood apologetically at her door.
"The—the word is all over town," he told her in a stricken voice.
"There's a lot of excitement, people talking on every corner. Mrs.
Jackson, most of them can't believe it." His emotion moved her
deeply. "If the General goes away, what's going to happen to us?
He can't leave the army. We need him too much; the whole
South needs him."

Too upset to answer, Anna merely nodded. She closed the door
and remained in seclusion as long as she could. In the late afternoon she and Mrs. Graham were due to call on a friend, and dully
she dressed for the visit. They left the house in silence; once on
the street they were startled at the sight of hundreds of General
Loring's men, streaming back into town with an air of triumph.
They had put Jackson in his place, and were roaring and shouting
over their accomplishment.

"Richmond's fixed the crazy yap!"

"Old Stonewall's gonna think twice before he pulls anything
like that again . . ."

Somehow Anna got through the rest of the afternoon. Tom returned late that night, but when he joined her in their room he

looked quiet and composed. "*Esposita,* it may be nice to get back to the Institute after all. Won't you enjoy reopening our house and seeing Maggie?" Although she nodded, she was conscious of the signs of doubt and solemn concern in his face.

To resume his classes under these conditions, to surrender the place he had won with such effort and determination . . . Suddenly Anna made up her mind. The South required Tom Jackson's services; he could do work no one else had been able to. And now she realized what her role was; she had to make her husband understand the part he must take.

"Tom." Her throat felt tight and her first words were barely audible. "Tom, I don't want to go back to Lexington because of this . . ." Gathering strength, she ended with sudden force. "And you don't either."

He showed his surprise: "Anna, I have no choice except to leave the army."

"No." She could feel her anger growing. "No, you can fight Judah Benjamin and—and anybody else who's responsible."

Tom's head rose, and on his face she saw a flash of fury: "There's one man responsible for all this—Davis himself. Benjamin would never have done it on his own, without backing."

Anna turned his words back on him: "Then all the more reason to fight . . . Appeal to the people you know, make them realize what the issues are. If this can happen to you, it can happen to any other officer . . ." With each sentence her voice carried greater determination. Tom himself, she knew, was becoming increasingly resentful, and this made her hopeful. Finally, he agreed with her.

Would he have come to this view in any case? Perhaps. Be that as it might, she sank back content; she had done her part in charting her husband's course—and she knew it was the right course for their new nation. That night she scanned a note he had written to Governor Letcher of Virginia, who had considerable confidence in him. The Letchers were from Lexington, and the Jacksons had known them for some years. Tom's protest was strong: even though he was commander in the area, he wrote, he had not been consulted in this matter. An order such as Mr. Benjamin's wiped out the results of his whole campaign, and he had been forced to abandon a position that had taken preparation, heavy expense, and exposure to win.

Anna's eyes brightened as she read on. If war was to be carried on in this way, they were all ruined, and the best thing he could do for the South was to leave the service, but not before putting his complaint upon the record. Anna's heart beat quickly; surely Governor Letcher would agree with Tom's stand.

The next day Tom showed her a letter from his superior officer, General Johnston, whose authority had also been by-passed in this situation. Johnston, "begging you to reconsider this matter," appealed to Tom to help him "reason dispassionately" with Richmond. If their arguments had no effect, the General concluded, both he and Tom could feel free to leave the army. As she quickly read the lines, Anna felt new admiration for Joseph E. Johnston. The man had spoken out firmly.

From that moment on, developments were swift. A representative of the Governor, a member of the Confederate Congress, and two army officers came to see Tom. He conferred with one after another of them, often in the Graham house. "And look at this," Mrs. Graham approached with quivering hands, pointing to a newspaper. A swell of protest was rising from editors, state officials, and private individuals. Southern journals presented fuming objections and delivered slashing attacks on Secretary Benjamin.

From the papers Anna turned excitedly to two piles of letters that had arrived within the past few hours. Every note said much the same thing: Tom must remain in the army. "Without you we cannot succeed . . ." "You have been right in your course."

Already the military disasters Tom predicted had occurred. With Loring's withdrawal from Romney, the Union moved speedily to recover the town. Then all at once, now that the damage had been done, Richmond took action; it shifted Loring and his men to another front. "They're giving in," Tom told Anna with a bitter look, "but that means there will be even fewer men to protect this area."

One day, a note arrived from the Governor. Tom studied it for a time and then handed it to her. It contained assurances that there would be no repetition of Secretary Benjamin's action. "And so, *esposita*," he told her with a softened manner, "I've agreed to withdraw my resignation."

Anna was profoundly relieved, and a feeling of warm satisfaction coursed through her. Not only had Tom been vindicated, but the South as a whole would benefit. During the rest of February she was conscious of the lessened tension upon them. Since no

military action was possible for the time, Tom worked to get additional forces, and drilled and prepared the men he had.

Like others around them, Anna saw his endless concentration,
his concern with highly detailed data. Repeatedly he demanded
new maps and fuller maps of his engineers. When she paused
beside him one night while he labored at his desk, he glanced up,
and she smiled: "Tom, you've practically *memorized* this Valley,
haven't you?" He shrugged. "Well, I've learned the roads and
the distances. From there to Staunton, from Staunton to Kerns-
town . . ." And then to her surprise, he recited several dozen
figures and relevant details.

Watching him, Anna was reminded of their long evenings in
Lexington, when Tom had struggled with his back to her at his
high desk, training his memory or analyzing problems—and always completely oblivious of his background. Now she could see
some of the results of that hard work. Tonight he remained upstairs while the Grahams and Mrs. Magill entertained friends,
among them a group of young officers. Anna listened with amusement to the quips and jokes and took her place at the piano to
accompany them. As the party approached its close, an artillery
captain smilingly described a military maneuver to Mrs. Magill.

"Oh, it wasn't hard," he said. "The cannon pounded like this."
Wheeling around, the youth snatched up a chair and held it as if
it were a piece of artillery. Mrs. Magill chuckled, seized a second
chair, and imitated him. Mrs. Graham took another, and in a
minute or two the entire company, the minister and Anna included, had done the same thing. A ridiculous battle followed,
half the group taking one side, the rest the other. Feet pounded,
cries rang out, and Anna, like the others, was speechless with
laughter.

At that moment the curtains parted to reveal Tom. His eyes,
wide with disbelief, went from his wife to the matronly Mrs.
Magill, and his amazement made Anna roar harder than ever.
After a short silence he grinned and issued an order: "Captain
Marye, when the engagement is over, you will send me an official
report." And so the evening ended.

Later that week Anna saw their old friend Colonel Preston at
close range for the first time since her arrival in Winchester. He
approached with a smile. "Can't you stop in for a minute?" she
asked, and he gave a semiconspiratorial nod. "If you promise not

to tell Tom, I will." As he settled himself beside her on the sofa, Anna noticed that John Preston had changed for the better since the war. While he had not lost his debonair manner, he showed an application she had never before observed. His tongue had mellowed; people did not bristle at his comments as had some of their friends in Lexington. And how oddly fortune had shifted his and Tom's roles! On her husband's arrival, John had been the town's dominant figure. Now he had accepted a place as Tom's adjutant. But she found no signs of resentment in him, no hints of anything except the friendliest spirit.

Today, after a few preliminaries, Anna asked about the Junkins, and John Preston smiled again. "The Doctor's doing his part for the North, writing articles and making speeches everywhere he's asked. They say he even addressed Confederate prisoners in a Pennsylvania prison and told them he had been Stonewall's father-in-law." Colonel Preston chuckled. "When he mentioned Tom's name to those rebels, they all jumped up and cheered, and I suspect that the Doctor doesn't volunteer that information any more."

But Anna could not laugh with her friend. In her mind's eye she could see the suffering on President Junkin's face at their last meeting on the day he had broken his ties with the South . . . A moment later John Preston's look also sobered. "One of Maggie's brothers is a Union army surgeon, the other is a navy chaplain." For Colonel Preston and for his wife this must be an unhappy thought. Rising, he said slowly, "One of my own boys, Frank, is in the army now, and we're having a hard time keeping Willy out."

A first son in the Confederate forces, and soon, perhaps, even the young one, her own favorite among the Preston boys . . . "You know, Willy was pretty upset last year when his friend, young Page, was killed at Manassas," the father concluded. "More than ever he wanted to get in the fighting, and he was afraid things would be over too soon. Well, the war's still on." With a shrug, John Preston strode away.

That week brought Anna a happiness that was to change her life. After their years of waiting she could finally give Tom the definite word for which both of them had hoped so long. For hours she rehearsed what she would say, but when he walked in her words came in an awkward rush: "I've known since this morning, and I wanted to run out and tell you, but now . . . Well, the doctor's sure of it, and I'm going to have a baby." Tom's mouth opened and closed, and he appeared about to break down. Then, taking her hands, he kissed her and led her to the sofa, where they talked for a long time.

"The war may be over when the baby arrives," Anna ventured.

"It may, *esposa querida . . .*" But his words had no conviction, and Anna asked herself as she did more and more of late, how much longer this fighting would go on.

She woke the next morning to find Tom regarding her tenderly, with a heightened love. During the next few days he often drew her aside; these were hours of new understanding. Several times he asked the same question: "You'll be especially careful this time, won't you?" The thought had already occurred to her; no matter what happened, she must watch her health for the sake of their child.

One morning she left Tom behind in their room and went downstairs, where she found Sandie Pendleton waiting. Sandie had advanced so rapidly on Tom's staff that Anna had heard rumors of resentment against him. Tom had to compose an answer to a message; while he worked, Sandie joined Anna, and as they talked her mind went back to the day she had first met this young friend with his father. How boyish, scholarly, almost ineffectual he had appeared that afternoon! Today Sandie, still only twenty-two, was one of Tom's most dependable aides.

Sinking into the chair beside her, the young officer grinned, "Ma'am, it's the first time I've sat in something as comfortable as this since—since the war began." Then he grew enthusiastic: "Mrs. Jackson, you're going to see great things happening next spring with this army of the General's. When we get some more men, to build around the forces we have now, and when Richmond just helps out a bit . . . Well, the whole Union army, or Lincoln himself, won't be able to stop us!"

Sandie's excitement had a contagious quality, and Anna's spirits soared. He bent forward intently: "Ma'am, General Jackson's just beginning to show what he can do. Give him a few more chances and he'll change this war." A moment later the minister's son in Sandie Pendleton made him add, "God willing, of course."

For a long time afterward Anna would repeat this prediction. Was it a burst of youthful optimism, or could he be right? For Tom to achieve even more, to go yet higher . . . Suddenly Sandie's remarks had taken a new direction: "We have men with us who can't be beaten. Jeb Stuart and Turner Ashby—they're both, well, invincible. It looks as if no bullet can reach them; the Yankee shots just whistle by and fall short." The boy went on swiftly, his eyes flashing.

"And General Jackson! He's the bravest man I've ever come across. He expects a lot from the rest of us, but never more than he gives himself. Why, in battle he goes right in, disregarding everything around him, while the bullets whiz within an inch. He'll just sit his horse, yelling to his men or riding in front of them with fire to right and left and under him . . ."

This was all too vivid for comfort. "Please, Sandie." Anna knew that Tom ran risks. But did he have to go as far as this? And the youth's talk of the invincibility of her husband and Stuart and Ashby—that filled Anna with a vague uneasiness. Nobody was invincible, and it was not good to assume such things . . . After Sandie left, Tom came over to her. At once she started into a discussion of this subject. He shrugged: "These things aren't in our hands, Anna. When God is ready to take us, in His wisdom . . ."

Tom smiled warmly as they spoke of Sandie Pendleton: "You don't know how much I love that boy, nor how much I owe him. He has a fine mind, a cheerful manner, and a way of getting things done." After a moment's silence, Tom's expression hardened: "Also, Sandie always does just what he's asked." Anna gave him a quick glance; she had already heard of her husband's troubles with officers who considered his orders bizarre or harsh. As a matter of fact, by now she knew well that many of his men found Tom a demanding superior.

Today she sensed in his manner a growing anxiety and a touch of sadness. After a few more exchanges Tom left with an abstracted air, and soon Mr. Graham appeared before her. He hesitated, then spoke: "It looks as if the Union army's moving closer."

When Tom returned, Anna watched him closely; apparently he noticed this and made an effort to speak with his old playfulness. For a time he succeeded. But then he remarked, "Anna, by the time we're together again . . ."

Although he stopped, he had let her know that the hour of her departure was near. She could no longer hold back her questions, and finally he turned to her: "*Esposa,* things are unsettled, and I'm afraid it will be best for you to go soon. I still hope the army won't have to give up this old town . . ." His last words frightened her; until now she had not realized this was a possibility. In

Tom's face she read his reluctance and his sorrow at the prospect of abandoning a place that had such meaning for both of them.

One early March morning Tom returned from his headquarters with heavy steps. As he opened the door, Anna braced herself to hear what she knew he had to say: "I don't know yet just what will happen here, and every instinct tells me to stay and fight." As he continued, his pain became more and more evident: "But we don't have the men to do it, and I can only promise these people that if we go, we'll be back. I'm ordering stores and baggage, and also our sick, sent to the rear, and the army's going to stay until the last possible moment." After a pause he spoke sadly again: "You'll have to leave tomorrow, on the train that's taking the sick men."

However well she thought she had prepared herself for it, the word shook Anna. Tom squeezed her hand and left, and within the hour rumors of the withdrawal spread through the town. The evening was glum, and the Grahams could not conceal their alarm. In the morning Tom told her he would take her to the station at ten o'clock. Unable to say more than a few words, Anna cried as she took Mr. Graham's hand and embraced Mrs. Graham and Mrs. Magill. She waved back to them from the carriage with a feeling of heavy loss.

Tom lingered for a time at the train, and murmured, "Now that you've left, I don't think I'll ever want to go back to the room we had at the Grahams . . . Thank you for coming here. You've made everything easier and better, and I'll be—praying for you." He swallowed heavily, and for a moment Anna thought he would lose his control. When Sandie Pendleton galloped up, his face tense, his eyes urgent, Tom caught her in a quick embrace and rode off. For a long minute she watched as Little Sorrel gradually disappeared down the road. Then she nodded to the youthful aide who had been assigned to take her to Richmond.

Around her the gloomy station echoed to soldiers' pounding footsteps and to commands for the loading of the train. Gradually the sick and wounded, brought there by wagons and ambulances, were carried in to the railroad cars. Suddenly Anna became aware of the full plight of these soldiers, and of the element of risk in their situation and hers as well.

"Look out, his arm!" "God, you can't get 'im through that window . . ." The men were white, emaciated; despair was in many of their faces. Anna heard moans, low cries of pain, and one hoarse scream as a soldier in heavy leg bandages fell down on his wounded limb. She saw patients bleeding through coverings over their heads; she made out several young ones who had been blinded, others who had lost arms or legs, a few who had suffered double amputations.

For a moment nausea attacked her at the sight of tumorlike swellings, filled with running pus, on so many arms and necks and faces. And then Anna was ashamed. So many people, suffering so badly, and she allowed herself a sickly revulsion. Fighting back her weakness, she stepped aboard the waiting car and sought out the nearest junior officer: "Please, let me help. I can certainly do something."

Although Tom's aide made a protest, Anna reached out to assist in easing first one victim, then another, into place. "Isn't there water in the car?" she asked, and when the officer pointed to a bucket, she darted to it and passed tin cupfuls to the victims. A cluster of new patients formed near the door, and she went over to help them on, bringing the aide with her. As she did a shout lifted: "All aboard, all aboard now." A dozen voices answered, "Not yet! No, ain't got everybody on."

An authoritative order rang out. "God damn it, everybody on, right now. If we don't watch out, the Yankee bastards'll be on top of us!" A shiver of apprehension caught at Anna, and she bent forward again to give her hand to the desperate men who struggled to get on the train. With the help of Tom's aide she drew in several gasping youths. One, who appeared little more than sixteen, was clutching a fellow soldier's arm. Suddenly his grip slackened, he sank back, and she saw his eyes roll up in his head.

Sadly the attendant beside him lowered the dying Confederate: "Well . . ." A moment later he thrust another into the car: "Here's one we *kin* do somethin' fer." Choking back her despair, Anna stretched her hands to the next men. But the coach was already moving under her. On the ground several wounded soldiers cried out, "Don't . . . Wait, wait just a . . ." It was too late. The sight of that huddle of stricken figures as they watched the train roll away from them stayed in Anna's thoughts for a long time.

"Look, ma'am." A few minutes later the aide touched her arm, and she faced in the direction to which he was pointing. Behind them lay the beleaguered town, its quiet loveliness spread out in the afternoon sunlight. Her sorrow welled up. What would happen to their friends, and when would she and Tom be in Win-

chester again? Not until later would she realize that there she
had enjoyed the longest period with her husband she was to know
during the war. She would never rejoin him in the little town,
and thirteen months would pass before she saw Tom Jackson
again.

And now, as the day's shadows lengthened, Anna forgot for a
moment the agony around her. For, though she had left Tom, she
carried the fruit of their union, the baby who would keep alive
the Jackson name. During that night and many that followed, she
clung to this thought.

In North Carolina, Anna's mind went back repeatedly to the
Valley of Virginia, where so many fates were centered. Tom's
letters outlined his maneuvers in the uncertain weeks after he
left Winchester. He had instructions to stay close to the powerful
army of the nearest Union general, Banks, keeping it occupied so
that it could not be used elsewhere. Yet he was not to attack the
main force, which so heavily outnumbered his, and he was to
avoid head-on entanglement. Once he reported to Anna that he
had fought on a Sunday. That was a surprise, for he had always
told her he would avoid clashes on the Sabbath. When she ques-
tioned him directly, she received a reply:

I was greatly concerned, too; but I felt it my duty to do it, in
consideration of the ruinous effects that might result from post-
poning the battle until the morning. . . . I hope and pray to our
Heavenly Father that I may never again be circumstanced as on
that day. . . . I do hope the war will soon be over, and that I
shall never again have to take the field. Arms is a profession that,
if its principles are adhered to for success, requires an officer to
do what he fears may be wrong, and yet, according to military
experience, must be done if success is to be attained.

Rereading the note, Anna felt her husband's dilemma and understood the way he had debated the issue. Almost at once a line
in another letter gave her fresh cause for sorrow. George Junkin,
the nephew of President Junkin, who had joined Tom's forces,
had been captured by Union men. Here was another irony, and
George was already in or was headed for prison. Daily Anna read
stories about prisoners who died of disease or privation in Northern and Southern jails. And now poor Maggie and the other
Junkins had yet another reason for prayer . . . As Anna sighed
over this, she received a letter from Mrs. Graham, describing the

gray day when the Union had arrived to take over Winchester:

It was, indeed, a bitter thing to feel that our own army was gone, and then to see the Yankees marching to the music of their brass bands, but some tearing across the fields, up the alleys and in every direction—"monarchs of all they surveyed." It was too much for me, and I gave way completely. . . . The country is becoming completely desolated—the farms being stripped of everything, the fences all destroyed, and the farmers not planting any crops.

Whenever Anna thought of her Valley friends, she remembered this dismal picture, and Tom's emphasis upon the Valley's vital importance to their cause. And in late spring she caught echoes of growing troubles for Tom. In these days his discipline had become more rigid than ever. She heard of several deserters who had been captured and sentenced to death.

Though former companions and officers tried to save them, Tom had insisted that the punishments be carried out. In one case a chaplain appealed to him on religious grounds, saying that if the offenders were shot, they would "certainly go to hell." To this, the tale went, Tom replied, "That's my business," and ordered the chaplain from his tent. Learning of the episode, Anna closed her eyes. How desperate Tom must consider their position if he acted in this way! And to him, an army must be run by rigid rules; to pass over violations would be to endanger its existence.

Her anxieties mounted when her father told her sadly, "Tom's had a real fight with General Richard Garnett, the officer who's been commanding the Stonewall Brigade." Anna was shocked at his next words: "Garnett ordered a withdrawal in battle, and Tom removed him and had him arrested. There's a lot of bitter talk . . ." The dispute gained in harshness; Garnett was well liked, and the storm that resulted had repercussions that extended as far as North Carolina.

At almost the same time, her husband made a change in the forces assigned to the dramatic, individualistic Turner Ashby, and Ashby immediately resigned. Anna was disturbed; Tom himself had told her how great a part the dark-bearded raider played in his battles. Then Ashby was placated. A new commander also took over the Stonewall Brigade, but the case of General Garnett hung fire. Meanwhile Tom's army had fallen back in a hard fight, and fresh whispers arose. On a visit to Charlotte Anna overheard many angry comments:

"That Jackson's been mighty lucky so far, but folks are starting to see through him." "Just crack-headed. I had a half-crazy cousin like that, and you never knew what he'd do next."

Against Anna's will the idea intruded itself into her mind: perhaps Tom had gone as far as he could, and from now on his star would decline. Sandie Pendleton's sanguine words returned to her: Tom had "just begun to show what he could do." Nonetheless she thought of General Beauregard of Louisiana, whose fame had paled of late. What had happened to Beauregard? Was the same thing going to happen to Tom Jackson?

Now the Morrisons frowned at even more disturbing tidings. The Confederacy's entire Mississippi River line was endangered; at Shiloh a large Southern army had been forced to retire after an assault on Federal forces. New Orleans, anchor of the Mississippi line, surrendered after a brief Union pounding. "And this may be worst of all," Dr. Morrison told her as he tapped a news story. The greatest Union force yet assembled was moving up the Peninsula toward Richmond. Anna's mouth widened as she read, "President Davis is sending government archives out of the city, and offices are getting ready to be evacuated."

Her alarm increased when her father showed her on a map the military situation outlined in one of the letters from Harvey Hill, now stationed in Virginia. Harvey spoke of the Union General, "Little Napoleon" McClellan, who was facing Joseph E. Johnston near Richmond: "McClellan outnumbers Johnston three to one. And along the Potomac there's a second Northern army waiting to trap us in a double grip." Meanwhile, Anna did not have to remind herself, General Banks, with an army almost four times as large, confronted Tom Jackson. And still another Union army was poised near Tom. Could the Confederates hope to escape destruction? The signs had never been more ominous.

Anna could not be certain when she had begun to understand the things that occurred next in the Valley. Most Southerners (and also Northerners) had as little comprehension as she. One day, to her surprise, Tom's small organization struck at Banks and pulled back. Then silence fell, and Anna wondered what was happening. A dispatch in a Charlotte paper speculated that Tom Jackson had started from the Valley, to join the defense of Richmond. As she read it Anna frowned. That might be necessary, but could it mean that all of their Valley would be left to the enemy? As Tom had so often drummed into her, a lost Valley of Virginia might bring a lost war . . .

The next few days were glum, but then, on his return from town, her father burst into the house in high excitement. "Mary, Anna! I—I can hardly believe it." He stammered badly: "Tom's amazed everybody. He didn't move east toward Richmond at all; he may have started in that direction to fool people, but then he went the opposite way, beat at one of the other armies against him, Frémont's, and sent it running! The Union's still trying to find out what happened . . ."

Warmly Anna listened to the reports Dr. Morrison had brought with him; he told them of the roaring delight in the Valley, and also of increasing Federal alarm. From that day on stories arrived, emphasizing the question asked by both sides: Where had Jackson gone *now*? A week went by, and another had started when Harriet Irwin's carriage rocked in from Charlotte with yet more astonishing word: "Nobody knows how Tom's done it, but he drove his men until they got back to General Banks, surprised him completely, and beat him! He chased Banks for miles, drove him out of the Valley. Anna, they say it's the most remarkable feat of the war . . ."

Anna looked from one face to another; could this all be true? For days the family gaped as neighbor after neighbor brought them news of later developments. "Stonewall's got Washington in a black panic; they're sure he's going to sweep right in on them and capture the capital. They've had to change all their plans—call back thousands of men from the drive on Richmond to protect themselves against the General and his men!" "They say Lincoln and his cabinet are in a fury, and wild stories have the place in an uproar."

Another drawling voice cut in: "Mrs. Jackson, those Yankees can't guess where he's going to show up next. He's marching up and down the Valley, pushing over the mountain trails, crossing his own path to fool the Union. The Yankees are reeling, going in a dozen directions at once to be ready when old Stonewall smashes down. They're calling his men 'foot cavalry' because they move so fast . . ."

When their guests left, Dr. Morrison walked back to her with an air that approached awe: "Child, this is even bigger than we've understood. Tom's added something new to the war, something

—brave and flashing . . ." She had seldom seen her father so strongly stirred.

Tom had done what even his greatest admirers had not thought possible. When Anna paid a visit to Harriet in Charlotte she realized the extent of his fame; strangers came up to her on the streets: "Mrs. Jackson, we want to say how grateful we all are to your husband." "Ma'am, Stonewall's the best soldier we have, and he's showing Richmond what real fighting is." Close to tears, Anna could only nod in silence. And just a short while before she had been asking herself if Tom's career might not be on the decline!

Familiar Valley names rolled past her: Front Royal, Staunton, McDowell, Cross Keys, Port Republic . . . the Massanuttons, the Blue Ridge, and other ranges she had come to know so well, and also Winchester, their "war home." Then fuller details arrived of Tom's feats, details which made them yet more fantastic. He and his fighters had covered incredible distances, pressing on through searing heat, through rainy nights that turned roads into gruel-like earth, along ridges from which men slipped into mud that was even worse than the mired passageways.

Tom's army had scored in quick thrusts by small bands of raiders, by pounding advances through surprise concentrations. Outnumbered heavily, as usual, he had nevertheless used every soldier to maximum effect; every advantage was pushed relentlessly to its fullest extent. Surprise, attack, attack, surprise . . . Several times the Union commanders had felt certain they had Stonewall's army in a trap and had cornered him at last. But Jackson knew his Valley too well; he disappeared into the mists, to reappear many miles away on a new and slashing rampage.

"Anna, he's captured so many supplies . . ." Her father found the reports of Tom's fellow officers hard to believe at first. Tom's men had seized guns, wagons by the score, drugs and medical supplies, commissary goods, small arms, food. Dr. Morrison blinked: "Three thousand prisoners from Banks' army alone— nearly a third of all his men, I'd guess. More than nine thousand arms, and wagonload on top of wagonload of Union goods, stretching nearly ten miles at one point!"

The family chuckled at some of the reports: Tom Jackson was using the Union army to keep his forces going and, General Banks had become "Stonewall's commissary agent." Tom had captured so many Union wagons that he had a new name among the Confederates, "the wagon hunter." And Stonewall's soldiers took so many Federal uniforms to replace their own tattered clothes that orders went out to curb their habit of wearing Union garb.

Tom's letters reflected his own joy: God had blessed their arms; by the grace of the Almighty Father they had won again. In the midst of grim campaigning, he once halted to look for Weyer's Cave because he remembered that Anna had seen it on her travels. He put aside pressing calls to describe mountain scenes, crests that stood blue and gray in the distance, the pale tints of bushes blooming in the sun.

"I do want so much to see my darling," he assured her, "but fear such a privilege will not be enjoyed for some time to come." And her heart rejoiced when he pictured his triumphal re-entry into Winchester, and the hour he had spent with the Grahams. Another time he wrote, "Time forbids a longer letter, but it does not forbid my loving my *esposita*."

Stories sped back of Tom's ever growing secrecy in campaigning. "When he orders a march, his own men never know where they're going; his officers have to guess, and sometimes the first they realize of his scheme is when they find the enemy's tents ahead of them." Anna could smile at a newspaperman's tale of the civilian who tried, with one hint after another, to get her husband to reveal something of his intentions. At last, as Tom's train rolled slowly away, the man called, "General, where are you going?"

This time General Jackson made a response. Leaning from the window, he asked, "Can you keep a secret?"

"Sure can."

"So can I."

Now, however, Anna heard grim overtones. "The Union's sending two enormous columns after Stonewall from opposite directions." Her fears rose, and she asked herself how Tom could escape such a trap. Two weeks passed, as each day she expected a bleak message; at best, he might withdraw after heavy losses. Then, as she listened almost in disbelief, her father told her that the incredible had happened. Slipping between the two armies, Tom had picked a place to meet one of them, had struck it a furious blow; now he and his men had disappeared, and nobody could say where they were.

One day as Anna rested on the porch at Cottage Home, a neighbor, who was a veteran of the War of 1812, arrived to speak excitedly to her: "Miss Anna, do you realize that he's become a legend in the North as well as the South?" This was news indeed, and she could only stare fixedly at him as he went on, "Union papers are describing his operations in detail, saying he's a genius, using him as an example for Yankee commanders. One after another, they're demanding to know why their own generals can't fight the way Stonewall does."

To Anna's further amazement, he handed her a clipping from the New York *Times:*

One thing is certain, Jackson is equally eminent as a strategist and tactician. He handles his army like a whip, making it crack in out-of-the-way corners where you scarcely thought the lash would go.

Such comments—and in a Northern journal! This was stranger than ever, and more exhilarating. But soon afterward Anna came upon an item that made her heart sink. Turner Ashby, riding into a skirmish on his white steed, had fallen beneath an enemy volley, and Tom's forces had lost one of their greatest warriors—one of the three Sandie Pendleton had called "invincible." Anna had not known Ashby more than casually; nevertheless she felt sad as she thought of the magnificent fighter. The matter haunted her. Ashby had shared in all of her husband's fighting, the blasts of fire, the hazards. And now he was gone in a moment.

Meanwhile another shadow had lengthened over the South. The siege of Richmond tightened as the Union concentrated ever more powerful forces and moved closer, closer on the Confederate capital. Already Northern soldiers could see the city's highest steeple, and it was said that when the bells rang in Richmond, the enemy knew the time . . . Overnight the Confederacy suffered an unexpected loss, when General Joe Johnston was wounded near the capital, and his condition reported serious. "A bad blow," Anna's father shook his head.

Before that news could be absorbed, Jefferson Davis had chosen his successor—Robert E. Lee, his military adviser in Richmond. Immediately grumbling broke out, and Anna heard echoes in Charlotte: "Davis is daft, naming an old failure like Lee!" "A flat disappointment ever since the war started." "What's he ever done except sit on his rear and give paper orders?"

As she listened blankly, Anna recalled that Tom considered Lee America's finest soldier. Could her husband be wrong? After all, Lee had made no great mark in the war . . . While she sat reflecting, her father approached hurriedly: "What do you think's happened? Tom's right near Richmond, joining Lee's army. They fooled the Union—sent a reinforcement of seven thousand of Tom's men one way, and slipped them back. He went right over the mountains and took them to Richmond. Even the men weren't sure till they got close to the capital!"

Excitement enveloped Anna: then she realized that the war and Tom's fortunes had taken a new and grim turn. He would have his part in the climactic battle that might settle the war, and he would be fighting beside the man for whom he had so much respect. But, with such overwhelming masses of men and supplies against them, could the Confederates hold out?

Definite news came slowly as the Union tightened its grip on the countryside. From Virginia, a brief note made Anna's eyes brighten. In the middle of the Virginia fighting, Harvey Hill had looked up in astonishment to find Tom, dusty and bedraggled, beside him. The last he had heard of Stonewall, he was many miles away, racing along the mountains in the opposite direction. The two brothers-in-law would be together in Richmond's defense. This news made Anna happier; Tom and Harvey had always respected each other's abilities.

Yet a harsh situation was in the making at Richmond. Food had become scarcer than ever. The poor and hungry were rioting for bread. Other developments, too, made Anna wince. One of those big new balloons had appeared in the air over Richmond. On its platform stood a Union professor, signaling messages about Confederate troops to the Union ground forces. What a grimly scientific thing was modern war; could it ever be more mechanically organized? Telegraph wires, monstrous new guns, machines swinging in the air . . . And if Richmond fell, all their efforts might have been for nothing.

Anna spent her days walking nervously along the paths and the halls of Cottage Home. The recent weeks had brought one blow after another. Norfolk had fallen and Savannah was now closed; Nashville had gone to the Union, and also Memphis and Pensacola. Mobile lay under heavy blockade, and Charleston as well. Kentucky, much of Tennessee, large areas of Alabama and Mississippi . . . One vital area after another was lost.

Meanwhile, in the alarming atmosphere of this July of 1862, Anna and her family waited for the decision at Richmond. Thousands of men were slipping into place as "Little Mac" McClellan consolidated his position on both sides of the Chickahominy

River, while Robert E. Lee worked frantically to fill gaps in his
own lines. Anna blinked at the figures: nearly 86,000 for the South
against 150,000 for the Union. And the Northerners commanded
mountains of guns and wagons, cannon and equipment . . .

A sentence in a hastily scratched letter made her pause: Tom
Jackson had arrived at the last minute, close to exhaustion, de-
scending from the clear mountain air to the miasmic river bottoms, "and a rumor says he's had a touch of fever." Then followed
days of silence. "It's a terrible battle—a series of them, I suppose,"
her father said as the fighting went on, day after day. She caught
names—Gaines' Mill, Cold Harbor, White Oak Swamp, Malvern
Hill—names that would be repeated later by millions of Southerners. She heard more and more of the fetid swamp, of the heat
that rose in almost visible layers from the mosquito-thick bogs in
which the soldiers moved. And every day, remembering the story
of Tom's "touch of fever," she prayed to God to grant him good
health and let him come through unhurt.

Several times her father frowned over the reports: "It's hard to
tell who's winning, or just what's happening. No, no special reports about Tom or Harvey either." Each morning increased
Anna's uncertainty, her nervous tension. Had McClellan and his
men smashed through at last; had the murderous fire, the bloody
slaughter sent the Confederates to destruction? Her answer came
at high noon on a burning day. A dispatch rider almost collapsed
as he leaped from his horse and cried to them, "Yankees retreatin'
from Richmond, all of 'em!"

There was a long silence. "Thank God. We've been saved."
Anna's mouth was dry; she tried to continue, but she could not.
Turning from the others, she ascended to her room, where she
spent a half-hour in prayer. The next morning dozens of messages
arrived, and friends rode over to talk excitedly, exultantly. Then
and later, her delight was tempered by her memory of the way
some of these same people had spoken a short time earlier.

"General Lee—there's nobody quite like him! I *always* said to
keep an eye on R. E. Lee."

"I knew all along that if those fools in Richmond would only
give Lee his chance . . ."

Both speakers were men who had previously stared down their
noses at any mention of Lee. Again and happily she caught another name, coupled with the Virginian's: "Lee and Jackson, that's
a real team." "Stonewall and Bobby Lee—those are the two we

needed." All at once Anna remembered the cries that had risen
when the war first began: Beauregard and Johnston, Johnston and
Beauregard. How long would Lee's name and Tom's be cheered
as they were today?

Tom's own message arrived, and she read it swiftly: "An ever-
kind Providence has greatly blessed our efforts and given us great
reason for thankfulness . . ." She started in surprise as she continued: "You must give fifty dollars for church purposes, and more
should you be so disposed. Keep an account of the amount, as we
must give at least one tenth of our income." Even now, Tom
thought of his tithes!

Then slowly Anna became aware that some people did not view
the Confederate record at Richmond in a completely rosy light.
Nearly everywhere in the Southern ranks there had been delays,
some almost fatal. While generals fumbled, thousands of men had
moiled about in confusion. General Jackson had not shown his
usual decision, his determined attack. And Lee, some asserted
firmly, had lost a great opportunity by failure to press on after
the Unionists and crush the North's greatest army.

But for Anna Jackson this was a time of deliverance from fear.
Her husband had been spared, and their new country had been
protected from ruin. She felt safer as she awaited the child who
stirred inside her.

PART V

A Sunday in May

It was well that I could not foresee the future. It was in mercy that He who knew the end from the beginning did not lift the veil.

—*Mary Anna Morrison Jackson*

CHAPTER 15

As summer of 1862 gave way to early fall, Anna Jackson nursed her energies, preparing for the months that lay ahead. Again and again she told herself that she must be strong, that this baby must live . . . When she went to Tom again, she would take him his child. Or—the question came repeatedly to her—could he possibly make a trip to North Carolina for a few days, and be with her as he had been when Mary was born?

Anna heard of several officers who had received two-week furloughs so that they could be home on such occasions. In her notes to Tom she hinted, then wrote directly of her hopes. Each of his letters brought a firmer response. That was out of the question. Since he never granted such leaves for others, he could not take one for himself. Absences of that sort, he assured her, hurt the Confederacy, crippled its strength. On any number of occasions a small extra force might have turned defeat into victory . . . Anna nodded slowly; she should have known her husband's answer.

Another small hope rose, only to flicker away. Perhaps she could go to him for a visit before the baby's birth. Then slowly she realized that a trip of any kind would be impossible for her. "It would be delightful to see my darling," Tom wrote her with an air of finality, "but we know that all things are ordered for the best."

Anna asked no more, and, resigning herself, followed his progress from a distance. After the Seven Days' battle he made his first public appearance in Richmond, slipping quietly into a pew at the Second Presbyterian Church. Before long one member after another of the congregation recognized him. As the service ended scores of people elbowed their way to him, to shake his hand and offer good wishes. Anna smiled to herself when she read that his staff members had to retrieve him from his admirers.

Outside the church a woman had touched Tom's arm and whispered to him, and he left with her for his first "social call" in Richmond—on the mother of a boy who had died in his army . . .

Anna was stirred as others reported that whenever Tom appeared among his old soldiers, cheers broke out, in tributes of respect and admiration without parallel in the war.

At such times, officers wrote her, Tom would take off his hat and, flushing heavily, take up Little Sorrel's reins and ride off, while the Confederate fighters yelled louder than ever. True, she had been told that some men feared him as a commander and complained about his "harsh" orders. But most of his men had a strange, fierce affection for Tom. They might chuckle at his idiosyncrasies; nevertheless they followed him unwaveringly.

In the early days after the lifting of the siege of Richmond, Anna learned several upsetting things. Casually Tom wrote her, "During the past week I have not been well, having suffered from fever and debility . . ." Was this the reason he had not made a better showing at Richmond? Then she heard through an officer friend that Tom had wished the Confederates to push on after the retreating McClellan and smash his army. As always, attack, press the advantage . . . He had hoped for the same course at Manassas, and, she realized, he had repeatedly urged an invasion of the North.

But it appeared that Lee, President Davis, and others thought such pursuit impossible under the circumstances. Although she understood his point of view, Anna was relieved that Tom had not had his way; at least there would be no more slaughter for a time. A little later she bristled when her officer friend described the military conference itself. She had always suspected that Tom had not changed his opinion of Jefferson Davis; now she had confirmation of her belief.

President Davis had entered the room at the farmhouse headquarters where Tom and several other officers were awaiting him. The courtly Lee presented members of the staff, including Jackson, to their President. Tom had remained stiffly at attention and had not offered his hand, and Davis himself said nothing.

"Why, President, don't you know General Jackson? This is our Stonewall Jackson." Lee had gone to work with his usual diplomacy, but he met scant success. Tom's attitude was all too clear. He merely saluted, and Davis confined himself to a bow . . . Anna clicked her tongue. Had any of them expected her husband to throw his arms around a man who had acted toward him as Mr. Davis had?

By this time a wave of relief and returning hope was sweeping most of the South. Cannon fire was heard no more over Richmond; the town's life was beginning to revive, and with it the spirit of the Confederacy. Down the Mississippi, the city of Vicksburg remained in Confederate hands despite preliminary Federal threats, and Anna heard predictions: "It's our Gibraltar, and it'll stand there forever." Western armies prepared for new drives, and from the East came rumblings of fresh offensives against the Union.

And what of General Johnston, wounded before the main Richmond battles? Several times she inquired about the man who had served for many months as Tom's superior, and learned that he was recovering and would receive other assignments. Meanwhile General Lee's reputation soared ever higher, and Anna mused over the curious way in which fortune had dealt with the two men. If Johnston had not been hurt, and had continued to use his more cautious methods, would Richmond have fallen, or would Johnston himself have won out in his supreme test? To that question none of them would ever have an answer.

And Tom Jackson's own standing seemed to rise with the passing weeks. One night her younger brother Joe grinned as he drew out a sheet of music. "Look at this," he said, and took Anna to the piano. "They're playing it everywhere . . ." She read the title, "Stonewall Jackson's Way," and her heart beat in surprise and excitement. She listened intently as the boy's words rang out, and after a moment she concentrated on their meaning:

> We see him now—the queer slouched hat,
>   Cocked o'er his eye askew;
> The shrewd, dry smile; the speech so pat,
>   So calm, so blunt, so true.
> The "Blue-Light Elder" knows 'em well;
>   Says he, "That's Banks—he's fond of shell;
> Lord save his soul! We'll give him——" well!
>   That's "Stonewall Jackson's way."

The lines went on and on, until the final words:

> The foe had better ne'er been born
> That gets in "Stonewall's way."

As Joe Morrison pounded out the ending, he smiled up at her, but Anna's feelings were mixed. "Blue-Light Elder," "Old Blue Light" . . . Those terms for her husband did not sit altogether well with her. And still the song was friendly and affectionate. After a moment she faced Joe with a happy look . . . That evening a Richmond friend forwarded her a clipping that gave her a new pride. From all over the South, the Richmonder told her, Tom was being deluged with letters of admiration, messages of support, gifts of food, clothing, personal supplies.

A Raleigh connection of the Morrisons passed on a story from a London paper, presenting a glowing description of her husband's military operations. The ever growing English interest in Tom was amazing. Lithographers were making likenesses of him and Lee and selling them on the London streets; traveling Britishers had begun to call on Tom in camp, military observers made detailed queries, and journalists hunted for information to send home.

"I don't think Tom's giving the newspapermen anything," her father laughed. "If there's one thing he hates, it's stories that give military secrets." The British military observers, he pointed out, had a professional interest in the conflict and Tom's part in it. "You see, Anna, there's never been a war like this, with such masses of men and such use of concentrated forces and guns and supplies." The minister's face darkened: "We're learning to kill and maim one another so much more easily and so much more expertly. The fighting we're doing in America now is changing the whole course of warfare."

Anna looked away. Such talk disturbed her, and her father's remarks revived the questions that had been pressed upon her. Was the pressure piling too heavily on Tom? Was too much expected of him? He would turn from no responsibility, and someday an impossible demand, a burden beyond any man's strength, might be placed upon him . . . She frowned. She, too, had been educated to a concept of duty. She did not expect him, nor indeed would she want him, to reject any call to service.

Soon after the end of the fighting at Richmond, Tom left the steamy swamps of the Chickahominy to return to the Valley, where he would face new Union drives in Northern Virginia. Anna heard a new Union name, that of Major General Pope, transferred from Western Virginia. McClellan was in decline, and Pope had a newly created post as commander of all Northern forces. The Union effort had entered a new phase, perhaps still more dangerous for the Confederacy.

"And Tom's men have had some hard times," Dr. Morrison reminded her. When it moved out of Richmond, the army left hundreds of its men under markers in the humid river bottoms. Many of those who survived limped around the city or lay dying in hospitals. "They've been through so much," her father went on sadly. "They're ragged, almost spent. They haven't had the food they should have; you keep hearing that they went for days at a stretch with only a few biscuits, a handful of smoked meat. And so many of them don't have shoes. On every march, hundreds fall out because of their bleeding feet . . ." At these tales of want and suffering Anna's eyes closed. Her husband's men needed so much, and the Confederacy could give them so little.

And now the flamboyant General Pope supposedly made a roaring proclamation: "My headquarters are in the saddle." To this her father, echoing many others, including Abraham Lincoln, remarked, "The saddle is where most people put their hindquarters." Anna listened with amusement as her father spoke ever increasingly of war strategy. With three sons-in-law—Tom, Harvey Hill, and Rufus Barringer—Confederate generals, Dr. Morrison had become a student of military affairs.

She was not amused, however, when her brother Joseph approached her and her parents with a deeply serious air. For weeks Joe had been dropping hints, and today he addressed them directly: "I want to be with brother Tom, and if he won't take me I'll apply anywhere they will. I'm old enough and there's no reason why . . ."

As Anna's eyes met her parents', she realized that they could not stop the boy. But Joe finally agreed to wait at least for an answer from Tom himself. Several weeks passed, and Anna could not have said whether she hoped for an affirmative or negative reply. If Tom took the youth, he would be with someone who had an interest in his welfare. But, after all, her husband's army was always in the hardest fighting . . . Tom's reply was pointed:

If you will vouch for Joseph's *being an early riser* during the remainder of the war, I will give him an aideship . . . if you will vouch for him to rise regularly at dawn, I will offer him the position.

Though some might have thought Tom wrote in humor, Anna understood that he meant every word. Her brother seized the note in delight, and somberly the family watched him go. They had given so many—Tom, her oldest brother William, Harvey Hill, Rufus Barringer, Susan's husband Alphonso Avery, and now young Joe . . . In these days any courier might bring bleak word from one of several battlefronts.

Now came disturbing reports of another kind. While Tom's men moved forward, the Union was building up staggering new forces under General Pope. "Hills of tinned stuff, mountains of guns and bullets, and wagonloads of clothing . . ." Her father studied the reports. When he reached the Valley, Pope took a harsh step, ordering his men to live off the land, to destroy and confiscate left and right. The new policy made Tom Jackson storm; his letters made it clear to Anna that he regarded Pope with more contempt than any other Union officer.

Rumblings of other troubles reached her. Many of Tom's military subordinates complained because he refused to give them even as much as a hint of his plans; they protested bitterly that he would not delegate authority or trust them. Anna heard rumors of other mutterings against Tom by General Longstreet, a man who set a high value on his own importance. And, in this summer of mounting edginess, Tom was snapping at his subordinates. In one case, when he had planned a very early morning start, his staff did not get up in time. Furious, Tom ordered the food packed and the coffee (a true luxury, taken from the enemy) poured on the ground. Sadly Anna asked herself if Tom was under all too terrible a strain.

Before she could decide, she learned of a dangerous clash with Pope's men. Here her younger brother had had his first taste of battle. Joe survived, but his horse was shot from under him and he was bathed in spurting blood. The description did not make Anna happier. Unexpected tales came back; officers had found Tom galloping forward, ignoring hails of bullets, and had finally intervened to persuade him to return. Suddenly she thought of Turner Ashby, the "invincible," who had toppled before a Union shot. One bullet, even a stray one . . . And since so many of the enemy knew her husband from pictures, he would make an easy target. In this mood Anna glanced again at the Unionist New York *Times,* to see a line she had previously missed. "The mountain fox," a correspondent called him, and added, "We may run the mountain fox to death yet."

Her anxieties sharpened, and she could not ignore her fears. Her mother reasoned with her several times: "Anna, this is all wrong. You're hurting yourself." Anna knew that Mrs. Morrison was right, and yet what could she do? Hetty said nothing, but stayed closed to her side, stroking her hands, rubbing her temples. "You 'member the nice times we had at Lexington, the day the Major come in . . ." Anna smiled for a moment; no matter how many honors Tom won, to Hetty he stayed "the Major." Then her fingers tightened. If only he were still the Major; if only they were back in Lexington again, living quietly and obscurely!

Anna could not remain on the sofa. With a long sigh she jumped to her feet and paced the floor, back and forth, back and forth. And then she stopped short. Years ago Tom had told her she must not "take counsel of her fears." Firmly she repeated the words, and set to work to thrust aside her pressing concerns. At dusk Anna took a place at her window, fixing her eyes on the skies, as she had done that time in New York. The silence of early evening had fallen; the only sounds were the drone of voices in the back gardens. Slowly her tensions lessened, and she rested easily for the first time in days.

Her new spirit of peace was still with her when she received a message from a point close to her heart—Winchester. The Union had again taken over, but despite General Pope's control, Mrs. Graham had managed to slip a letter through the lines.

While you were here, it became so natural for me to go into your room to communicate with you everything that was interesting or amusing, that now, when anything funny happens . . . I feel an intense desire to tell you about it.

The sheet dimmed before her as the words brought back, poignantly, their last winter in the old town. And poor Winchester had changed hands so many times . . . Reading on, she discovered that Tom had paid a visit to the Grahams a few months earlier:

He spent two evenings with us; the evening he arrived here (which was Sunday) he came around and said he did not think it was wrong to come *home* on Sunday. . . . I don't remember ever experiencing more happiness than during that visit . . . our dear general in his old place. . . . When the Federal Army last retreated, some of the frightened fugitives reported that the ladies of our town actually *fired on them*. Mother was seen to *kill two!*

As she laughed, Anna recalled the mock battle started by the bright-hearted Mrs. Magill. It was not too hard to imagine that doughty woman fighting for her home. A moment later Anna's mind returned to Tom's reunion with the Grahams. If only she

could have been there, or if her husband could be here with her
and the Morrisons . . .

A more upsetting message arrived from Maggie Preston. Colonel Preston's son Frank had been in recent fighting at Winchester,
and was seriously wounded, his arm smashed, a ball in his side.
The Colonel went out in search of the boy. Permitted to cross
Union lines, John Preston located Frank, to discover that he had
suffered two amputations of his arm, the second at his shoulder.

Anna's eyes darkened when she read the story. Colonel
Preston was not allowed to remove his son, and had to leave him
among strangers. Maggie described her own agony. If Frank died,
they might not even know it . . . And now the youngest boy,
Willy, had joined Stonewall's army; after months of pleading, his
wish to get into the fight had been granted.

Despite their pain over Frank, the Prestons told of their pride
at Willy's bravery in his first action. Part of a regiment had broken,
until the boy rallied it and led it in a charge. Anna's spirit quickened at the last words. Young Willy, with his boyish charm, his
brightness of outlook . . . But from now on Maggie would have
one more member of the broken family over whom to worry, and
another face would rise in Anna's dreams.

Overnight a long-familiar place began to appear in the newspaper columns—Manassas, where a new climax was developing.
General Lee remained near Richmond, while Tom moved in the
direction of Manassas. Her father grumbled over the uncertain
accounts: "It seems they're sending another big Union army to
back up Pope. And when the two get together, Tom will be outnumbered more than ever, enormously."

As Anna tried not to let the news upset her, Dr. Morrison
returned with later accounts: "Now General Lee's bringing his
men toward Tom's, but"—he shook his head nervously—"they're
well separated, with the Union forces between them."

For days they waited. "Anna," Dr. Morrison told her, "they say
Tom's retreated somewhere." Was that good or bad? She could
not guess, nor could her father. Then at the week's end Dr. Morrison entered her room, a newspaper in his trembling hands:
"Look, look here. Tom's taken his whole army on a march *completely around* the Union flank—close to fifty-five miles in two
days! Anna, that sounds impossible, even for men like them, over
the country roads in the August sun . . ."

Around her Anna heard the gay voices of her neighbors as they celebrated this fantastic feat. But she was thinking of the exhausted men, their clothes filthy and ripped, thousands of them trudging shoeless for mile after mile, and her mind went repeatedly to Tom, pushing doggedly on. How was his health, and was he keeping from her the whole truth about his physical condition? "They've reached Manassas, and part of the Union army's drawn away, so that they've found enormous supplies—food and everything else." Anna laughed bitterly; for once the huge Northern reserves would have full use. Then she grew solemn. Nobody predicted what would happen when General Pope's heavy reinforcements joined him against the Confederates.

A little later the intent Dr. Morrison rubbed his chin and stared: "They say General Pope's gone practically crazy—can't decide what to do next. Started for Manassas and Tom was gone from there. Went to another place and missed him. The Union men are marching all over the landscape, trying to put their hands on him!" Anna did not smile; she could see no humor in this pursuit of her husband and his men by superior forces. Even now Tom's life might be at stake. There were more days of silence, and then one morning her father walked slowly to the porch and lowered himself beside her.

"Child, there's a battle on, tens of thousands on both sides, and it must be some of the most brutal fighting of the war."

The ordeal continued. Was this to be the struggle in which Tom and General Lee would suffer destruction? Biting her lips, Anna tossed through a sleepless night and arose in the morning to hear hard news. "Still fighting all around there, day after day, and that's all anybody knows." Another night saw her waiting cold-faced through endless hours. She fell asleep only as dawn broke, and jumped up when a courier clattered across the porch.

Her father's voice rose from below: "Anna, they've driven the Union army off the field, back into Washington City!" After a long, stunned silence, she dropped to her knees, crying in happiness. After giving her thanks, she added a plea: Please, God, let this carnage soon be over. How much more could these men take?

Next week she learned details that dismayed her. The struggle at Second Manassas had begun at a black risk. Had the bulk of Lee's men not merged in time with Jackson's, the Confederates would have been smashed by the sheer, hammering weight of their opponents.

Anna's breath quickened at the stories—some of Tom's men collapsing on the march, others limping, clinging to wagons or clutching the shoulders of their friends; some sinking to the ground to lie exhausted for a while before resuming their progress. "On their way they grabbed whatever food came in sight—heads of corn from the fields, anything, and shoved it raw into their mouths." "Those shoeless fellows left bloody prints on the battle-field." "They were so short of ammunition, a lot of 'em ran out and ripped cartridge boxes off the Yankee dead or dying, and used the enemy's own bullets against them."

The tales became worse: "The injured and dying everywhere you looked, men moaning in the dark, crying for help when you went by; you couldn't walk anywhere without stepping on a hand or a head." "One part of the field was like nothing you ever saw—corpses and wounded men in red and yellow Zouave dress from Texas, covering the ground like a fancy rug, and those that still lived twisting and turning before they gave up." "Toward the end our boys had so little ammunition that they used rocks and muskets to beat in the Yankees' brains . . ."

Tom's next note brought Second Manassas closer home. Hugh White, the son of their minister, who had been one of Tom's helpers in the Sunday school classes, had been killed there. Anna began to lower the note; then a familiar name caught her eye and she read on with new shock. Willy Preston had been fatally wounded.

At her cry, Hetty ran in, and when Anna told her the news, she wept with her mistress. Only two weeks earlier Maggie had written happily to report her stepson's record in his first battle, and now the boy was gone . . . After being struck, Willy had watched his friends gather around him and told them not to distress themselves: "I'm not afraid to die."

Badly shaken, Colonel Preston made a second trip in search of his son, but, as in the first case, he was not entirely successful. At the battle site he searched for some time among the graves and bodies rotting in the fetid air. In one gully John Preston saw a hundred corpses. At last the soldiers dug open a shallow grave. When he lifted the blanket, Willy's father could not make out a single feature. Tearing at the shirt, he found the name in Maggie's writing. It was impossible to remove the body, and Colonel Preston had left a marker.

Anna heard more about Willy's death. When he received the word, her husband had almost lost control of himself. Catching

at the arm of Dr. Hunter McGuire, his medical officer, he demanded to know why the doctor had left the youth. Finally he
regained his composure and walked into the woods to be alone
in his sorrow. And Jim, the body servant, had sunk to the ground
in tears.

Anna thought of her husband and her brothers. Each of them
had been under fire. And in her mind there echoed Maggie
Preston's words: all through little Lexington, other women were
crying over their own hurts. "It is like the death of the first-born
in Egypt. Who thinks of or cares for victory now!"

Without warning, worn and exhausted though Tom's forces
were, they were being sent with others into a new enterprise—
an electrifying one. Robert E. Lee had assigned them with his
own forces to the kind of project which her husband had long
urged, an invasion over the Potomac into Maryland, and from
there, perhaps, into Pennsylvania! They lacked supplies, guns,
ammunition; and the effort would be a great gamble. Yet Lee
had decided to run the risk.

For days the Morrisons read every line that reached them. General Lee issued a proclamation, declaring that the Confederates
marched into the neighboring state as liberators, and throughout
the South people wondered whether the Marylanders would respond to the Southern banner. If they did, the war's course might
change within a day. "Anna, it's a great hour," her father exclaimed. Yet she could not be sure how the people of Maryland
would regard the dirty, unshod men who had been through so
much, who carried all the marks of their hard experiences . . .

Almost at once the answer came. Although hundreds of Marylanders ran out to smile at the men, others showed only curiosity
or neutrality, and many more displayed a stolid hostility. Maryland would not rise up behind Lee and Jackson.

Night after night, as the warm September progressed, Anna
asked herself how Tom and his men would fare against the Unionists in the neighboring region. At Sharpsburg, the Confederates,
numbering 40,000, lined up against a massive Union army of 70,-
000 under McClellan, back in command for the time. Men roared
and blasted, knifed and lunged at one another. "Child, it must be
worse than Second Manassas—the bloodiest day of the war."

Anna winced as bits of information came by telegraph. Relentlessly Lee and Jackson pushed their men into the savage butchery,

and again and again the Confederates approached disaster. At
the end, the South drove back the enemy, but Lee and Jackson
had expended their full strength, and they had not won as they
had to. More than 18,000 men had been lost on both sides, and
worse faced the Confederates . . . Grimly the Southerners signaled a withdrawal into Virginia. The Union, similarly spent,
could not follow.

Only afterward was Anna to see the full significance of the
Maryland invasion. In his notes Tom insisted that it had accomplished something, had given Virginians a respite and had hurt
the Union. Yet were its great sacrifices justified? And now tales
reached her of Tom's mounting fatigue; he went for days with
only an hour or two of rest at irregular intervals.

Once he had fallen asleep as he stood against a fence post,
and another time, as he rode on Little Sorrel, a friend beside him
had to reach out and steady him. He called a subordinate for a
conference, only to doze in the middle of a sentence. "One night
he was so worn down, ma'am, that he put a piece of food in his
mouth and dropped off with it on his tongue." Anna's eyes
clouded; could Tom's health stand all this? More word came, with
an episode that made thousands argue. Tom had had a raging exchange with one of the leading generals of his army, the peppery
young A. P. Hill, over one of Jackson's orders to the troops. Stonewall arrested Hill, charged him with neglect of duty, and the dispute was to hang over them for many months.

A happier development diverted Anna—the choice of a new
commander for the Stonewall Brigade. Through one campaign
after another her husband had watched Frank Paxton's conduct,
his handling of men. He had made him his assistant adjutant
general, praised his bravery in battle, and now he picked him for
one of the most celebrated of Confederate posts. Anna smiled as
she mused over the situation. It was good to know that Frank had
won this recognition, and also that Tom was capable of such
forgiveness.

Yet the matter had not quite ended. In naming Paxton, her husband had passed over Colonel Andrew Jackson Grigsby, a Lexingtonian whom Anna remembered from many meetings. Grigsby,
a Mexican War veteran a few years Tom's senior, was vigorous
and hot-tempered. At Sharpsburg he had performed admirably,
taking over a division after successive commanders had fallen under fire. And now Anna's father pursed his lips as reports came in

of Grigsby's burning reaction to Tom's appointment: "The Colonel's really biting nails."

Furiously, Grigsby had quit the army and gone back to civilian life; he had been grievously injured, he said. For the army's good, he would let this insult go for the time. But the moment the war closed, he would challenge Jackson to a duel, and it would be man against man!

"Anna, this has its funny side," Dr. Morrison told her tentatively. She did not smile; she had heard frequent tales of bloody exchanges between Confederates over matters less serious than this. And if and when they returned to Lexington after the war, Colonel Grigsby would be there.

She was happier when she learned that Tom was himself not far from his old quarters at Winchester. Once more their old "war home" had shifted hands. He wrote her: "If I only had you with me in my evenings, it would be such a comfort! I hope it may be my privilege to be in Winchester this winter." That winter . . . October ended, and the baby was due in late November. The cheery Mrs. Graham informed her that Tom had visited the family:

It did seem so much like old times—those good old times of last winter; we were all so cozy in our dining-room, and around that table we did wish for you in your seat between us. . . . He is looking . . . far *handsomer* than I ever saw him—and is in such fine spirits, seemed so unreserved and unrestrained. . . . He certainly has had adulation enough to spoil him, but it seems not to affect or harm him at all . . . don't you wish *you* had been here?

Though her lively friend asked the question in good spirit, the words hurt . . . The baby was delayed and, although the doctor insisted there was no cause for concern, Anna felt disturbed. Harriet Irwin made a suggestion: "Why don't you and Mother come to Charlotte and stay here for a while, so that you can be close to medical attention?" Mrs. Morrison quickly seconded the plan, and after some thought Anna agreed. A day or so later her mother fell suddenly ill, and the doctor shook his head when she insisted she must accompany her daughter. "You need a lot of rest, right here," he ruled, and reluctantly Mrs. Morrison stayed behind. "Child, I'll join you the first day I can manage it."

Anna rode in a slow carriage from Cottage Home to the Irwin house and settled down in a sunny upstairs chamber. She missed her mother more than she had expected, and her anxiety gradually increased. "There's something wrong, I know it," she told Harriet and Isabella. And in spite of all her resolutions, Anna found it hard to be cheerful. The previous time Tom had helped her by his very presence, and now she wanted him here, more than she had wanted anything in her life. Angrily she pounded at her pillow. Who had worked harder in the war, who had more right to be there for the birth of his child? Breathing heavily, she called to Isabella, "Please take a telegraph message. Tell Tom I'm so sick I have to have him . . ."

Isabella Hill put out her hand for a pencil, then lowered it: "Anna, you know better than that."

By now Anna was crying, out of frustration and shame. Why was the baby delayed, and how much longer would she have to wait? After that morning, however, she was calmer. Several times during the ensuing week she caught herself at the beginning of a wave of self-pity, but she pressed back her tears, and also the fears that waited at the corners of her mind.

From Virginia Tom sent a request that made her smile. While he was eager for news, the family should notify him by letter rather than by telegraph; he wished to keep the subject entirely to himself. In spite of all his celebrity, Anna reflected, Tom remained completely reticent about his personal life.

On a bright Sunday morning, sitting uncomfortably against her pillow, Anna started a letter to him. She had finished only a few sentences when it began—the deep, throbbing pain that she remembered. "Hetty, Hetty!"

Before Anna could say more, the girl had called down the hall, and her brother-in-law hurried across the porch and to the carriage to fetch the doctor. With Harriet, Isabella, and Hetty at her bedside, Anna groaned, "Suppose he can't locate him on Sunday and . . ." She did not end the sentence, for agony had engulfed her.

The next hour was a haze of suffering. Once, as she twisted from side to side, Anna stared at the mirror and muttered, "Isabella, turn it around, right now. I don't want to look at myself." Then she seized her sister's hand and held it tightly. Her mind went to Tom, to her mother, to Dr. Morrison, and briefly to the other child, the dead one. When the doctor arrived she stared at him through waves of throbbing pain. Then, without warning, there came a wrenching worse than any of the others, and it was over.

Some time later the doctor's voice reached her through the dimness: "A girl, small but healthy." Someone murmured, "She looks exactly like the General." She . . . Anna was caught by a sense of disappointment; couldn't it have been a son? The feeling went quickly; they had their baby at last, she told herself, and that was enough.

After a time—she could not be sure of the hour—Harriet sat down beside her and placed the child in her arms. Anna stared down; the little one seemed so quiet. Only a rosy hand moved, and the mouth was tightly closed. She touched the almost black hair and the transparent cheek; a moment later she heard a loud, shrieking protest, and the eyes opened—a clear blue like Tom's. A sigh escaped Anna; she was satisfied.

Through the cloudy uncertainty another question came to her. "Have you thought of a name?" "I'll—I'll let Tom decide. If he wants . . ." Before she had finished the sentence Anna dozed away.

Through the next twenty-four hours she woke and slept, woke and slept. Her strength returned slowly. "Where is she?" she asked a little later, and when the baby was brought to her, Anna settled into a long, happy interlude during which she turned from her sisters to the child and back again.

"Listen." Harriet read her a brief note she had written to Tom, and, with a smile, another:

My Own Dear Father: As my mother's letter has been cut short by my arrival, I think it but justice that I should continue it. . . . I am a very tiny little thing. I weigh only eight and a half pounds, and Aunt Harriet says I am the express image of my darling papa. . . . My hair is dark and long, my eyes are blue, my nose straight just like papa's, and my complexion not all red like most young ladies of my age, but a beautiful blending of the lily and the rose. Now, all this would sound very vain if I were older, but I assure you I have not a particle of feminine vanity . . .

Anna smiled her thanks, and for some time thereafter Harriet continued this "correspondence" on the baby's part. Meanwhile Tom replied immediately to Anna:

Oh! how thankful I am to our kind Heavenly Father for having spared my precious wife and given us a little daughter! I cannot tell you how gratified I am. . . . Now don't exert yourself to write to me, for to know that you were taxing yourself to write would give me more pain than the letter would pleasure, so *you must not do it*. But you must *love your esposo* in the meantime. . . .

I expect you are just made up now with that baby. Don't you wish your husband wouldn't claim any part of it, but let you have the sole ownership? . . . Do not spoil it and don't let anybody tease it. Don't permit it to have a bad temper. How I would love to see the darling little thing! . . . At present I am about fifty miles from Richmond. . . . Should I remain here, I do hope you and baby can come to see me before spring, as you can come on the railroad.

At Tom's last line Anna suffered a dart of disappointment. Not until spring . . . and they had said good-by early last March. She continued to read, and found a "message" for the child. Anna was to "tell her he loves her better than all the baby-boys in the world, and more than all the other babies in the world." So he wanted to reassure Anna on that score, and he had. All of his letters described his gratitude to God, and his hope of seeing her and the child. Then, however, as if he had become fearful that he thought too much of the little one, Tom wrote:

Do not set your affections upon her, except as a gift from God. If she absorbs too much of our hearts, God may remove her from us.

For a long time Anna's eyes focused on the final sentence: "God may remove her . . ." He believed that; she could have no doubt of it . . . He must be trying to warn her. Nevertheless a chill went through her, and she wished he had not used the words . . . When she asked what he wanted to call the child, he suggested his mother's name. For their first baby he had chosen Mary, Mrs. Morrison's name. And now the new one would be Julia.

One morning she awakened to discover, with delight, that her mother, now fully recovered, had arrived in Charlotte. At the same time still another Morrison came in—young Sue, who had recently had her own first child. Sue's baby was, perhaps, handsomer than Julia, with something of her mother's pert brightness. But inevitably Anna's attention centered on her own child.

She lay for hours, nursing Julia, watching while she slept for long, unbroken stretches. She felt for Julia, more even than for her first baby, a warming, protective emotion. She chuckled once or twice over Tom's directions-from-a-distance: she must not let Julia have a temper, she must not spoil her . . . That might be precisely what she was doing, but she did not care.

For weeks she had heard little or nothing of the war, and then, from the faces of her mother and sisters, Anna gathered that something important was happening. One day she found that Mrs. Morrison had withheld two newspapers. "Please, I hope you'll never do it again," she said. "Whatever it is, I want to know." With some reluctance Mary Morrison spoke: "There's a big new battle brewing near the colonial town of Fredericksburg. General Lee's called Tom and his men to join him."

Fredericksburg . . . Anna recalled what she knew of the historic spot at the head of the Tidewater, the area that had produced George Washington, Jefferson, and Monroe. In this early winter the old town and its wooded hills were crowded with thousands of Confederates, while the Union massed its men across the river. Several times during the next few days, listening to the words of Mr. Irwin, her brother-in-law, Anna went numb with apprehension.

In heavy fog and freezing weather the two sides met in harrowing battle. The town was being ripped and gutted by Union shellings, as wave after wave of Federal troops crossed the Rappahannock to the attack. Then came days of frenzied street fighting, gasping exchanges between men using guns and knives to rip out eyes, to pin enemies to the walls . . .

"Anna, it says there are bodies lying all over, on the riverbank, in the gutters, wherever you look." Anna felt sick but the stories continued: "And thousands of wounded lie on the frozen ground, some bleeding to death, others moaning for help . . ." There followed a truce for burial of the corpses and care of the injured. "They've turned poor Fredericksburg into a graveyard, burying people beside the roads, in the gardens, wherever they can make a place. They've even shoved bodies into icehouses till they can dispose of them . . ."

Overnight, in a raging storm, the Union withdrew its men and recrossed the river. Anna stared at the figures: The South had lost 4500 men, the Union 12,000, and now, as before, each would build back its strength and get ready for still another meeting of the depleted armies. How long could this go on, she asked herself, how long?

A day later came word that shocked her in another fashion. In this murderous fight John Junkin, Dr. Junkin's son, had been a Union officer. How poignant was this war . . . During the truce one of Tom's men had recognized Maggie's brother, and the two had spoken in a friendly way. John asked the aide to remember him to Stonewall and Anna. Old Dr. Junkin had requested him to pass on his greetings to General Jackson if he ever had the opportunity.

A brief letter, written in pain, arrived from Lexington. Colonel Preston's son Randolph had been at the Institute, preparing to enter the Confederate service, when he contracted typhoid fever. Taken home, Ran was in a delirium for days, and now he had joined Willy in death. And Frank, the other son, had lost his arm . . . Anna's eyes darkened. The war was a trial for everybody, but was anyone undergoing a greater ordeal than Maggie and her husband?

That day, when she went over to Julia's cradle, Anna put her hand to the child's face. Was Julia's forehead too warm, or did she imagine it? A moment later the baby began to cry furiously; Anna took her up, and though she found nothing wrong, the screams went on. Before the hour ended the doctor was beside her.

"She's a lot weaker than I'd like, and I'm not sure what it is. We'll have to wait, but please try not to worry. I'll do everything I can . . ." Anna's heart turned as she heard him. That was precisely what the other doctor had said in Lexington, just before . . . just before it happened there.

From then on, hour after hour, Anna stayed at the child's side, listening to her painful breathing, watching as the baby moved fretfully beneath her covers. In the morning Julia appeared more flushed and agitated than before. "Go for him, right away!" Anna almost shoved the frightened Hetty out of the door. When he returned the doctor examined the baby again. He probed, listened and looked, and then slowly, as if trying to avoid her eyes, raised his head. As she stared at him across the cradle, she realized that her second child was struggling for her life.

CHAPTER 16

Through the windows of the Irwin house the dim echo of Charlotte's Christmas preparations reached Anna's ears. The happy season, the time of cheerful spirit . . . The phrases grated harshly. She had not slept for many hours; when she tried, she could only doze fitfully, to be waked almost at once by the thought that Julia had cried.

Every few hours she prayed, either in her own room or beside the child's bed. She coaxed spoonfuls of liquids and medicines between the baby's dry lips; she tucked the covers around the restless body, whispering, Let Julia live, let her live. To lose another baby as she and Tom had lost the first . . . Before she became sick, Julia was beginning to recognize her mother; the blue eyes had followed her about the room. And now Julia might be taken from them.

"Please, Miss Anna." Hetty had a message, and Anna read it rapidly. It was from Tom, who had written her the same night he received her letter advising him of their baby's illness. Eloquently he offered his comfort, and told her of his sorrow that he could not be with her at this time. As soon as he heard from her he had called on Dr. Hunter McGuire, his army medical director, and carefully Tom repeated a list of suggestions the doctor had given him. He finished by saying that he was praying as she was, asking divine aid to spare their baby, "if it is God's will that she be spared."

With an uncertain gesture Anna put aside the note. "If it is God's will . . ." At that moment, Mrs. Morrison entered. The older woman spoke, but Anna did not hear her; her mind was too intent on her husband's message. Mary Morrison pointed to the mirror: "Child, look at yourself."

The gray face that looked back at Anna, lines carved beside its mouth, made her start, and she sank her head upon her hands. "Anna, Anna," Mrs. Morrison told her gently, "if you don't take hold of yourself, I don't know what's going to happen to you. The doctor has done all he can for Julia, and so have the rest of us— and so have you. Everything rests now with a Higher Power. Don't you trust in It?"

Her mother's question, coming immediately after Tom's letter, had its effect. Anna sat up, passed her hand across her face, and nodded slowly. She must keep her faith and be ready for whatever happened. She took Mary Morrison's hands, and slowly a feeling of relief coursed through her. Thy will be done, Thy will be done . . .

When she retired that night, Anna was in a calmer mood, and she slept in dreamless exhaustion until Hetty shook her shoulder the next morning. She jumped up, frightened, but the maid's smile reassured her: "The doctor been here real early, and he say let you rest long as you like. Baby a whole lot better today . . ." Tears of happiness rose in Anna's eyes, and, shrugging herself into her robe, she slipped across the hall to the nursery. Julia looked weak and was still feverish, but Anna's first glance convinced her that the child was recovering.

With the burden lifted, she wrote Tom again. The war must be nearing its midwinter lull, and surely she could go to him soon? From Harvey Hill, still in the Virginia fighting, she had heard that several other officers' wives were already with their husbands. Tom's reply was prompt but disappointing. He was overjoyed to know that his daughter was much better, and also that Julia was "beginning to notice and smile when caressed. I tell you, I would love to caress her and see her smile." Nevertheless, to his regret, he could not receive them yet.

In another letter, Tom informed her that several cases of smallpox had developed in the area, and he thought Anna would "have to give up the idea of coming to see me until spring." Her heart dropped; that was months away. Then blithely he went on: "Mrs. General Longstreet, Mrs. A. P. Hill and Mrs. General Rodes have all been to see their husbands. Yesterday I saw Mrs. Rodes at church and she looked so happy that it made me wish I had Mrs. Jackson here too . . ."

Anna reread the passage. Tom's all-too-casual words hurt her, but as she read on, she forgot her resentment; Tom touched on another subject that disturbed her more deeply. His ears were troubling him again, and while his health remained "essentially good . . . I do not think I shall be able in future to stand what I have already stood." This was frightening, and all Anna's old fears about his well-being were reawakened. Suppose he were to collapse under the strain and exhaustion?

After some delays Tom's troops took up winter quarters. The well-to-do Corbins of Moss Neck estate had suggested that General Jackson occupy a wing of the family mansion. Anna learned that, much to his staff's annoyance, Tom declined, and instead set up a tent on the Corbin property. However, a spell of bitter cold descended, and after hours of pounding ear pains, Tom was persuaded to give up the tent. It was with relief that Anna read her brother Joe's message: Tom had agreed to the offer of a small library and office building off the main house at Moss Neck.

Joe described Tom's quarters. On the walls were engravings of
race horses, hunting muskets, mounted animal heads, and the tall
ornamented bookcases contained richly bound volumes. Wistfully
Anna read of the Christmas her husband had enjoyed in this
luxurious setting. Jackson admirers in the region, who had begun
to pour gifts upon him and his staff, now provided turkeys, an
enormous ham, a rich cake, a pailful of oysters; and for the festive
day Tom had invited General Lee, Sandie's father, now General
Pendleton, and other officers, to be his guests.

When a waiter appeared in a white apron, General Lee had
grinned; laughingly he told Tom that he and his aides were playing at soldiers. If they were to dine with him they would see how
plain fighting men lived. Jeb Stuart guyed Stonewall about the
pictures of gamecocks and a famous rat terrier that decorated the
walls, and snickered over the butter stamped in an elegant pattern—a gallant rooster which, said Jeb, must be Stonewall's favorite fighting cock! What a decline in character all of this
disclosed, Stuart sighed, and how it would grieve the pious folk
of the South to learn of it.

Anna chuckled to herself. But then she became pensive. Why
couldn't she have been up there, like the other women who had
joined their husbands? Then, Christmas festivities to the contrary, she learned how little Tom had really changed. An officer
friend reported that Robert E. Lee had sent word he would like
to see Stonewall at his headquarters. Soon afterward a swirling
snowfall began, but Tom nevertheless started out and pushed on
relentlessly through gusts and heavy drifts. When the General
protested that Jackson should not have made the trip, Stonewall
responded simply. He had received the message, and he had
come.

Meanwhile Julia was developing a greater curiosity about her
surroundings. Anna, Mrs. Morrison, and the baby had returned
to Cottage Home, and every day or so, in the warmth of the afternoon, Anna took her to the edge of the vegetable gardens, where
Hetty maintained several hen coops. There she sat with the little
girl in her arms, watching the hens and the yellow chicks that
scratched near her. For Julia this was a particular joy, and she
laughed and gurgled at the tiny things. But Anna noticed that the
child was shy with adults. Tom, studying his wife's letters with

care, seized on all such information and sent many instructions:

I am still thinking and thinking about that baby, and do want to see her. Can't you send her to me by express? . . . I am glad to hear that she sleeps well at night, and doesn't disturb her mother. But it would be better not to call her a *cherub;* no earthly being is such.

Shaking her head in amusement, Anna read on:

Don't you accuse my baby of not being *brave.* I do hope she will get over her fear of strangers. If, before strangers take her, you will give her something to please her and thus make her have pleasant associations with them, and seeing them frequently, I trust she would lose her timidity. . . . I do wish I could see her funny little ways and hear her "squeal with delight" at seeing the little chickens. I am somewhat afraid that you will make such an idol of that baby that God will take her from us. . . .

Again Anna turned quickly from that subject. For the time, she discovered, Tom had a partial substitute for Julia in five-year-old Janie Corbin, the daughter of the Moss Neck household. Janie, a vivacious little blonde, pleased him so much that he asked the family to let her spend some time with him each day. When she arrived, the General always dropped his work to talk and cut out paper designs for her.

One day, Tom informed Anna, he noticed that Janie's hair was falling into her eyes. Anna had made him a new gray cap with a gold band, which he considered too grand, and finding that Janie admired the gold, he ripped it off and wound it around her head. From then on Janie wore the band constantly. Anna sighed; she wished their child could be at Tom's side! His letters continued:

I haven't seen my wife for nearly a year—my home in nearly two years, and have never seen my darling little daughter; but it is important that I, and those at headquarters, should set an example of remaining at the post of duty.

Again:

Just to think our baby is nearly three months old. Does she notice and laugh much? You never told me how much she looks like her mother. I tell you, I want to know how she looks. If you could hear me talking to my *esposa* in the mornings and evenings, it would make you laugh, I'm sure. It is funny the way I talk to her when she is hundreds of miles away.

Speaking across the room, pretending that she was there . . .
Anna was close to tears. She was disturbed by another sentence:
"If peace is not concluded before next winter, I do hope you can
bring her and spend the winter with me." So they might not be
together again for another year! The realization struck her like a
blow. Obviously he was concerned about Julia's health and her
ability to withstand the long trip by stage and train. But surely,
Anna told herself, she and Hetty could manage . . . Nevertheless, she could only wait.

When an officer who had spent weeks at Tom's camp passed
through Charlotte, the Morrisons invited him to call. For several
hours they pressed him with questions. "Oh, no, there aren't too
many privations at Moss Neck estate," he smiled. "And there's a
lot of interesting activity for the young bucks on the staff. In fact
there's a real romance blooming. It's Sandie Pendleton and Kate
Corbin, a relative of the Moss Neck family. She's a beauty—been
engaged a half-dozen times, and they all joke with Sandie and tell
him she'll break this engagement the way she did the others."

Anna did not welcome the news. She had met several professional belles of Eastern Virginia, and she wondered whether the
dazzling Miss Corbin and the Sandie whom she and Tom admired
were a good couple. "Is he really in love with her?" she asked.

"*Is* he? So much in love he . . ." Apparently thinking better of
what he was going to say, the caller simply shrugged. Nevertheless Anna could not be certain in her mind. A minister's son, who
had still seen comparatively little of the world, might be better
off with a girl unused to the elegance Kate Corbin knew. However, this was not her concern, was it?

Her musing ended, and she caught their visitor's next remark:
"General Jackson is getting more religious than ever. His mind's
on the subject a great deal, and he talks about it to his staff, visitors, people he meets." Anna was not greatly surprised; she recalled passages in Tom's recent letters: "I don't know that I ever
enjoyed Sabbaths as I do this winter." "It is a glorious thing to be
a minister of the Gospel of the Prince of Peace. There is no equal
position in this world." "I think that if, when we see ourselves in
a glass we should consider that all of us that is visible must turn
to corruption and dust, we would learn more justly to appreciate
the relative importance of the body that perishes and the soul that
is immortal."

A new message arrived from Tom. "The time has about come for campaigning, and I hope early next week to . . . go into a tent near Hamilton's Crossing." The words gave her a sense of harsh loss. As soon as that? Then she could not hope to see him again for a long time! Another letter arrived, which had been written in a saddened mood. Just before he left the Corbin estate, Tom told her, little Janie had caught scarlet fever, and a few days later the blonde child had died, along with two other young cousins. Anna shuddered; three in one family . . .

After a few days she learned that when he had heard of Janie's death, Tom had dropped his head and wept at his desk. To prevent contagion, the clothes of the Moss Neck children were burned. Almost simultaneously came bad news from closer home. Sue's baby had died after a brief illness. Covering her face, Anna recalled the pretty infant who had played beside Julia a few months earlier. To learn to love a child and then to lose her . . . was it better not to have children and escape the corrosive memories, the self-reproaches?

Abruptly Anna turned away; it was not good to harbor such thoughts. Her hands went out, and she held her baby tightly. With death all around them, in their daily life as in the army, she yearned to be with her husband more than ever before.

Then, overnight, as if in reply to her prayers, Tom sent a swift message: no matter how short a time they might have together, she and the baby were to come to him! Catching her breath, Anna called to several people at once: her mother, Hetty, another of the maids. As she worked with nervous hands, in her mind's eye she could see the touching words he had written her only a few days earlier:

Last night I dreamed that my little wife and I were on opposite sides of a room, in the center of which was a table, and the little baby started for her mother, making her way along under the table, and finally reached her father. And what do you think she did when she arrived at her destination? She just climbed up on her father and kissed him! And don't you think he was a happy man? But when he awoke he found it all a delusion.

And now, at last, the three of them could be together. But in spite of every effort it took her several days to complete her preparation. Before then Tom had dispatched a second letter. Hadn't she left yet? "There is no time for hesitation if you have not started. There is increasing probability that I may be elsewhere as the season advances." When she read this Anna thrust aside all the unfinished details, and she, Julia and the dependable Hetty rode away.

It was mid-April, and the North Carolina mountains were spread with a carpeting of light green. For a time Anna drank in the richness and variety of the land. The child, not quite five months old, behaved well. She nursed peacefully at Anna's breast, cried occasionally, then dozed off. But the train moved slowly, halting repeatedly to let others go by. Had she ever known delays like this, or was it only her anxiety over the baby and her wish to be with Tom? Anna had difficulty swallowing the food Hetty brought her. Suppose, after all this effort, she arrived to find that Tom had been called away?

From across the aisle she heard two men deep in conversation. One mentioned her husband's name.

"I say the bullet's not been made that can get Old Stonewall."

"Never been hit, and he never will be!"

The exchange disturbed Anna for a moment: whatever God wished would happen. And yet of late, she admitted, she had begun to believe that Tom would escape the bullets and the cannon fire. The thought stayed in her mind as the train rattled into Richmond. There, close to exhaustion, she located a room for herself and the maid, and with Julia beside her went to bed for eight hours of broken sleep.

Tom had arranged for a passport, and at last they boarded another car for the point nearest to his new quarters, Guiney's Station. Wanting to look her best for her husband, Anna tried to make herself relax during these last hours of travel. She closed her eyes, but she could not force away the tension that tightened within her. Meanwhile, Julia slept peacefully in Hetty's arms; the baby at least would present her best appearance when her father saw her for the first time.

On the way to Guiney's Station it began to rain, and the drops blotted out the spring landscape. Noon, Monday, April 20 . . . The date and hour of her arrival would always be fixed in Anna's memory. Peering through the misty window, she could see nothing. Hetty touched her arm: "Look, Julia wake up." The baby opened her eyes, yawned, and gazed placidly at her. "It's a good omen," Anna assured herself.

The train ground to a halt, and other passengers pushed past her. Down the aisle she could see a figure in a long, dripping overcoat, features all but covered by a cap, making his way through the crowd. Involuntarily Anna cried out, and he moved toward them, face alight, eyes fixed on hers: "Little one, it's seemed like years . . ."

For a fraction of a second Anna felt an odd emotion; was it hesitation, a sense of strangeness toward this man whom she had not seen in more than twelve months? . . . She could not explain. But it went swiftly; she had her husband back with her at last. Uncertainly Tom glanced at his rain-glistening sleeves, and she reached out to clasp him to her: "It doesn't matter if I get wet, Tom. It doesn't matter at all!"

Releasing herself from his hold, Anna brought Hetty forward with the baby, and her husband stared, his eyes dancing as he took in every detail—Julia's plump fists, her flushed cheeks and light eyes. Anna and Tom had exchanged so many notes, written each other so much about this child, and now Julia was before him. Anna saw that he was close to tears.

The baby seemed to understand her father's eager regard, and she beamed. Anna smiled at the thought that crossed her mind: one appeared as fascinated as the other. "I'm afraid to touch her," Tom murmured huskily, and he stood stiffly in the drafty aisle, hands awkwardly at his sides, until Anna broke in, "If we don't get you home, Tom, you'll have a real cold and more trouble with that ear." She took his arm and he led her out.

Sandie Pendleton was waiting for them on the platform. Anna felt an impulse to inquire about his romance. But she contented herself with a general question. "Oh, we're all right here, ma'am! *Everybody's* well and happy," Sandie gave a sigh, and she decided that love became the boy. Nevertheless she intended to find out more about the matter at the proper time.

"We have a room at Mr. Yerby's place, a mile from my headquarters," Tom told Anna as they rode along. Although he had still not held the baby in his arms, his gaze was focused on her. "She's bigger than I expected, and beautiful. Beautiful . . ." For a time he was lost in speculation, and then his hand took Anna's and they sat in silence for the rest of the trip.

A large and pleasant house awaited them, and the smiling family bowed them toward a wide, high-ceilinged room. "It's usually held ready for military visitors," her husband explained, as Anna blinked at the three beds she could see through the open door. Tom laughed: "General Lee once occupied it, so we have a fine precedent." Closing the door, Anna placed the child on the nearest bed.

Tom shed his wet coat, and he and Anna clung together for a long time. As his lips traveled over her face Anna gave a long sigh. To be with her husband again . . . A small cry arose from the bed, and he drew Julia into his arms, showing all his happiness and also, Anna noticed, his inexperience in handling babies. "Here," she demonstrated, "you hold her like this."

Gingerly Tom lowered the child to the bed and sank beside her. Anna joined him, and for a happy hour they talked at length of Julia and the many things that had occurred since their last meeting. When Hetty knocked, they gave the baby to her, and Tom Jackson was alone with his wife.

For the next two days Anna thought of little except Tom and Julia. They had spoken often of their happy winter in Winchester; this visit meant even more, she assured herself, for now they had between them this symbol of their union. Whenever she looked at Tom he was holding Julia—sitting with her in his chair, or walking up and down, or standing at the window. He would lift her up to a mirror: "Now, Miss Jackson, look at yourself." Then he would turn toward Anna: "Mrs. Jackson, you can be proud of this little lady."

Most often, however, Anna would find Tom kneeling beside the cradle, watching the sleeping baby. "She's like an angel," he whispered to her, and Anna managed to cover her momentary amusement at the word he used; only a few weeks earlier he had reproved her for describing Julia as a cherub! Meanwhile, studying his face, Anna could see that he was well, flushed with health. The comparative rest of the last few months had been good for him. True, he had lost some of his hair; when he combed back the long ends it appeared thinner than before. But to her he was handsome, with a look of—what? Achievement, perhaps, or even dedication.

As she mused, she heard the baby cry. When Tom picked her up she quieted, but now Anna learned how firmly her husband intended to handle the child. He placed Julia on the bed, and she began to scream. Instinctively Anna reached out, only to be waved back: "No, we're not going to spoil her." Arms folded, Tom stood over the kicking child—almost, Anna noted, as if directing a battle.

"This will never do," he frowned. "Miss Jackson, you must learn to behave . . ." At last Julia grew silent, and Tom gave his old sign of approval: "Good, good." Only then did he pick the baby up again. And Anna noticed that, before long, Julia remained completely calm whenever her father appeared.

By now they could no longer lock out the world. Her brother Joseph, who had been away on her arrival, came to visit, and she enjoyed a happy reunion with him. The husky boy was leaner, and in his face were lines she had never seen before; nevertheless his bronzed skin, the beard that was beginning to sprout, and his general air of maturity gave him a becoming new dignity.

"Now I know why brother Tom's men will follow him anywhere he orders. I'd do it in a minute, no matter what was ahead." Joe spoke simply, forcefully, and Anna believed everything he said. "But when his temper's about to pop—I'd run anywhere to escape!" This comment was not quite so pleasant, and resolutely Anna took up other subjects.

One was an event scheduled for three days after their arrival. On this day Julia would be five months old, and Tom had said, "I'd like her baptized that afternoon." Anna agreed happily, but she was astonished to hear the excited proposals their plans produced. Officers' wives and other women of the neighborhood began to call, and all of them revealed an interest that made Anna slightly uncomfortable. One exclaimed, "General, why can't we have the baptism in camp, in front of the soldiers?" Another all but twittered, "And General Lee—he must stand as the godfather. How romantic that will be!"

While Tom sat silent, the lady gushed on, as if the ceremony would be a public affair. Anna, unable to contain herself, spoke up: "I'm sorry, but I'm accustomed to private baptisms, and since there's no church near here, we'll have to have it in the house." As for asking General Lee to be godfather, she felt certain it would embarrass the Virginian as much as it did them, and she passed over the suggestion.

Though the ladies accepted her decision, their lips were slightly compressed, and Anna could guess what they would say. General Jackson was a fine man, but that wife of his . . . Well, they would still have a private ceremony!

Tom fixed the hour, and at the last minute Anna took time to hunt for an extra ribbon. She looked up to discover her husband standing before her with a purposeful expression on his face.

"Anna, we arranged this for two o'clock." Before she could say anything, he took the child from her and preceded her to the room in which the minister waited. Guiltily she followed.

That day and the next Anna renewed her acquaintance with an old friend, Little Sorrel. She was not sure that the soft-eyed animal recognized her at first, but he nuzzled her arm and followed her about the yard. As she patted him, she felt an increasing affection for the tiny, plain animal. One day later in the week, when Tom sent an orderly for her, she descended to find him on a handsome new bay, a magnificent, high-spirited animal. Surprised, she praised the bay. Tom, who had dismounted to greet her, jumped back into the saddle, touched his cap to her, and, still more surprisingly, swept off like Jeb Stuart or one of the other young gallants.

Anna stared, and the orderly gave a start and spurred on his own horse. As Tom galloped away, the wind took his cap. He did not halt to retrieve it; the orderly did and pounded off again, bending low and racing to keep the General in sight. . . . Here was a Tom she had never seen. That evening, however, he came back riding Little Sorrel and thereafter continued to use his old mount. For Stonewall Jackson, glamor was a temporary thing.

Daily she wondered how long she would be able to remain here. Several times she heard the name of General Hooker, the Union commander who was mounting a new offensive. Their host, Mr. Yerby, observed, "Hooker says he has 'the finest army on the planet,' and it's the biggest, anyway." The shadow of an enormous new mass of men and munitions was moving closer, and Anna knew that she must make every day mean something to Tom and to her.

When a photographer knocked downstairs, she heard his question: "General, mayn't I get a picture? Everybody's asking for a better one than they got." Quietly Tom refused, but Anna hastened to him: "Please, do it for me. You're looking well, and you have on your fine new uniform." Reluctantly he agreed, and she ran upstairs to bring him a comb. As he sat in the hall, just inside the doorway, a wind swept by, and he tightened his eyes in a frown. Would that pose make him too stern? It was too late; the cameraman had finished the picture, which would soon be distributed throughout the English-speaking world.

Several times Tom had assured Anna she would meet the Confederate officer in whom she had the liveliest interest of all, Robert

E. Lee. And as usual, he neglected to give her advance notice.
One day she was sitting with the baby in her arms when their
hostess darted in with a flustered air: "General Lee is calling with
his staff."

Anna's face flushed, and a glance in her mirror told her how
awestruck she was. Nervously she handed the baby to Hetty and
descended. She felt relief with her first step into the parlor. General Lee was, of course, the tall, white-bearded man with the kind
face, cordial manner, and fatherly air. His staff consisted of three
or four smiling men, and her calm returned.

"Mrs. Jackson." The commander bowed as he spoke in a low,
clear voice. "I've wanted to meet you ever since I heard you were
coming." Then he gave a lighter glance around him. "Does the
Yerby family still have the three beds upstairs? When I stayed
here, I wrote my wife and daughters that if they visited, I could
accommodate everybody in one room."

It was easy to talk to this man, with his sympathetic manner
and quiet poise. As they chatted, she studied the impressive face,
the figure, the clothes that fitted so well, and she could understand how Lee's tact and patience won others to him, how he
gained trust and devotion. Yet she wondered where were the
daring, the lashing determination that people talked about—the
qualities that led Lee to take high risks and gambles? She caught
herself short. How many people, meeting Tom Jackson, might find
it difficult to believe that he had gifts which were concealed under
his quiet manner?

As Lee and his staff were leaving, Anna heard one of the officers
casually mention a name: "Jim Walker . . . General Walker from
Western Virginia—the one General Jackson recommended." She
remembered the name vaguely, and later, as she was combing her
hair, her hand halted in midair. The cadet who challenged Tom
to a duel ten years back was named James Walker. Could this be
the same one?

When her husband rejoined her, Anna led the conversation
gingerly to the subject. "Tom, the General Walker I heard about
today—did he attend the Institute?"

About to cross the room to the washstand, Tom gave her a bland
look: "He did, and I remember him well."

She smiled: "It must have been somebody else I heard about."

There followed a silence, during which Tom applied soap to his
face. Then he spoke again: "Anna, it's the same one." As she

swung around he faced her: "The cadet I had that trouble with."

Tom had never discussed the topic with her, and she could think of nothing more to say. After a moment he resumed, "Jim's been with me during several campaigns and battles, and I've helped him when I could. He's a true soldier."

Anna hesitated, and her eyes widened. Then she went across the room and touched Tom's bare shoulder. As he turned she reached up and, ignoring the soap on his face, gave him a quick kiss. He was evidently pleased at this sign of affection, but he also seemed to be thoroughly surprised.

Sunday approached, and Tom sought her out: "I'd like you to come to camp for services." She agreed eagerly, and early that morning an ambulance took her to his headquarters, where the event was to be held in the open air. On the way Anna stared at the hundreds who were traveling in the same direction—on foot, on horseback, in wagons. When she whispered, "Is this some special occasion?" he shook his head: "No, the usual services."

A tent shielded part of the pulpit. The young minister, Reverend B. T. Lacy, Tom's chief chaplain, took a place at the front. Anna looked around; before them, sitting or standing, were nearly two thousand men. And General Lee faced her, as dignified as ever. Today, however, it was the soldiers who drew her attention. Most of them seemed far older than she recalled—worn, grizzled, as if they were close to exhaustion, between rounds in an unending fight. In their eyes she read a dogged acceptance, a calm resignation to whatever the future might hold.

Here and there she spotted others, younger than she had ever noticed—beardless boys in their teens who looked hardly more than children. Wincing, she thought of something her father had said: the machine of war was eating up more and more Southern men, leaving mainly the aging and the half-grown. And yet the faces in the long lines ahead of her were not devoid of hope. No matter how tired, how spent, these soldiers would march on . . .

Reverend Lacy lifted his hands, and silence fell. He spoke of the soldier's life, of the wives and children behind them at home, the farms and offices they had left, "to which you will return in God's good time." Anna was caught up in a wave of feeling, as, obviously, were many others around her. She saw men with heads bowed, staring at their clenched fists. Some were crying as they stood there. This was a day of profound significance to them all.

At the end the minister raised his hand and they sang one of the Psalms, and then solemnly the assembly closed.

Tom had arranged to spend the rest of the day with her, and they stayed in their room beside the baby, talking together seriously, serenely. As she had several times in the past weeks, Anna reminded herself that a roaring conflict might begin near them at any moment. Yet she felt no alarm; she was comforted by her recollection of the faces she had watched that morning.

Another countenance rose before her, that of Jim, Tom's body servant. Only the previous day Jim had shaken his head as he groaned over the food supply: "Things jus' ain't good, Miss Anna, and they ain't gettin' better." Meanwhile the blockade continued to tighten about the South, and each month it lost new areas, additional thousands of men. True, the North also was losing man power and supplies, but it had so much more to spare . . .

"What are you thinking, my dear?" At Tom's question Anna turned to him: "How—how badly is the war really going for us?"

Her words took him by surprise. He lowered his eyes and then looked directly at her: "To a lot of people things may seem worse than ever. But, Anna, we can still win if we have a mind to it, a determination, and if we follow God. Once we learn to sacrifice more than we've ever done, and fight with the right in our hearts . . ."

Tom Jackson's face flushed, and she was deeply stirred. Now he bent forward with news of something she had never known: "When I was at Harper's Ferry again some months back, I had word that Reverend David Junkin, President Junkin's brother from Pennsylvania, was near the Union line and wanted to see me.

"He was only a little way off, and I was happy to make the arrangements. I rode out, and for two hours we met under Maryland Heights—one of the most remarkable conferences I've ever had." Her heart was beating quickly, and Anna missed none of his words. "Both of us spoke in a friendly way, and frankly, about secession, theories about the war, the terrible clashes. He told me I was entirely wrong in my course, but I couldn't agree . . ." Tom's voice held traces of the pain he must have felt during the interview, and now he became solemn.

"At last we said good-by. He said he hoped we'd meet under happier conditions, if not in this world of trouble, then in . . . The Reverend began to cry, and I pointed above and finished for him, 'In heaven.'" A moment later Tom had left this Northern representative of the family with which he had so many ties.

The incident moved Anna as much as it had her husband. She squeezed his hand and sat beside him, and after a few minutes his voice came to her again, gentle and contemplative: "Anna, I'm content. I have as much to love on earth as any man, I suppose, and the days ahead are full of hope. Still, I'm ready to go any time, without a moment's regret, if the Almighty wishes it . . ." It was true, Anna told herself, that during this past year Tom had become more meditative, more responsive to spiritual influence.

Now suddenly he added, "No, I'm not afraid to die. But I hope I'll have a little while before I meet my Maker, to prepare myself." His tone was solemn, and he spoke as if he wished to impress her with his meaning. Time to prepare himself for his God . . . Although Anna inclined her head, the trend of his remarks disturbed her, and she was happy when they went back to little Julia, forgetting their problems as they bent over her cradle.

Tom left early the next morning, and several times that day members of his staff left messages for her. When Hetty brought Sandie Pendleton in, Anna led him to a chair. She could control her curiosity no longer: "What's this I hear about Miss Corbin?" Sandie flushed, grinned, and answered in a flood of warm words. As he talked, Anna's concern left her. If the courtship delighted Sandie so much, it must be good, and she hoped nothing would stand in its way. Then the boy halted and grew redder than ever. "Oh, it isn't definite yet, not quite," he warned her.

Anna assured him that she would keep his secret, and Sandie left. It made her happier to know that he had fallen in love. But an hour later she was saddened; she received a visit from a second friend, General Frank Paxton, now commander of the Stonewall Brigade. Frank, usually bright-spirited, was withdrawn, almost sorrowful, and she had the impression of mounting melancholy.

"I'd certainly hope to go back to Lexington, too," he nodded as she spoke, then added, "I know General Jackson wants to return as soon as the war's over, but who knows where any of us will be a year from now, or even a month?" All at once, as if he regretted what he had said, the young General made an effort to talk more easily. When Tom came home Anna mentioned the incident, and her husband was puzzled: "He's had troubles in the war, but no more than any of us. Still, he's been more and more serious of late. I'll talk to him when I have the chance."

Tonight the war appeared close to Tom's mind. Twice he referred to the size of the Union forces, and he mentioned several men whose wives had written of conditions close to starvation in their homes. "And still they stay on here, Anna," he told her with feeling, "because it's their duty to stay." Before she could say anything he bent toward the baby: "Look, I think Julia recognizes me now." Gradually his earlier words faded from her mind, and their Sabbath ended in calm happiness.

The next morning had disquieting moments. From a distance Anna glimpsed a slight officer whom she recognized from a previous casual contact. "Yes," Mrs. Yerby said, "that's General A. P. Hill." From the silence that followed, Anna realized that the matter of A. P. Hill remained a delicate one in and around camp. Of Tom's various disputes with his associates, this was the most unhappy—a cold feud. While Hill continued in service, Tom's charges against him awaited trial. From a murmur here and there, Anna learned that he and Hill met only occasionally and then saluted or bowed, but that was all. Anna sighed; to her husband A. P. Hill was another of those "deceived men."

When Tom returned for a moment he silently handed her a message from a West Virginia friend. For his sister Laura the war had brought still another unhappy development. Her husband, though too old for active service, had come out for the Confederacy, and young Tom Arnold sided sharply with his father. And now Laura, so earnest and so conscientious, had still another division in her life . . .

Wednesday, April 29 . . . Tom came and went several times, and Anna had the feeling that he was trying to be with her every possible moment. When she spotted Sandie Pendleton in front of the house, the youth was clearly nervous; something was in the wind. When he arrived home that night, however, Tom had a broad smile and during the hours that followed said nothing at all about the war. Fitting her mood to his, Anna enjoyed a long and peaceful evening.

Before dawn she heard a rush of feet and a knock at the door, and Tom called to the man who waited there. Instantly awake, Anna listened to the exchange: "General Early's adjutant wants to see General Jackson." Turning, Tom murmured to her, "Looks as if Hooker's crossing." He threw on his clothes, descended, and returned at once: "He seems to be moving right now. I have to go."

Anna stood beside him: "Julia and I can stay here, can't we, till things are clearer?"

In the rays of the lamp she had lighted, she saw her husband struggle between his natural caution and his deepest wishes. He replied at last, "No, this is too exposed a place, Anna. Get ready to start for Richmond at a moment's notice. I'll come back to see you off if it's possible, or I'll send your brother."

She seized his arm: "Can't we talk at breakfast?" She was grasping at any possibility.

"*Esposa,*" he began, and his voice had a vast sorrow, "there isn't time for breakfast today." As he worked at his buttons Anna realized that this might be their last moment together in many months. Her arms went out, and they kissed several times. He leaned down to caress the cheek of the sleeping baby, gave Anna a long look, and stumbled out of the building. They had had only nine days together.

At the window Anna watched him go, Little Sorrel galloping off into the gray-pink dawn. How many times had she peered after him from windows, seeing him leave her? Before the horse and rider disappeared, a deep pounding broke the silence. It went steadily on, volley after volley, and windows rattled and the house quivered under her. Mrs. Yerby ran into the room, and from below she heard frightened cries.

Although she trembled, Anna clenched her hands to still them. She must be calm, she must be sure to leave with her child precisely as Tom had asked. Hetty entered, terrified, and she directed her: "Julia's not awake yet; will you pack her things and yours while I pack mine?"

She had almost finished her preparations when the chaplain, Reverend Lacy, arrived with an ambulance: "Your brother Joseph told the General he wanted to stay there and fight, and asked him to send me to help you get off." The young minister spoke swiftly: "I'm to take you to the station, to catch the morning train to Richmond. They—they mayn't run another one."

The fighting must be far closer than she thought. Throwing her belongings into the bag, Anna picked up the baby, made her hasty farewell, and stepped into the waiting vehicle. On the way she opened a note the chaplain had given her. Pressed though he was, Tom had found time to write a letter, speaking tenderly of the baby, asking God's protection for both of them.

As they rolled off, Anna caught a quick, continuous rattle of muskets; the clash was already on, almost within sight. "Oh!" she cried out involuntarily when a man appeared around a corner of the road, supporting another who had a gaping neck wound that sent a red stream down his coat.

A wagon rolled by, in it three men all heavily stained with blood. One of them had apparently died on the way. Anna closed her eyes.

She and Hetty jumped when a new pounding sound began. From then on, for the several miles that lay ahead, the din of battle echoed close at hand. Her heart filled with alarm, Anna approached Guiney's Station and the train that would take her away. Settling inside the almost deserted coach—few passengers were riding at this tense moment—she listened to a young Creole woman, originally from New Orleans: "Madame, I've been here with my child, like you, to see my husband. Ah, madame, how is this to end for us?"

Sadly Anna shook her head and stared back as the train creaked under way, carrying her long miles from Tom Jackson. Yes, how was it to end for all of them?

CHAPTER 17

As the train pulled into Richmond that April afternoon, Anna puzzled over her course. In the past few days she had received several invitations to stay with Virginians outside the capital, but she had hesitated. Once a lull occurred in the fighting, she hoped to be able to return to her husband, if only for another eight or nine days . . . They would be worth the wait, however long.

At the station an orderly stepped up with a note for "Mrs. General Jackson." It was from the wife of Governor Letcher, their friend of Lexington days, who asked if Anna would make her temporary home at the official residence. After a moment's consideration, she nodded. Mrs. Letcher was a forthright woman who did not like a great deal of entertainment, and Anna could have the quiet interlude she wanted. Gratefully she followed the young man.

The Confederate capital seemed more tense than she had ever known it to be. Wagons rocked by, soldiers marched in files, military ambulances rolled around the corners, and crowds clustered in front of the hotels. In the early evening she caught the momentary fragrance of a flowering bush, but then it disappeared, and everywhere was the smell of tar and dust and the incessant clatter of military vehicles.

"Anna Jackson! We're so glad you could come." The Governor's wife installed Anna, Julia, and Hetty in two large rooms, and for the next few days they were left largely alone. Scattered reports reached Anna: "A heavy battle starting near Chancellorsville . . ." The Governor spoke gravely: "I don't believe we have half of Hooker's force, but Lee and Stonewall are attacking." As she listened, she remembered Hooker's boast that he had the "finest army on the planet," and she thought of the bedraggled, shoeless men who were fighting under her husband. In spite of all her efforts to remain calm, she began to pace up and down her room.

Then, over Mrs. Letcher's objections, outsiders intruded. The official residence was all too available. Hetty brought in note after note, each left by a person who "insisted on an answer." Several determined women thrust their way in to see her. "Surely you'll want to be there, in behalf of the General," a plump matron said, urging Anna to attend a theatrical event. Another spoke with calculation: "I'm sure people will wonder *why* you don't show yourself, as the loyal wife of Stonewall Jackson . . ."

By then Julia, wakened for the fourth time that day, was crying, and Anna made up her mind that something must be done. She had received a number of invitations from Mrs. Moses Hoge, wife of the minister of the Second Presbyterian Church, whose family had several connections with hers. "She told me they have an upstairs wing where we'd be remote from everything," Anna explained, and Mrs. Letcher, much disturbed by the situation at her home, quickly understood and helped arrange the transfer.

That evening Anna found herself part of a cheerful family circle. Dr. Hoge was in Europe, on a mission to obtain Bibles for Confederate armies, and the Hoges' friends, Dr. and Mrs. William Brown, were sharing the big house. Their hostess seemed to be the kind of woman who did things with dispatch; Mrs. Hoge gave her guest a look of quick sympathy, and the visit started well. Anna was calm and relaxed until Dr. Brown appeared: "Mrs. Jackson, the fighting around Chancellorsville is getting worse and worse."

Even as he spoke, a knock sounded, and a newspaper friend arrived with a message: "Things aren't settled yet, but something phenomenal's happened, one of the greatest feats of the war!"

Anna leaned forward as the journalist explained, "Lee and Jackson divided their forces in the face of the Union. That's against all the rules, and a terrible gamble. Well, Stonewall took three whole divisions and marched them completely *around* the Union's right flank . . . It's been a matter of timing. If the Federals had known just what was happening, everything could have ended. But they didn't."

Anna breathed quickly. "That's—that's very fine. But is the fighting still on?" When the man nodded, she slipped out to pray. Through that evening and most of the next day she waited with nerves on edge. What was happening now? At last, with dark, another rap came, and Dr. Brown entered in high excitement: "We've sent them reeling! Our gamble succeeded, and it looks as if it may be one of the biggest victories of all!"

Again, however, the unspoken question was in Anna's eyes, and Dr. Brown nodded: "They're still in the battle tonight, in a place called the Wilderness, a forest of underbrush and pine, a thick tangle . . ."

Anna could not follow the rest. Alone in her room, her last thought that night, after putting the baby to sleep, was of Tom and his men, and the way the grim fight was proceeding. The next day was Sunday, and she woke to the realization that five days had passed since she had seen her husband. The Hoges and Browns greeted her cheerfully, and they began the morning with brief worship in the parlor.

They were on their way to the dining room for breakfast when Anna halted, her body suddenly tense. In the hall before them stood Dr. Brown, his face a waxy color: "Mrs. Jackson, won't you sit down? I have something to say to you."

"No! What is it?" Anna almost shouted the question.

"It's—word from the front, a few minutes ago. General Jackson was wounded last night, but they hope it isn't serious."

Anna found that she could not move. Her eyes went from one to the other, and Mrs. Hoge led her to the nearest chair. When her hands touched its arms, she discovered that they were trembling badly, and a numbness settled over her. She seemed to be looking at her friends from a distance; it was almost as if she saw them through the wrong end of a telescope.

Mrs. Hoge and Mrs. Brown were talking to her, gently, persuasively, but she missed most of what they said. Was something going to happen to him; was he going to——? She could not use the word, even to herself. While she sat there, Hetty entered with the baby and silently handed Julia to Anna. With an automatic gesture her arms went to the child, and the small, warm body somehow made her confidence revive. Tom would be spared!

Holding to the thought, she let herself be taken to her room, and there, white-lipped, she stayed for most of the day. Dr. Brown rejoined her with a look of pity: "All communication is down between here and the battle area, but it should be open soon, and Governor Letcher and a lot of others are trying to get word."

Mechanically she thanked him, and nursed the baby in new anxiety. Communications down, cut off . . . She had to reach him, somehow. Late in the afternoon Dr. Brown returned again: "A courier came with a message that Stonewall's doing all right, but——"

"But what?" This time her voice was low in her throat.

"The way isn't clear for you to go to him yet. Federal raiding parties are moving through the country, stopping passengers, and if you went by ambulance or carriage, you might be captured."

Anna got up. "I'd be willing to take the chance."

Her new friend reasoned nervously with her: "Please . . . It would be mighty dangerous, and the railroad people say they hope to have the way cleared in another day or two." At dusk Mrs. Hoge entered Anna's room and took a place at her side.

"My dear, let's pray together." The minister's wife took her hand, and gratefully Anna accepted. In the silent chamber, she clenched her fingers together and sent up a long petition. Relieved, her mind calmer for the time, she went to the window. On the corner she saw a huddle of men, and one called to another, "Battle's over . . . Trounced 'em good, and they're runnin' back!"

Like a distant echo the words eddied around her, and she caught further snatches from the Browns and Mrs. Hoge. The victory Tom launched had been carried forward, and thousands of Confederates had charged in the dark with a cry: "Remember Jackson!" To Jeb Stuart had gone the command that Tom dropped, and the flamboyant Jeb had shouted the words when he led the men in crowding the heavy Union forces toward the Rappahannock River.

Hours later, almost without emotion, Anna heard talk of a great, crushing blow that the South might now launch to wipe out the Union forces. The Confederates had used the words so often. The war must go on, go on as before. So far neither side had the power to destroy the other and end this hell-like slaughter.

Somehow the evening passed, and at eleven o'clock Mrs. Hoge and Hetty went to her: "My dear, you've got to lie down, even if you don't sleep." Wearily Anna agreed, and Mrs. Hoge took a seat in a big chair across the room: "Hetty will be with the baby, and I'll be here if you need me." The combination of kindness and firmness worked, and Anna obeyed like a child. She dropped into a restless slumber, waked several times, and slept exhausted as dawn approached.

When she roused herself after seven o'clock, the situation pressed upon her like a hand on her heart. Hetty brought the child, and Mrs. Hoge pleaded with her. Yes, Anna agreed, she must think mainly of the child; she must keep telling herself that before long she and Julia would be at Tom's side. Dr. Brown arrived, and his first words reached her as if from a mist:

"We have some details. General Jackson has three wounds, one in the left upper arm, another in the same forearm, and an irregular one that broke the bones of his right hand. He must have lost a lot of blood, but we can thank God there are no complications as far as we know . . ."

Anna returned quickly to attention.

This was the first definite word she had, and it did sound encouraging. A moment later she heard a startling sentence: "They say he was shot by his own men."

Her head jerked up. Dr. Brown obviously regretted what he had told her, and he added, "That is, by accident, in the dark and confusion. Lines were breaking everywhere, and nobody could be sure where the front was. Stonewall and several of his staff approached a North Carolina regiment, and they mistook them for Federal officers."

He had escaped so many Northern bullets, and now this. Men of her own state! . . . Through that morning and afternoon Anna sat alone; occasionally she overheard the family's remarks:

"The newspaper offices are crowded with people asking about what happened to Stonewall . . ."

"Questions and wires arriving from everywhere . . ."

Once or twice Anna stared at those around her. Were they holding something back? That night Mrs. Hoge sat near her as before, and through the long hours she prayed. When she rose wearily on Tuesday morning, she told herself that they had to do something today, those railroad people, to get her to Tom. Nothing happened that morning, and then, just before midday, there was a stir and a husky figure moved quickly toward her—her brother Joseph.

"Anna, Anna! Tom asked me to reach you, and I'm to take you and the baby to him at the first chance." They embraced, and his trembling hands and stained uniform made her appreciate what a difficult trip he had had. As she searched Joe's white face, he explained, "It took me almost three days to work my way around the Union raiding parties."

A moment later Anna sensed that he had much more to tell. Without a word he led her to the sofa. "You see . . ." Joe hesitated, and then spoke with determination, "you might as well know the truth. They had to take off his arm, his left arm, just below the shoulder."

She needed a few moments to absorb what he had said. After the first shock Anna felt an automatic revulsion, and then she thought of Tom, lying there after the amputation. More than ever she had to be with her husband, to comfort him.

"Anna." Her brother appealed to her. "It needn't keep him from going on in the war. Other men have fought on just as . . ."

That hardly counted, she told herself. The important thing was to talk to Tom, encourage him . . . Nevertheless, she listened as Joe resumed, "I happened to be with him when he was hit, and I stayed at his side till I was sure he was in safe hands. But for a while, Anna, I thought none of us would get out alive."

For the first time she began to understand the hazard and the terror of the scene. "Brother Tom had gone forward to reconnoiter, and we found the enemy a little way off. We turned back, and then the volleys poured on us from the North Carolina boys. General A. P. Hill was right at the spot and yelled to them to stop firing. But it was too late, and we saw Little Sorrel running wild in fright, and Tom holding on, bleeding and being cut by tree limbs and branches . . . We got him down, and then General Hill went to work. Anna, he couldn't have been more anxious, or have done more than he did."

Anna's breath tightened. A. P. Hill, the officer with whom Tom had clashed so bitterly. How ironic that was! "For a while General Hill took Tom in his arms and held him while others ripped off his sleeve, found the hemorrhage, and applied a tourniquet . . . Then we heard sounds of Yankee fire. General Hill started away—and he was shot. The enemy fire came from only fifty yards off, and we had to get Tom away."

As Anna shuddered, Joe relived the nightmare that followed: "He walked for a while, holding to us for support. Then he was bleeding again, and we managed to get a litter. One of the litter bearers fell under fire; bullets were whistling by, shells shrieking. There was only one thing to do. The rest of us kept Tom on the ground and huddled around him to take the bullets ourselves if necessary."

At her brother's quiet words Anna felt an overwhelming gratitude toward him and the others who had risked their lives for Tom. "For a while we had trouble getting more litter bearers until we let them know who the victim was. Then we could have anyone we asked. But now one of the bearers tripped on a vine, and Tom fell heavily on his mangled arm."

When Anna closed her eyes in pain, Joe added, "Sandie Pendleton helped save his life. The minute Sandie heard he rode off furiously to locate Dr. McGuire. By the time he reached the doctor, Sandie was so wrought up he dropped in a faint, but when they revived him he went right into battle again. Dr. McGuire says that Tom lost a great deal of blood and was suffering badly from shock; in the ambulance the doctor put his finger over the shoulder artery to stop the flow, and finally they reached a field hospital. And there, Anna, Tom ordered his officers back to the fight."

Anna's eyes shone; how all of these men had struggled for her husband, not least among them her brother, who had proved himself that day . . . Joe Morrison suddenly tottered with fatigue, and Dr. Brown took him away. That night Anna slept in complete exhaustion; she awakened at dawn, and her apprehensions returned with new clarity. Through the next day, Wednesday, they waited for word from the railroad, and Anna kept her belongings near her, ready to leave in a moment.

Joe brought her a message sent to Tom by General Lee, and at one sentence her eyes filled: "Could I have directed events, I should have chosen for the good of the country to be disabled in your stead." Lee had also passed on his affectionate regards, and urged Tom to hurry and get well: "He has lost his left arm, but I have lost my right arm." The great Virginian had spoken, as usual, out of a full and generous heart.

"And General A. P. Hill—how is he?" Anna asked her brother.

"Getting better," he assured her, and for that she gave quick thanks. "But Little Sorrel's missing," Joe added. "Hasn't been seen or heard of since the shooting." Anna sighed. Surely the fine animal, who had served Tom through so many hard campaigns, would be found again . . .

Wednesday night came, and still there was no definite word. Hardly had they risen on Thursday, however, when a laconic soldier appeared: "Train ready for the first run-through; it will go in an hour and a half." At the station Mrs. Hoge whispered to Anna, "If you need a friend, send for me, and I'll come." Now they slowly left Richmond, armed men riding the engine, standing at the doors. "Ma'am," one of the young officers told her, "if we give warning, drop right to the floor. We may have to shoot our way through at some points."

Anna's arms tightened around little Julia. The baby slept peacefully through it all, and Anna looked at her tenderly; the round pink face was the only bright thing in sight. By now she knew that Tom had been transferred to a private home, after the battle moved too close to the field hospital, and was at the Chandler farm near Guiney's Station.

At last, hours later, they rolled toward the station. Joe offered Anna an encouraging thought: "As soon as Tom gets some of his strength back, they say they'll send him to Lexington to recover." These words cheered her; so they might be returning to that long-happy home, and sooner than she had expected. When the train slowed down at Guiney's Station, Anna looked out the window reflectively. The last time she had come here, less than three weeks earlier, everything had been so different. Her husband had been waiting at the station for her, moving briskly about. And now . . . Touching her eyes, she hurried down the aisle, her brother and Hetty with the baby behind her.

A young officer greeted her: "Ma'am, the General's at a small building on the Chandler place. The main house is filled with wounded soldiers, a lot of 'em with erysipelas, and doctors said the side office would be safer." Silently Anna nodded, and of the short ride that followed she later had no recollection; the closer they approached their destination the more agitated she became. When the vehicle halted before a gray-white building shaded by several oaks, a soft-voiced woman bowed to her: "Mrs. Jackson, we've been friends of the General this winter, and I'll be near if there's anything . . ."

Mechanically Anna thanked Mrs. Chandler, and a moment later a staff officer came up and saluted. "Please," she asked as she caught his arm, "please, how is he?"

There was a brief pause, and the man lowered his eyes. "He's doing—pretty well."

His manner only increased Anna's anxiety. She started to go into the house, and hurriedly he put out his hand. "You can't go to the General for a little while, ma'am. They're dressing his wounds. There's a room for you right over here."

Not to be able to see Tom, after so long . . . It came as another blow. A few feet off she recognized several familiar faces, among them Tom's body servant Jim. But she could not talk to anyone now; she must first go to her husband. Settling Hetty and the baby, she stepped to the porch again, to walk up and down.

A moment later she saw soldiers digging; it must be a grave for some poor man. But as she watched she discovered with a shock that they were pulling out a coffin for reburial elsewhere. One of the officers spoke softly: "Ma'am, you might want to know. It's General Frank Paxton. He was shot a day after General Jackson."

Anna's hand tightened on the doorframe beside her as the man continued, "He took General Stonewall's wounding real hard. He had a sort of premonition, said he himself wouldn't live through the fighting. Made a will and wrote a note to his wife. You know, it was the first real battle with him commanding the Stonewall Brigade. Now they're taking him to Mrs. Paxton."

To Anna there returned the memory of the day the war began, and again she saw Frank's young wife, her children about her, crying to herself. And today Frank Paxton was going home. She turned away, but she could not wipe out the picture of the mud-covered wooden box, or the face of Elizabeth Paxton.

"Mrs. Jackson, could you make some lemonade for the General?" Her hands quivering, she prepared it, badly. Why were they still keeping her from Tom? A few minutes later the officer stood beside her again: "Ma'am, they're ready." Her heart thumped heavily as she followed him into a small, dark room.

With her first look Anna almost gasped. Below the thick white dressing on Tom's left shoulder the sheet lay empty; his right hand, held in a splint, was heavily bandaged; his face and neck were torn with cuts and bruises. Worst, the well-loved face had

a heavy flush; it obviously cost him effort to breathe, and seemingly he was unconscious of her presence.

Uncertain what to do, she remained near the doorway. They
should have prepared her better for this sight. Next to Tom, she
could now see, was young Dr. McGuire. The doctor touched his
patient, and then, receiving no response, touched him again.
Drowsily, Tom opened his eyes.

"Anna, Anna! I'm so glad, so glad . . ." His voice, low and
husky, sank in his throat, and he struggled to continue.

"Sit down, please . . . near me so I can see you—see you well."
When Tom's remaining hand, thick with its splint and wrappings,
approached hers, she could not keep back her tears. After a moment she forced out a phrase or two, and he responded, "Louder,
esposita, I want to hear every word."

Through her pain she continued to speak until he interrupted
her, "My darling, you must cheer up. I love cheerfulness and
brightness in a sickroom."

Anna made herself smile, yet almost at once Tom's head fell
back and his eyes closed. Dr. McGuire explained, "It's the mor-
phia. He's semiconscious most of the time, but you should speak
to him. He's been thinking so much of you, and talking about you."

As she leaned forward, Anna told herself that Tom would not
be returning soon to Lexington; he was far more sick than they
had let her know. He woke again and addressed her gently: "My
darling, you're very much loved. Little one . . ." Almost immediately he slipped away, and after some hesitation she raised her
voice to get his attention: "Tom, I have Julia outside. Wouldn't
you like to see her?"

The flushed face brightened, and then his eyes fell: "Not yet.
Wait till I feel a little better."

Tom did not think he could look at the baby for whom he had
sent. He must be in great pain . . . Anna put her handkerchief
to her face and would have sobbed if it were not that she was
afraid she would waken him. As the doctor turned away, Tom
said in an intent voice,

"Whatever happens, *esposita*, I know you'd—you'd gladly give
your life for me, but God knows what's best. Remember that."

Her eyes filled as Tom lapsed into sleep again. He was obviously
suffering, yet he made no complaint. She spent the next hours
in a haze of apprehension. Several times Tom sank into delirium:
"Send the infantry . . . Get ready for the charge!" And twice she

caught the same name: "A. P. Hill . . . General Hill . . ." His thoughts were reverting to the sharp little man with whom he had had so much trouble. As he struggled for his life, he was also refighting the war that had become his life.

Each time he regained consciousness she suggested that she bring in the child; each time he shook his head. When he finally dropped into a deep slumber, Dr. McGuire took her into the hall, and there she quickly asked, "What's happening? Is it—complications?"

The doctor spoke compassionately: "Pneumonia, in his right lung. His wounds are healing well, but it's his chest that disturbs us. It may have been the fall from the litter, when the arm and chest were struck. Anyway, more doctors are coming tomorrow to look at him, and we have good hopes."

Dr. McGuire's words lifted her spirits. And yet he seemed to be trying almost too hard to reassure her. "I'd like to be near him every minute I can," she said softly. The doctor paused: "Would you want a woman friend to be with you?" She nodded and mentioned Mrs. Hoge's name, and the matter was immediately arranged; the older woman would be brought to the farm at the same time as a Richmond expert in pneumonia who was coming to examine Tom. Leaving the doctor, Anna went through the dim hall to her room. On the bed the baby gurgled, and Hetty quieted her. A steady rain had begun to fall, and Anna's whispers rose above the beat of the drops against the windows.

Anna caught Julia in an almost spasmodic grasp. Please, God, for Julia's sake if not for mine, spare him. If it be consistent with Thy will, let him live . . .

In the morning she rejoined Tom, and she stayed beside him for long hours as he dozed, woke, and sank into quiet again. Forcing himself into consciousness, he smiled and struggled to be cheerful, and yet the effort to stay alert came hard. He spoke at intervals: "Anna, you're one of the most precious little wives . . ." "*Esposita*, you're very dear to somebody."

Though the Richmond train which was to bring Dr. David Tucker, the specialist, was delayed, other medical men appeared, among them Dr. S. B. Morrison, Anna's cousin. When she caught sight of him, Anna remembered the night he had brought his daughter Mary to their home in Lexington, and she recalled that Tom had crept into the little girl's room to make sure she was sleeping well . . . At the thought she turned her face to hide her emotion.

As the doctors left, their faces had a gravity that frightened her. Dr. Morrison and Dr. McGuire were both kind, but they were also noncommittal: "We can only wait . . ." "He's fighting his condition." When she re-entered the room she wondered if his breathing was harder, or if she only imagined it.

Tom dozed steadily, but once he woke to say in a clear voice, "Lexington, Lexington. Oh, yes, Lexington," and Anna decided that he must be reliving their years in the town. It was hardly six years ago that they had gone together to Lexington; two years back, in another spring season, he had left it for the war. How could so much have happened in so short a time?

That night Mrs. Hoge arrived with Dr. Tucker. She took charge of Julia and helped Anna to bed. There Anna slept in exhaustion, until she woke at dawn on Saturday. "Did somebody call, Hetty?" She had dreamed it, and Hetty took her hand to soothe her. Her old servant and her friend . . . how good they were to her. The day began brightly, the sunlight cutting through the shutter openings, and when Anna walked to the window she discovered a glory of dogwood and a richly flowering peach tree a few feet away. The vista was the kind her husband had always loved.

Hearing a noise in the hall, Anna watched a man go quickly by—Dr. Tucker. After a time she went to the room and found Tom addressing Dr. McGuire: "I see from the number of physicians that you think my condition serious. But I thank God, if it is His will, that I'm ready to go." Her heart sank, until she noticed that he had become more alert and that his eyes had a look of determination. That was a good sign, wasn't it? Firmly she told herself it was.

"Little one"—he spoke with new energy—"I'd like to see Julia." Her mood lifting, Anna brought the baby to him. Julia was beaming, moving her arms up and down. "Tom, I think she recognizes you," she called to him. When her husband extended his one bandaged hand, Anna placed the child on the bed beside him. Lightly, despite his splintered fingers, he touched her, and Julia looked up at him smiling, murmuring.

"My little comforter," he whispered. "Little comforter . . ."

He grew drowsy, and Anna took the baby away. But he did not appear to know what had happened. Suddenly she noticed that he was breathing with greater difficulty than ever, and Dr. Mc-

Guire whispered, "His lungs are very filled." Nevertheless Tom turned and spoke in a firm voice: "Please call Mr. Lacy."

Anna and the doctor exchanged glances, and Dr. McGuire protested that he must not exert himself. Impatiently Tom shook his head: "This is important." The moment the chaplain seated himself, the patient began a discussion: "What is the nature of grace? . . . Are you working to develop the full Sabbath observance?" For a few minutes the two talked religion, and Tom struggled to explain his views, but Anna felt he was tiring badly. Understanding the situation, Dr. Lacy prepared to go: "Sir, I'd like to stay with you tomorrow."

"No." Stonewall Jackson responded at once. "You must spend the day as usual, preaching to the soldiers." When the chaplain left, Anna approached Tom again: "Let me read some of the Psalms." He gave her a troubled look: "I'm suffering, Anna. I don't think I could listen." It was the first time he had spoken directly of his pain. Then, however, his voice came quietly to her: "Yes, get the Bible. We must never refuse that."

For a time Anna's words lifted above the sound of his hoarse breathing, but she sensed that he had become very weak. Nevertheless his head rose: "Sing to me—the most spiritual hymn you can think of." Anna made a choice, only to realize that if she tried it alone her voice would give way. She had caught sight of her brother Joseph a few minutes earlier, and she sent for him. Together they sang several hymns for Tom. She thought he was asleep until he moved and spoke: "Sing 'Show Pity' . . ." Together she and her brother intoned the appeal:

> Show pity, Lord; O Lord, forgive;
> Let a repenting rebel live;
> Are not Thy mercies large and free?
> May not a sinner trust in Thee?

Her head dropped. Who was less a sinner than he, and who deserved mercy more than Tom Jackson? As the words ended he seemed to rest peacefully, and after a time Anna went to her room, her spirit heavier than ever. As she nursed her baby she wondered if there was any hope, if he might not still rally. He was a young man, only thirty-nine, and during this past year his health had been good. Yes, he was going to live! She clung to that thought with a tenacious grip, and it was her last on dozing off.

But when she saw him on Sunday morning, her hands went cold. He looked far worse, his face was beet-red, his mouth was open, his breath rasped. He spoke listlessly and then slipped off. Dr. McGuire touched Anna's arm. As she faced the young man she knew what he would say: "Mrs. Jackson . . ." He paused. "I have to tell you. We're afraid he won't last more than a few hours longer."

Her lips opened, but she could not speak. This could not be right. Then she tried to remember: to Tom and to her, death was only the opening of the gates into another world. She must think of that, press it into her mind . . . After a moment she recalled his recent words at the Yerby house. Although he was ready to go whenever he was called, he wished to have time for preparation before entering the presence of his Maker.

Slowly Anna forced up her head. She had her duty before her, as harsh as it might be. If she had ever been brave in her life, she must be now. Alone, she went back to her husband: "Tom, Tom. Do you know . . ." Her voice died, then rose again: "The doctors say you must very soon be"—how could she tell him? and yet she had to go on—"very soon be in Heaven?"

His eyes were almost shut; perhaps he had not understood. She repeated her words and added gently, "Are you willing to accept God's allotment, if He wills you to go today?"

Gradually Tom realized something of her meaning, and his eyes widened: "I—I prefer it." The first words were torn from his throat, but then they issued more firmly: "I prefer it . . . I will be an infinite gainer—to be translated." Yet she felt he had still not understood the full situation. The doctors interrupted to examine him, and after a bleak few minutes she returned, to say the hard words a third time.

He came back to full consciousness, and she knew that her meaning had registered. "Oh, no, you're frightened, my child. Death isn't so near; I may yet get well."

At that Anna lost her control. Dropping across the bed, she cried brokenly, "Tom, Tom. I—I have to tell you. Tom, the doctors say there's no hope!"

For the next few minutes she was lost in her grief, and then she fell back to her chair. Tom was looking upward, as if considering the subject: "Good, very good. It's all right." He used the words he had uttered so often on the battlefield and to her.

Through her sobs Anna heard his voice: "I have a great deal to say, my dear, but . . . I'm too weak."

Then she must talk for him: "What do you wish for Julia and me?" Her voice gave way. "Should—should we go back to my father?"

"Yes. You have a kind and good father . . ." A moment later, as if by habit, he added, "But there is no one so kind and good as your Heavenly Father."

"Tom." She had to thrust the next question from her: "Tom, where—where do you want to be—taken?"

For a moment she did not draw his full attention, and then he murmured, "Charlotte . . . Charlottesville." He could not mean that, and she asked, "Lexington?"

"Yes, Lexington, and in my own plot." It was the place he had chosen when their first child died, that quiet field with the mountains spreading to the horizon. A moment later Anna realized that Mrs. Hoge was standing in the doorway, Julia in her arms, and Tom looked up, suddenly alert.

"Little darling!" He smiled at the baby. "Sweet one . . ." Anna lowered the child to the bed, and for a few minutes Stonewall Jackson continued to smile, his eyes missing no detail of Julia's face, as if he had to print on his mind the outlines of the features he would never . . . Anna bit her lip, fighting back the thought.

With the pink face beside Tom's, she saw how emaciated, how wasted her husband had grown. But Julia beamed steadily at the bearded countenance she had come to know.

A sob reached them. It was Jim, Tom's body servant, near the door. The doctor's hands went to his eyes, and one or two other men, who had slipped in, began to cry. "Sweet child . . ." Once more Stonewall drifted away from them.

Another hour, and in the hall there appeared someone for whom Anna had been watching, Sandie Pendleton. The boy looked haggard, and he could not conceal his sorrow. As Tom glanced up, Anna read his love and admiration for Sandie.

"Who's preaching at headquarters today?" At Stonewall's query she started; he had forgotten his order to his own chaplain to perform the service. Sandie mentioned Lacy's name, and added in a muffled voice, "The whole army is praying for you, sir."

"Thank God." The words were soft. "They're very kind." Silence settled over the warm, dim room with its smell of many medicines, and again Tom spoke: "It's the Lord's day . . . and my wish is fulfilled. I've always wanted to die on Sunday."

Sandie Pendleton sobbed, and a moment later went into the hall, where he stood with his head against the wall. And Anna heard a low voice from one of the other officers: "What are we going to do without him? What are we going to do?" Anna's thoughts went to Tom's sister Laura, from whom he had been separated for so long, and whom he would never see again, and to her own family, and the Prestons and the Junkins on both sides of the war . . . Dr. McGuire offered Tom a glass of brandy, but he shook his head: "It will only delay my leaving . . . I want to preserve my mind, if possible, to the last."

While Anna clenched her fists, Tom sank into the past, and now he was calling out military orders, directing an assault. Then he left the battlefield, and his mind returned to their years at Lexington, to the house with the golden hinges.

"*Esposita*, where are you?" He was still reliving the Lexington days, and he seemed to be hunting her about the place. Was he remembering one of the months she spent in New York or in North Carolina, when he wrote that he missed her desperately?

"Mary, little Mary." With a pang almost too great to bear, Anna realized that Tom was thinking of their first child, the baby who was waiting for him now, somewhere beyond the gates. The doctor moved quickly at the sickbed, and Tom, his mind shifting, muttered incoherently, "Order A. P. Hill to prepare for action! . . . Pass the infantry to the front! Tell Major Hawks . . ."

Outside, the sun had brightened, and the green earth of Virginia lay shining in the May air. Anna thought of a distant land, the land of everlasting repose, where "Sabbaths have no end." The clock struck three on this Sunday afternoon; five minutes passed, ten, fifteen.

Through his heavy breathing Tom's voice reached quietly to Anna and the others: "Let us cross over the river . . . and rest under the shade of the trees."

His own journey was nearly over, and the shadows awaited. Slowly the light seemed to fade from his eyes, and they closed. Agony welled up in her, and when she heard a low cry, Anna realized it was her own. Sinking upon him, she kissed the beloved face. "Doctor, can't you do something—something more?"

Dr. McGuire stared down hopelessly. But her voice did what no other could have done; it drew him back from the silences. His eyes opened wide, and he gave Anna a long, full look of love and deep perception.

His last sight on earth was of her. His eyes shut, and his breathing stopped, and she was alone in this crowded room . . . Some day they would be together again, Anna tried to tell herself, she and Tom and both of their children, and forever. Now, however, she was alone, and the future stretched far ahead.

Unsteadily Anna Jackson got to her feet. She would soon be taking Tom on his last trip. They would be going back, after all, to Lexington, and she must prepare herself and her baby for whatever lay before them.

Epilogue

For two more years Anna Morrison Jackson waited for the war's conclusion. To her, as to so many others, it was a time of successive heartbreaks, of slow realization of the inevitable that came with the meeting of Grant and Lee at Appomatox.

Joy and tragedy, an occasional happiness, harsh destruction . . . Anna Jackson felt them all. Her recollections of these and subsequent years were part sweet, part bitter. In those memories there was a particular place for Sandie Pendleton, the boy who had been so close to her and her husband. Following Jackson's death he married Kate Corbin, the girl he loved. For nine months after Anna told him good-by, he fought on with zest and spirit. He had become a major at twenty-two, then a colonel, and had been a mainstay of Jackson's staff.

Then, in the fall of 1864, as he tried to rally retreating Confederates, Sandie fell under Union bullets. His men had to leave him in enemy hands, and there he died, not quite twenty-five. Sandie and Kate Pendleton had a son, born after the father's burial.

For Anna Jackson there was also special meaning in an announcement made soon after she returned from Lexington to Cottage Home. Colonel James Walker, who had figured in the unhappy episode of the near-duel at the Institute, became the new commander of the Stonewall Brigade. Like Frank Paxton, whom he succeeded, Walker had begun the war under Jackson's supposed hostility. Each officer had found Stonewall a man of forbearance, and had risen with his approval. Now, under Walker, the famous band won a still further reputation.

Anna learned of another kind of irony for her friend, Margaret Junkin Preston. While her father, Dr. George Junkin, and two brothers continued with the North, Maggie Preston saw more and more suffering among the Southerners with whom her lot was cast. Toward the close of the hostilities, she wrote *Beechenbrook; a Rhyme of the War,* a book which won her a phenomenal popularity in her adopted region. Southerners hailed her as a kind of laureate of their struggle.

At the war's end, Anna discovered happily, Maggie re-established affectionate relations with the Junkins of the North. Yet she remained in Lexington, and welcomed warmly a man who took the position her Unionist father had held as president of Washington College—Robert E. Lee.

Mrs. Laura Arnold, Stonewall's sister, never ceased to admire and praise her brother in later years, and also never ceased to uphold her own views. In time, Laura Arnold was honored by the Grand Army of the Republic, the Union organization. Here is a phase of Jackson's life, and his wife's, which has curiously escaped general notice.

Meanwhile, for Anna Jackson there was a life to be lived with her child. In a way she could not have predicted, her husband was to become the central figure in a great story, a brightly threaded narrative, a legend. In the year of 1957, with the unveiling of a statue of Stonewall Jackson in New York's Hall of Fame, the deacon-soldier's place in history is perhaps a more celebrated one than ever before.

Had Stonewall not died, would the war's course have been different? Many thought so, and Sandie Pendleton spoke for them when, in a tense hour in later fighting, he cried out, "Oh, for the presence and inspiration of Old Jack for just one hour!" In such questionings Mrs. Jackson expressed no view. With the war's close she went to work with two purposes: to serve her husband's memory and also to help bring about reconciliation between North and South.

She had known Stonewall as had no one else. Now she saw him become a subject of intense interest to millions, as one of history's great military figures and also as a man of true greatness of character. Gently, energetically, without recriminations, Anna Jackson lived out a long life in the shadow of her husband's fame. Not quite thirty-two when he died, she lived until 1915 and the age of eighty-four. During those many years thousands of Americans and Europeans who met her recognized her as a remarkable figure. One observer described her as a "fragile little woman with keen, bright eyes and the alert air which characterizes those whose interest in life and its best endeavors is undimmed by sorrow or the passing years."

As the decades went by, Anna Jackson knew personal trouble, harsh blows, and disappointments. Her mother died within a year after Thomas Jackson, and there were other family losses as she moved between Cottage Home and Charlotte. Six years after Chancellorsville Anna wrote a letter in which she said, "Our home is very retired. . . . It is a sad thing to be left almost entirely alone in a homestead where there has been a large and happy family. But I would not mourn, for I have many more blessings and mercies than I deserve."

Mrs. Jackson never married again, though she might several times have done so. "To her that would have been unthinkable," says one who was close to her. She wished simply to live out her life as Mrs. Stonewall Jackson.

Her husband had left no great means, and in the postwar South it became known that at times she approached, if not need, then a situation in which she must be extremely careful with her small funds. At times it was indicated that finances worried her a great deal. Nevertheless Mrs. Jackson declined repeatedly to take help, though it was offered with extreme tact. When the North Carolina legislature voted her a lifetime pension of one hundred dollars a month, she asked that it go to a welfare program. The result was the Jackson Training School of Concord, North Carolina.

Repeatedly she turned down offers to write about her husband. As she said, "The shadow over my life was so deep, and all that concerned him was so sacred," that she could not do so. "But time softens, if it does not heal, the bitterest sorrow," she declared later; and eventually she set down her memories of the man.

By then Anna Jackson knew the great sadness of her postwar days, her "sorrow's crown of sorrows." Her existence had centered upon her daughter Julia. At twenty-two Julia married W. E. Christian, by whom she had two children. Four years later, in 1889, Julia died of typhoid fever. In these days, the mother wrote, she tried to remember Stonewall's "lessons of submission and fortitude."

Upon her grandchildren she turned all the affections of her later years. In time her granddaughter Julia became Mrs. Randolph Preston, wife of the grandson of Colonel John T. L. Preston.

Thus the families that had been such friends were united more closely.

Many still recall Mrs. Jackson, a cheerful, energetic woman, her hair white, her face ever more lined, who followed the methodic program she had learned from her husband. Rising daily at the same hour, she followed a careful schedule: two hours for correspondence, another for callers, the afternoon for her grandchildren, and so on.

Through the decades she was visited or stopped on the street by men who told her they had fought under Stonewall and what he had meant to them. Curiously, or perhaps not so curiously, thousands of Union veterans also let her know how they regarded the man who had been their enemy. She smiled when she sometimes quoted a grizzled mountaineer who had a long talk with her, then complimented her: "Ma'am, you're real fine. Just as plain and common as my old woman." Others, their minds flooded by memories of Jackson and the war, would be unable to speak and would begin to cry as they stood before her: "So you're Stonewall's wife, ma'am." "He was the best . . ."

As Anna had hoped, Jackson's mount, Little Sorrel, was found after Chancellorsville. Governor Letcher of Virginia sent the horse to her at Cottage Home, and he lived to be more than thirty years old, she estimated. "Treated to the greenest of pastures and the best of care," he served in harness and under the saddle, and for a time carried the venerable Dr. Morrison to his country churches.

At times Little Sorrel was sent to Confederate gatherings. Ancient though he was, he would jump to attention when the band played "Dixie" or when he heard the rebel yell, and often he would break into an unsteady gallop before a shouting crowd.

American Presidents and their wives paid their respects to Mrs. Jackson, and distinguished continental visitors asked to be presented to the widow. Usually she remarked that she understood these tributes were not to her but to her husband. As she told her granddaughter, Julia Christian Preston, hers was a "reflected glory," and she tried not to forget that fact.

In 1910, at seventy-nine, she accepted an invitation to go to Washington for the first time in many years, and her reception was phenomenal. President Taft, a Republican, gave her marked attention. At a great banquet for the judiciary, attended by governors, senators and other officials, she received striking tributes. She remembered her first visit, she said, when she had gone to

Washington as a guest of her Uncle Graham. Now, so many years later, she rejoiced in "this great capital of my country, that is so glorious and prosperous and united."

She continued, "Seeing so many of those whose names link the present with the past, brought back old memories, but all memories have been sweetened by the passing of time." The kindness of Southerners understandably conveyed a great deal to her; no less meaningful were the marks of interest by "those who have not the same reason to show me courtesy." And, as always, "all this loving-kindness lavished on me was a tribute paid to my hero-husband."

In 1915, with members of her family around her, Anna Jackson died in Charlotte. In death she returned, as had her husband, to the Virginia town in which their life together had centered. The Virginia Military Institute provided an honor guard to escort her body to Lexington.

There she rests today beside her husband, in the quiet cemetery with the eternal hills as a backdrop.

Acknowledgments

More than in the case of any of my previous books, I have had the benefit of generous assistance by many individuals, libraries, and other sources of information in America and Europe.

Mr. and Mrs. E. Randolph Preston, of Washington, D.C., and Winston-Salem, North Carolina, grandson of Colonel J. T. L. Preston and granddaughter of Stonewall Jackson, received me on a series of visits, opened their extensive collection of material on the General and his wife, loaned innumerable manuscripts, and introduced me to dozens of others who were also of great help. Mrs. Preston, reared by Anna Jackson after her mother's early death, was invaluable in presenting a clear, sharp picture of Stonewall's wife.

Roy Bird Cook, the best authority of Jackson's early life, welcomed me to Charleston, West Virginia, and gave complete access to his magnificently indexed and annotated collection of Jackson data. Mr. and Mrs. Cook also answered many inquiries and directed me to many other people.

In Lexington, Dr. W. G. Bean of Washington and Lee University made available several valuable manuscripts, made specific replies to many inquiries, and discussed at length his findings for his future book on Sandie Pendleton. Colonel William Couper, major authority on Virginia Military Institute, called my attention to many little-known facts about Jackson and gave time to detailed points which I raised.

At Charlottesville, Virginia, Jay Johns, founder of the Stonewall Jackson Memorial, gave me a happy welcome, introduced me to many individuals connected with the Jackson story, and showed me some of the country Jackson knew so well. With him and Mrs. Johns I also visited the Jackson home in Lexington, which figures in this book, and studied documents and other items which have been collected for this new museum in honor of Stonewall.

About five years ago, while at work on *The Lady of Arlington,* dealing with General and Mrs. Robert E. Lee, I first discussed the subject of the Jacksons with the distinguished authority, Dr. Douglas Southall

Freeman. Dr. Freeman encouraged my plans for a book on Jackson
and his wife, noting the care with which Mrs. Jackson set down her
personal recollections, deploring the tendency of some to caricature
Jackson as a scarecrow-hayseed, and directing me to a number of rare
items.

Mrs. Marie Jackson Arnold Pifer, of Buckhannon, West Virginia,
granddaughter of Mrs. Laura Arnold, proved of strong assistance in
gathering data about that remarkable woman. Additional aid was given
by others of that branch—Miss Isabelle Arnold, Deland, Florida, and
Mrs. Beatrice Giffen, Topeka, Kansas.

Unusual help came from Miss Margaret V. Jones, librarian of Virginia Military Institute, who located individuals connected with Jackson's days in the town and clarified dozens of points. In Charlotte
similar assistance came from Charles R. Brockman, assistant director
of the Public Library of Charlotte and Mecklenburg County, who
traced newspaper accounts and out-of-print books.

In London I conferred with the skilled researcher, Miss Patricia E.
O'Driscoll, an expert in this period, who counseled with me on Confederate data and then carried on additional investigation for me. Mr.
Patrick Courtney, of London, was similarly helpful. Officials of the
British Museum and of the Foreign Records Office made available material on Jackson and the war, continuing the help given in my research
for *The Smiling Rebel* and *Spies for the Blue and Gray*.

In Paris M. Albert Krebs of the Bibliothèque Nationale directed me
to French books, magazines, and other sources. M. Guy Quoniam de
Schompre, French consul general at New Orleans, and Captain Robert
Estachy of the French Line, New Orleans, helped clear formalities for
a ready use of the materials in Paris.

Dr. Frank Vandiver, brilliant new biographer of Stonewall Jackson,
gave me considerable bibliographical help in Houston and New Orleans
and responded to scores of inquiries. Monroe F. Cockrell, Evanston,
Illinois, made available his detailed analyses of Jackson's character.

Miss Margaret Preston of Atlanta loaned me considerable data re-
lating to Colonel J. T. L. Preston and others of that family. Professor
Chalmers Davidson of "Hurricane Hill," Davidson, North Carolina, an
authority with close ties to the Jacksons and Morrisons, arranged for
use of Davidson College data and of information from his own
collection.

Colonel Robert Hall Morrison, Charlotte, and Mrs. Ronald Wilson,
Charlotte, received me, counseled with me, and later corresponded at
some length. Charles Shetler, curator of the West Virginia collection,
West Virginia University, Morgantown, arranged microfilms of many
original Jackson letters.

Junius R. Fishburne, of Charlottesville, loaned me the long, detailed reminiscences of his grandfather, Clement B. Fishburne, with invaluable recollections of Jackson in the prewar period. Miss Anna Barringer, of Charlottesville, granted an interview and replied to subsequent inquiries. Mrs. William J. Bryan, of Jacksonville, wrote several long letters with detailed data.

V. C. Barringer, Richmond, John Barringer, Richmond, and Dr. J. Morrison Hutcheson, Richmond, contributed manuscripts, family stories, or suggestions. Mrs. Henry R. Carter and Mrs. J. M. Cox, Ashland, Virginia, on whose family estate Stonewall Jackson died, made special efforts to provide recollections for the final chapter.

J. Walker Caldwell, Roanoke, his sister, Mrs. W. W. S. Butler, Roanoke, and Mrs. W. F. McFarland, Florence, Alabama, aided me in obtaining manuscript recollections of General James Walker.

Others of particular assistance were:

Mrs. Irwin P. Graham, Greenville, South Carolina; E. B. (Pete) Long, Oak Park, Illinois; Miss Elizabeth Jarrett, Chattanooga, Tennessee; Mrs. Ed Vandergriff, Blacksburg, Virginia; Mrs. Lee Ransom, Atlanta, Georgia; Vernon Spencer, Brooklyn Heights, New York; Thomas C. Barringer, McLean, Virginia; Hal Bridges, Department of History, University of Colorado, Boulder, Colorado:

Miss Frances Brown, Department of Chemistry, Duke University, Durham, North Carolina; Mrs. Henry R. McVay, Luray, Virginia; Mrs. Minnie Hite Moody, Atlanta, Georgia; Harry B. Wright, clerk of Rockbridge County, Lexington; Dr. George H. Preston, Atlanta, Georgia; Herbert Preston, Baltimore, Maryland; Mrs. Edward Waller, Jr., Richmond:

Stuart Moore, Lexington; Mrs. Virginia Wiltshire, Martinsburg, Virginia; Dr. Robert D. Meade, Randolph Macon Woman's College, Lynchburg, Virginia; James R. Anderson, Chapel Hill, North Carolina; Dr. Benjamin R. Lacy, Jr., Hampden-Sydney, Virginia; William S. Lacy, Jr., of *Commonwealth* magazine, Richmond:

Dr. J. Randolph Graham, Winchester, Virginia; Mrs. Betts Morrison Sales, Lexington; Paul Barringer, Jr., New York; Morrison Irwin, Charlotte; Charles Glasgow, Lexington; Rev. John R. Richardson, Westminster Presbyterian Church, Atlanta; Osmond L. Barringer, Charlotte; Clifford Dowdey, Confederate authority of Richmond:

David C. Mearns, chief of the Manuscripts Division, Library of Congress; Jesse Cunningham, librarian, Cossitt Library, Memphis; Mrs. C. I. Norton, librarian of the Handley Library, Front Royal, Virginia; C. Vernon Eddy, librarian of the Handley Library, Winchester, Virginia; Mrs. Dorothy Elliott, librarian of the Martinsburg Public Library; Miss Euna Faye Campbell, librarian of Wythe-Grayson Regional Library, Independence, Virginia:

Miss India Thomas, house regent, and Eleanor S. Brockenbrough, assistant house regent, Confederate Museum, Richmond; Randolph W. Church, state librarian, Richmond; Milton C. Russell, head, Reference and Circulating Division, Virginia State Library, Richmond; H. M. Brim, librarian, Union Theological Seminary, Richmond; Mrs. W. W. Griffith, librarian, Fredericksburg, Virginia:

Mrs. B. B. Clarkson, curator of the museum, Virginia Military Institute; William S. Powell, North Carolina Collection, University of North Carolina, Chapel Hill; James W. Patton, director, Southern Historical Collection, University of North Carolina:

Mrs. Grace Carnahan, librarian, Pulaski County Free Library, Pulaski, Virginia; Mrs. M. R. McVey, librarian, Morganton-Burke Library, Morganton, North Carolina; Miss Josephine P. Etchison, C. Burr Artz Library, Frederick, Maryland; H. G. Jones, state archivist, Department of Archives and History, Raleigh, North Carolina; Miss Carrie L. Broughton, North Carolina State Library, Raleigh, North Carolina:

Mrs. Kate Pyron, librarian, Salem College, Winston-Salem, North Carolina, and Lelia Graham Marsh, alumnae secretary, Salem College; Sarah Gray, assistant in Manuscript Department, Duke University, Durham, North Carolina; Harlan C. Brown, director of D. H. Hill Library, State College Station, Raleigh, North Carolina:

Francis R. Berkeley, Jr., curator of manuscripts and William H. Runge, assistant, Alderman Library, University of Virginia, Charlottesville, Virginia; Mrs. Adrian Belt, librarian, City of Morgantown, Morgantown, West Virginia; Christine L. Reb, reference librarian, University of Chicago Library; Harold W. Thompson, Jr., reference librarian, Lafayette College, Easton, Pennsylvania; Sylvester Vigilante, Ossining, New York, formerly head of American History Room of the New York Public Library; R. N. Williams II, librarian, Historical Society of Pennsylvania:

Hudson Grunewald of the Washington *Star;* Miss Cornelia Bowie, Washington, D.C.:

Miss Mavis McIntosh, New York; Mrs. W. J. Kane and Miss Anna Marie Kane, New Orleans; and Mrs. Florence Kane Reynolds, for long assistance in preparation of the manuscript:

John Hall Jacobs, librarian of the New Orleans Public Library, and George King Logan, assistant librarian; Dr. Garland Taylor, librarian of the Howard-Tilton Library of Tulane University; Mr. James W. Dyson, librarian of Loyola University, New Orleans; Miss Ruth Renaud, Miss Margaret Ruckert, Miss Gladys Peyronnin, Miss Lily Mouton, Mrs. Alice V. Westfeldt, Miss Marion Mason, Mrs. Ellen Tilger, and Mrs. Bernice Zibilich of the New Orleans Public Library:

Mr. Robert Greenwood, Mrs. Clayre Barr Lewis, Mrs. Dorothy Lawton, Miss Betty Mailhes, Mrs. Clare Low of the Howard-Tilton Library staff, New Orleans; and Miss Martha Ann Peters and Mrs. Evangeline Thurber, formerly of the staff.

Robert Meyer, Jr., of Festival Information Service, New York; Mrs. Fidelia Anding of Anding Bookstore; and William Fountain of Fountaine Library, Columbus, Ohio, aided in locating many out-of-print items.

Ralph Newman of the Abraham Lincoln Bookshop, Chicago, gave general encouragement and assistance in war research, the locating of early manuscripts, and similar help.

Manuscript sources of particular help were the large Thomas Jonathan Jackson Collection at the University of West Virginia; the Jedediah Hotchkiss Papers at the Library of Congress; letters of Daniel Harvey Hill, Mary Anna Morrison Jackson, Robert Hall Morrison, A. R. Boteler, and others at Duke University; papers of Charles W. Dabney, Clement D. Fishburne, Thomas Jonathan Jackson, and Henry Kyd Douglas; Morrison family papers, including fifty-three from Dr. Robert Hall Morrison to his cousin James; Thomas Jonathan Jackson Papers at Virginia Military Institute, and Thomas Jonathan Jackson Papers at Virginia State Library. Among about three hundred books and magazine articles which were used, the most valuable included:

ALLAN, ELIZABETH. *Life and Letters of Margaret Junkin Preston.* Boston, 1903.

ARNOLD, THOMAS JACKSON. *Early Life and Letters of General Thomas J. Jackson.* New York, 1916.

BRYAN, ANNA. *A March Past.* New York, 1932.

CABLE, GEORGE W. "The Gentler Side of Two Great Southerners." *Century,* new series, XXV, 1893–94.

CASLER, JOHN. *Four Years in the Stonewall Brigade.* Girard, Kansas, 1906.

COOK, ROY BIRD. *The Family and Early Life of Stonewall Jackson.* Charleston, West Virginia, 1948.

COOKE, JOHN ESTEN. *The Life of Stonewall Jackson, by a Virginian.* Richmond, 1863.

COUPER, WILLIAM. *One Hundred Years at V.M.I.,* 4 vols. Richmond, 1939.

DABNEY, ROBERT L. *Life and Campaigns of Lieutenant-General Thomas J. Jackson.* New York, 1866.

DOUGLAS, HENRY KYD. *I Rode with Stonewall.* Chapel Hill, 1940.

FREEMAN, DOUGLAS SOUTHALL. *Lee's Lieutenants,* 3 vols. New York, 1942–44.

———. *R. E. Lee,* 4 vols. New York, 1934–35.

HENDERSON, G. F. R. *Stonewall Jackson and the American Civil War.* New York, 1949.

HILL, DANIEL HARVEY. "The Real Stonewall Jackson." *Century*, new series, XXV, 1893–94.

JACKSON, MARY ANNA. *Memoirs of Stonewall Jackson*. Louisville, 1895.

———. Series of articles on her husband, *Hearst's Magazine*, XXIV, 1913.

JONES, J. B. *Rebel War Clerk's Diary* (Howard Swiggett, ed.), 2 vols. New York, 1935.

KINSOLVING, ROBERTA C. "Stonewall Jackson in Winter Headquarters." *Confederate Veteran*, XX, 1912.

MARSHALL, CHARLES. *An Aide-de-Camp of Lee* (Major Gen. Frederick Maurice, ed.). Boston, 1927.

MOORE, FRANK, ed. *The Rebellion Record*, 12 vols. New York, 1862–72.

PRESTON, MARGARET JUNKIN. "Personal Reminiscences of Stonewall Jackson." *Century*, new series, X, 1886.

SMITH, JAMES POWER. "With Stonewall Jackson." *Southern Historical Society Papers*, new series, V, 1920.

TAYLOR, RICHARD. *Destruction and Reconstruction* (Richard Harwell, ed.). New York, 1955.

War of the Rebellion: A Compilation of the Official Records of the Union and Confederate Armies, 70 vols. Washington, D.C., 1880–1901.

WAYLAND, JOHN W. *Stonewall Jackson's Way*. Staunton, Virginia, 1940.

Concerning the four pictures of General and Mrs. Jackson which appear as end sheets in this book, it is interesting to point out that the front end-paper portrait of Stonewall Jackson is by Matthew Brady from an unidentified earlier photograph. Curiously enough, the uniform was added to the original picture at a later date. The front endsheet picture of Mrs. Jackson is from a reproduction of a painting apparently made from a tintype. The portrait of Mrs. Jackson on the back end sheets is taken from a photograph made from a daguerreotype, and was found in an album belonging to a Richmond family which contained other contemporary photographs of local people and Confederate leaders.

—HARNETT T. KANE
5919 Freret Street
New Orleans
May 29, 1957.